DECEPTIONS

DECEPTIONS

JUNE
CONSIDINE

**NEW
ISLAND**

DECEPTIONS
First published 2004
by New Island
2 Brookside
Dundrum Road
Dublin 14

ISBN 1 904301 60 6

British Library Cataloguing in Publication Data.
A CIP catalogue record for this book is available
from the British Library.

Typeset by New Island
Cover design by Fidelma Slattery @ New Island
Printed in Ireland by ColourBooks

New Island received financial assistance from The Arts Council
(An Chomhairle Ealaíon), Dublin, Ireland.

10 9 8 7 6 5 4 3 2 1

The author would like to express her gratitude to the Arts Council
(An Chomhairle Ealaíon) for their support.

To my family with love: my husband Sean, my son Tony, daughters Ciara and Michelle and my son-in-law Roddy. Also, a special welcome to the first of the next generation, my granddaughter, Romy.

PROLOGUE

Dublin is a city with eyes. A gossiping great-aunt who sees around corners or peers suspiciously through the walls of quiet pubs and dimly lit restaurants. For this reason he has booked overnight into their favourite hotel, a discreet, old-fashioned country house buried in the seclusion of the Wicklow hills. Over the years the Oakdale Arms has remained an oasis in their busy lives. They are familiar with the narrow corridors and thread-bare carpets, the flocked wallpaper that no longer has any discernable pattern and the grandfather clock in the lounge which, on the hour, gives forth a doleful boom, reminding them that time may only briefly be stolen. Its shabby ambience is due to neglect rather than a contrived nostalgia and, with no stylish attribute to lift it from the mundane, it remains a hidden place where none of their friends or acquaintances would dream of staying.

The bell jangles when they enter the lobby and a porter, stooped and worn as a cliché, insists on carrying their overnight bags to their room. Over the years they have laid an affectionate claim on him, as they would to a favourite pet, and have named him Igor. He exists in their minds only for the length of time they stay at the hotel and is as much a part of the furnishings as the curtains that drape with tired indifference from brass hoops or the faded paintings of fox hunts adorning the walls.

She showers and dresses for their evening meal. Satin and lace lingerie are concealed beneath a sheer silk dress of midnight-blue. She pirouettes before him, laughing in mock-protest and pointing at her watch when he tumbles her onto the bed. They tussle, not seriously – the night is only beginning and they are at an age where anticipation is more enjoyable when it smoulders across a restaurant table. His mobile phone rings as they are about to leave the room. His shoulder is hunched when he answers, his voice lowered, as if protecting her from the intrusion.

She closes the door behind her and walks towards the lift. The smell of turf smoke, pervasive and homely, reminds her that an open fire burns in the lounge. Later, after they have eaten, they will relax in the shabby chintz-covered armchairs with a glass of brandy before retiring for the night. A tour bus has arrived and the lobby is filled with big-boned American men in comfortable shoes, enquiring about the availability of ice-making machines. Their wives, an authoritative twang to their accents, busily supervise the removal of luggage to their rooms.

She has reached the restaurant when he calls her name, an apologetic sound, and catches up with her. Their waiter, deferential in black, greets them without a flicker of recognition and leads them to their favourite window seat. Weary-wise in the ways of illicit passion, and armed with a generous tip, he will forget their existence as soon as they walk from his table.

The food on offer is as unimaginative as ever, an emphasis on roast meats and over-boiled vegetables. The dessert menu reminds them of childhood treats: Banana Splits, Knickerbocker Glories, strawberry jelly and ice-cream. While they eat, their conversation skims over the names of forgotten toffee bars, sweets and biscuits. They regale each other with food horror stories, remembering their most hated meals and the tactics they used to avoid eating them. On holidays in Trabawn, she says, her uncle gathered mushrooms in the morning and fried them in butter for breakfast. Disgusting. They reminded her of slugs sliding down her throat. She makes a slight moue of disgust and traces her index finger across the rim of her wineglass. This is a trivial conversation yet preferable to long, tortuous discussions that move in a widening but nowhere circle. Surrounded by noisy tourists demanding jugs of iced water and a detailed analysis of the menu in case allergies lurk among the overcooked vegetables, they can relax and touch hands, lean over the table and stare into each other's eyes, whisper words that promise much in the hours ahead.

Their meal is almost over when an elderly couple enter and are led to the only available table at the opposite end of the restaurant. Casually dressed in slacks and chunky sweaters, their sturdy boots well-worn and dusty, they have obviously been hill-walking. The shock of their arrival is so instantaneous that her hand freezes as she raises the wineglass to her lips. She remains in that position, her attention fixed on the couple who accept the menu and listen intently while the waiter describes a certain dish. Her companion has not yet noticed them. He continues talking until she quietly utters their names. His cutlery clatters against his plate. She winces, imagines the sound strumming across the room, can almost feel the jolt of disbelief between them and the couple should their eyes meet.

They must leave immediately. She makes the decision without hesitation. Their love is a two-edged blade where discretion and passion hone each other to a dangerous edge. This balance must be respected. She will collect their luggage from the room. He will settle their bill at Reception. He nods agreement. Observing his stricken face, she hopes he will have the necessary self-control to leave the restaurant without attracting attention.

Sheltered by sturdy American shoulders, she looks neither to right or left as she walks away. Within a few minutes she has packed their clothes and switched off the light. She avoids the old-fashioned lift and moves swiftly down the back stairs, which are steep and have a way of meandering off into culs-de-sac or laundry rooms. Eventually, she exits from the side entrance of the hotel. She recognises the hill walkers' red Toyota, which is parked behind bushes, and hurries onwards to where he is waiting for her, already strapped into the car and with the ignition running.

"Can you believe it? Jesus Christ! Can you credit that for a *fucking* incredible coincidence?" He drives down the avenue and out through the high spiked gates. Trees line the road on either side, oak, beech and chestnut, leafless now that November is here.

"Did they notice you leaving?" Her pulse still races and she releases her breath in a long drawn-out sigh when he shakes his head.

"What shall we do now?" he asks. "It's too risky to stay around here."

"We can't risk a hotel in Dublin," she replies.

"What then?"

"Your house is empty."

"I think *not*." His foot presses harder on the accelerator.

"Just a thought." She rests her head against the back of the seat then slumps, relaxing her shoulders. "We should do the sensible thing and call it a night. I'm still in shock after that experience."

"It could be difficult explaining why you're home tonight instead of tomorrow?"

"Not really. I'll tell him the seminar was so well organised it wasn't necessary to stay overnight."

"Will he believe you?"

"Oh yes, I expect he will."

He leaves the quiet roads and speeds along the motorway. He bypasses Bray, heads towards Blackrock, stops at the level crossing beside the Merrion Gates. A DART speeds northwards, windows flashing. Traffic is light along Strand Road. They pass the Martello Tower and the tall palm trees, the empty park benches and esplanade, the sand palely gleaming on the retreating tide. She stares across the sea towards the jetties and wharfs glittering reflectively on the waters of Dublin Bay.

"Remember the time –" She touches his wrist and he nods, instantly picking up on the memory.

"It'll be quiet there now." He turns right at the end of the road. His smile washes over her. "We can't let our night be completely ruined."

She laughs, unsure whether or not he is serious. "You're asking me to make out in a car?"

"It's been a while, eh?" He is relaxed now, his hand teasing its way between her knees.

"A while," she agrees. "And it's a daft idea."

"But a good one. What do you say?"

She nods and thinks, this is crazy, the two of them behaving so recklessly, but there is also the long-forgotten thrill of being in the open, playing perilous deceptive games.

He drives between houses and parklands, passes a factory with jagged rooftops, follows the flow of cars heading in the direction of the East-Link. Before reaching the toll-bridge which separates the north and south of the city he turns at the South Port roundabout and drives deep into the industrial zone.

The terrain changes, becomes darker, more isolated. This is a place with few charms, filled mainly with offices, oil-storage depots and an occasional abandoned factory site. He continues towards a small car-park overlooking the bay. A number of cars are already parked, possessively claiming space in the shadows. Without a word he reverses back out onto the pitted road leading to the Great South Wall. As he brakes beside a shed with high brick walls, the headlights flare into the dark recesses of the pier.

He cups her face and bends towards her. They are impatient now but she moves slowly, teasingly. He watches the sensuous glide of her dress along her legs, the revealing glimpse of lacy stocking tops and lingerie. He sighs, moves her hands aside to draw down the first stocking, then the other. She arches against him, knowing by the urgency with which they touch each other that this will not last long. They are not teenagers, even though they feel ageless, and there is some discomfort as they awkwardly manoeuvre themselves beyond the reach of steering-wheel and gear stick.

The headlights of an approaching car swamp them. The presence of strangers feels like shivery fingers on her neck. They are safe, hidden in steamy seclusion, but even the hint of exposure brings the all-too-familiar tension to the fore. The driver brakes and turns off the lights. A door is opened. Her stomach clenches, imagining the indignity of a vice-squad intrusion but there is no rap on the window, no gruff demand for identification. A voice does call out, male and almost inaudible. It floats towards them. There is something urgent in the sound that unsettles her. The driver returns to the car and once again illuminates them before departing.

When they kiss again there is no conviction in the feel of his mouth. His aftershave, her perfume, the cigarettes they smoked, even the subtle, intimate odour of sex, which she senses rather then smells, suddenly seem oppressive, heavy. She is only now beginning to notice the faint fumes of paint which grow stronger even as she tries to ignore them.

"Why couldn't we spend the night in your house?" she demands.

He pulls away from her, peers at her face to see if she is joking. "You can't *really* be serious."

"Try me." She hears her voice, sharper, demanding she knows not what. They are floundering, she suspects, within this intimate sphere they have created, unable to move back but equally incapable of moving forward. They need more from this relationship – yet when she tries to imagine what this "more" entails she is unable to give it shape or substance.

"Are we going to totally destroy the night with a row?" he demands.

"It was destroyed the moment they walked into the hotel," she retorts. Ignoring his protests, she slips on her shoes, straightens her clothes and steps outside. The night air refreshes her. For November the weather is exceptionally mild. She begins to breathe freely again. Behind her, the tall Pigeon House chimneys funnel smoke into the atmosphere. This place, with its cracks and warning notices, is hazardous, he warns, following her, trying to calm her down. She allows him to catch up with her and soon they are walking with one step. He steers her towards the shelter of the shed. They walk cautiously along the narrow path surrounding it and stop when the pier is out of sight. Only the cry of seabirds and the wash of waves on the rocks below disturb their solitude. They are impatient now. No time or space for the slow removal of clothes. He opens her coat, pulls her dress to her waist. She is ready when he enters her and their pleasure, heightened by their argument and the events of the night, is swift and intense.

When it is over he lights two cigarettes, hands one to her. Their rituals are as exact as if they have been married for many years. But the familiarity created within marriage has never touched their relationship and even this simple act of smoking, their exhaled smoke mingling unseen in the dark, is imbued with meaning. They are about to return to the car when the shriek of the alarm freezes them. The noise ceases for an instant, almost teasingly, then starts to whirr again. The reverberations press against her ears. He begins to run. She flings her cigarette towards the sea and follows him.

When he presses the off-alarm the instant silence is almost as shocking as the high-pitched clamour. The door on the driver's side is ajar, the window broken. Loose wires hang from the dashboard and there is a gap where the stereo has been pulled loose. She hadn't locked the boot in her haste to leave the hotel and the intruder did not have to force it open. Inside it, wooden picture frames still lie on top of each other but their briefcases are missing. She is relieved to see their overnight bags have not been touched. The pier now seems deserted yet this only increases her nervousness. She senses eyes watching them, violence waiting, preparing to strike again.

A short distance away she finds their briefcases. Documents are scattered along the pier. Some have already blown into the sea. She gathers those she can find and watches the remainder flutter eerily above the water before floating away. Back in the car she glances through the salvaged documents, sorting them into individual batches and stuffing them back into the briefcases. Glass has been scattered across the driver's seat. He carefully picks up the pieces, cries out when a shard cuts deep into his hand. His handkerchief is quickly saturated with blood and he reaches into his briefcase, cursing with frustration as he tries to locate a packet of tissues. Silencing him, she bandages the wound, finding a clean cloth among the jumble of paint-stained rags and brushes in the glove compartment. Her movements are swift and efficient. The night has turned into a fiasco which she wants to end as soon as possible.

Ignoring his protests, she insists on driving. On the first try the engine fails to start. She gently coaxes it into life and drives carefully towards the road. In the distance a ferry looms out of the night, sailing towards the North Wall terminal. Its lights glitter on the black sea. It begins to rain. The wipers are no longer working but the rain is light, a slight drizzle gleaming on the windscreen. Across the bay the lights from the ferry terminal blur against the glass. She accelerates, passes the car-park, empty now, and wonders if any of the other cars were vandalised in the same random way. He is still clasping his hand but blood has not yet seeped through the wad of tissues.

A plastic bag, bloated with air, startles her as it flaps past the broken window. It flutters like the wings of an injured seagull and forces her eyes off the road. At first, when the figure looms before the car, she believes he is in her imagination; a spectre born from terror and the mixed emotions of the night. Somewhere at the back of her mind she knows this is a man, his figure elongated in the glare of headlights, but it takes a heart-stopping instant before she brakes. Her companion appears to be in the same suspended state of disbelief and shouts a warning when it is too late. The figure rises in the effortless poise of a dancer, pirouettes before them with an almost-obscene gracefulness before sinking back again to the road. Even the squeal of brakes, the shouts of her companion who has covered his eyes, fail to banish the impression that she is witnessing a surreal ballet sequence performed on a wet, glistening stage. But this is a fleeting impression, instantly registered then forgotten, and all she will remember in the months to come are the crack of his body hitting the bonnet and a duller thud when he tumbles back to the road. The car seems possessed of a manic energy, shuddering, screeching, bucking against her hands as she fights to bring it under control. She brakes and slumps across the wheel. A guttural sound rises from her abdomen and escapes from her mouth. She is disassociated from the sound yet she knows it belongs to her – and to the horror that awaits her when she steps outside.

Her companion is already bent over the sprawled body. The young man lies to the right-hand side of the car. In the headlights, she sees blood trickling down the side of his mouth. Otherwise, his face seems unmarked. A woolly hat is low on his forehead. His head appears dwarfed by the width of a padded anorak and his hands, in fingerless gloves, are limply splayed across the concrete. Compact discs, stolen from the glove compartment, have fallen from his pockets – The Chieftains, U2, Bob Dylan, Billie Holiday – but there is no sign of the stereo.

She pulls her coat collar over her cheeks. The wind sweeps in from the sea and lifts her hair, blowing it over her eyes, offering a blinkered protection from the sight in front of her. Darkness presses down, threatens to engulf her. Her companion shudders as he reaches out to touch the young man's wrist. His breath escapes in a sob. He draws back on his heels, sways unsteadily to his feet. The horror of what has occurred makes words impossible. Fear and self-preservation overwhelm her. Already she is thinking like a different person. She ignores his protests and insists they leave now, before they are discovered. The car is a beacon, flaring a signal for anyone to witness. She takes his arm and pulls him towards its protection. Once again she moves into the driver's seat. This time he does not protest.

When they reach the roundabout he looks around, as if awakening from a nightmare.

"We have to make a call." He searches his jacket pockets for coins, fumbling loose change which spills across the seat.

"Not here," she says, pressing harder on the accelerator. "It's too close ... too close —"

"Jesus Christ! We must call an ambulance. He could still be alive."

"He's dead." Her voice fills the car. "It doesn't matter when the ambulance gets there."

For an instant she thinks he will wrench the steering-wheel from her. Instead, he stares through the window, defeated by her determination. She does not stop driving until they reach a road filled with small terraced houses and a phone kiosk. The houses are in darkness, the road empty. She parks the car and picks up the coins, unable to remember the last time she used a public phone. It will provide anonymity and, if their call is traced, they will be many miles away. She holds a scarf before her mouth and names the location of the accident, wondering how long it will take an ambulance to arrive. Not that it matters. The twisted angle of the tramp's body, his utter stillness, can mean only one thing. Street lights illuminate the car. She notices a deep dent in the bonnet but the main damage was done during the robbery.

Her companion is back in the driver's seat. His injured hand is clenched painfully on the steering-wheel. His face remains expressionless as he drives towards the late-night car-park where they met earlier when their night held nothing but promise. They do not kiss each other goodbye.

An ambulance should have arrived by now. The police will find shattered glass and a shattered life. Nothing else. She does not hover on the edge of this chasm but leaps it cleanly. The young man had been drinking. A vagrant, homeless. She knew by the smell underlying the alcohol, unclean, musty. Probably a junkie as well as a thief. A deliberate criminal act had been committed, not by them but by a vagrant who believed he had the right to violate their property before staggering drugged and drunk into their path. They will not be held responsible for the consequences. Too much is at stake: reputations, marriages, investments, friendships, their future.

When she reaches her house the outside lantern is shining. She steps into the amber glow and glances at her watch. It is later than she thought. Stolen property, stolen hours; thievery has many faces. She opens her front door and closes it quietly behind her.

PART ONE

CHAPTER ONE

Dublin Echo
10 January 2002

POLICE SEEK INFORMATION ON HIT-AND-RUN ACCIDENT

The parents of a young man critically injured in a hit-and-run accident which took place on 20 November 2001 between 11 p.m. and midnight on the approach to the Great South Wall have renewed their appeal for witnesses. Killian Devine-O'Malley (18) remains in a coma, having suffered serious head injuries, a cracked pelvis and severe bruising to his body.

Shortly after midnight on the night of the accident a telephone call was received by the emergency services from an anonymous female caller. The Gardaí have appealed to this woman to come forward to help with their inquiries. They are also anxious to contact any persons who were in the vicinity at that time and may have noticed anything suspicious, especially the occupants of a silver car, make unknown, which was seen on the pier shortly before the accident occurred.

The victim is the son of financial analyst Jean Devine-O'Malley and screen writer Michael Carmody, best known for his cult teen TV series Nowhere Lodge.

Brahms Ward
9.30 p.m.

Your name was in the papers again this morning, Killian. Eddie used the same photograph. Not one of your best, I'm afraid. The Gardaí have sent out another plea for information. No response, as yet, but we live in hope. I rang Eddie and thanked him for the coverage. He's good at keeping your name to the forefront. Killian Devine-O'Malley. Your mother's name, not mine. Eighteen years of age, hazel eyes, short auburn hair, freckles, of medium build, loved.

Did it shock them, that headline, when they opened the paper this morning? I'll bet it curdled their milk, snapped and crackled their crispies. They probably hoped you'd fallen into the great void the media leaves behind when the headline changes. But Eddie is a pal and he'll stay on your watch until there is an ending to your story.

I saw their car that night. I know it was the one. Only problem was that I was too preoccupied to notice anything that would later prove invaluable in tracing it, no toy dog nodding in the back window, no furry dice dangling from the rear view mirror. Nothing except a fleeting glimpse of silver, steamy windows and an arm raised protectively. No wonder my information is gathering dust in a police file.

I'd been searching for you, Killian. High and low along the pier, the same hopeless search. I shouted your name until I was hoarse. You never answered. I left too soon … too soon. I was thinking about the deceived when I left them to their pleasure. You were the only thing on my mind that night but, just for an instant, I found myself wondering. A wife, a husband, who knows? There had to be the deceived, the trusting partner waiting at home, counting down the hours, believing lies, excuses, the false smiles of reassurance. Why else would they hide in furtive places? Why else would they drive away and leave you crushed like a wind-blown leaf under the wheels of their car? Hit and run. The crunch of metal on flesh, no competition.

Can you hear me, Killian, wherever you are? Is my voice

reaching beyond the black drift of your mind? Are you sleeping in the past, reaching into the present, dreaming of the future? Is your memory short term, long term, long forgotten? Are you listening to me, my lost boy? My foolish ... *foolish* boy.

Black ... black ... black night ... black hole ... black eyes ... eyes ... drowning eyes ...

CHAPTER TWO

March 2002

The removal men arrived on time, their truck almost filling the
width of the small terrace. They were efficient, descending like a
swarm of locusts to divide the bric-à-brac of sixteen years of
marriage into two halves. They packed them neatly into separate
crates and departed, leaving nothing but a skeletal frame behind.

Lorraine Cheevers gazed around her house for the last time.
Bare walls surrounded her, stripped of paintings, posters, calen-
dars and the many photographs that charted the years of family
life. Already, the walls were expanding away from her, the bare
windows glinting coldly; even her footsteps on the wooden
floorboards sent back an unfamiliar tread.

"Running away never solved anything," Donna Cheevers
declared when she heard about her daughter's decision to move
to Trabawn. "It's not easy breaking into a closed community.
Trabawn was holiday time, nothing else. You'll suffer on your
own instead of allowing us to support you through this."

"I've a broken marriage, not a broken leg," Lorraine retorted.
"I don't need a crutch."

"Yes you do," Donna stoutly replied. "You need strong shoulders to cry on. Your life is here. And your work, what about that?"

"I can work anywhere. Trabawn's not exactly on the other
side of the moon."

"Think carefully," her mother warned. "And if you can't think about yourself, think about Emily. Fifteen is the worse possible age to uproot anyone."

"Emily will be fine." Lorraine brought the argument to a decisive close. "You have to allow me to be the judge of what's best for my daughter."

Donna's expression left her in no doubt that such judgement was way beyond her grasp and, when it came to parting, she had held Lorraine fiercely, dry-eyed, knowing the utter futility of uttering banal words of comfort.

Even in her numbed state of mind, Lorraine had been impressed by the amount of money people were willing to pay to live so close to the city. Only ten minutes walk from the city centre, the terrace of red-brick houses where she and Adrian had lived throughout their marriage was as drowsy as a suburb at night. Their neighbours, mainly elderly, retired people, were a close-knit community, watching over the house when they were on holidays and always willing to look after her daughter if Lorraine was delayed at her studio. Their street mascot, they called Emily, remembering her birthdays, fussing over her with presents at Christmas and Easter.

As the estate agent predicted, the house was sold within a few days of going on the market. The couple who bought it were young professional types. He mentioned something about the law library. She worked in the Financial Centre. A starter home, they said, their eyes dismissing the fixtures and fittings, assessing how soon it could be refurbished in their own image.

With the ease of long practice, Lorraine reversed from the terrace. Goodbyes had already been said but her neighbours came to their gates to wave them off. An elderly man walked past and raised his cane in salute. The Liffey had a sullen gleam as it channelled through the quays. Seagulls swooped between dun-coloured walls, fanning their wings against the high-tide markings. Emily clasped her hands on her lap. She stared straight ahead when they passed Blaide House. Fine blue veins etched against her skin. The quays dwindled behind them and the car surged forward, racing westwards towards Trabawn.

CHAPTER THREE

Brahms Ward
9 p.m.

The clinic is quiet tonight. There's stubble on your chin and your nails are growing long again. Your fingers move, clutching the sheet, knuckles braced against imaginary foes. So much life still within you. Skin dying and being renewed, your heart beating steadily. Your hands are beginning to clench inwards. Do you feel us massaging you, straightening your fingers, trimming your nails? Those are the good days, Killian. A sense of purpose to our visits.

They know me now, the staff. They've become my extended family. There's the nurse whose heart has been broken three times since you came here and another who can speak of nothing but her forthcoming wedding. Camila, the little nurse from the Philippines, is my favourite. She's sad and gentle, misses her family like crazy. I suspect you also love her quiet ways. I found her crying one night in the nurse's station. She was sending an e-mail to her daughter who hopes to go to university on her mother's earnings. Soon ... soon, she said, she'll be able to go home.

Maggie is another stalwart. She handles that tea trolley like a runaway train approaching a tunnel. Your fingers twitch when you hear her coming. We're tuned to the nuances of your movements, the flicker of your eyelids, the depth of your breath as it brushes the air around us.

The word "coma" is derived from the Greek. *Koma*: a sleep-like state. How benign it sounds, resting peacefully, ready to awaken to a new day. Brahms Ward, that's what I call this silent place where we wait out time with you. A place of lullabies and lost souls. Your medical team tell us you *cannot* be roused. They speak of vegetative states and the dim possibilities of an "awakening". We refuse to believe those experts with their charts and stethoscopes dangling like chains of office from their necks. Our belief is that you have *not yet* been roused from this sleep-like state – have not yet – have not yet! Hold on to our belief in you, Killian. Hold on.

Hold on ... hold hands ... hands ... join hands ... clap hands ... daddy home ... cakes ... pocket ...

CHAPTER FOUR

In the mornings Lorraine awoke to the crowing of a rooster and the barking of a dog. Rooster and dog seemed determined to outdo each other in verbal energy, and even the birds created a shriller chorus than their city cousins, as if driven by a need to fill the vast empty spaces with their song. Apart from the two bedrooms where she and Emily slept, the long L-shaped kitchen with its stone-flagged floor and smoke-varnished ceiling beams was the only other room in use. Occasionally, driven by a desire to restore some order to her life, she opened crates and stared at the contents, shifted furniture, pushed armchairs under the window then moved them back again against the far wall. This busyness never lasted long, although there was much to occupy her time, and soon she would stop arranging things. She would sit on a chair or a window ledge and stare through the window at the distant hills. She watched the diminutive figure of Noeleen Donaldson strolling the fields with her dog and heard the growl of Frank Donaldson's tractor as he drove past her gate.

When necessary, she drove to the shopping centre that had been built on the old carnival site and stocked up on food and wine. Donna Cheevers was right when she reminded her daughter that Trabawn belonged to idyllic summer days. The years since those annual holidays had wrought much change and little remained of the one-time quaint seaside resort. A large housing estate and an apartment complex marked the approach to the main street and the road, recently widened and lined with go-slow warning signs, had acquired a roundabout with a floral arrangement spelling "Trabawn" in a mix of pink and white petunias. Bed and Breakfast signs beckoned from the front of split-level bungalows and O'Callaghan's pub, with its half-door and low, smoky ceiling, was now a luxurious hotel and restaurant. The old fish-and-chip shop – from where salivating smells had once wafted through the evening air and a portion of chips was the reward for good behaviour – had been turned into a busy video rental shop. But when Lorraine drove beyond the village and its environs, when she indicated left and followed the narrow, sharply twisting road along the coast, everything was as she remembered. Another left-hand turn brought her to Stiles Lane. As rugged as she remembered, tunnelled with overreaching branches, it shook the foundations of her car if she drove too fast. Branches whipped the wing mirrors and pebbles slapped danger-ously against the windscreen. Donaldson's farmhouse created a cul-de-sac and, apart from her house, it was the only other building in the lane. On the opposite side of the farm an old-fashioned stile, almost obscured by high ferns, gave her access to the beach.

A fortnight after her arrival, she received a letter with a New York postmark. She recognised Meg Ruane's handwriting and laid it to one side until after Emily left for school. Her daughter's determination to hate everything about her new home was unrelenting. Trabawn was depressing, dismal, disagreeable, desolate, deserted, dead. She had adjusted to her surroundings with a fondness for alliteration and a tendency to shriek with disgust whenever cattle swayed past the gate or the smell of silage drifted on the wind. She made gagging noises when Lorraine tried to explain the workings of the septic tank and had, on three occasions, declared her intentions of ringing Childline. The school bus – which she approached with the reluctance of a death row prisoner facing an electric chair – picked her up at the top of the lane in the mornings. In the evenings she entered the house and flung her school satchel into the farthest corner of the kitchen. Desperate, despairing, dull, diabolical days. Lorraine was the only buttress for her anger and Emily, being young and energetic, never lost an opportunity to butt.

"Why was it necessary to bury me alive when, like, you know, there was the rest of the world to choose from?" The question had become rhetorical by this stage and was uttered on the slightest whim. "Why am I being forced to endure this hellhole when I should be getting on with my real life?"

"This is real life, Emily. It's different, that's all. I spent the happiest days of my childhood in Trabawn." Lorraine tried without success to convince her daughter of the yet-to-be-discovered delights of the small Kerry village. "It's a wonderful place when you get to know it. Just give it a chance and you'll love it as much as I did."

Emily ordered her mother to stop projecting. "Just because you loved living in this dump when you were a kid means nothing – except that you were easily pleased. I hate living here and I hate the way you keep pretending it's all a great big adventure when it's the most traumatic experience of our lives. A broken marriage is *not* an adventure, it's a tragic failure and I'm the victim. Can't you make it up with him … *just* this once? For my sake? *Please* do it for my sake."

Her pleas seemed to echo from the mildewed walls. But there was no fairy godmother, not even a sprinkling of fairy dust, to disguise the truth. Reconciliation was not an option and Emily, realising the hopelessness of her request, was growing into a changeling, a defiant, hurting stranger whose world had been kicked apart by the folly of adults.

Meg Ruane had taken a more sympathetic view in her letter, which Lorraine read sitting by the window with a cup of coffee cooling on the ledge.

Dear Lorraine,

I simply had to write and tell you how shocked we were to hear about you and Adrian. Eoin's mother rang us with the news and passed on your new address. At first I thought she was joking. You seemed so content when we met in New York. I'd no idea anything was wrong. I don't want to pry – and I'm sure you don't feel like talking about it right now – so this letter is just to let you know that we're thinking of you and wishing you the very best for the future.

We're all keeping well – although the dreadful happenings of 9/11 have cast a terrifying shadow over everyone. New Yorkers are giving the finger to terrorism and there's a jaunty image out there that we're all defiantly getting on with life, but, believe me, it's grim and it will get worse. I'm really looking forward to coming home when Eoin's sabbatical ends in October. His schedule of lectures and performances takes its toll on our time together. The two younger ones have settled down but Aoife remains determinedly home-sick. She spends her time texting and e-mailing her friends in case they're allowed forget her existence for an instant.

How's Emily coping? She and Adrian were so close. We must meet up as soon as I return. If, by chance, you're back again in New York for another of those crazy workshops, I insist you stay with us. Do keep your chin up, darling. It's a new beginning and you're very brave to take that first step. Drop me a line – or an e-mail, if you're on-line. Aoife is not the only one to pine for home and friends.

Love
Meg

She would write back immediately. Her mind raced with sentences that would sound strong, ruefully brave, even witty, and Meg, in her new York apartment, would marvel at her courage. She stared at the unpacked crates. Somewhere in one of them she would find a writing pad. Tomorrow she would search for it. There was a computer dumped under the stairs. She would set it up, go on-line. Altavista … Google … go, go, go. She folded the letter and placed it on a shelf. She sat by the window and watched the day away.

Noeleen Donaldson had welcomed her to the lane with home-made gingerbread and two jars of crab-apple jam. Her eyes had darted around the cluttered hall and kitchen, summing up the general air of desolation. They were dark eyes, shrewd and knowing as she offered to help. Politely but firmly Lorraine shook her head and guided the bird-like woman with her chirpy voice to the front door. The thought of a stranger's hands efficiently unwrapping the contents of her life and assessing them was more than she could tolerate. The older woman had taken the hint and had not visited since. Before she left she pressed a business card into Lorraine's hand. Her two sons had trades, plumbing and carpentry, they were dab hands at bricklaying and painting too – not to mention the contacts they had in the construction industry. Who could blame them for turning their back on farming, she sighed, what with the backache and documentation and the EU regulations that would strain the tolerance of a saint. If Lorraine wanted anything done to the house – her voice trailed discreetly away as she closed the gate behind her.

Her sons, Con and Brendan, came and cast experienced eyes over the rooms. An expensive job, they agreed, nodding ominously. Dampness had disfigured the walls with mottled purple blotches. Lorraine smelled the mustiness in the air, felt it seeping into her lungs. An expert on damp was coming soon. He would banish the mould and the brothers would paint the walls in vibrant defiant colours: Radical Red, Outrageous Orange, Bravado Blue, Yodelling Yellow, Give-Me-a-New-Life Green. Yes, colours could talk and dampness could be vanquished – but the echo, now there was a problem. The rooms were filled with furniture, even if haphazardly arranged and unused, yet still the echo dogged her footsteps, ricocheted around her, reverberated in the chilling aftermath of shock.

On the beach there were no echoes, only memories. Waves pounded against the rocks, arched towards her like beckoning fingers. At every turn on her path, every bank and hollow, in the humped rock and brooding sand dunes, they waited to leap upon her, clutch her throat, laugh in her ears. They would destroy her, those memories, yet she had fled towards them, battling against her parents' disapproval, her daughter's rebellion, her friends' advice; and, now, alone with the past, she felt herself sinking under their weight. She wondered what it would be like to walk through the sea until there was no sand beneath her feet, only bubbles, light as champagne, floating above her as the drift of the tide filled her senses and dragged her deeper ... deeper ... into a gentle green oblivion. On such occasions, she held Emily tightly in her mind and concentrated on the tasks that needed doing: a school skirt to be altered, jeans that Emily had dumped on the table with the request, no, the curt demand, that they be washed, the unpacking of the groceries she had bought earlier; trivial but essential tasks that forced her footsteps across the strand and back to the house.

Evening time and the settling dusk brought the bats flitting silently from a cleft in Donaldsons' barn. They swooped fleetly under the wind-break trees, skimmed around the walls of the old house. At first, she had been frightened by their arrival, imagining their frail fluttering bodies tangled in her hair, their invincible antennae searching for a chink, a tiny crevice in the fortress she had created. But they marked the close of another day and she had grown used to their sudden appearance. When they disappeared into the gloom she knew it was time to heap logs on the fire, light candles, open another bottle of wine. She listened to the clock ticking down the hours towards bedtime. There had to be an easier way to pass the time but she had yet to discover it.

The promise of spending a weekend in Dublin with her grand-parents silenced Emily's complaints for a short while. She was their only grandchild and they treasured the close relationship they had with her. Lorraine debated going to Dublin with her but she was still unable to endure the transparent attempts by her parents to tip-toe around her grief. For this reason she had refused to invite them to Trabawn. The house was still unin-habitable, she insisted every time Donna rang, refusing to hear the hurt in her mother's voice, salving her conscience by looking at the chaos she was accumulating around her.

On Saturday morning she drove Emily to the railway station in Tralee and waved her off. The town was busy, the streets congested with traffic and shoppers. When she was a child, on holidays in Trabawn, a night at the Rose of Tralee Festival had been the highlight of the fortnight, providing the adults and children with an opportunity to dress up and become part of the boisterous crowd that attended the annual beauty contest. Swimsuits and shorts were abandoned for the "Rose" dresses that she and Virginia donned for the occasion. Holding hands, they paraded up and down the thronged streets, admiring themselves in shop windows, imagining themselves on stage, surrounded by envious Roses as they received their crowns and the audience rapturously sang "The Rose of Tralee". For that night and the days that followed she would refer to Virginia as "London Rose", while she gloried in the title "Dublin Rose".

Shrugging aside this dip into childhood, Lorraine drove into a shopping-centre car-park and hurried towards the supermarket. She filled her trolley with basic items, impervious to demonstrators tempting her with cheeses and sauces. On leaving the town, she drove past Blennerville where the sails of the historic windmill whirred busily over Tralee Bay. She should spend a day in Tralee with Emily. They could tour the windmill, ride on the old steam railway line, visit the aqua dome, buy new clothes, have a meal together. By the time she reached Trabawn, she had sunk once again into the familiar lethargy.

Emily rang later in the evening to announce her safe arrival in Dublin. A music gig in Temple Bar with her friends was planned and they were eating afterwards in Thunder Road Café. Lorraine was relieved to hear the lightness in her daughter's voice, even if it was only a short respite from the resolute air of martyrdom Emily carried on her shoulders. Later, the telephone rang again as Lorraine was uncorking a bottle of wine. Only one person would ring her at this hour of the night. She tensed her arms and waited for the answering machine to switch on.

"Lorraine, pick up the phone. I know you can hear me." Her husband's voice faded into background noise. He was ringing from a pub. She could almost smell the perfume in the crowded bar, the vigorous crush of bodies around the counter, the exhaled smoke spiralling as high as the laughter. The noise faded as he moved to a quieter place. "Please talk to me, Lorraine. Emily called to the apartment this evening and created quite a scene. She's very distressed."

She lifted the receiver and pressed it against her ear. "Is she with you now?"

"I followed her but she insisted on going off with her friends. They'll take care of her. We have to meet soon. This is a ludicrous situation. It can't continue."

"*No.* I've told you already. I can't meet you. I'm not ready –"

"But this is not just about us." Impatiently, he cut across her protests. "Whether you like it or not, we have to sort something out for Emily's sake."

"I'll ring her on her mobile. Thanks for contacting me, Adrian. Goodbye."

"Don't hang up, please. You know I'm right. We must work out some kind of routine –"

"That's up to Emily to decide. I'll discuss it with her when she returns."

"You did a cruel thing by removing her from everything that was familiar to her and this is the result." His breath rasped down the line, judge and jury, accusing. He once had the power to cajole and comfort her, to raise her to heights of pleasure. But as she hung up the phone she felt nothing except an aching regret that tightened like a fist, knuckles digging deep into her chest.

She poured a glass of wine and flung another log on the fire. The glow from the flames reflected ruby splinters off the glass, imbued the kitchen table with a tawny sheen. She liked cottage furniture that had absorbed many lives into its grain and the table, an ancient hunk of wood with scrubbed ridges, bleached of colour and slightly hollowed in the centre, had once belonged to Celia Murphy, the original owner of the house. Lorraine had discovered daffodils among the weeds in the garden and had heaped them in vases around the kitchen. They added to the illusion of comfort and lifted her briefly into a future where she could imagine how everything would look when the house was restored. Small gestures she could manage. Illusions she could create. But nothing drowned the echoes. She sat by the window and stared into the impenetrable darkness of the countryside. Such silence. She breathed into it. The stars shone with a clarity she had never seen in the city but they only made her yearn more fervently for the glare of street lights, the noise of traffic, sirens, burglar alarms, the acceleration of motorbikes passing too close, too fast, the march of footsteps across the Ha'penny Bridge, the loud pealing of bells, the whispering sighs of passion satiated. Her hand was steady as she poured another glass of wine. In the past, on such a night, she would have lifted the phone to Virginia. Perhaps she would have driven to her cousin's house in Howth and they would have sat on the balcony overlooking Dublin Bay, sharing laughter and confidences, and everything would seem manageable again.

The bottle was empty, the glass smeared. Her breath shortened. Her skin shivered. As loneliness gave way to all-consuming grief, Lorraine Cheevers began to weep. Her crying echoed, unheard, throughout the empty house.

CHAPTER FIVE

Brahms Ward
10 p.m.

Don't look so lost, Killian. I'm here beside you. The moon is tossing high in the sky and the wind would slice the nose from your face. You're warm and safe here. Snug as a bug in a rug. I dreamt about you again last night. A wonderful dream, filled with colour and movement, but silent, as if sleep had granted me this one concession. I was standing on the Great South Wall and you, light as a feather and aged about six, were perched on my shoulders. A red lighthouse winked and warned at the foot of the pier and we were flanked by the Dublin Mountains, the curve of Sandymount strand and the Bull Wall jutting like a crude finger into the sea. How strong I felt standing there, the tide lapping the rocks below. A Saturday father again and you were mine for the allotted time span.

Do you remember our walks on the pier? How long ago it seems now. We trained our binoculars on the ferries as they sailed back and forth across the bay. We made up stories about the passengers: spies, pirates and gangsters, monsters, ghouls and werewolves too. You'd a taste for the bizarre, my son. A chip off the old block, some would say. When it was time to return to your other world, you sometimes cried as I drove away from the docklands; a dead place in those days, filled with derelict warehouses and empty wasted sites. How short those hours seemed then, hard-fought and won. But it was real time. Our time. Not stolen from dreams.

I'm going to slip away. It's late now and I've an outline to finish before tomorrow. The writing's not going well, I'm afraid. No inspiration. How Harriet would snort if she knew. She doesn't believe in writer's block. "Let your fingers do the thinking and your mind will catch up," she always says. "It hates being left out of the action."

So, it's black coffee and a long night. I'm working on the problems between Gary and his father. Can't sort it out, Killian. They spar with each other, old bull, young buck, but their dialogue has no life. It's fake, contrived mush. I've always found fathers to be tricky characters to handle. I never knew my own father, not on Saturdays or any other day. So there you have it, Killian. No role model. It's not an excuse for failing you – or for bad dialogue. Just a fact of life.

Father ... Our Father ... heaven ... father ... daddy ... Saturday Daddy ... cakes ... pocket ... daddy come home ...

CHAPTER SIX

The Donaldson brothers started work on the studio, converting the old stable where Celia Murphy once stabled her donkeys and, in a time before then, her father kept his two plough horses. With their sturdy bodies and strong, ruddy faces, the brothers were so alike that Lorraine had difficulty distinguishing one from the other. They sang in harmony as they worked. Garth Brooks fans. Although they harmonised surprisingly well they stopped self-consciously whenever she entered the studio. Their taste in music drove Emily to despair. Discordant, desperate, dreary, dreadful dirge. What had been an amused tolerance for country music had swelled to a passionate hatred. Every hammer blow they made was a reminder that her young life was changing inexorably.

One evening, while unpacking a crate that had been blocking the landing, she discovered an old photograph album of Lorraine's. Listlessly, she turned the pages that chronicled her mother's childhood holidays. Lorraine discovered her sitting cross-legged beside the crate, the album open on her knees. She knelt down beside her and stared at the photograph of two small girls sitting on a dry-stone wall, bare legs dangling, their swim-suits clinging to their tanned, skinny bodies. Virginia's straight black hair swung over her cheeks. Her eyes peered from under a long fringe. She was thin and leggy, her stomach almost concave in a red bikini. She held a dead crab which, seconds before the camera clicked, she had pressed against Lorraine's face. Lorraine, in an identical bikini, looked startled, as if she was trying desperately to hold her balance on the wall. A pair of donkeys grazed in the background and the old two-storey house looked exactly the same as now: dingy grey pebble-dashed walls, a hall door in the centre with a window on either side. Three windows on the top floor, two large and a small one in the centre, offered a distant view of the ocean. Celia Murphy stood in her doorway, her hand raised in a wave as if she was personally greeting the camera.

Emily turned the pages: the girls older now, tank tops and bell bottoms, outrageous platform shoes, standing outside O'Callaghan's pub. Mr O'Callaghan stood between them, an argyle jumper stretched across his imposing stomach. Everyone smiling, always smiling.

Emily pressed her nail into the last photograph. "People used to say I look like Virginia. But I can't see the slightest resemblance, can you?"

Lorraine stared at the young Virginia, thinking to herself that the hoydenish grin did indeed resemble Emily in one of her more impish moods, but before she could reply Emily flung the album back into the crate.

"Live in the past if you want to. I've more important things to do with my time." She entered her bedroom and defiantly turned up the volume of her stereo in a determined effort to separate herself from the poisonous, putrid prison her mother had imposed on her.

Lorraine could empathise with her daughter's sense of dislocation. The local women smiled when they met her in the supermarket and asked how she was settling in. But it was the politeness they showed to a tourist, superficial conversations about the weather and the rising price of groceries.

"You probably intimidate them," Emily had declared, shortly after their arrival. "They think you're a *celeb* just because you were on the *Late Late Show* with your nudes. Naked, naughty, nauseating nudes. It's *so* embarrassing."

In Dublin she had basked in the brief notoriety that had followed her mother's last exhibition but in her new surroundings she took no delight in being the daughter of an infamous artist.

The controversy that followed the exhibition had hardly touched Lorraine. Was *Painting Dreams* an erotic or a pornographic exhibition? Such an argument was always bound to evoke a strong reaction, offering a platform for anyone with an opinion – and there were many who had much to say. In a splintering world, how easily we are aroused by the unimportant issues, she had thought, listening to empty words, puffed up rhetoric, reviews that praised or criticised her work. As far as she was concerned, it was a trivial spat compared to the private battle she waged against herself and her fears.

By mid-May, her studio was complete. The exterior white-washed walls and green window frames had a crisp newness that demanded more than an indifferent nod of approval. She forced enthusiasm into her voice as she thanked the Donaldson brothers. It amazed her that she had once been unable to tell them apart. Brendan was the taller of the two, a tenor who played guitar in O'Callaghan's lounge bar at the weekends. Con was a baritone and a skilled horseman. She had noticed a rough-and-ready jumping arena in the field where the holiday caravans once stood and sometimes saw him riding on the beach, horse and rider cantering through the incoming tide. He had offered to teach Emily to ride, a suggestion that reduced her to hysterical laughter at the thought of coming into contact with hideous, horrendous, horrible horseflesh.

The shelves Con had built in the studio looked solid, practical, like his posture on his horse. Into this high-ceilinged space with its white pristine walls, a sink had been plumbed and a table, shelves and presses built to Lorraine's specifications. A small outhouse, adjoining the stable, was converted into a dark room. She could fill her new studio with clutter and colour if she so chose. But as the weeks passed the crates containing her painting materials remained unopened.

Emily arrived home from school one evening shortly before the start of the school holidays and announced that her art teacher had requested a meeting with Lorraine.

"He actually *owns* one of your paintings." She cupped her hand around her mouth and hissed. "The one with Cherie. I nearly died of mortification when he told me. Of course he pretended it was meant to symbolise the universal repression of the anarchistic desire of the male species – but he wasn't fooling me. Not for one single minute. I know a lap dancer when I see one."

John Falmer, Emily's art teacher, was far too handsome to instil knowledge into a class of pubescent girls, Lorraine thought when she sat down in front of him the following afternoon. He was quick to reassure her that Emily had adjusted well to her change of school and appeared to be enjoying her art classes.

"I'd an opportunity to view your last exhibition when I was in Dublin. An unusual concept. Well executed ... provocative, to say the least." He cleared his throat and briskly tapped his pencil off the desk. "Emily told me you used to give art classes. Have you heard about the adult education programme we run at St Peter's?" Without waiting for her reply he added, "I hope to persuade you to run a series of night classes when we reopen in September. We've excellent facilities available, especially our studios. It would be an honour to have you as part of our tutorial team."

Lorraine explained about the pressure of work. Commissions, deadlines, maybe some other time. He seemed genuinely disappointed when he shook her hand and said goodbye.

"So? How did it go?" Emily demanded on her return from school.

"He asked me to take on art classes in September."

"Oh my *God!*" Her daughter screamed in mock-horror. "Promise me you'll stick to still life. I'll die if you start teaching the population of Trabawn to paint nudes."

"You needn't worry. Trabawn is quite safe. I haven't the slightest intention of teaching anyone to paint."

For the first two weeks of her school holidays, Emily lay in bed, her Walkman to her ears, appearing only to raid the fridge or watch the latest episode of *Nowhere Lodge*. In Dublin, as soon as each episode of the teenage series ended, it had been earnestly analysed on the phone with her classmates who formed the *Nowhere Lodge* fan club. She still watched it three times a week, blankly staring at the screen and displaying little pleasure in the antics of the characters whose lives had become as familiar to her as those of her best friends.

By the third week of her school holidays she began moving the crates containing Lorraine's painting materials into the studio. She unpacked the paints and brushes, erected the easels, stacked half-finished canvases against the walls, filled the shelves with books and the compact discs Lorraine always played when she was working.

"Can't you at least slosh some paint on the walls and let me know you're alive?" she snapped one evening when she returned to the kitchen and found Lorraine lying on the sofa, a rug draped over her knees. "What's the big deal about painting a picture? You've done nothing since your nudes. Am I supposed to face a life of destitution, deprivation and despondency?"

Lorraine sighed. "Emily, do me a favour. Turn the page to E."

"Emotional, empty, enraged." She chanted the words with grim determination. "Endurance, entombed, excrement. Would you like me to move to the F words?" Her smile was brittle, her attempt at humour barely disguising her fury as she glared at her mother. She lifted an empty bottle and held it upside down. A trickle of wine spilled across her fingers. She placed it back on the table and waved her stained hand before Lorraine's face.

"When can I have my life back again? Are you listening, Mother – or am I communicating with a zombie? You turn my world upside down then lie around all day drinking and feeling sorry for yourself. I'm sick of it, do you hear me? Sick … *sick* … *sick!* I keep trying to help you but you can't even be bothered thanking me. What do you think I am? Your skivvy?"

"I never asked for your help." Lorraine pulled the rug across her knees. "Nor have I deprived you of anything, not now, not ever. All I'm trying to do is build a new life for us both – "

"No – no! Stop it right there. That's a lie. You want a new life for yourself, no one else. I *loathe* living here but you keep treating me like some kid having a tantrum that will soon pass. Where do my needs come into any of this? I've lost my friends. They're getting on with their lives while I'm stuck here with a mother who won't even comb her hair in the mornings. I'm sick of it, do you hear me? I can't stand what's happened and, what's even worse, no one cares how I feel. I don't want to live with you any more." Tears ran down her cheeks. "I want to go back to Dublin and live with Sharon. She says I can share her room. Her mother won't mind, I know she won't … and that's what I'm going to do so don't try and stop me." She ran from the kitchen. Her footsteps thumped against the stairs, her bedroom door slammed.

"What's the sense in talking," she screamed through the door when Lorraine tried to gain entry. "Nothing's going to change. I *hate* you."

In the bathroom where they were plumbing in a new sink the Donaldson brothers fell silent. Oh well – Lorraine collapsed back onto the sofa and closed her eyes. Let all of Trabawn know that the new arrivals drew blood when they fought.

Later, after the brothers had left for the evening, she entered Emily's bedroom. Her daughter lay sleeping, her face buried in the pillows, crumpled tissues on the floor. Lorraine touched her hair, stroked the thick black tresses. A montage of family photographs had been mounted on one of the walls. A close-knit family of three, their arms around each other. A day on the beach. Another at one of Emily's birthday parties. The candles on the cake numbered ten and Emily's cheeks ballooned as she blew them out. All the small and big occasions, the milestones, the forgotten incidents, the oft-remembered excursions, they were all there; a constant reminder of how much she had lost. Lorraine left the room and silently closed the door behind her.

In her studio, she switched on the lights. How clinical it looked, the white walls and harsh overhead beams. Con had screwed a large mirror into the wall. She placed a chair in front of it and removed a sketch pad from the shelf. Using charcoal she began to sketch, her eyes darting from her reflection to the page. It was years since she had drawn a self-portrait, probably as far back as her student days. She had no idea how long she had been drawing, an hour, probably two if the darkness outside the window was any indicator. Some sketches were abandoned, others finished. Her movements grew more frantic as she slashed and scored the paper. She pulled the mouth downwards in exaggerated grimaces, added violence to the eyes, stretched the lips in a scream.

Finally, exhausted, trembling, she flung the sketch pad on the floor. Perhaps she would never paint again. The thought would once have terrified her, forced her to contemplate a vast emptiness in her life. But, as she looked towards the easel, the weight of a paint brush in her hand was more than she could tolerate.

Emily entered, wraith-like in a pale yellow dressing gown. She picked up the sketch pad and stared at the drawings. "Please tell me it's going to get better." Her voice was almost inaudible. "I need to find you again."

"I'm still here, Emily," said Lorraine and she held tightly to her daughter's hand as they walked back to the house.

CHAPTER SEVEN

Brahms Ward
6 p.m.

Hi there, Killian. Let's take a look at you. Maggie says you've been fretful today. How can she tell? She rattles her tea trolley and pronounces on the state of your moods with the authority of a pope. Your grandmother must have been here earlier. She's left the glass snowball by your bedside. You'll shake it again some day and watch the snowflakes fly.

I met Jean on the way in. We talked for a while. It's a start. No, it's more than that. It's a bloody miracle. One thing we can both agree on is that the trail from the Great South Wall is dead. The police have no further information, no leads. The glass they found on the pier was further back from the scene of the accident so they don't believe it's a related incident.

Two guards came to my apartment that night. Boys masquerading as men. I've heard it said that the first realisation of aging comes when policemen and doctors cease to intimidate and start to imitate our children. But those young lads did not remind me of you. They were stalwart, square of chin, solidly earthed. They'd found my address in your pocket. The words they used were careful, regulation kindness, not overtly alarming. But

I knew, oh yes, even as I ran towards the hospital entrance, I knew what I would find. Tubes and machines, monitors bleeping and you, my son, clinging grimly to life. I wanted to kneel on the floor, throw back my head and howl. Old women once wisely keened their departed but nowadays we need a canyon or a cavern, not a white sterile room, to calm the fury, make the pain more bearable.

I rang your mother from the hospital. Laura answered the phone. Your sister is only fourteen but she's aware that late night calls come to her house for one reason only. When I asked to speak to Jean, she called her immediately. I listened to the sound of your mother's footsteps hurrying nearer and had no idea, no earthly idea, how I would break the news to her. She hung up when she heard all she needed to hear and arrived at the hospital shortly afterwards. How shrunken she seemed, as if some vital vertebrae had been removed from her spine. Terence supported her against his chest. Laura and Duncan clung weeping to her. Your grandparents came also. A tight family circle. Nurses brought us tea and comfort, spoke in hushed nocturnal voices. A doctor with sleep grit in her eyes told us of horrendous decisions we might have to make. These are the memories I carry with me from that grief-filled night. They are memories I'll carry to my grave.

I can't stop thinking about that voice on the phone. Anonymous, of course, muffled by something, probably a scarf or handkerchief, but with enough clarity to send an ambulance speeding through the night. Does she have children, I wonder? Does she worry about them at night? Has she ever felt that hand clutching her heart when the knock comes to the door and she knows the fear, the bleak, terrifying moment that nudges her awake from nightmares, is about to come true?

At first it was impossible to imagine an hour passing, then two and three, a day, a week, months. But time is an indifferent monitor of grief and two weeks went by before Jean had the energy to come to my apartment. And when she came, she was ruthless in her need to apportion blame.

"You got your way at last." Her anger was a wrenching cry, far beyond my comfort. It took nineteen years, she said, but I destroyed you in the end. I promised to look after you and I failed. I threw you out on the streets when I knew how desperately you needed my help.

"Tough love ... what kind of love is that?" she demanded. "You never wanted Killian. *Never!* I don't know how you can live with yourself."

What use is truth when it's buried in such anguish? She placed her head in her hands as if she couldn't bear the sight of me. Her words didn't hurt me. They were trite accusations compared to my own self-indictment. Like me, she is unable to rest at night. There's no closure, Killian. You were born from a careless love and it tied us both in an enduring knot. We have two stories, same source, different strands. Some day soon I'll write our story. Once upon a time there was a young man and a young woman. They made a homeless child ...

There's a grand stretch to the evenings. Soon it will be the longest day of the year. The cherry blossom is fading and the rooks are swirling past your window.

Homeless ... home ... less home ... show way home ... home on range ... home sweet home ... sweet Chariot ... coming ... carry me home ... no home ... Bozo ...

CHAPTER EIGHT

Cars drawing caravans chugged through Market Street and banners advertising a country music festival appeared in the windows of the restaurants and pubs. Trabawn settled into a more leisurely pace as visitors in sun-dresses, shorts and t-shirts took over the pavements. In the supermarket a trim, bespectacled man in denim shorts and sandals stared openly at Lorraine as she approached the fresh bread counter.

"Lorraine Cheevers! My God, you haven't changed a bit, not a bit. I'd recognise that flaming mop of curls anywhere." He laughed at her blank expression. "Don't tell me I've changed so much that you don't recognise Máirtín Mullarkey?"

"Mad-Dog?" She tried to silence the laughter bubbling up inside her. "My God! It can't be."

He chuckled, raised a long, slim finger to his lips. Pale and instantly familiar blue eyes gleamed behind his glasses. "*Shhhh!* I'm a respectable science teacher these days. Emily is one of my pupils, as a matter of fact. I hope you're not going to fling my past at me now, are you?"

"I wouldn't dream of it, Master Mullarkey." She lowered her voice to a dramatic whisper. "As long as you're not giving my daughter any lessons in horticulture, especially the grow-and-roll-your-own variety."

"Perish the thought. I'm a rock of respectability these days, with five daughters to keep me in hand. How've you been?"

"Oh, you know. Getting by. One daughter, one broken marriage and a career in painting."

"I saw you on *Artistically Speaking*. Interesting documentary. But I'm sorry to hear about you and Adrian."

She shrugged. "It's water under the bridge now. Life goes on."

"That's a fact, sure enough. Whatever happened to the gorgeous Virginia?"

"She's in the PR business."

"A spin doctor, is she? Well, who'd have thought it. I always imagined her in films or on the catwalk. I was mad about that woman. Is she still breaking hearts?"

"Oh yes, I suspect she is." Lorraine moved her trolley to one side and allowed a woman to pass them by.

"What about her brother, what's his name?"

"Edward. He's an economist in London. One marriage, still very much intact, and three children."

"Emily reminds me of Virginia in appearance. Your daughter is a charming young girl, very bright."

"But not a happy one, I'm afraid. She's finding it difficult to adjust to her new surroundings. So much has happened so quickly in her life and I feel guilty —"

She broke off, embarrassed at revealing so much about herself to a man who had once prided himself on the quality of his home-grown cannabis.

He smiled, shrugged. "I'm in the throes of rearing five daughters so you can't tell me anything I don't know about the guilt trip. As soon as Emily starts making friends you'll be home and dry."

Their conversation was interrupted by a woman who stopped beside them, obviously anxious to speak to Máirtín. "You and Emily must come and visit us," he said before Lorraine moved on. "Jan, my wife, would love to meet you. Give me your number. I'll ring and arrange something soon."

She unloaded groceries onto the kitchen table and handed a container of Pringles to her daughter. "As requested, madam. By the way, I met your science teacher in the supermarket."

"Sparky Marky?"

"I suspect we're probably discussing the same person."

"He's not the worst. Did you tell him I'm part of a dys-functional family set-up?"

"I could have. But he wouldn't have believed me. He says you're an excellent student."

"Of course I am." Emily snapped a crisp between her teeth. "You don't need to be happy to be brilliant. In fact, it helps when you're despairing, depressed and dumped in hell. His daughters are in my year. They're twin goths, Janice and Joplin."

"That figures."

"A man rang while you were out. Bill something or other. He wants to commission a portrait. He said you're a difficult woman to pin down and that you've ignored the two phone messages he left on your answering machine."

Before leaving Dublin, Lorraine had instructed the receptionist at Blaide House not to disclose her new address or telephone number to anyone. Abruptly, she stopped unpacking the groceries and walked outside. From where she stood, she could hear the faint break of waves on the rocks and, closer, the frenzied barking of Hobbs, the farmyard dog. These outbursts had become familiar to her, erupting whenever she approached the stile on her way to the beach or a stranger entered the lane. The collie's barking only subsided when Noeleen came to the door to scold him. On hearing her voice, Hobbs always collapsed into abject obedience, slinking towards the shelter of the wall so no one could witness his subjugation.

Bill Sheraton's arrival would break through the protective fug that had surrounded her since she came to Trabawn. She wanted to ring him back, postpone his visit, make excuses, invent a terminal illness – could a broken heart be classified as a "terminal illness", she wondered – and, if he still insisted on coming, hide behind the sand dunes until he left. Despite her annoyance, she smiled at the idea of crouching like a frightened rabbit behind the eroding, sandy embankments. He was arriving tomorrow, Emily said. She would meet him, hear what he had to say, then send him politely on his way with a firm refusal ringing in his ears. When she was ready to start painting again she would make the decision herself.

Noeleen opened the farmhouse door. Her voice rang out and the barking stopped as suddenly as it had started. Despite the dog's desire to tear her apart limb by limb whenever she came within sniffing distance, Lorraine felt a certain affection for the brute, having guessed, correctly as it turned out, that he was a direct descendant of Celia Murphy's dog, Old Red Eye. The past manifested itself in many shapes and forms. She stretched her hands before her and watched them tremble. The tremor was faint, almost invisible, like the first stirrings of a palsy. Virginia was the only person who would pass her telephone number on to the businessman. She claimed he was her most demanding client and charged him lavishly for his abrasive ways.

When Lorraine grew calm again she returned to the kitchen. Her hands were steady as she helped her daughter stack away the last of the groceries.

On the following afternoon when Lorraine returned from the beach, Bill Sheraton's BMW, which almost spanned the width of the lane, had offended Hobbs' territorial instincts to such a degree that he was barking an octave higher than usual. Unperturbed by the dog's hysteria, Bill was leaning against the front wall, observing the smoke rings that wafted in clear circles above his head. His broad hands looked more suitable to handling a shovel than the slim black cigarillo he was smoking but Virginia believed he was addicted to them. He had smoked in the gallery on the opening night of Lorraine's *Painting Dreams* exhibition, deliberately ignoring the No Smoking signs, and no one had had the courage to rebuke him.

"Leave him to it," Virginia had advised. "He'll buy quickly and leave. Andrea has a full schedule lined up for the night." Her judgement proved to be correct. After only a cursory glance at the collection, Bill Sheraton purchased two of Lorraine's most expensive paintings and departed with his wife to attend another function.

"Don't be fooled by his rough manner," Virginia had said, switching off her public relations smile and casting a speculative glance at the two sold stickers. "He knows exactly what he's buying and how much your paintings will appreciate in value. He's a rough neck with impeccable taste."

"What's with the mutt?" Bill brusquely swept aside Lorraine's apology for keeping him waiting and followed her around the side of the house. "Has it got rabies or something?"

"It's an inherited gene," she replied. "You can relax. He's yet to prove his bite is worst than his bark."

"I'm all in favour of a good bark but only when it's accompanied by a sharp bite." He entered her studio and blew smoke into its pristine interior. "So this is where you're hiding out." His tone was non-committal as he took in the bare walls and tidy shelves.

Emily was right. Her studio should be paint-splashed and haphazard, reeking of turpentine, breath-catching spirits, varnish. Instead, she stood in a white, sterile room that breathed loneliness from every corner. "How can I help you, Mr Sheraton?" She lifted the electric kettle and filled it with water.

"First of all you can tell me what the hell you're doing bolting off to the arse-end of nowhere when you should be in Dublin creaming off the publicity after your exhibition?"

She tried to hide her annoyance as she switched on the kettle. Her sudden departure so soon after the exhibition had obviously been a subject of gossip and speculation. "I'm not a horse, Mr Sheraton. I don't bolt. I make decisions. Trabawn is ideally suited to my needs."

"I'll say it is. I'll be lucky if there's any suspension left on my car after driving down that boreen." He blew a derisive puff of smoke towards the ceiling. "I heard some of the callers to *Liveline* giving out about your exhibition. Crackpots, all of them. You should have stood your ground and fucked the begrudgers. Every fruitcake in the country with a view on anything thinks the rest of us have nothing better to do than listen to their cock-eyed opinions. I still can't make up my mind if the paintings I bought are erotic or pornographic. But I'm not losing sleep over it." He deliberated for an instant. "Erotic, I suppose. Pornography leaves nothing to the imagination but — well — I imagine something different every time I look at the damn things." He chuckled deeply, suggestively. She almost expected him to nudge her and say, "Know what I mean, eh?"

"Mr Sheraton, I assume you're here for a reason?" She gestured towards a chair and placed two mugs on the table. "Would you like tea or coffee before we begin?"

"Coffee sounds about right. Call me Bill. No sense in formalities. Andrea is interested in commissioning a family portrait."

"I'm sure Virginia told you I'm not accepting any new commissions at the moment."

He drew deeply on his cigarillo and continued as if she had not spoken. "Andrea's been on my back for weeks with this latest notion. And that's to have a family portrait by Lorraine Cheevers. How soon can you begin?"

"If you want a family portrait I can give you the telephone numbers of excellent artists who'll be delighted to oblige."

"Give me a break, Lorraine." He sighed impatiently. "It's you she wants and what she wants she gets – or I get hell. Can I ask when you'll be available?"

"I'll ring and let you know."

"That's not an answer. When are you next in Dublin?"

"I've no immediate plans to go there."

"Is this a hermitage then – or can I assume you'll venture forth into the real world sooner or later?"

Without replying, she walked to the window. Such a wilderness of weed and briar. Nothing for it but to clear everything out. She would hire a digger, get things moving. He stood beside her, puffing his foul smoke into her fresh air. "I'll phone you when I've made my plans, Bill."

"Do that. We'll have lunch together. But, for Christ's sake, don't wait too long. Andrea gets what she wants or I get hell." He handed her his business card and nodded approvingly. "That's a nice kid I spoke to on the phone. What age is she?"

"Fifteen."

"Has she settled here?"

"It's taking time."

"At least it's a safe environment. Keys in the car, the front door on the latch, that sort of thing. Dublin's a cess pit and our kids are swimming in it."

"All Emily thinks about is returning to live there."

"Keep her here. She'll settle eventually." She sensed him hesitating, choosing his words. "Young people. I don't understand what the hell they're on about most of the time – or what they want from life. Our son went badly off the rails for a while but he's out the other end, thank God." He shook his head vigorously. "I was running my first travel agency when I was his age. Eighteen years and I could already smell my first million. But Lorcan! Even if luck bit him hard on the arse he wouldn't recognise it."

He left the studio and faced the farmhouse where Hobbs was once again making his presence heard. "Some people make a lot of noise but they say nothing. Keep your eyes on the future, Lorraine." She had expected a bone crushing handshake but his grasp was firm and oddly comforting. "I've been on the ropes a few times in my life. Yet I've always known when it was time to rise again and face the next round. You will too. Ring me when you get to Dublin and we'll talk again."

Máirtín Mullarkey kept his word. The following week he rang Lorraine and invited her to a barbecue on Sunday afternoon. As soon as they arrived at his bungalow, Emily disappeared with the goth twins, whose appearance suggested they had ventured forth from the confines of a vampire's bridal suite. Apart from a brief dash to the patio for sausages, burgers and baked potatoes, Lorraine did not see the young people again until it was time to return home. Coloured lights had been hung around the garden where friends and neighbours gathered. Some of the people were local but Lorraine heard other accents, an Australian twang, the deep, melodic cadences of an African voice and the heavily accented English of a young Italian couple who had set up a holistic health centre in the village. She heard, also, a London accent, the inflection so reminiscent of Virginia that for an instant she thought her cousin was sitting on a deck chair, her face shaded by a wide-brimmed straw hat. During her childhood summers a visitor from Dublin was a stranger in Trabawn. Now, only two decades later, Lorraine was simply another unremarkable face in a multicultural gathering.

She sat beside Sophie, a Sudanese woman married to an Irish

farmer. They had met in Sudan, she told Lorraine, when he was engaged on an agricultural project and she was working as a nurse in a local hospital. They had moved to Ireland sixteen years ago.

"A big adjustment?" Lorraine asked.

"At first, yes. Now, not so bad. I ignore what I don't want to hear and draw strength from those who are close to me. And you?"

"I don't know why I'm here." She made the admission frankly. "I came to escape from a marriage that was no longer working. At the time it seemed a good idea. Now I'm not so sure."

"The house where you live, it's lonely, yes? A woman on her own, now that, I know, is definitely not a good idea." Sophie's laugh rolled across the garden. "You must come to dinner soon. I have many handsome friends who would love to meet you."

"Dinner, yes. But no friends, handsome or otherwise." She smiled, spread her hands as if to brush away an unwelcome idea. "I'm not ready for anything like that, Sophie."

"How do you know? Stuck down in that lane." She touched Lorraine's hair, smiled. "Don't let the fire die, girl."

The fire is well and truly quenched, Lorraine thought, preparing for bed that night. She stood naked before the mirror and stared at her reflection. Outwardly there was nothing to suggest she had become a dried up prune. It should show on her face but, apart from the dullness in her eyes, she looked refreshingly healthy. Her hair, still tossed from a late-night walk along the beach, glowed red under the bedroom light and her skin was tanned from the sea breeze. Divorce proceedings had to begin. If she was to move on with her life she must make decisions instead of living in limbo-land. But she was unable to comprehend the reality of no longer being a wife. Would it be like losing an arm or a leg? Would she be limbless and free, suffer phantom sensations, imagining Adrian beside her in the morning when she awoke, hearing his key in the door, his music on the stereo, his body above her and she below him, sinking into the familiar rhythm of passion? And memories, what happened to them when they no longer had a structure to keep them intact? Did they, like love, dry up and die?

As Máirtín had predicted, Emily was making friends: a boy with bleached hair called Ian, Sophie's son, Ibrahim, and a willowy young person called Fran, whose gender still remained a mystery to Lorraine. Máirtín's goth twins completed the group. They cycled down Stile Lane and descended on her house to devour great quantities of popcorn, toasted cheese sandwiches and pizzas. They were noisy, untidy and unfailingly polite to Lorraine. Their tolerance for loud music would, she suspected, leave them with significant hearing loss by the time they were twenty.

"Can I ask you a fabulously fantastic favour?" Emily asked one evening after her new friends had departed. "It's to do with my birthday."

"Ask away."

"Will you and Daddy make up?" She spoke too quickly, nervously curling her fist against her chin, but her tone was so determined that it stalled Lorraine's instinctive rebuttal. "I know you're not going back to him but I want the three of us to have a meal together, the way we always did on the night of my birthday."

"Emily, please don't ask me to do that −"

"Please ... *please!* Can't we be a family again? Just for one night? He wants to come to Trabawn and stay in O'Callaghan's Hotel. If he books a meal in the restaurant will you come with us?"

"I don't need this discussion, Emily. It's not as if I've prevented you from seeing your father as often as you wish, but you've made no effort to stay in touch with him. Except for that one time −"

"It'll be different if he comes here." Emily flushed deeply. Her mouth puckered. "Just one night, that's all I want for my birthday and you can't even give me that."

"If it means so much to you, then that's what we'll do. But I don't want him in the house. Do you understand?"

Her daughter nodded. "Do you think you'll ever get back together again? Not now but maybe in a year's time − two years'?"

"Darling, that kind of talk gets us nowhere. Your father and I have made our decisions. Nothing's going to change. But time will make things easier, you'll see. After all, we did one wonderful thing together. We had you. You'll always keep us in touch."

Noble words, she thought, after Emily had gone to bed. She took a bottle of wine from the fridge and fiercely twisted the corkscrew in the bottle.

Her daughter had one last favour to ask. Could she bring Ibrahim O'Doherty to the restaurant? She blushed, tried to look casual when Lorraine agreed.

On the evening of Emily's birthday Lorraine collected Ibrahim from Sophie's house and drove to O'Callaghan's restaurant, where Adrian was waiting for them. Emily approached him cautiously. He held out his arms. She ran forward with a muffled sob and sank against him. His eyes were moist when he looked towards Lorraine. Stiffly, refusing to hold his gaze, she walked to the table that had been reserved for them.

Emily sat close to her father throughout the meal. Ibrahim sat opposite her. He was respectful to Adrian, was charming to Lorraine and fastened his black flirtatious eyes on Emily. He was the lightning rod upon whom they directed their attention. The waitress, whose name-tag spelled "Angie", took Adrian's camera and ordered them to smile, to look happy, to share Emily's excitement. *Click, click, click*, smiling, always smiling.

CHAPTER NINE

Brahms Ward
8 p.m.

I've had a hectic day, Killian. Don't pay attention if I snooze off after a while. I met my script editor this morning. Remember Roz O'Hara? Jangling bracelets, chain smoker, pink highlights? It was a terse meeting, to say the least. Not that I blame her for being annoyed. Despite a hefty advance, she's yet to read a single page of my promised draft. She reminded me that I'd other responsibilities besides family ones but she relented before I left and asked how you are.

"While there's life there's hope." She sounded apologetic, a woman who abhors clichés – but your deep sleep has left people bereft of meaningful comment. I've promised her the rough outline two weeks from now but Roz O'Hara can jangle her bracelets all she likes. I'm a dry stone, no blood. All I want to do is write about you. Perhaps it will help, writing it down, a cathartic cleansing. Perhaps not. Either way it passes the night when sleep is impossible.

You must remember *Nowhere Lodge*? Your favourite programme? My path to fame? Of course you remember. What a dab hand you were at making suggestions, my trusty barometer, bringing me on-the-spot reviews from school friends, thumbs down or up – I could always rely on you for an honest opinion. Fairy tales with an edge, that's what I write.

I never realised the vein I was opening when I cut into the teenage psyche. I knew the issues, the language of the street: ganga, shit, weed, barbs, downers, rock, wash, Charlie, disco burgers, doves, junk, skag, horse. You brought Lorcan Sheraton to meet me. Can you remember that weekend? You were twelve years old and ready to make your own decisions. I knew that when I introduced me as your *real* father. Such pride in your voice. It was the only recognition that mattered. Your mother was not pleased but that's another story, another era.

She's lost weight since the accident. These days she seldom visits her office and her diary only has one entry. But she's also needed at home. Duncan's being a bit of a problem. Sibling rivalry. Not that I'm an expert on the subject but, apparently, it can be quite an issue in families. We're working out a rota for visitors. Your friends want to be involved, Lorcan in particular, also Marianne. She rang last night and sent you her love. She's still working on the film. Remember? Street people, drug culture? For a while I thought the two of you might ... but what does that matter now?

We're going to bring you back to us, Killian. Music, words, massage, prayers, whatever it takes. Your mother has faith, such sublime faith. Jesus walks beside her. Her eyes glow when she speaks his name. I envy her, Killian. If only I could believe so fervently that prayer triggers the attention of a benign Christ with inexhaustible energy, an ear to the ground and eyes that see everything.

Yellow eyes ... blind eyes ... blind mice ... hickory dickory dock ... tick tock ... mouse ran ... ran ... whirr-whirr-whirr ... yellow eyes ... blind eyes ... blinded ... eyes ... headlights!

CHAPTER TEN

"I've fallen hopelessly in love," Emily announced one evening, stamping mud from Donaldson's farm on the back doorstep. "It's incurable, indestructible, indescribable –"

"Just give me the facts, Emily. Obviously his name begins with I."

"Do you mean Ibrahim O'Doherty?" She blew coyly up towards her fringe and laughed loudly. "Don't be ridiculous. My true love is a *she*. Her name is Antoinette and she has four legs."

"Come again, Emily?"

"She's my horse."

Lorraine set a dish of lasagne on the table and sectioned it onto their plates. "Are we talking rocking horses or the ones who eat oats and live on Donaldsons' farm?"

"Ha, ha. *Very* funny. Want to see me riding her?"

"Are you serious?"

"Absolutely."

After they finished their evening meal they walked to the end of the lane and entered the farmyard.

"Shut up, Hobbs," Emily ordered the dog and hunkered to fondle his ears, a gesture that caused Hobbs to pant devotedly and press his head against her knees. Before Lorraine could stop her, she lifted the latch on the back door and walked into the farmhouse. Noeleen, reading a newspaper at the kitchen table, greeted her so casually it was obvious she was used to Emily's unannounced entry. She noticed Lorraine hovering in the open doorway and gestured. "Come in, come on in yourself. I'm just about to wet the tea."

Emily joined the brothers in the room adjoining the kitchen where they were watching a soccer match on television.

"You're settling into the old house all right then?" Noeleen pulled out a chair from the table and invited Lorraine to sit down.

"More or less."

"It must seem strange after the city. It did to me when I first came here."

"I remember that time. Celia called you a townie."

"Sure you must have been only a tot then." Noeleen moved around the kitchen with quick, light steps, setting mugs and plates on the table.

"It doesn't seem all that long ago. You were originally from Tralee, if I remember rightly."

"Born and bred. But I went to London when I was fifteen and lived there until my mother became ill. I came home to nurse her. She didn't live long afterwards, God rest her, and I met Frank at a dance in the town about a year later. The quietness really got to me in the beginning but I'd Frank to warm my bed which helped settle me down." She stopped, suddenly flustered, and busied herself pouring tea. "Not that a warm bed is everything. Many's the woman managed on her own and made a far better fist of rearing her kids than if she had a man hanging out of her apron strings. Emily's coming on grand, despite everything. She told me about the art classes you're going to start in September. We've had some grand night classes altogether here. Computers, pottery and salsa dancing. I loved the salsa. But no painting until now. When do we start enrolling? I can guarantee you at least four other women who'd be delighted to get out of their houses at night."

"Noeleen, I don't know what Emily's been saying but she seems to have given the wrong impression to people. I didn't agree to do the classes. I'm too busy —"

"The furthest I've ever got to painting is dipping a brush into a bucket of whitewash." Noeleen swept her excuses aside. "I'd like to tackle something like portraits. I've no interest whatsoever in landscapes. God knows I spend enough time looking at the scenery around here."

"But I *haven't* agreed to do the classes."

Noeleen sighed, tilted her head to one side and surveyed Lorraine. "I'm sorry to hear that. You think you've all the time in the world to do the things you want but then you suddenly realise the clock's running ahead of you. Suppose I'll never get to paint a portrait of Frank now."

Despite her exasperation, Lorraine smiled. "Noeleen, are you trying to manipulate me?"

"Why would I want to do a thing like that?"

"That's what I'm asking you?"

"You need to mix with people again, Lorraine. You're here nearly six months now and you've hardly moved outside the house except to walk the beach. Emily worries about you."

"Does she talk about what happened between myself and her father?"

"She doesn't have to. I see it in her face. But yes, she did tell me. I wasn't trying to pry."

"I know. And I appreciate your concern."

"You'll do the classes then?"

"I'll think about it," Lorraine promised.

"Keep yourself busy," Noeleen advised. "I usually find it's as good a reason as any for rising in the morning."

Voices came from the dining-room, where a heated discussion had broken out. Emily laughed at a remark made by one of the brothers who had loudly expressed his opinion on the mental state of the referee.

"It's great having a girl around the place again," said Noeleen. "I've two daughters in the States and one in London. I miss them something terrible." She sat in silence for a while, a half-smile playing across her lips. Her kitchen had a comfortable feel, despite the modern built-in units which her sons had installed. A dusty St Brigid's cross hung above the door and she had kept the old-fashioned range in preference to a modern oven.

"It's a relief to hear Emily laughing again." Lorraine stirred her tea and wondered what it would be like to wave goodbye to children as they boarded a plane to begin a new life elsewhere. She listened to Noeleen talking about her daughters, relaxed in the company of this friendly woman who had been the first to welcome her to Trabawn.

When the match ended, Lorraine accompanied the brothers and Emily to the stables. Con led an old mare forward and stood back, observing Emily as she saddled the horse. Sitting gingerly on the saddle she rode Antoinette in a wide, slow circle around a fenced-off sand arena, waving excitedly at her mother when she passed her by. Con spoke in a low voice, obviously encouraging her to relax, and her posture settled. Her smile grew more confident as the mare responded to her commands. To Lorraine, watching from the sidelines, it was obvious that the love affair was well underway.

"Of course, Antoinette's very old," Emily explained when they returned to the house. "But Con says I can practise on her until I get a proper pony. Do you think there's any chance of that happening? If I'm going to be a culchie I might as well have the trappings."

"We'll see what's possible down the road. For the moment, though, it's out of the question. All this is costing an arm and a leg." Lorraine pointed towards the central-heating pipes which had been delivered that afternoon. She needed to start earning again. With the sale of the house and her *Painting Dreams* collection, she was financially secure for the time being but the costs of repairing her new home and setting up the studio were making serious inroads into her savings. "We're going to Dublin for a few days," she said. "You'll have a chance to see your friends again … and your father, if you want to?"

"I'll meet him in McDonald's. Isn't that where all the Saturday dads hang out?"

"You can meet him anywhere you like."

"Seeing as how you refuse to let him set foot in this house, McDonald's will do fine."

Lorraine moved to the window and stared out into the gathering dusk.

"Bat watch time again, is it?" Her daughter yanked open the fridge door and removed a plate of left-over lasagne. "I'm going

56

to feed Antoinette. She may be old and bony but at least I can rely on her not to wreck my head."

It was dark when she returned from the farm. "I'm sorry." She came straight over to Lorraine and hugged her. "I can't get used to it. I just *can't*."

"It will get easier." Lorraine brushed her daughter's hair back from her forehead and kissed her. "I don't know when ... or how. But I know it will."

On Wednesday evening, Emily flung herself into the car and waved out the window at the Donaldson brothers who intended painting the bathroom Bravado Blue while they were away.

Brendan stopped singing "If Tomorrow Never Comes" and closed the gate behind them.

Back in familiar childhood surroundings, witnessing the pleasure with which her parents greeted them, Lorraine felt guilty over her long absence. After dinner, when Emily had persuaded her grandfather to drive her to her friend's house, Donna had an opportunity to speak alone to her daughter.

"Teenagers are resilient." She cleared dishes from the table and stacked the dishwasher. "Emily looks well and she appears to be settling down. I'm glad she's decided to meet Adrian again. Her birthday must have been difficult for you."

"I got through it. There'll be other occasions. It's something I have to accept."

"Have you been able to make any decisions about – " Donna's voice quavered then strengthened again. "Are you going to look for a divorce?"

"As soon as it can be arranged." Saying the words gave authenticity to her decision but the words had a dream-like quality, as if some other person, someone cold and empty of emotion, were uttering them. Later, trying to sleep, she forced herself to think about tomorrow's meeting with the Sheratons. Her distracted thoughts were not helped by the sounds of road-works on the pavement outside her parents' house. The road was an artery into the city, busy during peak hour, and an emergency had arisen that meant the work had to be carried out during the night. The interminable trench was cordoned off by red and white striped plastic barriers, and leaflets delivered to each house on the crescent had apologised in advance for the inconvenience. She covered her head with a pillow but the noise penetrated. She had no idea who was responsible; electricity, gas, telephones, they all seemed to operate independantly. At last she slept but her dreams were disturbed by crashing sounds, thuds and the relentless thump of heavy machinery.

CHAPTER ELEVEN

Brahms Ward
8 p.m.

Killian, I know what happened that night. I want to weep but I've no tears left. Bozo Daly gave her an identity. He put flesh on her bones and turned her from a phantom into a living, breathing being who can be traced and be held accountable. He's ill, I'm afraid, very ill. A nurse rang to tell me. She referred to him as Luke Daly. Did you know that's his real name? Neither did I until she described him. He wanted to see me urgently and so I went immediately to his bedside. He's in the Mater Hospital, frail and old in his striped pyjamas. I can't imagine him as a Luke. Too biblical. But he's sober for a change and his nose, that humped and cratered structure that belongs to an alcoholic, not a clown, no longer resembles an angry weal. It was the first time we'd spoken since your accident.

Lorraine Cheevers is her name. I wonder if she noticed a clown on the pier that night? Probably not. Bozo Daly is used to being invisible. But he saw her take her lover's hand and pull him back into the safety of her car. It's a crazy story, Killian, and will be impossible to prove in a court of law, not that Bozo will ever get that far. From the look in his eyes I'd say he's already hearing the beat of angels' wings. He refuses point blank to talk to the police. He's well-known to them and they, for their part, have little faith in a clown with selective memory lapses. I could go to them myself but what can I say? A robbed bracelet, a television programme and the opinion of a wino who lived the last ten years of his life on the edge of a river.

Remember *Artistically Speaking*? Talking heads and boring art farts, you used to say. They made a programme about her. I know the producer. We shared a flat for a few months when we were students. He used to wear knitted bedroom slippers. Now he wears Gucci loafers. We've all moved on, I guess, since those days. He gave me a copy of the tape.

Last night I switched on the video. Red hair, blue eyes. Her neck is long and slim. I could fit my hands around it easily. I could squeeze it until the life fades from her eyes and they are lustreless, empty. Like your gaze, Killian. So far removed from us. Yet you weep tears. I see them ooze from the corners, trickle down your cheeks. Where do they come from, those tears? Are they the last ripples in a dried-up riverbed, flowing heedlessly from a wasted reservoir? Or do they signify emotion, the possibility of hope, the glimmer of a nightmare ending?

Jean touches your tears and signs the cross on your forehead. I see them fall and I think of revenge. Last night I watched Lorraine Cheevers. I studied her face, her willowy frame, her smile, her white, straight teeth. I switched off the machine and waited for the mist to pass from my mind.

Misty man … Mister Men … Mr Dizzy … Mr Bounce … Mr Bump … bump … smash … crash … whirr-whirr-whirr-whirr …

CHAPTER TWELVE

"Mount Subasio" was engraved on a granite slab outside the gates of the Sheratons' residence. Lorraine drove slowly along an avenue that curved into a wide-angled view of the house. The style was mock-Georgian, or had started off as such, but other influences had created a startling edifice of pillars and turrets. A flag with the Sheraton crest hung from one such turret and gave the building the appearance of a massive but ill-designed conference centre. Stone lions crouched like sentinels at either side of the steps and, as Lorraine approached the entrance, a massive studded hall door opened to reveal Andrea Sheraton.

She waited until Lorraine mounted the steps then lightly brushed her fingers, coolly establishing the fact that this was a business rather than a social lunch. Gold hung from her neck, gleamed on her wrist and fingers. Her hair fell to her shoulders, sleek and flawlessly blonde. She led Lorraine into a dining-room where the windows offered a spectacular view over the Dublin mountains. Throughout lunch she toyed with an avocado salad, unable to hide her impatience whenever she glanced at her son.

Lorcan Sheraton had the fidgety unease of a landed fish, flapping and helpless under his mother's scrutiny, his shoulders twitching involuntarily every time she addressed him. He crumbled a bread roll on the damask tablecloth and replied in monosyllables to Lorraine's questions. He was not going to be an easy subject to paint. From his comments it was obvious he hated the idea of a family portrait. She would have to work on him, reassure him without sounding patronising, focus on his strong features which, looking into his woebegone eyes, could be difficult. His father, after a few failed attempts to include him in the conversation, ignored him completely.

Andrea insisted that Lorraine paint from photographs rather than sketches. "Photographs will give a truer representation of our family, don't you agree?" She gave up all pretence of eating and lightly dabbed her lips with a napkin.

"Whatever you wish." Usually Lorraine preferred to work from sketches but on this occasion she was determined to spend as little time as possible with this family, whose combined unease in each other's presence was unnerving.

"And I insist on seeing all the preliminary work," Andrea continued. "I adore your work, Lorraine, but 'quirky and cheekily Cheeverish' is not what I'm looking for on this occasion."

Lorraine winced away from the affected laughter of the woman sitting opposite her. The phrase had been used by the presenter of *Artistically Speaking* and it had annoyed her as much then as it did now.

"Just as well you won't be organising regular sittings." Bill glanced at his son and grinned wryly. "As you can see, Lorcan wouldn't be capable of sitting still even if he was encased in cement."

His attempt at humour settled wearily across the table and was rewarded with a glare from his son. When the meal finally came to an end Lorraine made excuses and left, after arranging to return the following day for the photographic session.

Throughout the night, the road-works continued outside her parents' house. She stood by the window staring down at arc lighting which illuminated the workers in their yellow jackets and hard hats. The lateness of the hour added a surreal image to a scene she would have passed without a glance during the day. She remembered the old night watchman from her childhood who used to guard the cordoned-off trenches and how he called out to her when she passed him by, his hunched figure sitting before a glowing brazier, his gloved hands clasped around a tin mug of tea.

Before she could change her mind she slipped on her clothes and took her camera outside. The foreman was defensive at first, believing she had come to complain and was using the camera as a means of gathering some evidence of wrongdoing on his part. But she was persuasive and after consulting with the workers he gave permission. As she approached the crew she realised one of them was a woman. She worked silently alongside the men and paid no attention to Lorraine, who moved among them as unobtrusively as possible.

When they stopped for a tea break she was still photographing them. They began to talk to her, the men striking macho or provocative feminine poses, asking if they were going to feature in a *Playboy* centrefold. When they heard she intended painting them they whistled and sang "Mona Lisa", the woman joining in, a husky voice, one of the lads. She looked wiry and skinny against their hulking masculinity. Lorraine studied her tough face with its give-as-good-as-you-get expression. Did she suffer sexual harassment? Was her bottom pinched, patted, stroked? Had she been lewdly teased? She did not look like a woman who would suffer silently. Lorraine took their addresses and told them she would send invitations if the painting was ever exhibited.

Bill Sheraton fretted about time-wasting. Lorraine fretted about missing the light. Lorcan, glowering and inflamed, fretted about her close scrutiny of his skin. Andrea piled clothes on the bed and fretted over the most suitable outfit to wear. A hair stylist and beautician attended to her hair and make-up. Tempers were frayed by the time the photographic session started.

Lorraine photographed the family in the garden, grouped before a copse of blazing redwood trees, in the drawing-room, in the conservatory and at the foot of a curving staircase. Lorcan's head jerked defensively whenever she approached him for a close-up shot. His bottom lip was cracked as if he had bitten down hard on it.

"They want to play happy families," he muttered. "I told them it was a sick idea but nobody around here gives a fuck what I think."

"Trust me. You'll be pleased when it's finished." She tried to reassure him, hating her glib response but unable to think of anything else to say.

"Will I?" His eyes rejected any comfort. "What are you going to do, airbrush out my face?" He glared at his mother whose lips were again receiving attention from the beautician. "Don't bother inviting me to the unveiling."

He reminded her of Emily. The same angry struggle to break free from the decisions of adults. Following in the footsteps of a man who smelled his first million when he was eighteen was a hard burden to carry and Lorcan's slouching posture revealed his determination not to try.

In a clipped, cultivated accent Andrea questioned Lorraine's fee, convinced that anyone who provided a service to her family was out to exploit their wealth. She fixed her rigid smile on Lorraine and suggested that, as she could work more easily from photographs than time-consuming sketches, surely her fee should not be so exorbitant.

The temptation to walk away without a second thought from this elegant, spoiled woman was almost irresistible. Such an action would be gossip fodder for Andrea and her friends but what did it matter. Let them say what they liked. They had probably said it all anyway and she was far removed from the circles Andrea frequented. But, suddenly, it seemed important that she hold her ground. If she walked from this house she would do it calmly, on her own terms. "As it was your husband who commissioned the portrait, then you must make your views known to him. My fee is not negotiable. But if you decide to cancel the commission I'll accept your decision." She spoke crisply, reverting to the business-like attitude she always displayed when dealing with difficult clients and heard, as she expected, Andrea's sigh of capitulation.

"You've such a long journey ahead of you," she said when Lorraine was leaving. Her tone suggested that Lorraine had settled somewhere far beyond the Russian steppes. "Bill says you've gone quite rural. It must be incredibly difficult to adjust.

You've had such a busy lifestyle –"

"I've adjusted very well, thank you."

"I've suppose you've heard that the studio in Blaide House is being turned into an art gallery. It should be quite a transformation." She smiled, offered Lorraine a limp handshake. "I really am looking forward to working with you. Safe journey."

The neighbouring houses were mainly hidden behind dense shrubbery. As Lorraine drove down the driveway she caught tantalising glimpses of roofs and balconies. The road leading back to the main junction was narrow and sharp with dangerous bends. The sense of affluence, hidden wealth screened behind high walls and overhanging trees, was a tangible presence when she slowed on the corners and cautiously approached the main road. She reached the centre city in the late afternoon.

Before moving to Trabawn, she had driven through Dublin without a second thought, equally at home in traffic grids or on the crest of busy motorways. Six months of driving along country roads where she was more likely to be held up by the rump of Frank Donaldson's cattle than a set of traffic lights had made a difference. She drove slowly past Blaide House, averting her gaze from the glossy exterior, the grey hammered limestone walls and marbled entrance. The windows reminded her of opaque eyes, staring outwards, slanting inwards. She imagined hushed footsteps on carpets, the silent glide of an elevator rising to the first floor where Ginia Communications was located. On the ground floor, the discreet brass plate signposting the direction to Strong–Blaide Advertising would have been changed by now and her studio, that slanted attic space, would soon be stripped bare, the last remnants of her personality removed, the walls hung instead with expensive paintings. On the car radio Bob Marley sang about slavery and freedom of the mind. Music will undo me, she thought, remembering the summer of '82 – and her memories blended with the plaintive voice of the singer, so alive and in tune with a moment, a movement, his star dying in the throes of fame. Sirens shrieked and traffic grid-locked around her. The trail of the river followed her along the quays. Firmly, she switched channels and listened instead to politicians slugging it out across the airwaves.

CHAPTER THIRTEEN

Brahms Ward
9 p.m.

I called to her studio today. The clouds were heavy with rain. It suited my mood. Blaide House overlooks the Liffey. It's only a short distance from my apartment yet how often have I passed its walls and never once looked upwards towards her attic where she was busy painting dreams? I climbed the spiral staircase and entered a room with windows in the ceiling and a view of a grey sky. The walls were streaked with paint. Abandoned canvases and broken frames lay on the floor, the remnants of a dream turned sour. Workmen were putting a new shape on the place. They'd no idea where she'd gone. A carpenter gave me the name of the owner, who has an office on the premises. Ginia Public Relations is written outside. A woman with sculpted black hair introduced herself as Virginia Blaide. The lease had changed hands, she told me. The artist was out of town and had left instructions not to be contacted. Her attic is being converted into an art gallery.

I demanded her new address. I refused to leave without it. The woman's anger was contained but visible when she flashed her dark eyelashes, a beautiful face but formidable. In the end I left. Short of beating her up, what else could I do? She escorted me to the ground floor. We walked past the frowning receptionist whom I'd successfully evaded on my way in. Glass doors slid open and released me to the streets.

How can someone fall off the edge of the world? No forwarding address.

Glass ... glass snowball ... shake snow ... glass ... bottle ... Bozo ... glass ... smash ... crash ... whirr ... whirr ...

CHAPTER FOURTEEN

The crates blocking free passage along the landing could no longer be ignored. Lorraine gazed at the ornaments and cutlery, the table mats and linen tablecloths, the numerous sets of glasses, champagne flutes, whiskey tumblers, the Waterford Crystal goblets she had received as a wedding present. Since moving into the house she had not needed them – which seemed like a good enough reason not to bother unpacking anything. Tomorrow, she would ask the Donaldson brothers to move the crate into the attic. Anything that was not necessary for survival would be left inside. As she continued sifting through the contents, she noticed her jewellery box. Music tinkled when she opened it. A ballerina spun in a slow circle; a present from her daughter for one of her birthdays. She lifted out a pendant and laid it against her chest. Adrian's present. A sapphire, the same shade as her eyes, and a bracelet to match. He presented them to her on their wedding night, the two of them exhausted from the celebrations and the flight to Portugal yet still eagerly seeking each other. It was dark outside, the hotel lights shimmering on the swimming pool, the beach chairs empty, the dance-floor silent. Sapphires woven into a silver weave and love as durable as the hardest stone.

She straightened, her legs cramping, and walked unsteadily down the stairs. Emily had rung earlier and asked to be collected from Ibrahim's house. Time had slipped by while she was searching the crate and it was now after eight o'clock. She drove without further delay to Sophie's house. After knocking repeatedly on the front door and getting no response, she walked around to the back of the farmyard. The back door was open but no one answered when she called out. A mournful bellowing came from a large cavernous building which she recognised as a cubicle shed. She had seen one on Donaldson's farm and often, when she was passing it on her way to the beach and the wind was blowing in the wrong direction, she had held her breath against the pungent smell of cow dung. She heard raised voices and made her way towards it. The shed was empty except for a penned-off area within which a small group of people hunkered around a cow. Lorraine, hesitating at the entrance, resisted the urge to run from the sight of her daughter at the rear end of a pregnant animal, its tail firmly grasped in her hand. Ibrahim appeared to be in charge of a torture machine which was, Sophie calmly assured her, a calving jack used to assist the birthing process. The jack had two ropes attached to a lever which would be used to draw out the calf.

"It's going to be a hard pull." Sophie beckoned Lorraine closer. "We're having some difficulty with one of the legs." The cow had gone into an early labour and Joe, Sophie's husband, was on his way back from Killarney where he'd been attending an agricultural conference. Ibrahim had already phoned the vet who was out on another call and had promised to be with them as soon as possible. The cow, however, was not prepared to wait for the experts to arrive.

"We're in trouble if we can't manage this ourselves. Ibrahim's trying to ease the leg free. He's done it before with Joe but never on his own." In the village, Sophie always cut a dash in her vibrant costumes and traditional headwear but this evening she was wearing jeans and wellingtons. The sleeves of her red t-shirt were already stained with perspiration. The animal, in distress and lying exhaustedly on a bed of straw, raised dull agonised eyes towards her. She spoke in a soft Arabic tongue to the cow as Ibrahim eased his arm into the animal's back passage. Emily uttered a tiny shriek which she stifled with her free hand, her other hand engaged in preventing the tail swiping Ibrahim's face. She stared fixedly in the opposite direction as he probed, his arm disappearing up to his elbow, his face crumpled with the effort of locating the calf's bent leg and drawing the two forelegs parallel.

"I've got a hold," he grunted.

Emily allowed herself a horrified peek before settling her gaze once more into the middle distance. Lorraine, feeling no calmer than her daughter, replaced Sophie at the cow's head. Tentatively, she touched the sleek neck, jumping back when the cow gave vent to an enormous bellow, its bloated belly shuddering in another spasm.

"We've no time to waste." Sophie's voice shook as she assisted her son with the calving jack. It was a large frame, six feet or more, Lorraine reckoned, but they handled it deftly, securing it to the cow's back end and attaching the ropes to the calf's first joints. Together, mother and son began levering the handle of jack. They paused frequently to allow the exhausted animal a short respite then continued with the slow, laborious process until the feet and head appeared and the calf slithered free.

Emily dropped the tail and sobbed into her hands. She walked to the wall and stood facing it, her shoulders heaving. Ibrahim disinfected the calf's navel then turned Emily around and pointed. Together they watched the mother revive her new-born calf. Gently, persistently she stroked her tongue over the glistening flesh, her pansy eyes resting protectively on the wriggling animal who began, under her gentle persistence, to stagger upright before collapsing again in a sprawl of knobbled legs.

"At this stage we leave the rest to nature," Sophie spoke softly as she gathered detergents and disinfectants. She splashed water from the buckets and led the way back to the farmhouse. Darkness had fallen while they worked. A full moon dragged the hedgerows. How close it seemed, touchable almost, and splendid in its ripeness, as splendid as the experience of watching life come into being. And so Lorraine Cheevers paused to savour its beauty and to fleetingly touch the rising beat of happiness.

"*I've just given birth to a calf. It was a laborious process. Mother and baby both doing well.*" On the car journey home, Emily texted the message to her friends in Dublin. "See what they make of that!" She giggled and sat back to await their response. She was high with excitement, still shaking from the birthing experience. "Wasn't it absolutely, awesomely amazing?" she said. "Wasn't it the most wonderful thing you ever saw in all your life?"

Lorraine nodded, her hands still trembling from shock. Her daughter's capacity to recover was more immediate.

"I've made two life-changing decisions tonight," she announced when she reached the house. "I'm going to study to be a vet and I'm going to marry Ibrahim O'Doherty. Any man who can put his arm up a cow's backside and still turn me on deserves to spend the rest of his life with me."

CHAPTER FIFTEEN

Brahms Ward
10 p.m.

Killian, I've to break some sad news, I'm afraid. Bozo Daly is dead. His liver finally gave out. Live by the bottle, die by the bottle. He was a good patient, the nurse said, one of the quiet ones, fading out like a whisper. No second-guessing death, no outrage that his day was done and lady luck, that elusive, bitchy lady luck, had flicked the dust of departure with her high-buttoned boots.

We buried him this morning. Your mother attended his funeral, Marianne also. The woman with the silver boots was there and some young people from the squat. They tell me it's ear-marked for demolition soon. We were a small gathering around a pauper's plot. Jean says she will erect a wooden cross with his name inscribed and place it on his grave. Luke (Bozo) Daly. R.I.P.

It's hard to believe that two years ago I'd never heard of him. I probably passed him on the quays and turned my face away or, feeling magnanimous and in tune with the world, gave him coins if he stretched out his hand. The destruction of his squat won't be the cause of preservation angst or street protests. But until the time comes for the developers to move in it will still provide shelter for the young people who crawl nightly into its dark corners.

I wrote about it last night. My fingers flew over the keys, cut, copy, paste, delete. How easy it is, with the passing of time, to write with clarity. How simple it becomes to chart the mistakes, the unthinking actions that spin the future from our grasp. I never wanted to write a memoir. Screenplays, quick action, instant dialogue, that's usually my style.

I'm still searching for her, Killian. I've checked her out on the Internet. She had a web site but it's out of date. Her e-mails come back with a delivery failure message. She's out there somewhere. She's running from me but I will find her, Killian, that I promise you. And when I do … then we shall see …

Run … run … run rabbit run rabbit … whirr-whirr … smash … crash … glass … pick up … pick up … bracelet …

CHAPTER SIXTEEN

The Sheraton portrait was ready. Andrea's hands had been gracefully elongated and draped across her lap. She sat regally on a throne-like armchair, chin tilted, mouth softly curved. Her husband, solid and substantial, stood behind her. Then there was Lorcan, miraculously transformed, fresh-faced, smiling, his elbow elegantly placed on the mantelpiece, his gaze fixed fondly on his parents. The perfect composition of a successful family unit.

"Do you mind if I say something insulting?" Emily arrived into the studio one evening when her mother was applying some final strokes to the portrait.

"Why should I mind? I'm a mother." Lorraine sighed and braced herself for the worst.

"That painting is actually *awesomely* awful."

"Thank you."

"I mean it's brilliant as a portrait but it's awful because there's nothing of you in it. It's just like a *really* posh pretentious photograph."

"But the woman who commissioned it will love it. Believe me."

"She looks like a proper poser. Who's the guy hanging over the mantelpiece?"

"Her son."

"Mmm … does he *really* look so groovy gorgeous in the flesh?"

Lorraine shrugged, remembering Lorcan's scowling

countenance. "A few brush strokes of artistic licence. But given time and the right circumstances, who knows what the future holds?"

Andrea Sheraton removed a bottle of champagne from the fridge. "We must celebrate." She perched herself on a high kitchen stool and poured the champagne into two glasses. "Here's to you, Lorraine. Long may your talents last." One spiked high-heeled shoe beat against the breakfast bar, the other dangled from her toes. "I must say you're looking wonderfully healthy. Must be the country air. The wild Irish image suits you but I still can't get used to the idea of you in wellies. It quite boggles the mind."

"The mind can get used to anything." Lorraine took a sip from the glass and laid it back on the counter. The cloying sincerity in Andrea's voice was as irritating as her comments.

"No, I mean it sincerely. You've been through a wretched time. It's inspiring to see you coming out the other side. This portrait will attract a lot of attention. Expect commissions from my friends." She held the glass carefully by the stem and studied the bubbles. "I was talking about you to someone the other night. Your ears must have been burning."

"Not that I noticed."

"It was at the opening of the Spiral Staircase Art Gallery. You remember I mentioned it a while ago? Such a wonderful night. Everyone but *everyone* came. Check out this month's *Prestige*. The photographs are in the centrefold."

For an instant Lorraine was too shocked to reply. How the wineglasses must have clinked as invited guests gathered in Blaide House to celebrate the opening. She leaned her elbow on the counter. The chill of the marble surface sent an involuntary shudder along her arm. "I'm afraid there's not much of a demand for *Prestige* in Trabawn."

"No, I shouldn't imagine so." Andrea released a trill of laughter. Her eyelids closed over her slightly protruding eyes and Lorraine was reminded of a bird of prey that waits for the exact moment to strike.

The tapping shoe quickened its beat. "Do you know Mara Robertson?"

"We were in college together."

"She's running the gallery. I hope I'm not upsetting you, Lorraine?"

"Of course not. Time has moved on, Andrea. My studio was on prime city space. It's the perfect location for an art gallery."

"I admire your spirit. I really do. So courageous. Mara's hoping you'll do your next exhibition with her. Rather an insensitive aspiration, under the circumstances." Her accent was contrived, too many drawled vowels, each word carefully pitched to provide maximum hurt. "Bill invested in another painting. Cost him well over the odds. It's staggering the prices you artists demand. I'll show it to you before you leave. I'd like your opinion on its market value."

"I have the utmost trust in Bill's investments." Lorraine eased off the stool. "I'm sorry to rush off but I'm already late for an appointment."

"Oh, dear." Andrea's fingers fluttered to her lips. "This has upset you. I can see it in your eyes. No, no, don't bother denying it. Bill says I'm far too sensitive for my own good. I pick up other people's vibrations so easily."

"Andrea, I never impose my personal life on my professional relationships and I expect you to extend the same courtesy to me." She stared coldly at the other woman until Andrea was forced to look away. "If you'll excuse me, I'd like to leave without engaging any further in this inappropriate conversation."

High gates opened at the end of the avenue. Distracted by her anger she drove too fast onto the road. A car exiting from an opposite driveway stopped with a screech of brakes and the driver, shocked by her sudden appearance, was jolted forward. She signalled an apology and smiled through the window at him. He reversed back and allowed her to drive ahead.

A van, parked illegally and too close to the T-junction leading onto the main road, blocked her right hand vision. She advanced cautiously, unable to see if the road was clear of approaching traffic. As she drove forward, nosing past the rear of the van, a car came into view, travelling too fast, the headlights flashing warningly, forcing her to slam on her brakes. Within a few seconds the car coming from behind thudded against her bumper. She saw the driver raise his hand to his forehead. He sat in that position for an instant, his hand obscuring his face, then opened his door and walked towards her.

Together, they surveyed their cars. There appeared to be little damage to her own, apart from a dent on her bumper and some scratches.

"We seem destined to *almost* do serious damage to each other's cars." She spoke jokingly but his lips tightened, as if he resented her attempts to lighten the situation. He walked around her car, examining it from all angles, then leaned his hands upon the bonnet, breathing deeply, still obviously shocked by the collision.

"Twice in five minutes would certainly suggest we were destined to meet." His voice was low, as if addressing the words to himself. "But it could have been worse. We could have knocked someone down."

"Thankfully, we didn't. There's hardly any damage done. If you're happy to leave things as they are, then we needn't bring it any further."

He held her arm as she attempted to open her door. "Don't go yet. We've both had a shock." He gestured towards a hotel across the road. "At least allow me to buy you a coffee before you begin your journey?"

Black hair hung low over his forehead and on his neck. His strong dark eyes observed her, an unnervingly intimate stare. His face would make an interesting study, she thought, and was conscious of a slight, almost-forgotten response, an awareness of a man's attention and the challenge it excited within her. Once more she attempted to open the car door, aware that there was strength in his grip on her arm. "I'm afraid I haven't time. But thank you for the offer."

He released her arm but still stood in front of her. "You're Lorraine Cheevers?" His voice lilted over her name, as if it was a cherished sound. "I recognise you from *Artistically Speaking.*"

"I never watched that programme." Tears rushed to her eyes. Horrified by her reaction she sucked in her breath and released it slowly.

"Meeting you today is such a coincidence." He spoke hurriedly, a slight frown furrowing his forehead. "I've tried to make contact with you for months but you seemed to disappear into thin air. I called to your studio a while back. The person I spoke to refused give me your address."

"Those were my instructions. What did you want to discuss with me?"

"My son … I was thinking of a portrait."

"My studio is now in Kerry."

"Can I call and see you?"

She wrote down her address and telephone number on a piece of paper. "I only recently returned to work so I haven't an up-to-date business card."

"Trabawn." He stared at the address. "I spent a holiday there when I was a child."

"So did I, many holidays." She smiled, feeling a sense of kinship with him. " I only remember sunshine summers. But it's changed quite a bit since those days. You probably wouldn't recognise it."

"I'll have to check it out." His handshake was firm. "I'll be in touch with you soon."

"I'll look forward to hearing from you."

She watched him walk towards his car. He was not as tall as Adrian, or as handsome, but he carried himself well, a confident stride, easy movements. He lifted his hand in salute and watched her drive away. Only afterwards, as she was driving through the city, did she realise that he had forgotten to tell her his name.

CHAPTER SEVENTEEN

Killian

Sometimes, there is a glimmer in the dark. A chink. Memories roll across the waves. Coil like fish seeking escape. Flash like lightning in a stormy sky. Voices call. He holds the sound in his fist, hugs it to his chest. Reaches into the dark and listens ... listens ...

He looks strong today, Missus. Have a cup of tea. A biscuit, take two. You're skin and bone, God give you strength. How do you keep doing it? He knows what I'm saying, don't you, Loveadove? You mark my words, Missus. He'll be drinking tea with the best of them before you know it.

Come back to me, my darling boy. Dreams are good but you can't live in them forever. We're all here, Terence and Laura, and Duncan's come too.
　　Always here! Always here! Smelly ward. Wanna go home.
　　Hush at once! Killian can hear you.
　　Can't! Can't! Retard. Wanna go home!
　　Knock Knock. Who's there? Tinker Bell. Tinker Bell who? Tinker bell is out of action. Ha ha ha.

I've got a belly stud, Killian. Look. Mum did her nut when she saw it, didn't you mum? I can play your guitar now. I listened to REM the other day and heard you singing clear as a bell in my head. Everybody hurts ... hold on hold on ...

Your temperature is good, little soldier. Normal. My daughter ring from Manila. She pass her exams for university. I am very proud of her. Let me fix your pillows. Your father – he is late tonight. He is lost like you. How sad to see such unhappiness when family are near and can hold each other.

Bridesmaids! Jealous whores, more like. They won't turn up for fittings and they keep making remarks about my dress. It's not a meringue, it's not! Blood pressure's stable. Good lad. Wish mine was. They refuse to wear pink shoes. Say they look tacky. I ask your holy pardon! Whose wedding is it anyway?

Wake up, mate. How long does a trip last? Sorry I fucked up. Left you on the pier. How crazy were we? Wired to the fucking moon. What were we fighting over anyway? Some shit piece of junk jewellery.

Lay thee down now and rest: May thy slumber be blest. Lay thee down now and rest: May thy slumber be blest ... Granny is here, Killian. Look, I'm shaking the glass snowball. See the flakes dancing. Stop fretting. We're with you every step of the way ... Lay thee down now and rest: May thy slumber be blest. Lay thee down now and rest: May thy slumber be blest.

I'm late tonight, Killian. Give me a chance to catch my breath and I'll tell you everything. I found her ... found her ... found her. I thought she was an apparition, my fury summoning her from the ether. It was too easy, you see. All that searching, scanning cars, the faces of drivers, wondering if she was among them, watching her on video, she had taken over my mind – and there she was in the flesh, driving impetuously and much too fast from Sheraton's driveway. I thought I'd lost her when she accelerated away but she had to stop at the end of the road, you know how dangerous that junction can be, and before she could escape again I forced my attention on her. A light bump, skilfully executed.

She was puzzled rather than angry as she surveyed the damage. Not that there was much to see, at least outwardly, but all I saw was the dent of your body beneath a sheen of polished silver. I wanted to strike her, watch her fall helplessly at my feet. Instead, I offered her coffee. There was a hesitancy in her smile — how well I know it now, how familiar her gestures seem. She refused and drove away.

What would we have discussed if we had sat opposite each other sharing a pot of coffee? A portrait of my son? How could I have uttered such foolish words? I spoke without thinking yet in that instant I wanted her to know you, to stroke you to life with her brush, capture your innocence, the hopes you once cherished.

She lives a long ways down the road, Killian, hours away. I'll have to make time, leave you for a while. She talked about childhood holidays and sounded nostalgic for sunshine summers. But she too suffers from selective memory. Of course it rained. Just as it rains tonight, splashing silverfish off your window pane.

I was nine years old when I went to Trabawn with Harriet. We stayed in a guesthouse that smelled of gravy and toilet cleaner. Under the shelter of rocks on a windswept beach we shared sandy cheese sandwiches. Waves swept me off my feet. My mother had died in the spring. Harriet cried and pretended it was rain on her face. There were children in raincoats, jumping from high sand dunes. Was she among them, I wonder. A young freckle-faced girl running through the summer, engraving memories on her soul that would last forever?

PART TWO

CHAPTER EIGHTEEN

Trabawn
1969–1980

Trabawn never changes. That's the most wonderful thing about it. Lorraine is convinced the population of farmers and fishermen falls into a magic slumber when the Cheevers leave at the end of their summer holidays and only awaken again on their return the following year.

Soon Market Street is left behind and the countryside spreads greenly before her. Uncle Des pulls out into the centre of the road and passes them, loudly honking his horn. From the back window Virginia and Edward shake their fists triumphantly. The two cars race each other to see who will reach the caravans first. Old Red Eye, the one-eyed dog, is crouched, waiting in the lane.

"Barking mad as usual, daft mutt!" Lorraine's father laughs loudly as the dog ducks and dives beneath the whirring wheels. He enjoys this annual contest of wits which he wins every time – for who, he shouts, slapping his leg for emphasis, but a suicidal mongrel will argue with a blue Toyota Corolla?

Celia, the owner of the caravans, waits at her gate to welcome them. She wears hobnailed boots and a long red skirt. Her hair is tied in a hairnet which sparkles with coloured beads. Two donkeys graze in her garden. A cat with yellow slanting eyes watches them from the gate post. The Strong family from Galway have already arrived. Mrs Strong is shaking mats at the door of her caravan and shouting at her husband to fetch water from the pump. Adrian Strong runs down the caravan steps to greet them. He is an only child and too spoiled for his own good, claims Aunt Josephine.

"Spare the rod and spoil the brat," she says every time he comes to the beach with his surfboard and fancy snorkelling equipment. Lorraine's mother says he will break hearts when he grows up. Uncle Des calls him "a nancy boy" and Lorraine's father always has him on his team when they play beach volleyball. Soon Adrian and Edward are lost in the heart of the sand dunes. They shout and fling fistfuls of bubbling seaweed at those who dare to follow, especially small girls.

The abandoned car at the end of the field is a little more rusted than the previous year but the door opens with a shriek and the steering-wheel still turns. The tree with a branch like a sofa that serves as a swing is still standing but each year the hidey-hole hedge has a little less space in which to hide. The girls rush to Celia's garden to greet the donkeys. She calls her donkeys The Philosophers and allows the girls to ride them bareback up and down the lane. The one with the darker coat is called Aristotle. Plato is skinnier and has a white mark on his ear. Celia's gingerbread is fresh from the oven, cooling on a wire rack, and there is fresh milk in a bucket behind her kitchen door. In the evenings she tells them stories about banshees and fairy forts and how the rat-a-tat-tat on their caravan roofs is not from crows pecking, as the adults believe, but is actually the step of tiny dancing fairy feet. In bed at night, Virginia whispers that Celia is actually a witch with warts on her left breast. Lorraine cannot imagine the old woman in a witch's hat riding high on a broomstick but she pretends to believe her cousin, because Virginia, being a year older and from London, knows everything.

London is much better than Trabawn, says Virginia. It has trains that run under the ground, Spangle sweets, fireworks in November, pop stars with fur coats and a queen with a crown. Once, when Virginia curtsied and handed Queen Elizabeth a bouquet of golden roses, the queen shook her hand and said, "Thank you, my most loyal subject. I will treasure these flowers forever."

"Liar, liar! Dirty knickers on fire," chants Edward when Virginia tells this story, which she does many times. Lorraine is not sure what to think. She is an only child, fanciful and shy, but for the next two weeks she has a make-believe sister and her world is perfect. How she envies Virginia's self-confidence which comes, Lorraine is convinced, from being English. But she never says this aloud because when Virginia's father drinks too much he shouts, "Up the IRA," and sings "A Nation Once Again" with tears running down his cheeks.

Virginia swings upside down from the branches of the highest trees. On the beach she is the fastest runner. Faster even than Adrian Strong. When everyone else obeys the Golden Rule and swims parallel to shore she heads like a shark towards the rock where the cormorants perch. Once she pretends to drown, flailing her arms and shrieking *Help! Help!"* until Adrian dives in fully clothed to rescue her. Her father slaps her afterwards. Hard, stinging slaps across her legs. But she doesn't cry, not once, just as she never apologises for the rows and the tantrums that come without warning and swallow Lorraine like a giant rumbling wave.

At the end of the lane there is a farmhouse with a byre where Frank Donaldson milks his cows. He tilts the cows' udders and squirts milk towards the girls, laughing loudly when they scream and dash for cover. Celia warns them not to fall in love with Frank who has turned twenty-two on his last birthday and has a townie girlfriend called Noeleen. Virginia says she would prefer to be a buried alive in quicksand than settle on a smelly manure farm. Lorraine imagines marrying a farmer like Frank, only with Adrian's face, and wearing her jeans tucked into wellingtons as she herds cattle down the lane. At night they signal messages with their torches towards Adrian's caravan window and he answers – dots and dashes, short flashes, long flashes, see you tomorrow, girls.

In the evenings the adults gather around the campfire to sing the same songs they sing every year. They grow noisy and drink from long glasses then order the children to perform their party pieces. They won't take no for an answer, even when Edward hides his head in his knees and curses softly, chanting each word like a slow litany. When Adrian plays guitar and sings "Puppy Love" he sounds far better than Donnie Osmond.

"Young ladies! Don't hide your lights under a bushel. Virginia! Lorraine! On your feet immediately." Aunt Josephine encourages them forward. They sing and dance, swaying together while the moths spin crazily above the campfire flames and the vampire bats with blood in their eyes flit between the trees.

"Time for sleep, young ladies. Tomorrow is another day," Aunt Josephine shouts when she hears them giggling. On alternate nights, the girls sleep in each other's caravans. Lorraine lies under Virginia's bunk and thinks about tomorrow, imagines it waiting outside in the darkness, a closed flower preparing to open yellow petals and release the sun. She knows exactly what the next day will bring: games of hide-and-seek, treasure hunts, picnic dinners on the caravan steps, the shivery ache of sunburn, the soothing touch of calamine lotion on hot skin.

On Friday night there is music in O'Callaghan's pub. Aunt Josephine calls it "our night out on the red hot tiles of sin". She snaps her white handbag closed and herds them down the caravan steps. The seats in O'Callaghan's remind Lorraine of church benches. Those who come late have to sit on beer barrels. They arrive early to avoid the beer barrels and Mr O'Callaghan shouts from behind the counter where he is pouring pints; "Begob! It can't be that time of the year again. The Cheevers have arrived." He wears a beige cardigan with leather patches on the elbows and calls Lorraine and Virginia "the lovely little girleens from the big smoke".

Musicians with beards and peaked caps play endless tunes that all sound the same to Lorraine. Her father recites a funny version of "Galway Bay" and everyone laughs, no matter how often they hear it. Uncle Des puffs out his chest, raises his fist and sings "A Nation Once Again". Someone always shouts, "*Tiocfaidh ár lá,*" which, Uncle Des explains in his loud bossy voice, is Irish for "Our day will come".

Aunt Josephine's face turns bright red. "Don't bite the hand that feeds you, Des Cheevers, or your boat may rock in mid-ocean." She has a proverb for all occasions. If she can't think of a suitable one she invents her own.

Virginia and Lorraine clap each other's hands in the clapping game and chant, "*My mummy told me if I was goody that she would buy me a rubber dolly. But when I told her I kissed a soldier she wouldn't buy me a rubber dolly.*"

As the night wears on Mr O'Callaghan's cheeks turn puce and his eyes disappear into narrow slits. Lorraine thinks his face will explode and his skin shrivel like a burst balloon.

"Blood pressure, poor man," says her mother.

"Drinking the profits, more likely," insists her father.

"Drink and be merry for tomorrow we fall upon the sword of Damocles," intones Aunt Josephine.

Uncle Des says nothing. He is gazing at Roisin O'Callaghan's bosom. She is Mr O'Callaghan's wife and whenever she leans over their table to place a glass of whiskey before him, his hand brushes against her knee.

Virginia swears Lorraine to secrecy. She must promise on her heart that she will never tell this secret to anyone, even under pain of torture and violent death. Uncle Des has a girlfriend in London. Her name is Sonya. She wears red stilettos and dyes her hair blonde.

"Peroxide," says Virginia and her mouth puckers just like Aunt Josephine's when she says, "Eyes to the front, Des Cheevers," every time women in bikinis walk past him on the beach.

Sonya is being hunted by kidnappers who will kill her if they find her. Virginia's father is her protector and Virginia must not tell anyone – even Aunt Josephine, who leaves Uncle Des in charge of Virginia when she has to bring Edward to the eye hospital. But as soon as she drives away Virginia's father dresses in his happy shirt with the pineapples printed over the front. He holds her hand and they take the bus to Sonya's hideaway house. Sonya giggles just like a little girl. There are ladders in her tights and her hands are hidden under the sleeves of her jumper. She owns a pet canary called Cassie who sings for Virginia when her father and Sonya are in the other room where she must not go. Sonya makes whimpering noises that sound like pups – whimper whimper. Virginia and Lorraine giggle, hands across their mouths in case the grown-ups hear. But when Virginia imitates her father – snort snort snort – they collapse against each other, helpless with laughter.

"Laughter is the best medicine," says Aunt Josephine, coming in to kiss them goodnight.

"Castor oil," shrieks Virginia.

"California Syrup of Figs." Lorraine gathers her knees into her chest and splutters. She has absolutely no idea why she is laughing but it is the funniest thing in the world. Nor does she know if this is one of Virginia's tall tales but in the pub she watches her uncle's hand trailing across the curve of Mrs O'Callaghan's dress and his mouth becoming moist when he chats to women at the bar and how he always stands too close to them, as if their words are precious pearls.

Sometimes they fight; they are, after all, small girls. Lorraine's cheeks sting as she sulks behind the sand dunes, wondering why she is being punished. What words or deeds have triggered her cousin's indifference? There are no clues. No rules to follow. Nothing she can do to prevent it happening again. She watches Virginia swimming with the boys and playing French cricket on the hard sand. The bat looks as light as a feather in her hands. She hits the ball every time and the boys groan loudly when it sails above their heads. The boys from the village join in. Those who manage to catch the ball fling themselves across the sand, hoping she will pay attention. When she is bored with their company she climbs the rocks, singing loudly, ignoring Lorraine but looking as happy as if her cousin is beside her, joining in.

Lorraine imagines a switch in her cousin's head that clicks on and off. The "off" switch makes Lorraine disappear. She is breathless with resentment, knowing that Virginia does not care. On such nights she sleeps alone, watching Virginia's caravan to see if her cousin will signal an apology. No torch flashes in the night and she vows never ever to forgive her. No matter how often she begs on her bended knees, even if she's kneeling on broken glass or nails, she will never *ever* forgive her.

When morning comes Virginia knocks lightly on the window. She stands bare-foot in the damp grass. Cobwebs tremble on the bushes and Old Red Eye, no longer suicidal but quivering with excitement, tongue lolling, is waiting by her side. Lorraine leaves the caravan, moving quietly so as not to awaken her parents. They climb the stile. The faint pulse of the sea grows louder, beating time against the cry of seabirds flying low over the foam. The little girls lift their feet, dancing forward, toe prints etched on the sand ridges that wriggle like snakes away from the retreating tide. It is easy to believe they are the only children alive in this hazy white universe and, no matter how hard she tries, Lorraine is unable to remember why Virginia made her so cross.

Just when it seems as if time has sculpted the years into an unchanging blueprint, adolescence kicks aside the ramparts of childhood. Mood swings replace tree swings. The carnival they loved is, suddenly, too small, flaking paint, tarnished brass, commandeered by children who look *so* young. It's impossible to stop giggling and chests are curving into breasts with a tendency to wobble violently when dashing from the sea. The village boys come to the beach at night and light bonfires. In the mornings Lorraine sees empty beer cans and a circle of black ash on the sand. The beach parties are strictly forbidden but the caravan campfires are beginning to lose their charm. The repetitiveness of adult songs that once sounded funny or sad, or simply seemed wonderful because they were always the same, hum like a saw through her head. Virginia sticks fingers into her mouth and pretends to retch each time her father clears his throat to sing "Ireland Boys Hurray". The attractions of the beach parties are too much to resist. When the adults are sleeping off the effects of wine and gin, the young people escape to the dunes.

Across the driftwood flames, Lorraine watches Adrian Strong watching her. He has been her torment for years, dragging her under the waves or waylaying her in ambushes to pull her hair or war dance around her. Now he is sturdy and tanned. His hair is bleached even blonder from the sun and his eyes remind her of autumn, the deep gold of fallen leaves. They smoulder with something only she can see and the intoxication of first love sets her limbs shaking. On the beach he no longer drags her under the waves but lifts her high in his arms and shouts that he has captured a mermaid. She flails against him, unsure whether her screams are from fury or the sleek wet touch of his skin when he slowly lowers her back into the water.

Virginia has already kissed six English boys. In the shelter of the sand dunes she explains "French kissing" to Lorraine who, remembering the hard nudging pressure of Adrian's body, quivers. When he lies on a towel beside her, filtering grains of sand between his fingers and across her legs, she imagines opening her mouth, the way Virginia describes, so that his tongue can touch the sensitive spot that makes girls swoon. As the sand trickles between her thighs, she shrieks and feigns indignation. She pushes him away and yells at Virginia to come to her aid. They dash into the waves and are swallowed in another endless summer of sky and sea.

Lorraine is sixteen years old, light of step, charged with energy yet languid when the breeze plays across her skin. The fuchsia blooming on the hedgerows cuts a crimson swathe through the countryside and the fiery orange of the montbretia, nodding and swaying along the roadside, drives her from the caravan early in the morning to try and capture such hues on paper. She paints the sun melting on the sea and the pulsing jellyfish, washed ashore and abandoned by the tide. Her mind is a dreaming space of half-formed truths. The swell of waves, rising and falling, has a new rhythm that beckons her forward into the long grass beyond the dunes where she kisses Adrian Strong until their lips ache.

In O'Callaghan's pub she sips 7 Up and feels the persistent nudge of his knee. Surely people can feel the heat radiating between them. Virginia ignores them. She tosses her head and walks proudly through the beat of traditional music towards the ramshackle hall at the back of the pub which serves as a disco for the youth of the village. A disc jockey called Mad-Dog Mullarkey stands behind coloured lights. He wears black eye shadow and frizzes his hair. Virginia is allowed to share his platform and play her favourite Sex Pistols records. She is bored with school, bored with her parents who seek to destroy her with mediocrity, bored with the suburban estate where she lives, bored with everyone who walks outside her small closed circle. Her parents bicker constantly. Sonya is still a secret and her father is a coward, trapped in a loveless marriage, afraid to walk away. Lorraine thinks that a woman who keeps a canary and wears red stilettos must be an exotic change for a man whose wife's vocabulary has been robbed from a phrase book. But is it an excuse for adultery? Her heart aches for Aunt Josephine who advises her to "Gather ye rosebuds while ye may – for tomorrow we lie down to die in green pastures," when she discovers her in Adrian's arms behind the caravans.

By the following year everything is different. Adrian is studying marketing and working with Edward for the summer in Boston. Josephine comes to Trabawn without her husband. She walks the beach late in the evenings with Donna, the two women falling silent when the girls draw near.

Virginia has become a punk. Her hair is orange, spiky as the Statue of Liberty. She has pierced her ears with rings and studs, encircled her arms in metal handcuffs. A tiny silver dagger has been inserted into her bottom lip. Her eyes, sea-stormy, reflect her disgust at having to spend time trapped in a caravan with her mother. When Lorraine's father makes jokes about electric shocks every time she spikes her hair, she looks as if she is biting down on a freshly sliced lemon.

She explains the finer points of punk to Lorraine. It has galvanised her, given her anger a focus. The aggressive graffiti on her denim jacket shows her contempt for the world. She follows the Sex Pistols and the Buzzcocks. She threatens to vomit violently when Lorraine says she adores David Cassidy. At the disco in O'Callaghan's she dances on her own. Her movements are graceless and spasmodic, her head jerking violently. There is a recklessness about her that demands attention. She is like a honey pot but without the sweetness, challenging yet attracting the young men who watch her from the side of the hall and no longer know how to talk to her.

In London she has a boyfriend. She hates every minute they are forced to spend apart. Her mother hates every minute they spend together.

"There's plenty more sharks in the sea," says Josephine but

Virginia ignores this advice. Her boyfriend's name is Ralph Blaide but he refuses to answer to anything other than Razor Blade. He belongs to a punk band called Sulphuric Acid. They have an explosive sex life, she informs Lorraine, describing torrid sessions which involve biting, screaming at each other, sometimes spitting, hissing, kissing until their lips bleed, then making love, only she calls it "fucking".

The first time she uses the word Lorraine recoils. It sounds brutal, sickeningly different to the romantic ideal she still holds about passion and sand dunes – which she is unable to pass without her heart seizing up with longing for Adrian Strong in Boston. But Virginia throws it out with such indifference that it seems more like a manoeuvre undertaken in the front line of a battle field.

Mad–Dog Mullarkey grows cannabis in his mother's herb garden. He rolls a joint and the girls smoke it in Mrs Mullarkey's greenhouse, sheltered by enormous rubber plants and bulbous, thorny cacti. Lorraine inhales and is violently sick. Her face feels green. It is the colour of death, she tells Virginia, who says it is all in her imagination and floats the words above Lorraine's whirling head.

Her self-confidence grows even as her friendship with Virginia disintegrates. She refuses to allow herself to be dragged along in the wake of her cousin's angst. Her art teacher has encouraged her to study art when she completes her Leaving Certificate. She is anxious for the new school year to begin. Instead of seeking Virginia's company, she borrows a bike from Celia and cycles around Trabawn, sketching and taking photographs of the countryside. As the evening tide retreats she walks barefoot over the sand, her eyes exploring the mysterious depths of shadow and light. On the rocks she sits, her hair loose, visualising herself as Adrian's mermaid, maimed of heart.

Some months later her mother tells her they will not be returning to the caravans. Virginia's parents are divorcing. Uncle Des is marrying his red-heeled Sonya. The Trabawn summers have come to an end. She does not see Virginia again until the summer of '82.

CHAPTER NINETEEN

Ferryman
(an extract from Michael Carmody's memoir)

In the summer of '82, Jean Devine tied an orange bandanna over her long chestnut hair. She wore a tie-dyed t-shirt that revealed what it was supposed to hide and Doc Martens wide enough to walk on water. She was nineteen years of age and I, one year older and not any wiser, grabbed for around her waist and spun her into my arms. The Rolling Stones were in town and those of us who had not emigrated to shape the great Irish diaspora gathered in Slane to hear them play. In that grassy amphitheatre we danced to the beat of "Brown Sugar", high on freedom and the amplification shuddering through our bodies, carelessly swaying towards a future where we would love and maim each other with equal fervour.

In my sagging two-man tent, we dined on pineapple chunks and cold beans. The closeness of our surroundings, the thin, flapping canvas straining against the guy-rope, the sense of people moving around us yet being separated from them within this flimsy space, added to the intensity of our time together. We drank cans of tepid beer, exchanged life stories, revealed secrets, admitted insecurities. When we could no longer contain our impatience we slipped into the padded warmth of my sleeping-bag. Her jeans were slashed across the backside. Three rips. I counted before I pulled them off. Afterwards, I would think of that small tent as a fantasy stage where we, without inhibitions and constraints, found the freedom to be different people for a short, searing time.

She'd gone to Slane with friends from university. Business students studying for Bachelor of Commerce degrees and secure positions within the money sector. Nowadays, they work in the heart of the Financial Centre or other similar spires of glass and steel. Occasionally, on the business pages of broadsheets, I notice their photographs – head and shoulder shots, their smiles growing in confidence as they climb another rung on the fiscal ladder. Monica, Gillian, Jennifer. Would I remember their names if something as incidental as a condom, torn in the force of passion, had not changed everything? Would I even remember Jean Devine?

When we returned to Dublin, the funny, passionate girl I knew in Slane seemed like a figment of my imagination. The striped bandanna had disappeared. Her hair was washed free of grass and mud, her dress patterned with sprigs of daisies. A pair of espadrilles had replaced the Doc Martens which she never wore again. Our awkwardness when we kissed belonged to the feinting and dodging of a sedate courtship. She came to my bed-sit with a plastic bag full of detergents to dust, polish, brush and bleach. New sheets were laid upon the mattress and I, whose only desire was to lay her flat upon the narrow bed and run my hands over the hidden curves of her body, felt trapped and angry as she cleaned up my act. I decided it was time to end our brief relationship but nature had other options in store for us.

Two months after the departure of the Rolling Stones we sat opposite each other in my bed-sit.

"I'm late," she said. "I'm always on time … to-the-very-day, actually." Her breath broke on the last word. She looked around my bed-sit and began to cry. I was an arts student with ambitions to become a playwright and a compulsion to write bad poetry. I had no parents, just an eccentric aunt who was walking her way around the world. My only secure employment was waiting tables part time in an Indian restaurant and shifting props for a drama company. It had sounded wonderfully eclectic when we discussed it at Slane but, without the liberating beat of rock music to enliven her imagination, the peeling wallpaper and empty beer cans beneath my bed told a tale of poverty, sloth and lack of ambition.

A pregnancy test confirmed our worst fears. We talked about abortion or, to be fully honest, I talked, Jean listened. My script was word perfect. We were too young, still students with our lives in front of us. We would scrape the money together somehow and go to London for the abortion, sharing the pain, the loss, then move on again.

Her voice cracked with fury. My argument was no match for her outrage and conviction. She was terrified of what was happening to her but abortion was a sin, unforgivable, unforgettable. I argued the line which I'd heard debated so often in university among my feminist friends. What about a woman's right to choose, autonomy over her own body? Her eyes glazed me out.

Under duress, I agreed to meet her parents. They lived in a modest bungalow but it was in a respectable location, she told me. Such things, I was beginning to discover, were of importance to her. I took a bus to Monkstown, feeling the snare tightening around my neck. Noel Devine's shoulders are stooped now but then he was tall and straight as an exclamation mark. Greta was as plump as she is today and her hair was only beginning to grey. When I stood before them, expecting Noel to brandish a shotgun and march us to the altar, he showed concern for our situation, rather than a desire to load and fire. They agreed that we were too young to marry but if that was what we wanted they would be happy to accept me as their son-in-law. Jean watched my face, judged my expression to be less than enthusiastic and shook her head defiantly. Marriage was out of the question, she stated. We hardly knew each other. I agreed, perhaps too whole-heartedly, but promised to support her and our child in every other way.

We battled our way towards Killian's birth. Despite Jean's brave words, the term "single mother" terrified her, conjuring up a one-bedroom flat in the inner city with drug addicts needling their arms on the stairwells and money-lenders crashing through doorways. The question of marriage kept cropping up in conversation. My future was being shaped by her vision of the perfect life; an incremental salary and a secure pension plan. I, too, was equally limited in vision, imagining myself joining an army of grey suits marching with one step from grey office blocks towards the grey uniformity of suburbia. Our child was also without identity or colour; its presence visible only in the growing bump on Jean's stomach which she disguised with loose dresses and a refusal to go anywhere people might recognise her. Since this effectively ruled out the pub, cinema, rugby club or disco, our dates mainly consisted of sedate walks in the Phoenix Park where, one evening, in a hollow of fallen leaves, we spotted a deer standing perfectly still for an instant before bounding silently away. I envied the ease with which it moved into the trees, leaving nothing, not even a trembling leaf, as evidence of its swift escape.

Perhaps that was the reason I also ran, deserting her at a time when she needed me most. We'd had a row before I left. A family gathering had been planned. I was to meet her relations. They waited in vain for my arrival.

I hadn't realised I was running away from everything until I reached Harriet's cottage. She was home from exploring the snow caps of Chile and offered me her usual absent-minded welcome. I didn't tell her she was about to become a great-aunt, knowing her scorn would send me slinking back to face my responsibilities. I told myself I was doing the right thing. Far better to end it at the beginning. What kind of father would I make when I'd never known a father's hand on my shoulder? A ship that passed in the night, said Harriet when I questioned her about this nameless man. As an answer it lacked a certain clarity and so I gave him a personality; a buccaneer on a pirate ship, the commander of a submarine, a Viking on a longboat pillaging the Liffey.

I awoke one morning and sensed it, a shifting in the air, a quickening in the breeze. My head was clear for the first time in months. I needed to be with Jean. Whatever our future held, I wanted a share in it. I left a note for Harriet and hitch-hiked back to Dublin. Six hours later I rang her doorbell. Greta closed the door in my face. Killian had been born the previous day. Jean and her family never wanted to see me again.

In time Greta relented but Jean's forgiveness was more difficult to obtain. I phoned her every day, sent her flowers and letters, besieged her with phone calls until she agreed to meet me. Killian was three weeks old when I saw him for the first time. I held him in my arms and wondered how his frail bird-like neck would ever support his head. As he struggled to make sense of shape, smell and sound, I watched his gaze lock with bemused concentration into mine. Can anyone describe happiness? It is elation, walking on air, music of the mind. It is a fleeting thing.

At first it seemed possible to make amends. I was free to visit the bungalow as often as I wished. A tentative friendship grew between myself and Greta, who looked after her grandson when Jean returned to university. She had a sweet voice, Joni Mitchell came to mind when I heard her sing, and she sang often to Killian, lullabies and folk songs. "Hush little baby, don't say a word. Mama's gonna buy you a mocking bird."

I remember the afternoon he walked for the first time. We sat in her kitchen and watched him release his grip on the edge of a chair. He swayed forward with the uncertainty of a drunk who sees the floor rising and falling. He took one tottering step then another, his body wavering between disbelief and determination. I will never forget his startled smile when we applauded. The wonder with which he collapsed and stared at his feet. This ever-changing relationship between father and son was beginning to unfold in ways I'd never anticipated. I wanted to spend my life exploring it with him.

I proposed marriage. Magnanimous Sir Galahad, determined to do the right thing. As always, my script was out of date. Jean Devine had met a rugby player with wavy hair, a truncated neck and ambitions to take over his father's wine import company. As she waved me from her house that evening, Killian balanced securely on her right hip, I felt as if the lid of an unexplored treasure chest had been slammed across my fingers.

Terence O'Malley adored her. As soon as I saw them together I knew I'd lost. On Sunday afternoons she strapped our son into the back of his Jaguar and they drove to the mountains, to the beach. I imagined Killian's stomach heaving as the car mounted bridges or turned corners too sharply and how, on the way home, he would drift asleep to the strains of Terence singing "The Bog Down in the Valley O" – or drawing from his interminable store of Knock Knock jokes.

Jean and I found it impossible to be in the same room without arguing. Greta refused to take sides and ordered us to sit down together and discuss our son's future in a civilized manner. She was beginning to sound increasingly like a mother. At least, I assumed her scolding, exasperated tone was maternal. As far as I could remember, my mother had never raised her voice to me and Harriet had always treated me as a miniature adult disguised for a brief period in a boy's body.

Our meeting took place in the Shelbourne Hotel. In six months' time her father would escort her to the altar. An engagement ring gleamed on her tanned finger. A house had been purchased in the Dublin Mountains where Killian would begin his new life. *Her* son, she allowed the emphasis to settle between us, needed to acquire a strong sense of identity. If I persisted in believing I could come and go as I pleased she'd have to look at other options to protect him. My furious reminder that I had a natural right which could never be denied was met with indifference. That's how I remember our conversation. No doubt Jean would take a different view.

"My son would have been an abortion statistic if you'd had your way," she said. She'd checked out her rights and advised me to check out mine which, she added, almost as an afterthought, were non-existent. There was no father's name on Killian's birth certificate. How could there be when I'd abandoned her at a time when she had most need of my support? She closed her eyes, as if blanking out an indelible memory. Terence wanted them to be a family in the fullest sense. Total commitment.

The word "adoption" was cold and complete. It did not need an appendage or any further explanation. I veered between disbelief and outrage. What she was suggesting was inconceivable, obscene. Yet, she made it sound reasonable, even possible. Her hand was steady as she held a silver pot and poured coffee. She was deftly working my strings between her fingers and I had no option but to dance to her tune.

I met with a solicitor who warned of protracted court battles and partisan judges. I was a single father without any family structure, apart from an aunt whose life was an endless journey of discovery. The self-help group of lone fathers I joined reflected my own helplessness. Their stories of injustices terrified me. I contacted Eddie Wynn, a journalist who'd supplemented his income when he was studying by waiting tables in the Indian restaurant where I'd worked. Under the *nom de plume* of Patrick I told my story which was published in the *Dublin Echo* with the bold headline "SINGLE FATHER DEPRIVED OF RIGHTS". It sparked off quite a debate, made Killian famous in an anonymous way. Letters on the issues of single fatherhood were published. I was asked to do a radio interview, then another for television. My face was shaded from public view but my hunched, defeated shoulders told their own story.

Jean never admitted she guessed the identity of "Patrick" but in the months that followed she stopped insisting on adoption. I could have five hours every Saturday afternoon, providing I agreed to Killian's surname becoming Devine-O'Malley. My solicitor negotiated a full Saturday and an overnight visit once a month. I accepted these terms, having heard too many in-camera horror scenarios from the men in the group. They were an angry gathering. Many of them had good reasons for their anger but my own reality was becoming submerged under their experiences. I left the group when I realised I was beginning to feed off their collective outrage.

Do I sound bitter, jealous? Jealousy I will accept as an abiding emotion but bitterness was impossible to maintain when it came to Terence O'Malley. When he was not stamping the imprint of his boot into the head of his opponent on the rugby pitch, he was an affable, easygoing man without opinions. His love for Jean was uncomplicated. Killian was three years old when they married. He would not create an uneasy triangle within their union but form the complete circle.

Terence sings from his belly … The Bog Down in the Valley O … sing Killian sing … and in that bog there is a tree … clap, Killian, clap! What a lovely day. Look at the trees, mountains, rivers. Say thank you

to daddy. Say it! Thank you Daddy. Terence is daddy ... daddy is Michael ... Terence is daddy ...

Cinema circus concerts McDonald's playground bookshop museum ... wasn't it a great day, Killian ... wasn't it great to be together again ... what did you do this week ... tell me everything ... stop with those stupid Knock Knock jokes ... you're doing my head in ... sorry for being so cross, son ... sorry for spoiling our day ...

CHAPTER TWENTY

London
1982

Lorraine is adrift in a cacophony of sounds, spice smells, greasy-spoon cafes, dreadlocks, girls in saris with cockney accents, boot boys, ageing beatniks, Rastafarians and men in turbans who stare haughtily through her. Everyone hurries at a faster pace and snaps, "Excuse me, let me pass," if she dallies too long on the Underground escalators. She enters a crowded pub where young men with tight white faces move in an uncontrollable fury to the music of Sulphuric Acid.

"It's not quite O'Callaghan's, but you'll get used to it." Virginia laughs at her expression and leads her into the seething mass of bodies. Two years have passed since the cousins met and Lorraine is spending her first summer abroad. Her dread of being introduced to a man called Razor Blade – who spits and hisses when making love – has not lessened with time. His appearance does little to ease her apprehension. On stage he writhes his skinny body and contorts his face. His songs, bitter vitriolic lyrics which he writes himself, electrify his fans. His restlessness, so similar to the nervous energy Virginia projects, dominates the stage. Lorraine will share a flat with them for the summer.

Uncle Des has married his red-heeled Sonya.

"No sense crying over sour milk, young lady," said her aunt when Lorraine rang to sympathise. "Eyes to the front. Best foot forward." She now belongs to a ten-pin bowling club where she bowls with such ferocity that she has became the club's top scorer. She attributes her success to the belief that the ball she is rolling towards a strike is Des Cheevers' deceitful, cheating head.

One night, listening painfully to Sulphuric Acid in a basement club with no ventilation to release the sweating angst of its occupants, Lorraine is pulled backwards and held firmly against a lean masculine body.

"Virginia told me you'd be here tonight." A familiar voice growls in her ear.

"Oh my God!" She presses her hand across her mouth and turns into the laughing face of Adrian Strong. "I *don't* believe it."

He is dressed in jeans and a white t-shirt, his arms muscular and tanned the same reddish bronze she remembers from Trabawn. He is different from the crowd, both in the way he dresses and the ease with which he listens to the music. She wonders if they will beat him up for standing apart from them, relaxed and amused, his very posture suggesting contempt for their collective fury.

"I'm working in London for the summer." She has to lean closer to hear him. His Irish accent is music to her home-sick ears. His eyes rest on a Celtic cross glinting against her throat. She tilts her head back, allows her hair to sweep down her back. In college, an art student painted her neck and entitled his painting *Swan-song*. Ever since, she has been prone to showing off her neck and Adrian Strong seems to appreciate her efforts. He fingers the cross, drawing her closer with an almost imperceptible pull, then stops before they touch. He could swallow her in his gaze, shake her heart until it loses all sense of rhythm. She turns her back on him, pretending to stare towards the band. He needs punishing for never writing to her. She recalls the anguish of waiting for the postman, hoping to hear his voice every time the phone rang. The pain does not seem important any more. He tightens his hands on her hips, presses her more insistently against him then turns her around, his mouth hot against her lips. She had forgotten the desire he could arouse in her and cannot imagine how it will end, who will be the first to break away, not her, impossible.

"What say we escape from this harbour to hell and find somewhere quieter to talk?" he suggests.

"Don't you like their music?" She teases him.

"It's pure, unadulterated *shite*." She can see him laughing but the sound is lost in the frenzied clash of drums. Music blasts around them as Sulphuric Acid vent their hate and Razor Blade jerks the microphone in a grotesque sexual parody. They leave the packed snarling fans, fists raised, heads banging, and Virginia, like a flame, jumping higher than any of them.

In a pub where pin-ball machines ping and music plays too loudly, they talk about home, discovering mutual acquaintants from college, and when she says, "Isn't Ireland *such* a village," they moan with the contented satisfaction of those who have escaped its homogenous clutches. They discuss music and books, art, themselves, the past and the future. He has completed his marketing degree and intends to travel. To earn money he is working on a building site, his second summer in London with the same construction crew. She pictures him standing high above the city, bare-chested, running along thin strips of scaffolding, striding confidently along ceiling joists, stepping onto window ledges without hesitation.

Later, the band party in the old Victorian house where Virginia and Razor live. She holds Adrian tightly as they circle the crowded room. His voice whispers in her hair. His hand slides between them, touching her intimately, secretly and the lurching pleasure she feels remains with her long after he leaves.

London is an oven of grey cement, the sun bouncing off high grey walls. Lorraine seeks the shade of trees and overhanging balconies, shop awnings and the dark side of the street, dreading the long hours in the hotel where she works as a chambermaid. She can tell much about the anonymous occupants of the bedrooms she cleans: the signs of sex in the tangle of sheets and discarded condoms thrown carelessly under the bed, empty pill bottles, books by Jean-Paul Sartre and Barbara Cartland, pornographic magazines, the bible with the crushed rose as a book mark, a mountain boot in the bath, a lacy bra wound around a curtain rail. But the tide of life that flows around her only has relevance when she is with Adrian Strong. Mind domination. Lover takes all. And he is taking all, not just the time they spend together but also time spent without him, which she flings aside as heedlessly as debris.

"He comes and goes," says Virginia. "He'll be back. Just don't hold your breath."

The titian dye is fading from her hair. Dark roots show between the spikes but even they are losing their aggression and have a wilted look. She is working in public relations and a more chic image is being cultivated.

"Punk is dying," she informs Lorraine. "It's time Razor moved on to something more meaningful."

Lorraine does not want to move on anywhere unless Adrian Strong is beside her. His pattern of coming and going has no order and she is unable to organise her shifts around him. When he does turn up, always unexpectedly and days later than promised, he is as unapologetic as ever. The desire she experienced on the night they met has not been repeated. His kisses, although wonderful, are just ordinarily wonderful and, sometimes, in his arms she feels as if she has no identity. He talks about New York, San Francisco, California – he wants to experience the States and plans to leave London in September. All he has to do is beckon and she will go with him. She closes her eyes, imagines them sipping coffee in Greenwich Village and returning to their loft bedroom to lie entwined in each other's arms.

Despite his obvious contempt for Sulphuric Acid, he attends many of their gigs. Occasionally, the four of them drink in the local pub, The Pewter Tankard. When they stay in for an evening they watch films on television, slumped comfortably together on the long sofa. Razor dons a butcher's apron and cooks. Lorraine is surprised to discover that he is an excellent chef. He uses only fresh vegetables and introduces her to unknown seasonings and spices. Jamaican dishes are his speciality and even Marley, the Jamaican man from the flat next door, says his food has the authentic taste of home cooking. He also makes home-made beer. Bottles line the kitchen shelves and their corks pop with the velocity of gunfire.

Marley's real name is Earl Bradley but he is a dedicated Bob Marley fan, playing the singer's records constantly, even in the mornings before breakfast and late into the night. He calls to the flat one evening and presents a bottle of Jamaican rum to Virginia as an apology for keeping them awake.

"Believe what I say, sister. This is the fastest route to heaven."

"We must enjoy and suffer collectively," says Virginia, after he leaves. She places four glasses on the table. Later, when the bottle is empty, Razor opens his home-made beer. It seems like a good idea to drink as many bottles as possible.

The following morning Lorraine awakens, her tongue thick and furry, her brow pounding. She has no idea how she reached her bed. Under the bedclothes she is naked. Her clothes are heaped on the floor, her bra folded neatly on top. Did she remove it in front of the others or in the privacy of her room? A flush runs from the tips of her fingers and along her spine as she begins to gather fragments of the night around her. They played strip poker. She has no idea who suggested the game and can only remember sitting cross-legged on the floor in her knickers and bra, voices encouraging her to take off one or the other. She remembers Virginia walking across the room, tall and slight as a young boy except for the dark triangle of hair between her thighs and the curve of her small breasts. She swayed past the three of them, deftly swinging her hip away when Razor reached up to touch her. Adrian's eyes followed her, his mouth open and frozen on a silent moan. The air had been heavy, dense with a violent need that frightened Lorraine but Virginia settled back into the deep cushions of the sofa, a glass in her hand, cards fanned in the other, enjoying the vibrating tension her nakedness created.

Lorraine's hands shake as she sits on the edge of the bed and tries to recall what happened afterwards. Outside in the kitchen she hears Virginia's throaty laughter, Razor's deep voice, the clink of a frying pan. Her stomach heaves then settles queasily again as she moves towards the bathroom. Later, showered, her tongue and teeth scrubbed, she enters the kitchen where they greet her casually. She lost the poker hand and ran to the safety of her room, explains Virginia, when Lorraine insists on knowing. A game of Monopoly would be discussed with the same air of ennui. Razor does not bother joining in the conversation. He knows how Lorraine feels about him and is not willing to waste time changing her mind.

"You can take the girl out of the convent but you can't take the convent out of the girl," says Virginia which sounds like something her mother would say. Lorraine is angry rather than amused. Last night is a hole in her head and all Virginia can do is make patronising remarks. For minutes, or perhaps hours, she walked and talked and breathed in some unconscious sphere that was neither sleep nor wakefulness. Even dreams leave a residue but this – this was oblivion in the deepest sense.

Alone in her room she begins to draw on a sketch pad, using sticks of charcoal. Her hand moves freely over the pages. Sinewy, snake-like figures emerge. The shapes weave in a convoluted circle, sometimes hidden behind clouds or coiling around a bridge that hangs suspended in mid-air. Soon the shapes are obscured by a face, a lush expression, smouldering eyes, a half-open, pouting mouth. When Virginia bangs on the door and announces that Adrian has arrived, she guiltily shoves the sketches under the mattress. Dream analysis or doodling, she wonders, spraying perfume on her wrists and combing her hair. She looks tousled and childish, unawakened. The only exhibitionist tendencies she ever displays are on canvas. Perhaps if she was more daring – she frowns and her lips, which she is outlining, suddenly quiver. She sits down, her fingers gripping the edge of the mattress. Something flicks, a thought, a vision. She has no idea why she should visualise Adrian and Virginia entwined like snakes, their sleek, smooth limbs writhing silently in the deep cushions of the sofa where they often huddle, the four of them together, watching television.

She is crazy to think such thoughts. Razor and Virginia belong together. The sounds they make at night, such thudding force, as if their bed is unable to take the strain of their desire, and sometimes they make love against the wall, uncaring whether or not she hears. And she does hear. Even with the pillow over her head the sounds are audible. The moaning, urging sounds that hint at sexual violence and a passion she can only imagine.

Two months later the summer is almost over and Sulphuric Acid are touring the Midlands. Lorraine looks forward to spending time alone with Virginia before she returns home but her cousin has disappeared from the flat. She leaves nothing, not even a note to explain her whereabouts. Out of the corner of her eye, Lorraine imagines her flitting by but when she turns, the room is empty. Yet there is evidence that she calls into the flat when Lorraine is at work. Her underwear dries on a line in the bathroom, make-up is scattered across the window ledge, sunglasses lie on the mantelpiece. On the draining board two mugs have been rinsed and left to drain. Lorraine notices spilled granules of coffee on the counter. Virginia's bedroom door is open, carelessly tossed shoes are on the floor, rumpled bedclothes.

She takes the tube to Angel where Adrian lives. The front door bell remains unanswered. She stares upwards at the windows but no silhouettes or shadows suggest movement beyond the dusty Venetian blinds.

Marley is playing his reggae music when Lorraine arrives unexpectedly back to the flat on the fourth day. Her stomach is cramped with spasmodic period pains and the hotel housekeeper, taking pity on her, has given her the rest of the day off. She fills a hot-water bottle and lies on the sofa. From next door the beat of a calypso drum thumps heavy as a hammer against her head. To love Adrian Strong and not to be loved in return – that is all she has gained from a summer in London. Swamped in misery she goes to the bathroom in search of tablets.

The door is closed. Inside, someone is sobbing, the sound audible now that Lorraine has moved away from the reggae beat. She opens the door and stares at Virginia's huddled figure weeping against the side of the bath. The bath is old-fashioned with claw legs and a chipped surface that was never cleaned until Lorraine moved in. Virginia's hair is no longer spiky, just greasy and defeated, and her eyes, when she looks upwards in shock, are ringed with streaked mascara.

Without speaking, Lorraine drops to her knees, pulls her close. They rock together until the sobbing eases. She has never heard Virginia cry. Perhaps during the early summers in Trabawn there were tears but she cannot remember them – only her own tears as she floundered on the edge of her cousin's moods and indifference. Now, Virginia is clinging and needy and Lorraine feels as if she has crawled beneath barbed wire to reach her. She confirms what Lorraine has already guessed.

"I kept thinking it had to be a mistake." She releases a hiccuping sob. "Even when the doctor confirmed it, I had to check for myself. How can this happen to me?"

Remembering the nightly sounds from behind the bedroom wall, Lorraine figures this is a rhetorical question.

"Have you told Razor?"

"I don't want to tell him." Virginia shakes her head violently. "I can just imagine what he'll say."

"You don't know how he's going to react. He could be thrilled when he hears."

"That's just the problem. He'll be so thrilled he'll want us to get married immediately. This is exactly what he needs to twist my arm."

Lorraine sits back on her heels, startled by this new perception of Razor who has remained as enigmatic as when she first met him.

Virginia gives way to a fresh paroxysm of tears. "He's so possessive. He thinks he owns me. I don't want this baby … I don't … I don't." She is adamant, her voice rising as if she can already hear the words of caution Lorraine is about to utter. "Will you help me? I have to borrow money, oh God! How am I going to manage?"

"But you can't *not* tell Razor. He has a right to know … to be with you if you decide –"

"I *have* decided. I'm too young to be stuck with a baby. I don't want one – *ever*."

"At least talk to him about it." Lorraine forces authority into her voice. "You can't get rid of his baby without saying a word."

"Don't call it a baby. It's nothing yet, just a lump. Nothing! Do you understand?" Her face, ravaged by tears, is defiant.

"Razor – he is the father, isn't he?" Lorraine asks. The stifling heat of the day has gathered in the bathroom, making it difficult to breathe.

Virginia's hesitation is as painful as a skipped heartbeat. "Who else would be the father?" She snaps her answer with such fury that Lorraine dares not repeat the question. "I don't want him involved in this. Promise me you won't tell him … or anyone. I want it to be over as soon as possible. Will you come with me to the clinic? I need you with me, Lorraine."

"But you haven't looked at any other options. You could come to Dublin with me, stay in my house. You might change your mind and want to keep the baby or have it adopted."

Virginia's eyes are swept with long lashes. "No! No! No! Are you listening to me? If you won't come with me I'll go by myself. I'll get the money from somewhere and you can keep your priest-ridden, bog-Irish opinions to yourself."

The vehemence of this attack stuns Lorraine. She is a child again behind the sand dunes, struggling to understand. Virginia grabs her hand when she tries to rise, presses it tightly. "I'm sorry – I'm sorry. I didn't mean to say that. I'm so upset. Please, Lorraine. There's no one I can turn to except you."

Razor is back by the end of the week. He and Virginia are lying like spoons on the sofa watching television when Lorraine arrives in from work. *Coronation Street* is on – a programme they claim to despise but they watch every episode. They barely acknowledge her presence until the credits start to roll and appear so contented together that Lorraine is convinced Razor must know. She feels light-headed with relief as she switches on the kettle and makes tea for everyone.

Virginia pats a space beside her on the sofa and Lorraine sits down. Razor has love bruises on his neck, pinheads of red skin, raw and flagrant. She thinks of Virginia's sharp white teeth sinking into his flesh, imagines, also, him calling her "my vampire bitch", which he does at night behind the wall. She wonders how Virginia broke the news and what he said in reply – and if they made love afterwards – she suspects they did by the languid way they lie against each other, no tension, no urgency. They probably did it right there on the sofa where she is sitting. The thought makes her rise hurriedly and open the window, allowing the night breeze to cool her face.

"We're having a celebration party tomorrow night," announces Virginia.

"What are we celebrating?" Lorraine smiles knowingly across at her cousin, who fixes her with a cold warning stare and replies, "Sulphuric Acid's got a new record deal. Isn't that something worth celebrating?"

People lounge on beanbags, prop the walls, invade Lorraine's bedroom in pairs. The air reeks of hash and cigarettes. Sulphuric Acid have taken over the stairs which they block, refusing to move aside and forcing the late arrivals to squeeze past. Virginia dances in the centre of the room. Her head thumps the air, her fists raised high. Thick metal links around her neck remind Lorraine of a slave collar and she thinks about the bites on Razor's neck, a ring of fire, enslaving him, and how he no longer seems aggressive and controlling, just sad. The clinic has been booked, excuses made and the money Lorraine saved throughout the summer has been transferred into Virginia's bank account. Razor stands at the edge of the crowd and watches Virginia. His eyes follow every movement she makes.

Adrian arrives late and forces his way through the crowd.

"Where have you been all week?" Lorraine tries to control the question but it sounds angry, demanding. He frowns, mutters about working overtime. Is he under an obligation to send her his schedule?

"I thought something had happened. I was worried, that's all." She wants to have a row, scream and slap his face, make him aware that she exists. "The House of the Rising Sun" is playing on the stereo and the crowd sing along. Virginia sits on the floor, cross-legged, smoking a joint. She stares at Adrian, not smiling or even acknowledging his arrival. She passes the joint to Razor, leans like a cat against him. Lorraine almost expects her body to ripple with pleasure. The singing voices are a raucous chorus, parodying a song that Lorraine loves. She sees the same expression of distaste on Adrian's face.

"We need fresh air." He grabs her hand and leads her from the room. The crowd on the stairs has grown. She follows him downstairs, a pall of smoke stinging her eyes. The new moon, frail as a clipped fingernail, rocks between lucent clouds. It is difficult to see the stars. They seek the shelter of an empty shop doorway. She aches to tell him about Virginia but, as soon as she mentions her name, he kisses her, tells her how much he missed her, apologises for being rude. His kisses are deep and passionate. She is pushed further into the dark recess but she is conscious that the distance between them keeps widening, even as his hands seek her body. She begins to vibrate with his tension, unable to respond when he moans and snaps open the buttons on her blouse. Voices intrude, people pass too close, car lights sweep across their privacy.

"Not like this ... I can't." She pushes him away and returns to the house where young men sweep knowledgeable, indolent eyes across her flushed face.

A sloe-eyed Rastafarian refuses to budge from his position at the foot of the stairs. When she tries to climb past he stares up her legs, tilting his head provocatively. She senses Adrian's fury and is frightened he will lash out, igniting a fuse just waiting to explode. She grips his arm, warning him to calm down. The Rastafarian catches her ankle, slides his hand up above her knee, grinning when she tries to struggle free. She is aware of movement, his dark face jerking backwards, his mouth opening in shock but no sound emerging. Adrian punches him again. Blood spurts from the Rastafarian's nose and the men on the stairs stir like a choreographed group of dancers waiting for a signal. The fight is so instantaneous, so violent, that she has only a panicked impression of hurtling fists and boots kicking.

She is pushed backwards, her head cracking against the banisters. Razor appears at the top of the stairs, boots flailing, and notices her huddled against the wall. He grabs her, almost lifts her through the mêlée to the safety of the street. The police are called by an elderly woman in rollers who flings a bucket of water down the stairs before retreating to her flat and locking the door. The siren is heard in the distance and the crowd scatter, leaving behind stubbed out cigarettes and empty bottles.

Virginia greets the police at the front door. Her slave collar is missing. She addresses them with a demure smile and an apology. Her contagious laughter floats up the stairs where swollen lips are being nursed and tempers calmed. Marley's *Uprising* album is playing on low volume and the plaintive lyrics spill into the balmy night. The police warn of dire consequences if there are any further reports of trouble. The younger policeman asks for Virginia's phone number before they leave.

The house is silent. Even Marley has called it a night. Lorraine is restless, unable to sleep. On her head there is a bump, solid and painful. She thinks it is swelling. Perhaps she has concussion or a brain haemorrhage; the blood clot even now waiting to explode with deadly precision. She leaves the bedroom, opening the door quietly, and is startled to find Razor sitting by the window, his face in profile, a set of earphones on his head.

She has seen his record collection and knows he is probably listening to Vivaldi or Sibelius. He is a sham, a punk without conviction, a manipulator who enjoys unleashing the power and the fury. He looks up, equally surprised to see her, and flaps his hand in greeting. She moves past him into the small kitchenette and pours a glass of water, adding ice cubes, a slice of lemon. Her night-dress clings to her; she feels the static electricity in the air, or perhaps it is the antagonism he always displays on stage that is causing her skin to lift in goose-bumps. They have never been alone together without the presence of other people to buttress the space between them.

"Can't you sleep either?" He removes the earphones as she passes by him. The faint strains of a violin, the strummed rhythm of a cello are audible for an instant before he switches off the stereo.

"It's so hot." She fans her face, creating a breeze, and sits down beside him. Blood from a cut has congealed above his right eyebrow. "Does it hurt?" Her touch is light as she runs her finger over the wound.

"Not much." He grins. "You should see the bastard who did it to me."

"I can't," she replies. "He's in intensive care."

They laugh quietly. She tries to imagine him married like her parents, semi-detached in suburbia, wheeling a buggy past neatly mowed lawns, his trouser chains clanking, the skeleton on the back of his leather jacket terrifying children and setting the dogs barking.

"Thanks for rescuing me, Razor." She has found it almost impossible to address him by that name but now it slips easily from her.

"All part of the service." He pulls a curl of her hair and lets it run loose between his fingers. His grey hooded eyes remind her of a hawk.

"Do you think I'm scum, like her parents do?" The abruptness of the question, or even that he should ask it, astonishes her.

"Of course not. I'm sure her parents don't –"

"I know what they think." He allows his hand to fall heavily to his side. "She's going to dump me. There's some other fucker waiting in the wings to step into my boots."

"Who?"

"Could be anyone. I've seen the way they look at her, the guys in the band, that fucker Adrian. If I thought she was cheating –"

"Did she say that?"

"She doesn't have to. I know her mind, her thoughts. I feel them here." He taps his head, thudding his fingers against the side of his skull. He talks so low she has to strain to hear him. "I'd walk through fire for the bitch and she knows it."

"Her name is Virginia," she snaps back at him. "It's not a difficult name to pronounce if you try."

"She likes it. Vampire *bitch*." He watches her reaction and she sees Virginia, blood on her lips, draining him. It is such a vivid, disgusting image that she draws away from him with a muttered exclamation.

"Why is she doing this to me?" His mouth is tight, even his nose seems thinner, sharper, an urchin's face, unable to disguise his hurt.

"She's afraid of you, Razor. She doesn't think she can talk to you – tell you things that are important."

"What things?"

"Things like … oh, how should I know? If you stopped pretending to be on stage all the time it might help."

"Don't change the subject. She tells you everything. What's going on?"

"Do you love her?"

"What kind of shit question is that?"

"Do you?"

"She's my life. Anything else you want to know?"

"Why do you think that she and Adrian –?" Unable to complete the question she lets it hang between them.

"It could be him. It could be anyone. What difference does it make? She's breaking my heart and he'll break yours."

On the wall a spider scuttles slant-ways towards a crack. It slips and hangs suspended on invisible silken threads. Razor's arm slides around her, awkward and comforting. They sit silently together. It is the first time they have touched. She cannot remember even shaking his hand when they were introduced.

"I'll love her until the day I die." He makes this admission without embarrassment.

She rests her head against him, whispers into his hair. "She's pregnant, Razor … and she's scared to tell you."

After he leaves her and his bedroom door has closed, Lorraine sits alone on the sofa. She plays with the edges of a cushion, twirling tassels around her thumb, the skeins biting deep into her skin. A coral dawn steals over the rooftops and she listens for sounds beyond the bedroom wall where Razor and Virginia lie. There is only silence, a silence that remains unbroken throughout the house – except for the hoarse rasp of her breathing.

The following morning Razor has the exhausted look of someone who has run a long race and crashed through the pain barrier.

"We're going to have a baby." Virginia's laughter tinkles like delicate glass smashed against stone.

Lorraine's summer in London is over. The train sways through tunnels, hurtles towards Heathrow. Beside her, not speaking, keeping an eye on her luggage, Adrian sits with his feet on the seat in front. A word, a nod, a whisper, a hint and she will go anywhere with him, the two of them together, forever. He laughs defiantly when an elderly lady with rose-powdered cheeks, tells him to remove his feet. She waits to see if he will obey her and, when he ignores her order, she threatens to call the guard. Her threat is not carried out. He keeps his feet in the same position until the tube shudders to a halt at the terminus. He carries Lorraine's luggage to the check-in desk. He hugs her, promises to be in touch, a vague promise she knows he will not keep. Last night he announced his intention of moving to California to work in advertising.

It has been a year of conflict and famine. Argentina invaded the Falklands. The Brits took it back. Beirut is in rubble, besieged by Israel – while Iran and Iraq are slugging it out along the Gulf. The IRA continue to etch their message of freedom into the charred remains of bomb victims while Charles and Diana hold a temporary cease-fire to celebrate the birth of their first born. The world is spinning on its usual axis of war and famine and terror but for Lorraine Cheevers, as her flight is announced, 1982 will always be remembered as the year her heart was broken.

CHAPTER TWENTY-ONE

Ferryman
(an extract from Michael Carmody's memoir)

Regards from Aunt Anna, my first screenplay, was written shortly
after Jean and Terence married. Forget about pure streams of
consciousness. *Regards from Aunt Anna* – based on the adventures
of my roaming aunt and developed into a weekly half-hour
sitcom which brought me a moderate success and my first
realistic pay cheque as a screen writer – was written on a pure
stream of fury. But there was money in the bank, which enabled
me to make regular maintenance payments into a trust account
for Killian.

I struggled for recognition as a television dramatist. Some
screenplays are worth remembering, others best forgotten. I
moved into a larger flat where we spent rainy Saturday afternoons watching old movies, playing Snap and Snakes and
Ladders, and eating his favourite meal of sausages and chips, food
that was never allowed on the Devine-O'Malley menu. Meg
Golden lived in the flat above mine and always dropped in over
the weekend with her collection of classical records. Killian was
never too young to appreciate *real* music, she insisted. Van
Morrison, Bob Dylan, U2, Bruce Springsteen were dismissed

with a snap of her fingers, my taste consigned to the scrap heap of popular culture. Killian adored her bossy ways and listened with equal absorption to Chopin and Puccini as to Dylan or Morrison. One morning, finding her in my bed, he crawled between us, tickled her under her chin until she awoke and read him *The Cat in the Hat.* It was his favourite book, tattered, stuck together with tape on tape.

They had hats in common. Meg wore them like a badge of identity and could instantly change her image with the tilt of a brim. She was Killian's golden girl.

"Why can't she be my Saturday mammy," he demanded time and time again. "Why don't you love her best of all?"

The question was valid but unanswerable. I imagined our lives together, her hats tilted rakishly, mysteriously, sensuously, and the temptation to sink into the future she envisaged was difficult to resist. But I did resist and she eventually moved on to marry a musician who shared her fascination with Chopin. We remained friends – a painful transition, but one we worked hard to achieve. I was godfather to Aoife, their first child. Meg brought her to visit us one Saturday afternoon when she was three years old. Killian read her *The Cat in the Hat.* What goes around comes around.

After Meg, there were other women. They came and went, bestowing on Killian a casual affection. I met Roz O'Hara around that time. She was an assistant script editor who worked on one of my plays. We had a brief emotional relationship which we ended with mutual agreement after a month and settled down to a working relationship which lasts to the present day. As my script editor she cajoles and bullies the best from me. *Nowhere Lodge* is our most successful series. But I was never able to reach a compromise based on friendship or business with Jean Devine-O'Malley.

Killian was delighted when his mother gave birth to Laura. He was an inquisitive child, always asking questions. If I made a baby with Meg or Jackie or Roz or *anyone* – would it be his *real* sister or brother? Would the baby belong to Laura as well? Could he live with my new baby some of the time in Laurel Heights – or would the baby always have to live in my flat? He must have asked Jean the same artless questions. She rang after one of his

Saturday visits and accused me of corrupting his innocence. He must not be encouraged to form attachments to the women he found in my bed. Their presence in his life would be fleeting. She had first-hand experience of my definition of "commitment". If I continued to confuse my sex life with his welfare she would stop his visits.

The war of nerves we fought was carried out far from the front line, or so we liked to believe. But when Killian began to cry one Saturday afternoon and pressed his fingers nervously into his mouth, his face suddenly pinched and nervous, I realised we'd placed him in the centre of the fray. He was six years old and Jean had ordered him to call me "Michael". The word sounded foreign on his tongue, especially when he uttered it in front of me. He looked thinner that day, an unhealthy pallor, the skin around his eyes shadowed, puffy.

I tried to draw him out but he sobbed, "Mammy says you're not my proper daddy and I must never tell bold lies to Lorcan."

It wasn't the first time he'd mentioned Lorcan, his new school friend, who lived in the house opposite him.

"A castle," said Killian. "It's a really huge castle with flags."

Jean was adamant when I rang and accused her of using Killian as a weapon between us.

"You can talk." Her voice rose. "You keep asking him questions that have nothing to do with you. My life and how I live it is none of your business. Killian needs a strong sense of his own identity, not to be torn between two fathers. Terence is bringing him up as his son. He's willing to send him to a private school and pay for his education. He deserves the respect of a proper title."

"But *I* am his father. Nothing will change that fact. I'll drag you through every court in the land to prove my point." I parroted the same familiar clichés and she replied in kind, reminding me that I was a struggling writer with no visible means of educating *her* son.

The school Killian attended was select and private. It had an avenue of beech and a statue of the Sacred Heart, arms out-stretched, above the entrance. The school principal was well known for her views on the sanctity of family life, which she enshrined in the three R's – Reverence, Respect, Rectitude. The fact that Sr Maria was never likely to endure the slings and arrows of the marital state made no difference to her belief that the family who dined together should whine together. Jean had been appointed treasurer of the school fund-raising committee, which was presided over by Andrea Sheraton. When it came to status and wealth, the Sheratons were in the premier league and Jean Devine-O'Malley, successful businesswoman, mother and wife of a managing director with a nose for fine wines, had an image to maintain. Reminders of a heedless weekend on the slopes of Slane did not feature on her social agenda.

The following Monday morning I rang Sr Maria. She spoke with crisp authority but her voice grew warm, almost human, when I introduced myself as Killian's father. She thanked me for the wine I'd contributed for the school's fund-raising auction. For a short while we discussed the distinguishing qualities of wines from the old and new worlds. When we had exhausted such pleasantries I told her my son had a dental appointment. I would collect him from her office at twelve that afternoon.

I timed my watch for Jean's phone call. Twenty minutes after midday she rang, demanding to know what game I was playing. She'd been in the middle of a business meeting when Sr Maria rang her office, wanting to know why Killian hadn't been collected by his father. I've no idea what Jean said in reply – but adding two and two and getting four must have been easy for a graduate of business studies. I imagined her sitting tall and straight, those chestnut lights in her hair, tapping her finger furiously against her desk as she struggled to bring me into line.

"This is blackmail," she said. "You'll be dealing with my solicitor if you dare contact Killian's school again."

Did she intend signing a barring order to prevent me attending the next fund-raising event, I asked. As Killian's father, it was time I met his principal and the parents of his friends. When I reminded her that my story was already in the public domain, albeit anonymously, I felt the satisfaction of a worm turning and striking back. This time I'd have no hesitation in going public. My friend, the journalist, was not one to avoid tabloid ink on his fingers. His editor could be guaranteed to provide an appropriate headline and a photographer outside the school gates where I would be waiting, hoping to catch a glimpse of *my* son. She fought back valiantly but I'd touched her Achilles heel. By the end of our conversation she'd bought my silence in exchange for a full weekend with Killian once a month and a week's holiday during the summer.

The following Saturday we were sitting together in McDonald's when Killian asked what an abortion meant. He lowered his voice, as if he instinctively understood the question should not be asked amidst the clamour of birthday parties and family gatherings. Was it a big gun with bullets – or a dagger? He'd overheard Jean and Greta arguing. Greta may have been fighting on my behalf, demanding more time with him, perhaps. He did not know the details, just the essence.

"Mammy said you wanted to kill me when I was in her tummy." He pulled apart a Big Mac and squinted at the contents then, noticing my expression, laid it uneaten on his plate.

Greta, whose bungalow was our neutral territory, was working in her kitchen when I collected him the following weekend.

"How could you tell Killian that Terence doesn't love him as much as he loves Laura because he isn't his real father?" She scrubbed a counter top hard and determinedly, her face tight with an anger I'd noticed only once before – when she'd slammed the door in my face. "Jean said he cried for hours after he returned home."

I defended myself, made excuses. Self-justification is always an easier option than admitting shame. I always hoped Killian would forget that conversation. But I know now that such fractured incidents were stored in his head as carefully as a squirrel's hoard. He absorbed our anger through his pores, breathed it deep into his nervous system, heard it in our voices when we questioned him about the life he spent apart from us.

On the morning of his First Communion I sat at the back of the church. I watched Jean and Terence escort him to the altar. After the ceremony I was presented to the Sheratons as a family friend. Greta took photographs. Now, when I look at them, I see the tension that frightened our son so much. It's set like aspic in our fixed smiles, the strain in our eyes, the nervous clutch of our fingers on his shoulders.

I heard him acquire Terence's accent, repeat his jokes. I watched him imitate his confident stride, his skill on the rugby pitch. My son had a Saturday father who didn't exist, an invisible presence who walked beside him during school concerts, birthday parties, rugby matches. He no longer prattled heedlessly about family activities, aware that a careless remark could rouse Jean or myself to instant fury and retaliation. Tit for tat – tat for tit. I write with honesty, not with pride, and if there is a punishment for those who injure with words rather than knives then we, his parents, have served our sentence overlong.

He first asked about my mother, the grandmother he never knew, when he was eight years old. I spread photos across the floor.

"She looked like you," I said.

He spotted the resemblance immediately and swallowed her with his eyes. His smile was her smile. The way he tossed his head when he laughed brought her instantly to mind.

He said, "That's a weird name," when I called her "Shady".

"Her name was Sadie," I explained. "But her friends always called her Shady."

"Shady lady." He grinned and tried it again. "Shady lady … Shady lady."

He asked what age I was when she died.

"Seven years old," I replied. His eyelids flickered as he tried but failed to imagine a world without a mother.

Shady died in a head-on collision with a wall. It was an accident that should never have happened. The police found alcohol in her bloodstream and traces of LSD. Such carelessness when life was so fragile. No wonder I carry anger. I remember a coffin borne on shoulders and a graveyard with rain; muck piled high as a mountain. A woman in a headscarf stood close to me. She had a mole on her cheek. It reminded me of a beetle. I expected it to crawl across her broad face and down her chin, drop silently on the muck where it would burrow deep. But only her lips moved.

"That Sadie Carmody was a wild one," she said to the woman beside her. "Drugs, if you wouldn't mind. Who ever thought we'd see the day?"

They nodded vigorously, their mouths slanting, as if opinions must be cautiously released in the presence of death. Who knows but the wild one could be listening from that distant sphere.

"Poor little lad. Never a mention of a father and now this." They turned their eyes in my direction. I think they were surprised to see me standing so close. But they didn't see me, not really. Just a shadow child, hollowed out inside.

The coffin was lowered by a rope. Harriet threw clay into the hole. She held my hand with her left hand, the one with only three fingers and a thumb.

"Frostbite," she said when I asked. "I lost it in Alaska. It's my wedding-ring finger. Fate, I suppose. Like Shady, I was never meant to marry."

She held my hand so tight it hurt and I held her just as fiercely. I felt the space where her finger used to be and wondered if she had searched for it in Alaska. Did she miss it and, if she did, was it the same as missing my mother? My poor lost little boy, she cried. Lost like her finger. Shady was lost under the clay. Her eyes were brown as a bruise.

Harriet hung up her walking boots and we moved to Mayo. The cottage had a window overlooking Clew Bay. She tried her best to be a mother. I tried my best to be a son. We ended up being friends.

Killian stared at my mother's photograph, a blurred image, taken, I suspect, at a family party. Her lips looked black and thin against her white teeth. It did not reflect the beauty I remembered. He asked if she had been a drug addict. His face was troubled, as if he was forcing the words from a disturbed place within himself.

"Mammy says that's why you can't love anybody but yourself."

Jean was righteous when I rang. She reminded me of Slane, the anger I'd expressed over my mother's death. As if I needed reminding. The memory of the pleasure we'd experienced throughout that passionate weekend when we opened our hearts and minds to each other had long withered – but the knowledge we carried away with us had become a poisoned arsenal.

Granny Greta takes tablets for heart scald ... leave the child alone ... shame on you both ... carrying on like that over a little boy ... tug love ... tug of war love ... tough love ...

Stop standing up for him, mother. Killian could have been an abortion. A lump in a bucket. Why are you always hanging around, Killian? This is a private conversation. Go and play in the garden ... bucket baby ... rock-a-bye baby ... bang bang bullet baby ...

CHAPTER TWENTY-TWO

Virginia and Razor run through a shower of rice. Dressed in cream chambray with freesias in her hair, Virginia carries her stomach as if it is an awkward but precious possession. A scan has revealed the gender of the baby. They are going to have a son whom they will call Jake. Lorraine has flown to London to attend the registry-office ceremony. On the night before the wedding she rests her cheek against Virginia's stomach and feels the pattering feet.

"Have you forgiven me for telling Razor?" She is awed by the momentous event soon to take place and is relieved that the decision she made was the correct one.

Virginia smiles enigmatically, rests her hands on her stomach. "Time will tell."

"Marry in haste, repent in hell," intones Aunt Josephine who wears a lavender hat with a feather. Des Cheevers arrives with a frail blonde woman. Sonya does not look like a vamp in red stilettos – and Josephine is heard to say, "Those who sleep with dogs will rise with fleas."

No one is sure whether she is referring to her son-in-law or her ex-husband.

At home, Lorraine waits for the phone call that will announce the baby's arrival. It comes in the small hours of the morning. At first, she is unable to recognise Razor's voice. It rasps down the line, as if something is lodged in his windpipe. Tears, she realises, feeling her heart plunge in shock when he tells her that their baby died during delivery. A distressed heart. By the time a caesarean operation was performed, it was too late to save him. He talks for over an hour, endlessly repeating his story as if repetition will bring understanding, some form of acceptance.

Lorraine returns to London and is waiting to greet Virginia when she arrives home from hospital. She has tidied the apartment, removed the baby clothes. Her heart ached as she folded vests and baby shoes, removed the carry-cot and pram. Virginia lies in bed and gives vent to a low keening wail that reminds Lorraine of banshees, old Celia stirring the shadows with her ghostly tales. Her scalp prickles as the hours pass and Virginia continues to cry, dredges her past, lacerates herself for the carefree, dangerous life she led throughout her pregnancy. Razor is reticent in his grief, as if her overwhelming sorrow drains him of any energy or expression. Her outburst, its very intensity, cannot last and by the time Lorraine returns to Ireland Virginia is calm again. She will return to work and develop some really wild promotional ideas.

Punk is dead. Sulphuric Acid have buried the remains and Virginia now refers to Razor as Ralph. She sends Lorraine a photograph taken on Tower Bridge. Her hair is long and back to its natural black. Under a wide-brimmed hat, which she clutches with one hand, her eyes seem enormous in her heart-shaped face. The wind is blowing across the bridge, flapping her skirt against her legs. Ralph's hair is long at the back and he wears a sharp pinstripe suit with a pink shirt. Lorraine is surprised to realise he is handsome when he smiles. That night she uses the photograph to paint her first portrait. On her next visit to London, she presents it to them as a gift.

Their lives are in the fast lane, hectic. Razor and Virginia have gone into business together, setting up their own public relations company and working closely together on many high profile promotions. His briefcase has monogrammed initials and his Filofax is as essential as his right arm. The cramped flat where Lorraine lived for a summer has been replaced by a spacious apartment with a sun-filled balcony overlooking the Thames. With life in the fast lane there is no time for babies or hormonal urges.

Lorraine has a boyfriend, Louis, a sculptor who casts her hand in bronze and claims that life is a terminal illness. Their relationship, as far as Lorraine is concerned, is in terminal decline and even the dubious distinction of being a bronze casting no longer has any appeal. She is alone in her house one night when the doorbell rings. Afraid that Louis is returning to plead his case one last time, she does not open the door but waits, instead, behind the curtain until the figure retreats to the gate. He is taller than Louis, blonde, not dark, and there is no mistaking Adrian Strong's graceful prowl. She raps the windowpane, calls his name, flings open the door and blurts out explanations about bronze castings and terminal life patterns. He is equally excited and brings a blast of Californian sunlight into the kitchen where she makes coffee, suddenly gloriously, insanely happy. He has returned to Ireland to establish the Strong Advertising Agency. What does she think of the name, he asks, sitting opposite her.

"It's *strong*." She laughs back at him and resists the temptation to stroke the golden hairs on his arms. They talk until after midnight when her parents return, merry from too much wine and a chicken curry with the Ruanes next door.

Donna invites him to stay in the spare room until he has found accommodation. Three months later he is still living with the Cheevers. Afterwards, Lorraine will remember those months as an idyllic phase in a relationship that will change its shape in many ways, allowing them a marriage of consuming highs, painful lows and settling finally into a contented flow that carries them through the years of career building and parenting. But for those three months their passion burns like a subterranean fuse – which is carefully disguised under Donna's watchful eyes. At night Lorraine tip-toes across the landing to the spare room, it being furthest from her parents' bedroom. She is aware that Donna will probably awaken at the first squeak of wood and, as she slips into bed beside Adrian, that need for silence adds an exquisite tenderness to their lovemaking.

He is a charming lodger, praising Donna's cooking, respectful of her opinions yet able to tease her, to flatter her and compliment her sense of style when she dresses to go out for an evening. She remains adamant that he must find his own place and pencils rings around the rental sections in the evening newspapers before handing them to him.

"What's the rush?" Lorraine demands one evening when Adrian has followed up one such advertisement. "We have the spare room and he's not exactly eating you out of the house."

"Do you take me for a fool?" Donna retorts. "All that flitting across the landing at night. I know what's going on and it worries me. I don't want him to hurt you again."

"Why should he hurt me?" Lorraine's initial embarrassment fades when she hears the concern in her mother's voice.

"You came back from London looking like a scarecrow. And even before then, after Trabawn, he was handy with his kisses but it was another story when it came to keeping in touch."

"We were young then," Lorraine retorts. "Things are different now."

"How so?" Donna demands. "What's to stop him heading off again? His plans haven't exactly come to fruition, have they? I thought he was setting up his own business. So far, from what I've seen, he's talked a lot but done little else."

"That's because his loan didn't come through on time and the landlord let the premises go. It's all taking longer than Adrian expected but that's not his fault. He has brilliant ideas, you've said so yourself. Why can't you believe in him?"

"I said he was creative – and he is a talented young man. Full of ideas and dreams. But he needs to walk on terra firma more often, especially when my daughter is besotted with him."

"I'm not besotted. I'm in love … and he's in love with me."

"How can you be sure? Words come very easy to his lips."

Stung by her mother's comments, Lorraine feels herself floating back to the uncertainty that dominated her summer in London. For a shocked instant, she sees Virginia's head bent at the side of the bath, hears again her violent sobbing. She stares at Donna, her anger overflowing. "What is it with you? Why can't you be happy for me? You're forever making remarks, trying to undermine me. I want to live my own life, in my own way, and I won't put up with any further interference from you."

Besotted. She hates the word. It spells dependence, rose-tinted glasses, a love that weighs too heavily on one side. Such an image is far removed from the love Adrian whispers to her at night. When they are alone together she is incapable of doubt.

Shortly after her row with Donna, his loan is passed and a new premises acquired. He invites Loraine, her parents and his own parents, who travel across from Galway, out for a celebratory meal. Before leaving the house, he asks Brian Cheevers for his daughter's hand in marriage. Brian is flattered by his future son-in-law's old-fashioned courtesy and gives them his blessing. The sun shines on their wedding day and eleven months after their marriage Emily is born.

Lorraine tries to frame time but the shutter clicks too fast. One Sunday afternoon they sit on a bench in Stephen's Green and watch Emily running on sturdy legs around the edge of the duck pond. She flings bread towards the ducks and Lorraine imagines a small brother or sister standing beside her. She would like another baby. She was a lonely only child, envious of friends who came from larger families, but Adrian basked in the privilege of being the sole pride and joy of his parents and is happy with a one-child family. But on that afternoon they are of similar mind. When Emily is taking an afternoon nap they make love and lie contented in each other's arms.

She does not become pregnant and, as the months pass, Adrian becomes more insistent that they cannot afford another baby. These are difficult years and companies are reluctant to invest in expensive advertising campaigns. He rails against the Irish system of begrudgery and caution, the reluctance of banks to invest in the talent of young people who return from abroad with vision and energy. She agrees to wait another year, then another. Soon, the subject of a second child becomes so laden with emotion that they stop discussing it. When did that happen, she sometimes wonders. The moment she deluded herself it no longer mattered.

They have remained friends with Virginia and Ralph, regularly visiting each other for long weekends, flying back and forth between London and Dublin. They enjoy leisurely meals

around the table, the conversation spinning on until the small
hours, the women shopping on Saturdays, the men bringing
Emily to the zoo or other places where she can be entertained.
The conversation sparkles when they are together. Virginia is the
pivot of their attention, amusing them with anecdotes about
unmanageable clients and salacious gossip she has picked up on
the public relations grapevine. Lorraine settles into the role of
passive listener, often allowing her attention to wander and settle
instead on the other diners surrounding them, observing their
expressions, their gestures and body language.

The term "Celtic Tiger" has yet to be coined when the
Blaides sell their companies for a substantial sum of money and
move to Ireland. They purchase a newly refurbished building in
the Dublin docklands. It is, they have been assured, a dream
location with substantial tax benefits and, indeed, there is a
dream-like quality to the docklands; a fairy-tale sense of rejuv-
enation after many years of slumber. The building – which will
be known as Blaide House – is long and narrow with two storeys
and a spacious attic. Ralph (impossible to ever imagine him as a
Razor) is tired promoting petulant musicians and singers whose
music he despises. Nothing remains of the gawky, skinny punk
who used to sit on the floor of his London flat, dressed in shorts
and a singlet, scribbling down the lyrics he would later put to
music. Words that would ignite the anger of his fans, playing on
their anxieties, hatreds, vulnerabilities. It was a talent, he
discovers, that can be put to good use in advertising and so the
partnership of Strong–Blaide Advertising is born.

Adrian's ideas are as numerous and light as thistledown but
Ralph is the one who moulds them into successful advertising
campaigns, which cause outrage and controversy and much
admiration. They start small and grow at a steady pace. On the
floor above them Virginia decides to specialise on the corporate
sector and Ireland, poised on the crest of an economic boom, is
loaded with potential clients. She is sure-footed and self-assured.
Her cut-glass English accent impresses her clients and is a
decided advantage, she confides to Lorraine, when it comes to
making an impression. The Princess of Spin, says Ralph, which,
somehow, does not sound like an endearment – yet when he calls

her his "vampire bitch" it is as soft as a caress. As in London, their private and public lives are inextricably linked. A party at their house in Howth feels like a lively press function or networking launch – and Virginia's official receptions have an intimate, party atmosphere.

Lorraine subsidises her income through art classes and continues to experiment in the realm of dreams. She is fascinated by the depths of nightmares: the scream that turns to a whimper on waking, the terror of falling through dark spaces, the laden footsteps that struggle but never reach that safe destination. Her paintings achieve critical acclaim but few sales. One afternoon, shortly before an exhibition opens, Virginia and Ralph visit the warehouse where she has her studio. She belongs to an artist's co-operative and they are planning to hold a collective exhibition. Virginia shrugs aside any attempt by Lorraine to explain the concept behind her paintings and is obviously bored by what she sees in front of her.

"Rather too Gothic for my liking," she states. "I've never seen the merit of hanging nightmares on my walls." She has lost none of her ability to be blunt, nor her inability to understand why such thoughtless remarks should upset Lorraine. Her attention suddenly fixes on the portrait of a pianist with dramatic dark hair swept back from his brow. Lorraine has focused on the pianist's hands, the delicacy of his fingers as they rest on the keys of a grand piano. He is dressed formally in black with a white dicky bow and wing-collared shirt. But instead of the stately lines of a concert hall, she has placed him in the vaulted surroundings of a railway station. No spotlights, no candelabras, just the flashing overhead timetables and the headlights of trains in the background. The piano lid is tilted, a gleaming mirror reflecting the whirl of rushing commuters, their attention caught momentarily on the drift of music soaring above them.

"Tell me the name of this incredibly magnificent hunk," Virginia demands.

"It's Eoin Ruane. You must remember him? He was always practising the piano when we were kids."

"No." Virginia slaps her head in amazement. "Not the skinny kid with acne who lived next door to you?"

"That's him. It's a surprise for his birthday."

Eoin's family are musicians and Lorraine grew up listening to the strains of Mary's violin and Eoin's piano playing. The wail of his father's saxophone filled her with loneliness and she plugged her ears whenever his sister Sally took out her tuba.

"Portraits!" Virginia exclaims. "This is where your future lies."

Lorraine has been working on the portrait for weeks, snatching a few hours when she has time, enjoying the juxtaposition of images which link the pianist's past – when he busked on a keyboard in railway stations during his student days – and his present career as a concert pianist. As she paints she is conscious of this fusion of movement and music and hears, in her head, the notes rising to overpower the clattering footsteps. But the portrait is a diversion, nothing more, a gift commissioned by Meg, his wife, who will present it to him on the night of his birthday.

"Why don't you take over the attic in Blaide House?" The suggestion comes from Ralph who has had difficulty renting the space. The slanting ceiling and bulky supportive joists are too cumbersome to work around and there has been a rapid turnover of dissatisfied tenants.

Virginia shakes her head dismissively. "Not a good idea, Ralph. Lorraine would find it far too claustrophobic."

"I don't agree. It's got wonderful light, loads of space. She can bring her stuff through the back staircase. It's perfect for an artist."

"It's a crazy idea. Look around you." Virginia waves her hand at the warehouse with its high ceiling and cluster of studios. "Blaide House would be much too stultifying for her."

Lorraine is the catalyst for their argument but she is forgotten as they square up to each other. It is an on-going battle, this need to dominate, and Lorraine is never sure whether they are seriously fighting or simply playing with each other's tolerance. The arguments that occasionally flare between her and Adrian are short-lived; fire crackers that spark and splutter rather than the explosive Catherine Wheels that flash between Virginia and Ralph.

The warehouse is damp and cold in winter, an airless oven in summer. She has already seen the high, wide skylights in the attic and knows that the luminosity splashing across the floor and walls would be just right for her needs. She raises her voice and brings the argument to an abrupt close by agreeing with Ralph. Virginia's bottom lip pouts aggressively as she strides from the warehouse. She is not used to Lorraine disagreeing with her, but the studio is installed and she raises no further objections. Within a short time she is introducing Lorraine to her clients, who commission portraits and spread her reputation among the business community.

Virginia has had no problem adapting the odd Irish colloquialism to her cut-glass vernacular and at a party in her house one night she declares that Ralph is behaving like a "fuckin' bollox". She simmers with annoyance as she confides in Lorraine. "He's trying to tie me down," she adds and laughs reluctantly when Lorraine asks if she should take this statement in the literal sense – or metaphorically.

When Lorraine allows herself to think about Virginia's sex life her thoughts automatically return to the summer of '82 and the games being played in the bedroom next to her own. But times have moved on and Ralph, it appears, is playing the jealous husband, brooding over some slight indiscretion Virginia has committed with a young photographer. Virginia has the reck- lessness of a moth, always flying too close to the flame, and Ralph accepts these indiscretions as the price he is willing to pay for maintaining her love. Only occasionally does he confront her and when this happens Virginia acts as if he has personally chained her to a dungeon wall and thrown away the key.

They never mean anything, these "slight indiscretions", which she views in much the same way as she would a tonic or an energising pick-me-up. On occasions, Lorraine has suggested a multi-vitamin supplement as a safer alternative but her advice falls on deaf ears.

"Do you think they'll split up?" In bed that night she tells Adrian about the photographer and Ralph's furious reaction.

"He'll never let her go." Adrian switches off the light and yawns, pulls the duvet over his shoulders. "I'm *absolutely* knackered. You should see what I've got to face in the morning."

He kisses her forehead and turns his face to the wall. "I'd be better off with my own agency. Ralph struts around the place like he owns it but when it comes to pulling his weight he's off wining and dining and leaving the full workload to me."

"But you had your own agency. Then all you wanted was a partner. Why are you never satisfied?"

"All I need is a little sympathy, not the sermon on the mount," he says whenever she tries to lift him from his moods, which have the weight of stones while they last. For a man who makes his living through the meaning of language and its persuasive power, he has a curiously limited vocabulary when it comes to analysing his own marriage, she often thinks. She knows his body intimately yet his mind remains as mercurial as when they first met. Often, when he is doing some job around the house or undressing for bed, unaware that he is being watched, she has gazed objectively upon him and imagined him as a stranger, a blank canvas. She has observed his face, the long, narrow curve from cheek to chin, noticing how his facial bones had become more defined, his eyes deeper-set and hooded. But this is a gentle ravaging which adds to, rather than diminishes, his good looks. Even when he becomes an old man his face will still present that strong bone structure, the high Sphinx-like cheeks and sensuous eyes. His blonde hair, heavy on top and shaved close to his neck, shows no signs of thinning and regular work-outs in the gym have kept his body slim and supple. Observing him in this way, knowing he is not a stranger and that he will soon lie beside her – his body warm and responsive – gives her an intense, possessive happiness. Yet never once has she felt any inclination to paint him. She has not gazed upon his face and fixed on something – his nose, ears, mouth, the line of his neck or chin or the eyes that dance so easily away from her when she asks a direct question – nothing in him has ever challenged her to capture his essence on canvas. Sometimes, usually when she is pre-menstrual, she wonders if her reluctance to paint her husband comes from fear. Does she know, intuitively, that she will have to look beyond his handsome features and study what lies beneath.

In the busy rush of passing years, it is easy to ignore the little incidents that skim like pebbles over her marriage, spreading the ripples outwards and onwards until nothing remains except the smooth surface of denial.

For Adrian's fortieth birthday they go to Venice with Ralph and Virginia. Pink domed palaces and churches glow in the afternoon sun. This is a city whose existence flows on the tide and history rots silently in stagnant waterways. A city of dazzling deceptions and intrigues, carnal liaisons, amorous eyes flashing behind butterfly masks. Lorraine's mind is alive with impressions of a splendid, cruel time, paintings that glorify creation and the terror of annihilation.

They visit churches and art galleries, museums, restaurants. Gondoliers in their boater hats steer their gondolas beneath the Bridge of Sighs and in St Mark's Square a woman dances in the shadow of the Campanile. The woman is old, an ancient crone with sunken mouth and haggard cheeks. High above her, a golden archangel glitters in the afternoon heat. Lorraine studies the woman's wrinkled countenance and headscarf, wondering how she came to be among the pigeons and the violinists who play for the tourists under café awnings. The woman ceases her dance and begins to sing. Lorraine does not recognise the language. Not that it matters. Whatever nationality, whatever language, this is a thin, quavering lament that lifts the hairs on the back of her neck because the old woman is obviously mad – she holds a crucifix towards the sky and tears run from her eyes – yet her presence is as powerful as a dream, the discordant sounds hovering on the borders of reality. One truth. One vision.

Shaded by a canopy, Lorraine sketches the woman's ecstatic stance. She draws in a notebook she keeps in her bag, a habit from years ago when she was inspired to capture such fleeting moments. Those days have gone. She has become a skilled portrait artist, intuitive and imaginative, with more commissions than she can handle. But there still remains that yearning for something more, something indefinable, haunting, unfinished.

Before her, Adrian and Virginia stand in the square, feeding pigeons. Virginia flings her hand wide, scattering crumbs. Pigeons strut around Adrian's feet, swirl above him, and he laughs at their boldness, sharing his amusement with Virginia – and Lorraine, watching, feels something claw against her chest. The London summer is aeons away and if, in the years since then, it entered her mind she dismissed it as a distorted fragment of a distorted night. The high-pitched tuneless singing scrapes against her thoughts and, for an instant, she is infused with the woman's madness. One vision, one truth. She sits under a café awning and watches Ralph walk towards his wife, slide his arm around her waist, point upwards to the archangel flashing gold. The naturalness of his actions, Virginia's voice, Adrian's smile as he strolls back and sits beside her, orders coffee for everyone, reduces her suspicions to the craziness of a raddled old woman singing songs of praise. She draws the woman with bold strokes and listens only to the voice, the joyous, tuneless voice singing a requiem for all that is to follow.

As soon as they return home, she begins her dream paintings. The theme further clarifies in her mind when she attends a ballet performance with Emily. She is captivated by the effortless poise of the dancers, their graceful movements that can only be achieved through a punishing regime of fitness and near-starvation. As she watches their flamboyant leaps and subtle gestures, she is aware of images fleeing through her mind with the same ephemeral grace. The ballerinas are co-operative, allowing her access to rehearsals. She studies the movements of muscle, sinew and flesh. Dancers pose before her, moving freely, expressively. Through the language of dance she absorbs the complexities of touch, the hidden intimacy of a glance, the subtle gesture that has meaning only to the beloved.

She becomes friends with Cherie, a lap dancer who is perfectly at ease demonstrating her act in the privacy of the basement club where she dances at night. Watch, don't touch. Sex neatly, safely packaged. Loneliness briefly alleviated in the swing of a woman's hips, the velocity of satisfaction always out of reach. Yet it also has its own precise chorography and Lorraine, in a shocked but pleasurable fluster, sketches this lithe young woman who can move with the decorum of a ballerina or the gyrating energy of a women on the verge of orgasm.

Her imagination is riotous. She knows this is her strongest collection to date. In Venice she drew a dancing woman whose madness was a living dream and she is excited in a way that has not been possible for years.

When Adrian arrives home she is already in bed. She awakens as he slides in beside her. He had been dining a potential client. He describes the food as "indifferent" and turns to the wall. When she slides her arm around his waist and moves closely into him, he presses his face into the pillow, mutters goodnight. His body smells of smoke and something more subtle, fleeting. The seed in her mind takes root but still remains beneath the clay.

CHAPTER TWENTY-THREE

Ferryman
(an extract from Michael Carmody's memoir)

Is there such a thing as an instant revelation? A thunderbolt from
the blue? Or does the truth reach us by a more circuitous route,
ring-fencing our vision until we are ready to confront it? The
night was humid when I entered Killian's bedroom to check if
he had borrowed one of my compact discs. He had just turned
thirteen and his visits to my apartment had continued
uninterrupted over the years. He turned in his bed when I
switched on the light, disturbed but not awakening to my
presence. He was sleeping naked, the sheet thrown back from his
chest. Bruises spread like a flight of amber moths across his
shoulders and arms. I pulled the sheet further down and saw the
marks on his legs. I shook him awake, demanded to know what
had happened.

He sat up in bed, the duvet clutched around his chest. Only
the slight lift of his bony shoulder blades revealed his agitation.
He'd fallen down the stairs in the middle of the night. I imagined
his body shuddering from one step to the next and finally lying
still at the bottom. No bones were broken but Jean had driven
him to the hospital where he'd been X-rayed and later discharged.

Throughout Sunday she refused to take my calls. On Monday morning I rang Devine-O'Malley Financial Services and spoke to her personal assistant. Could Ms Devine-O'Malley contact the Society for the Prevention of Cruelty to Children. An official wished to speak to her on a personal matter regarding her eldest son. Jean allowed ten minutes to pass before she rang me back. We arranged to meet as soon as she finished work.

In the Westbury Hotel we faced each other. Her gaze was steady, revealing nothing, her explanation unwavering. A highly polished timber staircase and a young boy who never walked when he could run. Such a dangerous combination, she said. Killian had been going downstairs for a drink of milk when the accident occurred. A pianist played softly behind us as she discussed his X-rays, the doctor's diagnosis, the fuss made of him by the nurses. I wanted to believe her. Anything else was too appalling to contemplate. In a nearby armchair a Japanese businessman slept, his mouth drooping slightly, his ankles tucked neatly over his briefcase. Ice tinkled as Jean raised a glass of tonic water to her lips.

I accused her of beating our son. The skin on her neck tautened. She laid the glass carefully down on the table.

"You foul-mouthed bastard! How *dare* you make such an accusation." Her voice chilled me with its fury. She stared at the sleeping Japanese man, who awoke with a startled snort then allowed his head to droop forward again. "You'll have the full medical report posted to you by the end of the week."

Deny ... accuse ... deny ... accuse ... deny ... She walked towards the staircase without another word. A week later the medical report arrived as promised, complete with X-rays and medical diagnosis.

I watched over Killian. I checked his body while he slept, minutely scanning his skin for signs of bruising. Instead, I found only the early evidence of puberty, the thickening of his penis and thighs, the faint growth of pubic hair, the musky scent of sweat which rose from his body when he moved, realising, perhaps, at some unconscious level, that his privacy was being invaded.

A year passed before I met Jean again. She rang me in the

small hours of a Sunday morning to enquire if Killian was in my apartment. Her anxiety became more obvious when I assured her I hadn't seen him since the previous weekend. He'd slipped noiselessly from the house while they were sleeping. Duncan, his younger brother, had awoken from a nightmare and gone to his brother's room for comfort. He woke his parents when he discovered the empty bed stuffed with pillows.

I drove immediately to Laurel Heights. Outdoor lamps curved in an S below an avenue of laurel trees. A tennis net was slung across the lawn. By the time I arrived Killian had been discovered in a field about a mile from the house, drinking cider with a gang of older boys. Jean stood in the doorway, unwilling to allow me in. Everything was under control, she assured me, and attempted to close the door in my face. Terence came into the hall when he heard our raised voices. Overriding her protests, he invited me inside. I entered, knowing I was in the eye of a storm, and wondered what Killian had done to disturb the even rhythm of their lives. I followed him into a long drawing-room with oil paintings on the walls and scattered rugs covering polished floorboards. Velvet curtains blocked out the night. Jean left the room. I heard her footsteps on the stairs as she went upstairs to check on Killian.

I felt a tight glow of satisfaction as I listened to Terence. This perfect house had its own imperfections. Haltingly, as if he was betraying his family's privacy but unable to stop, he laid their problems before me.

Killian was becoming increasingly difficult to handle, bad school reports, his grades down on the previous year – which was not surprising, since he refused to study in the evenings. He demanded his meals in his room and refused to eat if he was forced to sit at the same table as everyone else. Terence was troubled and helpless. He was capable of flooring a rugby opponent with a lethal elbow but useless when it came to handling a young boy. As he poured whiskey and handed me a glass, I finally understood the reason for the bruises. This was not the first time Killian had left the house when everyone was sleeping and returned, drunk on cider and whatever tabs he'd taken. The bruises I'd seen occurred one night when he'd fallen down the stairs on his return. Terence had found him unconscious at the bottom of the staircase.

He walked with me to the front door. Perhaps, in other circumstances, we could have become friends, two uneventful men living out our uneventful lives. Except for Killian. He pulled us along routes we never envisaged. Perhaps there had been evidence beforehand that he was a doomed reckless youth, the signs already in place, genetically programmed while he was still forming in his mother's womb, a spoken word away from being an abortion. Genetics. That's what everything is about these days, a predisposition to cancer, heart disease, thrombosis, addiction, dandruff. Yet Killian showed little disposition towards any form of addiction. As a child he objected strenuously to my smoking, arriving at weekends with pamphlets and opening windows as soon as I lit up. I'd been amused by his crusade, the earnest nagging which, eventually, did succeed in making me abolish the habit.

He was older now, disturbed, a rebellious adolescent but I was on his wavelength. I refused to believe we were facing a crisis. Had I not dealt with similar problems through my characters in *Nowhere Lodge*? My research had been extensive. I knew that during those crucial teen years the risk factor was balanced against the survival factor. Under my care he would emerge bruised but complete. I knew everything in theory but nothing about the emotional wrecking of the heart that chronic addiction creates. I should have remembered. Instead, I'd locked those memories away, refused to travel back along the turbulent path of my early childhood. The apprenticeship that followed was swift and punishing. But that was all before me and, as I drove down the winding mountain road from Laurel Heights, I believed it was just a matter of time before Killian made his own decisions and belonged finally to me. I'd yet to come to the realisation that the son we'd created from a careless passion and loved with bitter possessiveness was already lost to both of us.

I fought with Jean over her decision to send him to boarding school. He ran away and was discovered by the police sleeping rough in a field. Sometimes he went missing for days. He walked out of counselling sessions or failed to turn up for appointments.

He no longer came to my apartment for weekends but would arrive mid-week in the small hours, often accompanied by Lorcan, their eyes glazed, their movements hyper.

He agreed to enter the Patterson Rehabilitation Centre, where he made friends with Marianne Caulfield. She'd dropped out of college where she had been doing a media studies course and was in the process of kicking a coke habit. Her spiky bleached hair and thin face reminded me of a dandelion puff but when she shook my hand her grip hurt. She left the centre rehabilitated and carrying the evangelical zeal of one who has seen the light. Killian, also, appeared to have settled down. For a while there was peace. The prelude to the storm. Marianne went back to her media studies course and began making a documentary about street life and drug culture. Killian had fallen in love with her. So had Lorcan. They wanted to be part of the film crew, currying favour with her, accompanying her on her nightly forays into the streets. Bozo Daly was the guide who brought them through the tunnels of a sub-culture my son was soon to join.

Jean rang one night from her mobile phone and told me to be ready in fifteen minutes. I met her outside my apartment. When I opened the car door her face, in the overhead light, was tense with exhaustion. I thought of her snobbery and acquired wealth, balancing it against the vulnerability I could see in her defeated shoulders. She refused to answer my questions as she drove along the quays.

"You'll find out soon enough," she warned. "Just settle back and enjoy the ride. This is your territory." She drove deeper into the side streets adjoining the docklands and braked outside a house with boarded-up windows. A favourite haunt, she said. She'd been there before with Terence, persuading Killian, bullying him, pleading with him to return home. She gripped my hand as she banged on the front door. Suddenly, we were parents together, staring into a terrifying vista. The years in between, the ugly struggles and petty manoeuvrings counted for nothing. It was a momentary ceasefire that could not last but, as we waited for someone to open the door, it was comforting.

Killian's body, wrapped in a sleeping-bag, was pressed tightly against the wall. Candles guttered in plastic containers. A gas ring hissed blue flame. The smell of a meat stew rising from a saucepan was surprisingly appetising. Bozo Daly sat down on a sagging armchair and lifted a bottle of cheap whiskey from the window ledge. He held the bottle towards Jean. It was obvious they'd met before. She shook her head and pulled the hood of the sleeping-bag from our son's face. I was shocked by his pallor. He looked so young and defenceless in sleep, his eyelids hiding the hard, focused stare I'd learned to dread. As if my thoughts had entered his dreams he opened his eyes. With the ease of a snake shedding old skin, he slid from his sleeping-bag and demanded money. He cursed us when we refused, forced Jean away when she tried to prevent him leaving the squat.

"You wanted him." She turned towards me. "He's yours. You keep claiming you have all the answers, demanding he move in with you. See if you can do any better. I've nothing left to give him." Her grief had an ugly, helpless sound. Tears ran down her cheeks. She made no effort to wipe them away. "This is where you'll find him when he runs away again."

Our son was seventeen years of age. He'd moved from Laurel Heights to an inner-city squat in a seamless journey while I sat idly by and wrote the script.

I soon became familiar with the pattern: his sudden disappearances, the lies, the missing money, the promises so quickly broken. I followed him into the streets. We walked beneath dangerous walls where his friends gathered. The blank stare, the menacing stance, I was familiar with it all. Graffiti was sprayed across the wall – cryptic messages, abusive threats, pleas to be fucked, shagged, screwed, an incongruous heart entwining Decco and Anita's undying love, and the not-so-cryptic demands, "Brits Out" and "Up the Provos". Someone had dumped a fridge against the wall. A burned-out car was a rusting hulk beside it. They called Killian Ferryman, those friends he made, those street-wise young men with their thin faces and hard eyes. Ferryman was a nickname with impact and power, capable of carrying travellers over dangerous waters. But I watched my son fade behind it until he was simply another lost face hanging around the quays. We tried again – and again. He begged my forgiveness, asked for one more chance. Over the next year, I clung to an emotional pendulum that veered between optimism and despair.

Once more, he agreed to enter rehabilitation. It was after midnight when I received a phone call. Killian had left of his own accord. I didn't find him that night or the following one. I called to the Garda station and reported him missing. The guard on duty was bleary-eyed, impatient, uninterested when he heard Killian had walked voluntarily from the centre. Free will. He shrugged and scratched his head with a pen, his mind moving on to the next event, a city-centre knifing, perhaps, or a domestic brawl behind lace curtains.

I drove to the squat but there was no sign of him. A woman arrived while I was there and left a bag of groceries on the floor for Bozo. We walked outside and stood under a tree which had grown from a crack in the cement. The branches cast wounded shadows over the lager cans, whiskey bottles and mouldering food cartons at its base.

"You his da?" she enquired and shook her head ruefully when I nodded. "Kids! They break your heart when they're under your feet and break it twice as hard when they scarper." A denim mini-skirt rode high above her thighs and her solid legs were squashed into knee-high silver boots. "He's a hard act to handle, your lad. If he were mine I'd lock him up and feck the key into the Liffey. He's a goner if you don't."

She lit a cigarette. Her tough red face was silhouetted for an instant in flame. Her lipstick was purple, glossy. I suddenly remembered my mother painting her lips, the tube delicately balanced in her hand as she opened her mouth then lightly patted her lips on a white tissue. It must have been shortly before her death. The tissue was still on her dressing table after her funeral.

Killian came home eventually, as he always did, moving between my apartment and Laurel Heights and back to the centre of nowhere. My stereo and television set were stolen, money was taken from my pockets while I slept. For the first time the words "tough love" were mentioned. When all else fails tough love is the only option, said the counsellor. He was young and idealistic, a text-book talking. Tough love – such a convenient category. Not harsh like banishment. No, love was my prime motivation when I told my son to go. He'd broken every promise he made to me and broken my heart in the process.

I met Bozo Daly the following afternoon on Custom House Quay. He sat on a bench studying the flow of the river, his chin thrust downwards towards his chest, a bottle by his side. His age was indefinable, his face creased like a chamois on which the world had wiped its indifference. We crossed the bridge and headed for a sandwich bar. He walked with a shuffling gait, as if he was pushing paper with his feet. His hair was the colour of dead grass.

Ferryman is a good kid, he told me. A bit wild but he'd settle down soon enough. He could have been consoling a disappointed parent at a school meeting.

"He's a thief and a drug addict," I replied. "Apart from that I know nothing about my son."

"F-ferryman doesn't b-b-belong on the streets." I heard a quick exhalation of breath before the words rushed from him, as if somewhere, in another life, he had acquired self-help techniques he still remembered. Some people choose it, he said, others have it thrust upon them.

"Killian has choices. He's fucked up every one of them." My anger, never far below the surface, was a zig-zag of lightning. At times, I hated my son. How hard those words look on paper. But I write them as unflinchingly as I write about love. They are opposite sides of a damaged coin.

Bozo said he'd seen too many troubled lads not to know the difference between the hard cases and the ones who had simply lost their way. I asked him where he got his degree in family psychology and he smiled, displaying stumpy yellow teeth.

"1976. F-first class fu–fu–cking honours." His laughter was a shield against my disbelief.

I wondered for the first time about his story, the road that brought him to a derelict squat and a ridiculous nickname. I ordered soup and baguettes. On high stools we sat together, our faces to the wall. He asked about my work. Killian had told him I wrote drama. His eyes glazed when I mentioned *Nowhere*

Lodge. He'd never seen it, hardly a surprising discovery. He did, however, display a flicker of interest when I mentioned *Regards to Aunt Anna*. Vaguely he remembered something – he forced his mind back to a forgotten time – then shook his head, no longer interested. He promised to watch out for Killian. An odd choice of guardian – but needs must. We agreed a payment. He would get in touch with me at the first sign of trouble. Trouble is a relative term and my understanding of what constituted 'trouble' had changed radically. After a short while he grew jittery and left, having pocketed his first payment with an indifferent nod of thanks. He was going in one direction only but, at least, he knew where to find the nearest off-licence. Where Killian had travelled was impossible to imagine.

Perhaps it could have worked. Killian phoned regularly, talked about methadone programmes and rehabilitation. A new beginning, old routines. I'd had the same conversation too many times to feel anything other than weariness over having to parrot the familiar responses. But there was always the desperate belief that this time … this time … things would be different.

He rang late one night, sounding distraught, and asked me to meet him. His clothes were still in good condition, a bulky puffa jacket and jeans, strong trainers, but his hair was lank, unwashed, and his face spotted, some of the pimples turning into sores. Spittle had dried on his mouth. Every part of me cried out to take him home but I was holding out, following the dictates of tough love.

He was living with friends in the inner city. Rented accommodation, he needed money. The landlord was a shit, demanding an exorbitant deposit. It was obvious he was lying. His sing-song voice, the pat answers, the ever-shifting gaze, his sudden outburst of fury when I shook my head.

"Fuck you … you're my father. You want to see me lying on the edge of the road, is that what you want? This is a chance to make it back. It's the least you can do seeing as how you kicked me out."

This meeting was no different to the others. In the past I'd given in, handing over the money in the belief that it would give him a roof over his head. My anger carried me swiftly into the night. I did not turn around when he called my name. It was the last time we spoke.

What did you do this week? Not playing bloody rugby again! Jesus Christ! Is he trying to turn you into a clone?

He left me Killian! He never wanted you! Never – wanted – you!

Ferryman is my name. Nicer than Killian. Too many Killians …

CHAPTER TWENTY-FOUR

In New York, Lorraine stares at an obscene gap on the skyline. Photographs of lost faces flutter from walls and railings. Standing close to where it happened, just breathing in the stultifying air, brings home to her the enormity of what has occurred more than the most horrifying television images which had reduced the collapse of the Twin Towers to a tormented, iconic image of a billowing curtsy. Two months have passed since September 11 and the city still vibrates with shock. A new vocabulary is being created. War on Terror. Axis of Evil. Global Terrorism.

In the aftermath of the tragedy, life grimly continues. Sally Jones has persuaded Lorraine to stay in her loft apartment for five days. They have been friends since they worked in the artists' co-operative and keep regular contact with each other through e-mail. Sally has organised a workshop on meta-physical art and believes Lorraine's work will benefit from participating in it. The challenge of being analysed and criticised, of having to justify and defend her work-in-progress, appeals to Lorraine but her main reason for making the trip is to be with Sally. She was the first person Lorraine tried to contact when news of the attack came through. The phone in her apartment rang out and it took two days before an e-mail from Sally arrived to her friends, assuring them that she was still alive. She had been swept along in the debris of the attack, had wandered through parks where candles flamed and people gathered to comfort and calm each other. She plans to return to Ireland in the spring and set up an artists' colony in a remote Wicklow location.

The workshops are as stimulating as she promised. Lorraine finds herself caught up in debates on surrealism, the power of the absurd and the enigmatic dream. The artists break early on the last day and arrange to meet in a nearby bar for a farewell drink. Later that night, she and Sally will attend a piano recital by Eoin Ruane and meet beforehand with Meg for a meal. She finds a quiet spot in the bar and phones home. She leaves a message when the land line rings out but, when she calls Emily's mobile, her daughter answers immediately.

"I'm sleeping overnight with Sharon," she announces. "We're watching *Home and Away*. Dad's on a business trip. How's it going with you?"

"Fine. Where is he?" Adrian had not mentioned any impending business trip.

"It's some big deal he's doing. I think he said Cork."

"I thought his car was being serviced."

"He took yours. Anyway, he's back tomorrow. Miss you, Mum." From her tone it is obvious she wants to turn her attention back to the television.

On his mobile, Adrian speaks so softly she has difficulty hearing him. He is dining with a client and promises to ring her later. She is unable to hear cutlery clinking or the murmur of voices in the background. The only sound that penetrates is his guarded tone and the click of a door closing.

Two bodies writhing on an old battered sofa. The image is so instantaneous that her breath thickens and she is forced to suck deep into her lungs. Suddenly she needs to speak to Virginia. Virginia is the only person who can calm her down.

Ralph answers the phone. He talks about a seminar. Virginia won't be home until tomorrow afternoon.

"So sorry to have missed you." Virginia's voice does not sound in the least apologetic when Lorraine rings her mobile number.

"Leave a message and I'll return your call as soon as I'm free."

She hangs up without speaking and returns to the bar.

Over the following weeks Lorraine listens for words, for meanings behind words, for gestures that display little but convey much. Denial is still an option. If there is something going on then surely Ralph, so worldly-wise, so perceptive and possessive, will know. She is unable to utter her suspicions aloud. If she is right – what then? The destruction of her marriage, the breaking of a friendship, never to be renewed. The severing of a business partnership that has stretched their finances to the limit.

She does not find them kissing in hidden corners or making love on the marital bed. There are no unexplained Visa payments, hotel receipts, lipstick marks on shirt collars, no silent phone calls. Instead, on a dull morning in November, shortly after she returns from New York, Adrian lifts his briefcase from the kitchen floor and balances it across his knee. He is searching for something, car keys or his mobile phone, his movements growing more impatient as he rustles the documents. The briefcase slips from his grasp. Sheets of paper scatter across the kitchen tiles. Lorraine picks up a report which contains a five-year development plan for Strong–Blaide Advertising. A jagged rust-coloured stain has smeared the cover. Beside it lies a press release. Virginia's distinctive company logo is visible on the front, a logo which Lorraine designed for her the previous year. The press release has "Sheraton Worldwide Travel" written on the top with "Confidential" stamped in bold print above the headline. It is in draft stage. There are handwritten notations in the margins. Lorraine glances down at the same faint but unmistakable stain. Blood, she realises, smeared and splattered.

"Why is this in your briefcase?" She hands it to him and awaits his reply. She is curiously disconnected from the question, an unnatural calmness descending on her as she watches him scrutinise the document before tearing it into pieces.

"Virginia ran it by me once. I thought it was fine as it was but you know how fussy she can be. If the 'i' is dotted she wants a second dot to be on the safe side." His gaze slides away and his voice – persuasive, drawing her inwards to share the joke –

sounds as empty as his explanation. He flings the press release into the rubbish bin with the swivel lid and slaps his hands together. "I must have forgotten to hand it back to her."

He leaves the house in a hurry, his waxed coat flapping open against his legs. He is a busy man with a business to run.

For the opening night of *Painting Dreams* a large crowd gathers in the gallery. Journalists arrive, tabloid diarists, critics from the arts pages, the television crew from *Artistically Speaking*. Virginia sails effortlessly through the crowd, a bird of paradise in her bright colours, her short black hair brushed upwards and highlighted in a titian quiff that would look outrageous on anyone else.

"You'll get the coverage," she whispers, gliding past. "It'll be serious and salacious. Keep smiling." She has organised the publicity and is delighted by the ripple of shock that reaches from one guest to the next as they view the exhibition.

"Sold" stickers are already on some of the paintings when Lorraine faces a television camera and the crew from *Artistically Speaking* gather around her. As the interview continues she glances beyond the spot where Adrian and Virginia stand togeth-her. Adrian's body language alerts her, the rapt concentration on his face as if he wants to block out every other sound in the gallery. Virginia touches his hand, a warning pressure, and he moves away, just a step or two, to stand before one of the paintings. A casual drifting apart that has been played out many times before Lorraine's eyes but this time she recognises the casual touch a husband gives to a wife, a wife to a husband, as if they are flesh on flesh, so familiar to each other that such gestures are exchanged with thoughtless ease.

She struggles to concentrate on the interview, to see only what is there before her eyes – an interviewer whose voice seems glazed with honey and whose every question is delivered like a speech from the dock – but all she can see is Adrian, his back now turned to her as he stands before a painting, intrigued, perhaps, by the flaunting impression of Cherie exposed on canvas. She watches him engage in conversation with the man standing next to him. Why does his laughter ring false and the set of his shoulders look tense rather than relaxed? Virginia is now at the opposite end of the gallery yet, in the beat of an eyelid and the touch of a hand, everything has changed and Lorraine knows with chilling conviction that her husband and her best friend are bound together by an unbroken thread that stretches back to another era when the air around her trembled with every breath she took, and how, standing in the doorway, the ceiling spinning above her, the floor swaying, she saw them, his supple back arched like a bow that will snap if not released, the dew of sweat on his shoulders and, as she moved closer, Virginia's upturned face, ecstatic. Her slender legs wrapped him secure and – before he reached for a cushion to press against her mouth – a cry soft as cat's purr crept across the room towards Lorraine. Dawn washed over the ceiling and in the milky light of a new day she left them, flitting from the room as silently as she entered. She closed her eyes on the tableau she had witnessed, allowed it to vaporise, to fade into the ether of oblivion.

But it was not oblivion, nor a frozen tableau: there had been much thrashing of limbs on the old four-seater sofa and that memory, quiescent for so long, is powerful enough to weaken her knees and cause her to wonder if she will collapse in front of the assembled gathering who have lifted the level of noise so that they too can be part of the televised proceedings. She pushes her hair from her forehead, the lighting is too hot, her face burns, she must concentrate. When the filming ends, she shakes hands, accepts congratulations, moves through the crowd – but she is a young girl again, lost in the summer of '82, and the pain is unendurable.

"How long has this been going on?" When they return home she confronts him. Her voice takes on an unfamiliar cadence. "I want the truth, Adrian."

"What on earth do you mean?" Of course he sounds perplexed, quizzical, his forehead wrinkling in bemusement. She feels nothing – that will surely come later when she has time to absorb the enormity of what is taking place.

"How long have you been having an affair with Virginia?" She links into his gaze, holding it. "Don't ask me to repeat myself. Just answer my question."

"Jesus Christ!" Colour floods his face. He draws back as if he can feel her fury blasting him. He will argue, bluster, fight for survival, tell her she is crazy, possessed, neurotic – but in the involuntary twist of his mouth she has seen the truth.

"How long?" she screams. She has never screamed before, not as far as she can remember. As a cherished only child it was not necessary to do battle with siblings or fight for parental attention.

"The apple of my eye," her father used to say, lavishing her with love, just as Adrian had placed his own daughter at the centre of his world. Or so she had believed. Emily, whey-faced, hearing her mother scream, refuses to leave her bedroom for two days and is finally coaxed from her retreat by Donna, who tries to explain what is taking place.

Adrian too attempts to rationalise, to talk his way through the myriad emotions swirling around them. He has always loved two women. It is as simple and as complex as that. The eternal dilemma, the cruel triangle, and so he agonised, prevaricated, fought with his conscience. Impossible to make decisions. She, in turn, drifted through the summers of Trabawn, through the airless streets of London, through the years of marriage, floating high above the scent of his betrayal.

"When did it start?" she demands again and again. When, where, why, how often, how could you … tell me … tell me! Her voice rises to a pitch that would normally horrify her. There should be power and energy in an unsuppressed scream but her screams are weighted with defeat and the knowledge that forgiveness is impossible. Perhaps if he had skulked in shadows with a stranger whom she would never know they could have managed a painful journey back together. Their marriage might have been secured with forgiveness and a wisdom that comes from understanding the dangerous underbelly of deceit. But as she reels back from her husband's confession, she understands only that her perception of the past and her expectations of the future have changed utterly. How can mere words bring about a reconciliation? What gesture can repair such a rupture to the heart?

How quickly decisions are made, driven by a manic energy

that has taken possession of her. In the turmoil following her discovery, Donna rings with the news that Celia Murphy is dead. At the age of ninety-seven, she sold her field to Frank Donaldson and died a week later. Her demise is marked by a notice in the *Irish Independant* and a well-attended funeral.

Lorraine is among the mourners who fill the small church and walk behind the coffin to the graveyard. After the funeral, she sups on soup and sandwiches in O'Callaghan's pub, its dust and upright benches replaced by well-sprung maroon armchairs and stained-glass partitions. Celia's nephew, Eugene Murphy, introduces himself to her. He has seen her on television, something to do with an exhibition. He knows little enough about art, he admits, but he recognised her at once and remembers playing with her on the beach when they were children. His aunt's house, which he inherited, is now on the market. It will sell cheap and need refurbishment. Lorraine leaves the hotel and drives with him to view it. When she expresses an interest in buying the house, Eugene assumes she intends using it as a holiday home. On hearing she is moving permanently to Trabawn he makes no attempt to hide his astonishment. "That'll be some lifestyle change."

In the kitchen he stands back from her, his hands clasped behind his back, puzzlement written across his face. She knows he is summing up her lacklustre eyes and strained expression but she is beyond caring what people think. They shake hands on the deal.

And so she comes to Trabawn. A flashback to childhood summers when pain was confined to stubbed toes and jellyfish stings. Ralph visits her before he leaves for London.

"Virginia always demanded more than I could give her." His emotions remain hidden behind his hawkish features. "But I was arrogant enough to believe she would never betray me with my best friend. They've moved in together."

Lorraine paces the floor, unable to stay still. Every part of her gnaws, burns, shivers and the weeping, she is convinced, will never stop. The business partnership of Strong–Blaide Advertising is over. Virginia will keep Blaide House. Their house in Howth now belongs to Ralph. The spoils of war, he calls it. His matter-of-fact acceptance of all that has happened diminishes her grief.

"I wish you wouldn't be so calm," she cries. "You'd discuss the break-up of a failed merger with more emotion."

He gathers her against him, forces her to a standstill. "Believe me, Lorraine, it's hatred that keeps me standing upright, nothing else."

But the person Lorraine hates most is herself, poor deluded, pliable, pitiful, gullible fool, hiding in the hidey-hedge, hiding behind the sand dunes while Virginia skipped over the rocks and away with the prize.

CHAPTER TWENTY-FIVE

Ferryman
(an extract from Michael Carmody's memoir)

The phone call from Bozo Daly came two nights after my last meeting with Killian. "F-f-*erry*man's d-d-down on the wa-wa-*wall*. Better co-come, mate." As usual, there was much stammering and puffing of breath. But I got the message. He hung up before I could ask questions. I wanted to roar into the silence that followed, strike the nearest object with my fists. I was weary of my son's endless destructive games.

I drove along the quays. The peak traffic had long dispersed but the trucks still headed for the ferry terminals. I drove towards the South Port and into the industrial zone. Boulders positioned on sections of the road prevented travellers parking their caravans. But a few defiant families had managed to penetrate this fortress and closed their curtains against the settled world. I passed empty warehouses. Bulky containers and giant oil drums were visible beyond high walls. Outside the gates of the ESB generating station, a row of cannons offered a silent salute. My headlights swept over the pier, hoping I'd find Killian running wild, chasing the moon, perhaps. I walked the pier, searched the shadows. Apart from the silver car parked close to a shed, the place was deserted. I drove to a small car-park overlooking the bay and removed a torch from the boot. Its beam was a feeble light in the vast abyss my son had created between us.

The last car was leaving the car-park when I climbed over the rocks banking one side of the South Wall. Seaweed squelched beneath my feet. I slipped, my foot wedging between rocks, and imagined Killian sliding, falling, his mind lost, wandering back to his childhood when he had my steady hand to guide him back to safety. He played my emotions like a mandolin, strumming my love with brutal fingers. Yet I remembered those same fingers clasped in mine as we explored the murky green depths of rock pools, coaxing crabs from under the cover of seaweed and following the rippling flow of minnows.

From the pier I heard a car door slam. Footsteps sounded, voices argued. On a quiet night sounds carry. I saw them walk out of sight behind the high walls of the shed. I left them to their pleasure. If only I'd stayed a while longer. If only ... only ... ten minutes more could have made a difference. Two hours later the guards came to my apartment.

Since that night, medical terminology has become a familiar language. Killian's neuro-surgeon uses words with a casual ease that terrified us at first; CAT scans, trauma, brain-stem damage, occipital lobe, Glasgow coma scores, the remote possibility of a "reawakening". We've become attuned to the nuances of meaning, the pitch of his information. His skill at breaking bad news into small digestible pieces is well honed. Temporal-parietal subdural haematoma. How's that for a mouthful? Killian was operated on in Beaumont Hospital and transferred to the Hammond Clinic when he was stable.

I saw Bozo Daly a few times after the accident. He walked past, his head down, not replying when I called his name. He had nothing to say or, to be more accurate, was incapable of saying anything. But he too had been searching that night for Killian. A short-lived search that ended when he found a shelter and settled down with a bottle. He heard the car alarm and later, against a skyline of high cranes and towering chimneys, he saw my son's fallen body.

He was yellow-skinned and wizened as a tough old nut when I visited him in hospital. Finally, nearing his end, he was willing to talk. Our last conversation was not an easy one. He was dying with a stammer on his lips. It was no longer a hindrance to our conversation but lent authenticity to words that must be true when they took such an effort to produce. As he spoke the walls of the hospital ward seemed to bend towards me and straighten again. A woman in a blue overall came with a trolley and poured a cup of tea, handed it to me. But I couldn't drink it and Bozo shifted on his hard hospital mattress, wishful, I suspect, for a sagging armchair in a dockside squat. He had stayed with my son until an ambulance arrived then slid back to the dark.

The following morning Killian's friend arrived at the squat. They had robbed the contents of the silver car. A stereo and a bracelet were the only things of value they had time to steal before they were disturbed. The lad was terrified, anxious to dispose of the proceeds of the robbery. Bozo shook his head when I asked his name. He'd occasionally seen him with Killian but he never stayed overnight in the squat. The stereo fetched a small sum, hardly worth the effort. But the bracelet was a different story. Bozo Daly knew about jewellery, having handled enough of it in his day, and this was a piece with a very specific design, probably unique, with the initials LC carved into the clasp. It fetched a tidy sum. Killian's accomplice never returned to collect his cut.

He had no idea who owned the bracelet until he saw a programme called *Artistically Speaking*. It was repeat of the original programme and he watched it from his hospital bed. He used to paint once. He shuffled the words as if he understood my disbelief, conjuring, as they did, the study of still waters and bowls of luscious fruit. He recognised the bracelet. It was a chunky, distinctive piece of jewellery with strands of silver intricately criss-crossed. The effect was the same as an Aran-type stitch, with sapphires embedded into its curious weave.

"Why didn't you bring it to the police?" I asked. "They could have traced the owner."

He laughed thickly and coughed. He did not bother replying. It was a stupid question. The bracelet is gone, sold on, money spent, a dead trail.

I've watched the video seven, perhaps eight times. I look at the bracelet flashing on her arm and think of drowned sailors. Mothers in black shawls identifying their sons' cold bones by the pattern they once lovingly knitted into their jumpers – and I think also of the Synge-like vengeance they keened towards the bitter sea.

Clips of earlier interviews were shown. She was shy of the camera in those days, uncomfortable when it stayed too long on her face. I heard and understood the struggle for acknowledgement in her voice. The bracelet hung on her wrist. The interviewer commented on its design and the camera focused when she moved her arm. Apparently, the silversmith was well known to them both. How could Bozo be sure it was the same bracelet? I asked him that question many times. He was definite it was the one he'd handled and Killian's friend had spoken about painting materials in the boot of the car.

The programme covered her entire career, analysed how her work had evolved to the present day. Her fascination with dreams was evident in her early work but in those days she painted nightmares. Then, as if a steady hand had calmed the beast, her work changed. The presenter referred to her portraits as "quirky and cheekily Cheeverish", an expression that made her wince and push her hair from her forehead, as if weary of its weight. She paints people in repose, smiling, pensive, animated. Knowledge of one's sitter, she stated, is the key to a successful portrait – and so she seeks to capture the essence of her subject's personality. He asked why she changed direction so dramatically for her last exhibition and she spoke of influences, the fantasy of Surrealism, the grip of imagination, the sexual ambiguity of the unconscious which has always fascinated her.

I understand why *Painting Dreams* created such controversy. Her paintings breathe with yearnings; a provocative dance of seven veils, evoking fantasies that cling to the senses long after the dreamer awakens. On the opening night of her exhibition she spoke with the assurance of a successful artist. Thin black straps rested on her shoulders. There were pearls at her neck. She looked older, weary, as if her thoughts were elsewhere. She gesticulated a lot, making language with her hands. Anticipation, perhaps, of the furore her paintings would create in the weeks ahead. Or perhaps she was remembering a desolate pier and the secret she left behind. She no longer wore a bracelet on her wrist.

Chapter Twenty-Six

Killian

Hands cover him, lull him, keep the pain away. They come and they go. Sound and silence. He sinks below the tide and rises. Light and dark. The moon is always out of reach.

Merciful Jesus, we have gathered around Killian's bedside to plead with you, in your divine mercy, to return him to his family and friends. If it is not your will that he be cured then carry him safely and painlessly into your everlasting light. Goodnight, darling. I must leave now. Duncan is being difficult again.

Knock knock. Who's there? Dill. Dill who? Dill we meet again … ha ha ha.

Listen mate, I'm going out with Marianne now. I'm sorry, Killian. Don't be mad. She's here with me now. You have to wake up! I miss you, mate.

I planted primroses on Bozo's grave today. They'll bloom in the spring. Remember the film Killian? It won an award. I'm going to bring it in and show it to you soon. Bozo liked you. Said you had the makings of a great director. He was right, Killian. You have to keep believing.

I tell my daughter about you, little soldier. She is going to pray to the Madonna. Like your mama, she has the faith. Smile, yes, you smile from your heart. No matter what they say I know you smile for me.

There you are, Loveadove. Did you hear me rattling down the corridor? Your da calls me the late-night express. How many fingers am I holding up? Is that a blink or a wink? Don't fret, Loveadove. You'll do it yet. Some things take time but it's worth the wait.

Killian, it's just too much. My veil still hasn't arrived. They promised delivery from France a week ago. And the invitations have a spelling mistake! I could chop straws with my tail. There you go. Isn't that more comfortable? God, I envy you. Lying there with fuck all to worry about.

Lullaby and goodnight, thy mother's delight. Bright angels around, my darling, shall guard. Don't be afraid, pet. I'll always be here to sing for you, just as I always watched out for you. I was your buffer zone as well as your granny. They will guide thee from harm, thou art safe in my arms. They will guide thee from harm, thou art safe in my arms.

Mr Carmody, I understand your anxiety but I must ask you to refrain from exciting the boy. That was a reflex action, not a conscious movement. Recovery of conscious awareness after a patient has been in a vegetative state as long as Killian is exceeding rare. I'm not suggesting it never happens but it is rare indeed. To give you hope would be cruel. I'm afraid Killian is in another world, a deep black hole. You must accept the reality of his situation.

PART THREE

CHAPTER TWENTY-SEVEN

His breathing was quiet and relaxed. Virginia was glad he did not snore. What was acceptable in a husband was intolerable in a lover. She traced her hand lightly across his chest and felt the regular thud of his heartbeat. He stirred, as if he sensed her restlessness, then settled into a deeper sleep. For a while she lay like this, buried in his warmth.

She looked at the clock, dismayed to realise it was only three in the morning. A busy day awaited her in the office. She focused on her meeting with Bill Sheraton, rehearsed in her mind the points she would make. Their business could just as easily have been discussed in his office but she was anxious to speak to him in a more relaxed environment and he had agreed readily to a working lunch. Her promotional skills guaranteed excellent coverage for his company and he had reason to be grateful to her. She was his bailiwick against troublesome journalists who asked awkward questions about his third-rate package holidays. How many times had she batted for him on radio phone-ins when clients complained of shoddy service? Too many to remember. As for his wife's hunger for publicity! Only someone with Virginia's numerous media contacts could satisfy it.

She slipped quietly from her bed and entered the living-room. The large sandblasted mirror on the wall reflected the elegant simplicity of the furnishings. She adjusted a painting and moved an occasional table into its allotted space. Minimalism, the interior designer had urged when she was commissioned to turn the dull square rooms with their boring magenta walls into a home. Clean lines, cool glass, pale wood, the clarity of chrome. Everything in the apartment should be a feature with a purpose, even if it was simply to gladden the eye. The idea of minimalism appealed to Virginia, suggesting, as it did, the removal of baggage, a new beginning without clutter or mementoes.

Insomnia was a new experience. Even at the height of their affair, when an inadvertent word or action would have brought the whole edifice tumbling down, Virginia had been able to sleep soundly, untroubled by the realisation that she was living a lie. Lies had not been an issue. She had stepped unhesitatingly across that threshold when she realised what the future demanded of her.

She opened the french doors and stood on the balcony. The globe-headed security lamps in the courtyard below her reminded her of pale winter moons shining over the lives of invisible people who lived side-by-side, enjoying neither comm-unication nor contact with each other. Even now, six months later, it was difficult to accept that the world they had crafted with such care had collapsed around them like a house of cards. Their love had cost a high price but if she had learned anything from her mother it was that change and challenge walked hand in hand. Eyes to the front, Virginia. Remember what happened to Lot's wife when she looked behind. Salt of the earth she was, poor thing.

Not that Josephine was prepared to apply that criteria to her daughter's decision. No phone call from London was complete without the terse reminder that a friend indeed was worth two in the bush – or that old friends were as scarce as gold bullion. Josephine's determination to condense life into an abused proverb has not lessened with age. If she did not catch Virginia in the office she left messages on her voice mail.

Virginia did not need constant reminders from her mother that she had destroyed both her marriage and the most important friendship of her life. Of course there was guilt and regret.

Friends did not attach themselves easily to her. Acquaintances, yes, satisfying, socially acceptable and fun. Lorraine was not always fun to be around. She had a dark side that brooded and tended to go off the deep end, like those crazy dream paintings and her decision to cut loose and head for the hills.

"Why Trabawn of all places?" she had demanded when Adrian told her where Lorraine intended moving. "It's a hole in the wall. She'll go crazy living there."

But Lorraine always clung to nostalgia. Sometimes, talking about those childhood summers spent in a hamlet – where even the sight of one horse was an amazing apparition – Virginia wondered if they could possibly be discussing the same experience. In the midst of publicity and controversy, just when her career was on the cusp, Lorraine Cheevers had turned her face away and hid. As if pain could be banished so easily.

When Virginia remembered the instant that shaped her future with Adrian Strong, she saw the past and the future connecting in a seamless join and the years in between – the lives that were lived within them to the full – were suddenly condensed and seen as marking time until that moment.

She and Ralph were spending a long weekend in Churchview Terrace. The days had followed the same lazy, predictable pattern and, after a late brunch on Sunday afternoon, they decided to walk the Great South Wall. Emily ran along the pier. Dressed in baggy dungarees, her hair in ponytails, she screeched with excitement as she released the kite Ralph had bought her. He had many nephews and nieces but Virginia often thought his affection for Emily was deeper than any familial one. He helped Emily ply the string between her hands, a falcon-faced kite, fierce eyes staring down on them. Lorraine's hair, tossing in the breeze, was as unruly as ever and she was smiling, sharing Ralph's pleasure as the kite quivered high above them.

Virginia walked at a slower pace, aware of Adrian beside her, talking about some play he had seen in the Abbey. Their footsteps slowed so that the distance between them and the others increased, and when she stumbled – the rutted pavement catching in the toe of her sandal – he steadied her, held her against him for an instant.

In Trabawn she had called him a little boy, taunting him when he kissed her behind the rocks, and he had turned to Lorraine with her day-dreamy innocent eyes that only ever saw what she wanted to see. Two years later, when he came to London, he held a bottle of sangria in one hand and a tacky toy donkey tucked under his arm.

"I'm not sure whether he's Plato or Aristotle." He presented the donkey to Virginia and bowed, sweeping an outrageously large sombrero from his head.

"Let me guess." She laughed and invited him into the flat she shared with Razor. "You've been to Iceland on your holidays?"

He smiled his lazy, sexy smile and stepped inside. His holiday in Spain was a respite before he started working for the summer in London. She cooked pasta and they drank the sangria which he poured into their mouths through a long thin nozzle and then, when they drank their fill, he licked the fruity taste from her lips. When Razor, on an overnight gig with his band, returned the following day, the bed was neatly made, fresh sheets in place. How torn she had been, how excited. Wings on her feet as she ran between the two of them. Razor, engrossed in his band, recording his divisive songs, never suspected. He did not register the laden silences or notice the sideways glances.

Adrian left at the end of the summer, returning home to complete his studies. He was back again the following year. Lorraine arrived shortly afterwards, shaking her mermaid hair, more attractive than Virginia remembered, and she had watched Adrian come adrift, swing between the two of them, but, always, returning to her. Jake had been conceived, she suspected, on a sultry night when reason, like their clothes, was flung aside. In a game of strip poker Virginia held a full deck. She had slipped from Razor's bed and quietly entered the living room where she found Adrian in the dark, sleepless, ready for her. She had plundered desire that night, thrown caution to the wind as she stormed high on the passion of two men, and, afterwards – how was she to know which one had fathered her child?

While Razor toured with his band and Lorraine wilted,

lovesick and confused, she ignored the reality of her pregnancy and discussed a different future with Adrian. They would move to California. His enthusiasm was contagious: open-topped jeeps and rollers, people dancing bare-foot on the beach, breath-taking sunsets, falling asleep to the sounds of the ocean. She wanted the fleet-footed happiness he could give her, or so she believed until she returned to her flat and collapsed to her knees, suddenly overcome with an incredible feeling of loss. This creature – not yet life and conceived in a maelstrom of lust, without thought or consideration – was assuming an identity that could no longer be denied. And there she was, her head against the bath, a towel clutched in her hands, when Lorraine discovered her.

Razor held her gently when he heard, no longer her rough, tough punk but a young man in love, awed by the realisation that he was to become a father. As soon as she made her decision to stay with him she knew it was the right one. Shortly afterwards, Adrian moved to California.

"How would you react if this was your child?" she asked, before he left.

"I'd stay with you, of course," he replied. "We'd work something out together."

"A termination?" she said.

His eyes glazed over at her direct question. "It would have to be a consideration. But only if it was what you wanted. Why are you putting me through this? It's not my child, not my decision to make."

Lightness and air against solid rock. She had made the right choice. No time for regrets. Life was too full, too swift, to waste time wondering.

But that afternoon on the South Wall the past leapt upon her unawares and Adrian, as if tuned to her thoughts, turned her towards him, and she knew from the sultry touch of his hands that he too was remembering. Without speaking, they moved out of sight behind the walls of a shed. They kissed, an ardent furtive embrace, and emerged again, shaken by the realisation that a summer madness was still upon them.

Emily's kite was lowered. Reluctantly, the falcon dipped, swooped once more, as if defying the pull of the string, and then settled with a last desperate flutter at their feet. Lorraine walked towards them. Did her step falter for an instant, her smile become more fixed? Virginia braced herself, steadied her nerve. She knew how to carry a secret. Sonya and her red high heels.

A small terrier dashed forward and tore at the kite. Emily sobbed as Ralph wrestled the kite from the dog. Adrian and Lorraine took her hands and swung her forwards and backwards, a well-practised manoeuvre, effortless, and Emily's tears turned to laughter. Lorraine's voice floated back, floated lightly past Virginia, who paused and stared towards the sea, aware there was a choice that could still be made. When she walked from the pier that afternoon, she had severed a lifetime of friendship. She exchanged it for the coded world of lovers, where innocuous words spoken in company had the power to transfix them with desire and the foreplay of yearning glances in crowded places was an unspoken language only they could interpret. Six months later she had persuaded Ralph to move to Ireland. The future had been ordained.

In the Blue Oyster restaurant, Bill Sheraton was waiting when she arrived. She ordered salmon and crab terrine with a dill mayonnaise. Easy to digest, no bones or flaky pieces that might drop inelegantly from her fork and stain her silk blouse. The businessman, having no such worries, wrapped a linen napkin around his neck and tucked into a steaming plate of Moules Marinière. It was their final meeting before the Sheraton Worldwide Travel fund-raising ball and memorabilia auction. The response to tickets had been excellent. Celebrities had offered personal possessions for the auction and a film made by an ex-patient of the Patterson Rehabilitation Centre would be premiered on the night. Virginia had already viewed the film with some distaste but – as the proceeds of the auction were going to the centre – her voice betrayed no such emotion when she discussed it with the businessman.

She politely waved aside the dessert menu and ordered an espresso.

"Same for me." Bill nodded brusquely at the waiter. "Make it strong enough to kick-start the afternoon." After a quick glance at his watch he turned his attention back to her. "You mentioned there was another matter you wished to discuss with me."

"It's a business proposition concerning Adrian's company."

"Ah yes. Strong–Blaide. But not any more, eh?"

"No indeed." Virginia offered him a rueful smile. "It's been a difficult time for all of us."

Understatement was an art she had polished to perfection in the early years of her career. Adrian's accountant had warned that closure was inevitable unless a sizable investment was made. She fell silent until the waiter served their coffee then leaned towards the businessman. "But life moves on, Bill. Adrian is restructuring his company and –"

"And you think I'd be interested in putting a rescue package together?" His non-committal tone interrupted her prepared speech, increased her nervousness. She smiled brightly, the espresso cup poised precisely in her hand. He was difficult to fathom, abrasive and rude when publicity was not to his satisfaction, and also capable of bringing business meetings to an abrupt conclusion when the point was not reached in the first few minutes.

"It would certainly *not* be a rescue package." She spoke more quickly than she intended and forced herself to slow down. "You've always been able to recognise a good investment. Adrian has some very exciting ideas in the pipeline. I was hoping you'd meet him, hear what he has to offer."

His questions came in rapid succession, stimulating and challenging her. She was always at her best when it came to selling ideas, influencing decisions, bringing like-minded people together, and Bill Sheraton, like Adrian, had a creative vision. There was no reason why the dynamic partnership created by Strong–Blaide could not continue in a different form. The two Cs, Ralph used to call it – creative genius and commercial sense. Ralph, the dynamic force, had provided the perfect balance for Adrian's ideas but with his departure a number of important accounts had been lost. Adrian had tried without success to interest two potential investors in his new agency but both men changed their minds at the last minute. Their excuses did not fool Virginia. She was certain Ralph was in the background, pulling strings, a subtle whispering campaign. His reputation as a ruthless competitor was well established.

Bill Sheraton was interested. Virginia could see it in his narrowed gaze and the almost imperceptible nod he gave when she outlined the reasons why his investment would reap a worthwhile return. He finished his coffee and signalled for the bill, slapping her hand aside when she insisted on paying. Outside the Blue Oyster, he hailed a taxi to bring her back to Blaide House.

"Initially, Adrian will have to convince my financial controller that this proposition is worth discussing," he repeated, before she stepped into the taxi. "You've made your pitch. The rest is up to him. I'll get my secretary to ring him and make an appointment. You needn't worry, Virginia. I won't keep him on tenterhooks."

A message from Adrian awaited her when she returned to the office. He was engaged for the afternoon with a client and would meet her back in the apartment. At seven o'clock she finally switched off her computer. Except for herself and Brenda, the woman who cleaned the offices and whose vacuum cleaner droned faintly in the distance, the building was empty. She hesitated on her way to the exit, suddenly oppressed by the silence. Strong–Blaide Advertising had been such a vital part of Blaide House, loud with young voices, the ring of mobile phones, the clatter of computers, laughter. Its premises would soon be taken over by a finance company and Adrian had moved to smaller offices on the first floor. At least the attic was up and running again. Spiral Staircase had been a brainwave and Mara Robertson, the owner of the gallery, was confident of its success. The transformation was startling yet each time Virginia entered the gallery she found it impossible not to think of Lorraine in her paint-stained shirts and trousers, welcoming her into her cluttered space, making coffee, lounging against the wall, the two of them relaxing down for a few minutes in a busy day. Mara used lilies to decorate the gallery, arranging them in glass vases, yet their scent had not succeeded in banishing the smell of paint, a cloying odour that drifted light as mist and clung stubbornly to Virginia's skin.

The door to Ralph's office was open. Brenda dusted it every evening, even though it was vacant since he moved to London.

Hesitating for only an instant, Virginia pushed the door further ajar and entered. His desk was clear, not even a pen or piece of paper to mar its surface, her photograph gone from its customary position. The drawers were also emptied, the flamboyant paintings removed from the walls. She sat into his chair and spun around, spinning faster and faster until it seemed as if she was physically breaking through his invisible presence, banishing a spectre that somehow, somewhere, still hovered in the air.

Josephine had rung shortly after Ralph's departure. "I thought you'd like to know that your unfortunate husband called to see me last night. He wept like a baby in my arms. As ye sow so shall ye weep." She sounded like an orator at a graveside.

The sheer audacity of this lie had enraged Virginia. To think of Ralph shedding tears, much less weeping in her mother's arms, would be amusing at any other time. But Virginia was not in a mood to be amused. She had walked from her marriage with a swollen cheek and the marks of her husband's hand on her skin. Before striking her, she had sensed the blow, watched it forming in the bleakness of his eyes, as if he was already separating himself from what he was about to do.

"Go on," she had taunted him, her head humming from the force of his hand. "Why don't you do it properly? You're strong, you can take me on. It's what you've always wanted to do."

"It's what *you* want me to do." When he stepped back she saw his pitiless determination. "I've no intention of making you feel better about yourself."

"You never owned me, Ralph. No matter how hard you tried, I was always my own person."

He jerked his palms before her but did not attempt to touch her again. "Then go, Virginia. Whatever prison you occupied with me never had a lock."

Her cheek was beginning to throb. The pain gave her the courage to walk from her house. The garden enfolded her, the heavy-headed pampas grass waving farewell as she drove down the driveway. Automatic gates slid open then closed slowly behind her.

Adrian had moved to a hotel and was waiting for her. A city

centre hotel, frequented by those they knew, but she walked
boldly through the foyer. No more lies. Lorraine had raged down
the phone, her voice hoarse from weeping, unrecognisable,
ranting about her exhibition and some unthinking gesture on
Virginia's part that had confirmed her suspicions. Unable any
longer to continue speaking, she had slammed down the receiver.

"Who were you talking to?" Ralph asked.

Virginia had turned to face him, the receiver fused to her
hand. One by one she unclenched her fingers. Disbelief gave way
to a slow dawning, her body already shivering in the aftermath
of lost affection.

She closed the door of the office her husband had occupied and
left the building. Outside Blaide House she hailed a taxi. The
driver, an elderly man who looked like a retired civil servant,
switched on Lyric FM. Perfect. *La Bohème*. She closed her eyes,
relaxed. The journey was short and the taxi driver soon drew up
outside the apartment in Clontarf. On the grassy promenade
across the road a team of young boys were in training. The
staccato commands of their soccer coach carried towards her. She
entered the elevator which, as usual, was empty. How could such
a large community remain invisible to each other, she wondered,
as it glided upwards to the fourth floor. She never met anyone
entering or leaving the red-brick blocks. Yet the small balconies
surrounding her held tables and sun chairs, potted plants and,
occasionally, a bicycle jammed against the railings. And beyond
the walls of each apartment there were other trapped sounds,
other struggles for supremacy, love, peace of mind, domination.

Adrian was slouched on a low armchair, his legs stretched
before him. His relaxed posture was in marked contrast to the
terse expression on his face as he spoke into the phone. Emily-
talk-time. She knew the signs. This ritual had been going on
since his daughter moved to Trabawn. She tousled his hair as she
walked past. He raised his head but continued speaking, his voice
low, persuasive. She heard him laugh at some remark made by
Emily, his laughter too hearty, as if his daughter needed reassuring
that she was the comedienne of the year. In the beginning, Emily
had been intent on slicing her father's heart into thin withered

pieces but there were signs that she was at last coming around to accepting his situation. He had driven to Galway so they could celebrate her birthday together. Neutral territory, he explained when Virginia protested at being left out of the loop.

"Just give her time and then we can organise weekends here with us. She needs gentle handling until the dust settles."

The dust always settled. It had nowhere else to go.

She placed her briefcase beside the work station, folded the newspaper he had scattered over the coffee table, added fresh water to a bunch of orchids. They had opened fully, their delicate, speckled petals reminding her of exotic butterflies in flight. A quick shower banished tiredness. She wrapped her hair in a towel and returned to the living-room, where Adrian was standing by the window, looking down on the football team.

"Where were you all afternoon?" she asked. "I tried to contact you on your mobile but it was switched off."

"I had a meeting with Brian Ormond. By the time it ended it was too late to return to the office."

"No problems, I hope?"

He leaned back against the wall and drew her into his arms. "Why should there be a problem?"

"Absolutely no reason. Just that he and Ralph used to be thick as thieves."

"Ralph's in London. He's happy now that the house is sold and he's pocketed his million. I was showing Ormond some ideas for the new campaign. It was a useful meeting." When the towel fell from her shoulders he fluffed her hair and called her his sexy punk.

She smiled, slapped his hand away. "Behave yourself. I've something important to discuss with you."

"Can we do it in a horizontal position?" He waltzed her around the room, then veered towards the bedroom, singing, "I'm in the mood for love," as they collapsed onto the bed.

She stifled her impatience, allowed him to kiss her twice before she told him about her meeting with Bill Sheraton. His arms stiffened, his playfulness instantly disappearing. He rolled over, pushed himself upright, a frown gathering between his eyebrows. "Why didn't you tell me you were meeting him?"

"It was a toe-in-the-water exercise. What was the sense in getting your hopes up? He might have said no at the outset and then you'd have had to deal with another disappointment."

"I understand what you're saying but meeting Bill Sheraton behind my back is way out of line. Ralph may have allowed you to interfere in the running of the company but that's not how I operate."

"For goodness sake, stop looking so offended." The enthusiasm drained from her voice. "I wasn't trying to interfere. If Ralph is trying to make things difficult, and those two investors had dust on their heels, Bill Sheraton won't be influenced by anything other than his own judgment. What does it matter who makes the contact as long as you're successful? His accountant is going to ring you next week. Check up on Siamese cats. She breeds them."

"You're quite a mover, Virginia." His eyes narrowed, studying her, then he smiled again, his mood lifting. "A real shaker and a mover. Dry your hair. We have to celebrate." He reached towards the bedside phone. "I'll book a table at Pascal's."

Their favourite French restaurant was within walking distance of the apartment. A violinist circled the tables and stopped to serenade them. Not so long ago they would have banished him with a cold warning look but Adrian smiled and slipped a twenty euro note into the musician's pocket. After their meal was over, they strolled along the esplanade, holding hands, enjoying the cool night air. No shadows walked in their footsteps. They made love when they returned to the apartment, not assuaging love, not seeking oblivion, but freely, as was now their right. It had been an enjoyable night. Throughout their meal they had avoided talking about business, Emily, Lorraine, Ralph – and not once had they mentioned the boy.

CHAPTER TWENTY-EIGHT

On a September afternoon when the clouds clung to the hills like dour grey sheep and the sea rolled queasily towards shore, the stranger Lorraine had met on the mountain road came to Trabawn. Hobbs' barking warned her that someone had entered the lane. A few minutes later he braked his car outside her house.

"You got my message?" His glance was enquiring, uncertain of his welcome.

"My daughter told me. I was walking the beach when you rang yesterday."

He stared around the overgrown garden, the cement and mud tracks, the crack running along the gable wall.

"I'm still settling in as you can see," she said. "You'll have to excuse everything. Would you like coffee or tea before we go into the studio?"

"Coffee sounds good."

They entered the kitchen and she gestured towards a chair, set a plate of buttered scones on the table.

"My neighbour's home cooking, not mine," she said when he made an appreciative comment. "She always throws my name into the baking bowl. I guess she thinks I need nourishing."

His eyes raked her but he made no comment. Self-consciously, she pushed her hair from her forehead and lifted mugs from the dresser. Slowly, as if he was memorising every detail, his gaze moved over the freshly painted walls, the spice racks, her jacket hanging from a hook on the back door; his eyes resting on the wooden table, the chairs with their broad backs and solid legs, the old-fashioned dresser filled with crockery. A red throw had been draped over the sofa where Emily usually curled watching television.

"I'm afraid your name meant nothing to me when you rang yesterday so I didn't know who to expect. But Emily was in quite a tizz. She believes you write for television. *Nowhere Lodge* – is that the name of the programme?"

He bowed his head in acknowledgement.

She heaped logs on the fire. The flames licked the wood and the blast of heat brought colour to her cheeks. "I can't believe it! Emily's one of your greatest fans. She adores that show."

"Where is she now?"

"At school. She should be home soon. Be warned. She'll pester you for autographs."

Emily usually arrived home from school with Ibrahim. They were now recognised in the gang as "an item" and, ostensibly, they went to each other's houses to study. Whenever Lorraine came in from her studio, she found them sitting at the kitchen table, their heads bent over their books. Such diligence would have impressed her had she not also observed the rumpled cushions on the sofa. Remembering her own dalliance behind the sand dunes and the delirium of first love, she knew the uselessness of advising caution. Instead, she found herself delivering the same heavy-headed lectures Donna had once delivered on the trauma of crisis pregnancies and thought, "It's actually happening. I'm becoming my own mother."

"When did you move here?" Michael Carmody interrupted her thoughts.

"Early March."

"Have you settled down?"

"Not really. You mentioned something about a portrait?"

"Yes. Killian Devine-O'Malley, my son."

"How old is he?"

"Nineteen."

"Is the portrait a present for his birthday?"

Coffee sloshed from his mug, scalded his fingers. With a muttered exclamation he laid the mug back on the table. Lorraine rummaged in a drawer and found a spray of aloe vera balm, which she applied to his hand. He flinched when she touched his skin. No wedding band or rings of any kind. His son called by a different name. He was separated from the boy's mother, she guessed. Early forties, had known tragedy, it was in his eyes.

"Don't worry," she reassured him. "This will work quickly and stop the stinging. Is the portrait meant to be a surprise or shall I have an opportunity to meet him?"

"I'd like to arrange a meeting." He drew his hand away and rested it on the table.

"Good. I prefer to meet the person. Sometimes, if it's a surprise present, I have to work from photographs which is not half as satisfying."

"I can show you his photograph." He removed a wallet from his inside pocket. To her surprise he produced a photograph of a young boy, about seven, she guessed. His front teeth were missing but, oblivious of gaps and gums, he was grinning widely as he stood on a pier and pointed towards a ferry sailing across the bay from the North Wall terminal.

"He's the image of you." She handed the photograph back to him. "Is he your eldest child?"

"He's my only child."

"Emily's my only child too. Do you have a more recent photograph of Killian? I'm sure he's changed a lot since that was taken."

A second photograph revealed a tall slim youth wearing a Nirvana t-shirt and jeans. He stared into the camera with the same challenging gaze as his father. Lorcan Sheraton stood beside him and Mount Subasio, looking like a fixture in a theme park, was the backdrop.

"I see we have a mutual acquaintance." She stared in surprise at the two boys.

He nodded. "Lorcan is Killian's neighbour. They've been friends for a long time."

"I'm afraid I was rather distracted leaving Lorcan's house that day we met. My apologies for almost slamming you back into your own driveway."

His coffee was cooling but he made no attempt to drink it. "I was leaving Killian's mother's house. My apartment is in the city."

"What a coincidence. I was delivering a family portrait to the Sheratons when we met. Lorcan hated the experience of being painted. He'll probably warn Killian to run for cover. You could check out the portrait with Andrea. See what you think of my style."

"I'm very familiar with your style."

"In that case, we might as well go to the studio."

A light drizzle was falling. The weather changed with a rapidity that amazed her. Mist could descend from the hills in minutes and rain swoop in from the sea, blinding her eyes, yet by the time she had completed her walk along the beach the sky would be milky streaked.

"Be careful here," she warned as they walked around a cement mixer. "I intend having this area paved. Everything takes so long." She unlocked the studio door and stood aside for him to enter.

"Was this originally a stable?" Again his quizzical glance, this time upwards towards the high arched ceiling.

"Two donkeys lived here when I was a child. Plato and Aristotle."

"Philosophical donkeys. Makes sense." He laughed abruptly and removed his jacket, placed it on the back of a chair. She was about to show him her portfolio when Con tapped on the studio door and entered. He took a step backwards when he saw she was busy and turned to leave.

"Sorry, Lorraine. I didn't know you'd someone with you. I need to check delivery dates but I can call back later."

"No. Go on ahead to the house. I'll be with you in a moment." She placed her portfolio on the table. "These are some samples of my work. Have a look at them while I'm talking to Con."

When she returned, Michael Carmody was leafing through one of her sketch pads. To her consternation she realised it was the one containing the self-portraits.

"Sorry, Michael. But those are not for public consumption."

"Such pain," he replied, making no attempt to close the pad. "It reminds me of your early work."

She walked quickly towards him and laid her hand protectively over the open page. "You know a lot about my paintings."

"But not a lot about you. Are these recent sketches?"

"As I already said, they're not for public consumption." Firmly she took the sketch pad from him and pushed it to one side. "We were talking about your son. Those drawings are not typical of my work but if you've changed your mind about the portrait I understand."

"No, I'd like you to meet him. When will you be in Dublin?"

Before she could reply his mobile phone rang. He turned from her, his voice changing, becoming more urgent. "No, I'm not at home. Why?"

His breath caught and was released on a whistling sigh. "I'm on my way, Jean." He had already reached the studio door before he clicked off his mobile.

"Are you all right?" She followed him outside. "Has something happened?"

"I have to leave right away." The drizzle had turned to heavy rain. Despite his protests, she took the umbrella she used when walking the beach on rainy afternoons and held it over him.

He fumbled for his keys and opened the car door. In the overhead light his face was haggard. "I'll be in touch with you again and then we'll talk." Without saying goodbye he accelerated away.

He had only travelled a short distance when his car swerved and came to a standstill.

She hurried towards him. "What's the problem?"

"Jesus Christ! I can't believe this!" He was already hunkered down before one of the front tyres. "I hit something sharp on the way down the lane and it obviously punctured the wheel."

He removed a jack and wheel-brace from the boot. When the car was fully jacked he tried to twist off the wheel nuts. Despite his strenuous efforts he was unable to loosen them. After ten minutes he wiped his sleeve across his forehead.

"I can't do it without a machine." His voice shook. She wondered if there were tears or raindrops running down his cheeks.

"I'll drive into the village and bring back a mechanic. I know the garage owner. He's very obliging. I'll get my car."

"Your car?" His furious voice stopped her in her tracks. He gripped the wheel brace in his hand and she thought for a shocked instant that he was going to fling it at her. Abruptly, as if he sensed her fear, he flung it to the ground. The rumble of Frank's tractor drowned out his reply. The ground seemed to vibrate around them as the tractor drew nearer and shuddered to a halt.

The farmer took in the scene at a glance. "Wait a minute and I'll get the lads," he shouted and juddered past them towards the farmyard gate.

He returned shortly with his sons who hunkered beside the wheel, each taking a side of the wheel-brace and holding it firmly in position while Frank in his muck-splattered wellingtons stood firmly on it. Lorraine winced as the men took their father's weight but they were obviously used to working as a team. As Frank jumped lightly and persistently on the wheel-brace, the bolts twisted and loosened. They watched while Michael put on the spare wheel, standing around him in a protective semi-circle. His frenzied movements, his haste, the tension emanating from him as he tightened the bolts increased Lorraine's nervousness. She wanted him on the road, speeding towards whatever emergency had drained the colour from his face. She was standing by her gate when he finally drove away, her face shaded under the brim of the umbrella.

He had left his business card with one of the photographs on the table. She studied his son's features, his fine cheeks and slim nose, the tremulous smile. A sensitive face, she decided, easily hurt or frightened. She recognised the Poolbeg lighthouse at the end of the pier and remembered a Sunday afternoon, two figures walking slowly. A vibration passed through her fingers and the photograph trembled, as if a breeze blew gently but persistently by her.

She entered her studio and opened the sketch pad containing her self-portraits. How haunted she looked, those skeletal cheeks and distraught expressions. She remembered the fury that had consumed her that night as she sketched, snapping sticks of charcoal, rubbing, shading, highlighting, shaping.

Trapped and vulnerable, without any concept of a future, she had sought refuge in childhood and the belief that the past held the key to what was to come. Perhaps it did. Sometimes it flickered, a will-o'-the-wisp taunting her to take a step forward, mocking her when she fell two paces back. Slowly, deliberately she ripped out the pages and flung them into the rubbish bin. She turned up the volume on her compact disc player and began to draw a boy standing on a pier. Michael Carmody's face came to mind. She remembered his whistling breath and the tremor in his voice when he spoke on the phone. The caller had been a woman. Lorraine had heard the high tones, her words inaudible, her panic unmistakable, and that same fear had taken hold of Michael Carmody and sent him speeding homewards.

The thudding guitar beat and world-weary lyrics of Bob Dylan singing "Just Like a Woman" echoed around her studio. When she finished sketching she tacked the drawings to the wall. She pinned the photograph to the top of her easel and painted without interruption until the small hours of the morning. She had no idea when it happened, the shift that lifted her over the self-consciousness and forced discipline that had gripped her for so long, but suddenly her mind was free and she was painting with free, easy strokes that created a blurred impression of ships sailing over the horizon and, watching them leave, a young boy standing lonely on a pier.

CHAPTER TWENTY-NINE

Killian

Black horses on the ocean. Riding through the waves. The sea sings, drum-beat engines, fog horns call. The lighthouse flares the rocks. He watches the lady. Daisies in her eyes. And in the moon, Bozo tumbling.

See where you're going, Ferryman. This road only has one signpost. I was your age once. The world in my hands. I flung it into an empty bottle.

Where's your stammer, Bozo? Where's your big fat red nose?

Left them on the shore. Stop asking stupid questions and go home to your family, you squandering, reckless boy. Don't you know where you're heading? One road, one signpost. Fuck off out of my sight. I want to sing with the angels.

Shady Lady, take me away. Smother me. Mother me.

I'll be waiting for you, Killian. We've all the time in the great beyond. But my arms can't hold you yet.

Why did you leave Michael? You did you make him sad?

I reached too soon for heaven. I squandered the daisy days.

Stay … Shady … stay … stay …

Killian, I'm here beside you. Keep breathing, please keep breathing. Don't leave us now. Not when you've endured so much. Feel my hand. Hold it tight. Jean rang. She said hurry … hurry. Pneumonia. They warned us it could happen. I scorched the miles from Trabawn, sparks on the road. I fought with my mother every inch of the way.

"Leave him with me," I yelled. "Get off your fucking cloud and take a look below. What the hell do you think you're doing? Why aren't you watching out for me the way a proper mother should? Open your bruised eyes and see my son. He's not ready, not near ready to go to you yet."

How I raged, Killian. Right on the chin, I gave it to her. I told her what it was like to be without a mother and a father who passed like a ship through my nights. I demanded from her, temper tantrums, kicking, screaming, the way I never could when I was a child. I demanded your life in exchange for my anger. When I came here I was punch drunk, reeling.

Jean said, "You were praying," and I laughed at the notion, even though there's no room for laughter tonight. She's drifted off to sleep on the chair beside your bed. Terence has gone to the kitchen to make tea and see if he can scrounge some biscuits. He loves you as much as I do. Love has no divisions. It's a river, an effortless flowing river. Flow with it, Killian. Let it carry you back to us.

CHAPTER THIRTY

The men, handsome in tuxedos and black ties, and the women, glittering in designer eveningwear, gathered in the reception room of the Congress Hotel to drink champagne. Bill Sheraton moved among the guests, an affable host, stopping here, stopping there, stepping out a skilful minuet between business and pleasure. Virginia cast her experienced gaze over the proceedings and welcomed a photographer from *Prestige*. He flirted with her, as he always did on such occasions, and obeyed her instructions to photograph Andrea. The Sheratons posed beside a prominent government minister. Lorcan, ordered by his mother to smile, looked as if his teeth were being pulled without an anaesthetic. His habitual look of boredom disappeared when a young woman shrieked his name and flung her arms around him. Marianne Caulfield. The name clicked instantly into Virginia's mind. She had directed the film which would be shown later in the evening.

The guests swept towards the ballroom where tables were laid for the gala dinner. Chandeliers shone kindly on bare arms and there was much excitement over the foil-wrapped gift resting beside each place card. Despite Andrea's insistence that the places at the top table could not be changed, Lorcan demanded that another setting be organised beside him for Marianne.

Waiters streamed from the kitchen with silver platters balanced on one hand. Throughout the meal the young couple sat closely together, locked in a conversation that excluded everyone at the table. Occasionally they giggled and lowered their voices in a conspiratorial whisper. No doubt the adults surrounding them were the source of their merriment.

The level of noise reached the animated pitch that accompanies good food and fine wine. How handsome Adrian looked compared to the other men present. Virginia willed him to meet her eyes across the floral centerpiece. How often in the past had they dined in company, separated by convention, yet linked by the magnetic pull of desire. He was seated next to Jennifer Dwyer, the financial controller of Sheraton Worldwide Travel. His gaze never wavered from her face as he talked knowledgeably about the breeding patterns of pure-bred Siamese. Her laughter suggested that his comments had a *risqué* edge but she seemed amused and behaved towards him in a mildly flirtatious manner. Virginia turned her attention to the accountant's husband, a barrister who would always look insignificant without his wig.

Marianne gestured dismissively at the wine waiter. Her voice had an assertive ring when she demanded a jug of still mineral water with ice and slices of lime. She bestowed a contemptuous glare on those around her who were drugging legally and merrily on alcohol and explained to the table at large that she and Lorcan were on an addictive-substance recovery programme.

"Marianne, *really*. This is not the time or the place –" Andrea coughed warningly into a table napkin and left the perfect imprint of her shocked lips on white linen.

"This is a fund-raiser for the Patterson Centre." Marianne was prettily defiant. "We have to talk about these issues."

"Of course, dear. But is it necessary to do so tonight?"

"Why not?" Lorcan placed his arm protectively around his companion. "Marianne made the film we're going to watch. I helped with the editing. I'm not ashamed to admit I'm in recovery."

The barrister gazed slyly at Virginia's cleavage and declared that addiction had many forms. He was occasionally tempted to steal items from Brown Thomas. In particular he enjoyed staking out the ladies' shoe department. Not that he would ever attempt to steal anything, he hastened to assure her. Being a pillar of the legal establishment had its obligations. It was just an urge. Like the desire of a recovered alcoholic to lean his elbow on a bar – or a reformed smoker to breathe in the carcinogenic fumes of other people's cigarettes. He glared peevishly at Bill Sheraton who unabashedly lit up his black cigarillos between each course.

At the end of the meal a large screen was lowered from the ceiling and the film began. Virginia had little interest in witnessing the daily routine of recovering junkies whose earnest revelations about life on the mean streets set her teeth on edge. Polite applause greeted the end of the film then increased to a crescendo when Sulki Puss, the drag queen who was conducting the charity auction, appeared.

Over six feet tall, Sulki Puss had become an overnight celebrity since the start of his late night game show on television. He cut a dramatic figure as he strode on stage in a red lamé dress, his height increased by an exotic turban in the same material. His dress was slit from ankle to hip and he was balanced gracefully on red stilettos, his muscular legs sleek under fishnet tights. Sonya and her red high heels. Virginia forced herself to concentrate on the auction but Sonya continued flickering like the faded rewind of an old long-forgotten film.

Sulki Puss was in full swing … titty-titty bang-bang … going, going, gone … he brought the hammer down on a black lace bustier donated by a famous cabaret singer.

"Jesus, I'd put myself on hard labour for those spikes." The barrister, enraptured by the drag queen's stilettos, chortled into his brandy. His wife cast a blistering glance in his direction before turning her attention back to Adrian.

"Why don't you check them out in Brown Thomas?" Virginia smiled serenely and wondered how soon she could politely slip away or, preferably, curl into a quiet corner and sleep.

"As always, Virginia, a splendid occasion." Finally, the night drew to a conclusion. Bill Sheraton was mildly intoxicated and jolly with it. He clasped her hand, glanced across the table where Adrian and the financial controller were still deep in conversation. "You can relax. Jennifer has assured me he's a worthwhile investment."

Energy surged through Virginia. "Wonderful. I promise you won't regret your decision."

"Don't worry, Virginia." His eyes glinted a warning. "I make sure I never regret my decisions."

Andrea brushed her cheek in farewell. "Marianne was most indiscreet tonight. I'm sure you won't mention —" She settled a steely glance on her son and his elfin companion who were talking animatedly to the director of the Patterson Centre.

"Of course not." Virginia rushed to reassure her.

"Sometimes I wonder … it's not easy being a mother." She pursed her thin mouth, which was beginning to develop deep-set commas on either side. "You're lucky, Virginia. No worries on that score."

No worries indeed. If Jake had lived he would be a few years older than Lorcan, handsome, charming, witty, polished. His hair had been black, like her own. She had never seen the colour of his eyes. It was so long ago, compartmentalised, placed tenderly out of sight.

As Josephine was fond of saying, "Into every life a little pain must fall."

Virginia closed her eyes on a velvet night. Velvet was how she classified events that flowed through her hands without a hitch. Tonight had been exhausting but worth the effort. Adrian was jubilant when he returned to the apartment and carried her into the bedroom. Her body still felt delightfully invaded and Adrian, always the first to drift away, uttered a languorous moan, as if his body was still infused with their pleasure.

Time to count sheep. There was something peaceful about their plump white bodies jumping over endless hurdles. She began to float with them, rising and falling, rising and falling. Wolves and red high heels. Her body jerked awake. Already the dream was fragmenting, leaving just a fleeting impression of Sonya in her red shoes and prowling wolves. Virginia did not believe in the significance of dreams. Life was complex enough without it being dominated by Jungian theories and in-depth analysis of the id. Unlike Lorraine, she had no intention of daubing her surreal fantasies across a canvas for all the world to view and dreams, when they did invade her sleeping hours, did so discreetly and had the good sense to be gone by morning, leaving nothing, not even a shadow of the unconscious to weight her down. She awoke refreshed, ready to take on the demands of a new day – or so she had believed until … well … she sighed and attempted to banish the vision of Sonya in her red high heels and laddered tights mincing across the floor of her little house in Blandsford Crescent. The image reminded her of one of Lorraine's painting – which was enough to banish any lingering hope of sleep.

Painting Dreams should have been another velvet night. Virginia had worked tirelessly to make the opening of Lorraine's exhibition a success. As always, her finger was steady on the promotional pulse of the evening – but the exhibition made her uneasy. There was a wildness in Lorraine's paintings, an unfettered imagination utterly at war with the portraits upon which she had built her reputation.

Adrian had moved purposefully through the crush and stood beside Virginia, his words muffled, inaudible. She smiled across the gallery at a photographer from the *Evening Herald* and noted with pleasure an art critic from *The Irish Times*, another from the *Dublin Echo*. Standing slightly apart from the main gathering, Lorraine and the crew from *Artistically Speaking* were engaged in the interview.

"Have you seen it?" Adrian repeated, insisting on Virginia's attention when she had so much to oversee.

She whispered, "We'll talk later," and waved to Bill and Andrea Sheraton, who had just arrived.

But he persisted, holding her arm until she stood still and allowed his words to blow warningly against her cheek. "He was mentioned again in the papers this morning." His voice shook suddenly. "His photograph was on the front page. Eighteen years of age. He's on a life-support machine, a vegetable from the sound of it."

She whispered that he must be calm. She touched his hand,

forced him to listen. No one knew. No one would ever know. She reassured him, strengthened him, told him there was nothing to fear but fear itself and resisted the longing to smooth the worried expression from his face.

Lorraine had turned from the camera, her eyes moving slowly, deliberately over them and in that instant, as Adrian moved away, Virginia felt on her skin the quivering pressure of velvet being gently stroked in the wrong direction.

CHAPTER THIRTY-ONE

Lorraine arranged a still-life of fruit and wine in the centre of the circle.

"Study the basic shape of each object before you attempt to draw anything," she advised. "Always take time to observe. It's only when you have a clear vision of what's before you that you can interpret it in your own individual style." Lorraine had forgotten how much she used to enjoy teaching and the people who turned up each Thursday evening settled easily around her. After each class they adjourned to O'Callaghan's for a drink, crowding together into an alcove that jokingly became known as The Artist's Colony. She was carried along on their laughter, their good-natured banter. A car pool had been organised with Noeleen and Sophie, the three of them taking turns to drive each other to the school on alternate weeks. The needs of the group were diverse. Sophie wanted to paint the Sudanese landscape she had left behind, Angie from O'Callaghan's restaurant was interested in fantasy illustrations and Lorraine noted with amusement that the vivid hallucinatory images produced by Máirtín Mullarkey definitely belonged to his Mad Dog phase. Noeleen wrestled gamely with her portrait of Frank and worried about the proportions of his nose.

Energy radiated from the group. Their rapt expressions and

concentrated silence suddenly reminded her of Michael Carmody. She had heard nothing from him since his abrupt departure. His discovery of her self-portraits had obviously scared him off. Noeleen waited until the class dispersed in the direction of O'Callaghan's before producing the portrait of her husband.

"His bloody honker is driving me to drink." She pointed to a rock-like structure that threatened to dominate her painting. Lorraine diplomatically pointed out that Frank's nose was one of his most noble features and made suggestions as to how it could be modified by cheating slightly on the brow, cheeks and upper lip. With a few deft rubs and strokes she demonstrated what she meant. Noeleen agreed it made all the difference and they joined the group in O'Callaghan's. An hour later, with Lorraine at the wheel, they left for home.

Sophie's house was the first stop. Lorraine had only driven a short distance from the O'Dohertys' farm when the dashboard blacked out, the headlights failing in the same instant. The sudden enveloping darkness terrified her. As Lorraine braked to a standstill she was unsure if she had swerved too close to the middle or the side of the road. Noeleen was also subdued as she peered through the windscreen.

"The speed some people drive around here they'll be into the back of us in no time at all. Have you got a torch? I can stand behind the car and shine it as a warning."

Lorraine removed a torch from the glove compartment and they stepped outside. By the torch beam Noeleen checked her mobile phone and tapped a number. "I'll give Fred a ring. He might still be in the garage."

Fred Byrne had closed his garage for the night but he promised to be with them as soon as possible. Ten minutes later he arrived in his jeep.

"If it's the electrics it'll take time to sort out," he said. "The best thing to do is leave it with me. I'll tow you back to the garage then drop you home."

The journey back to the village was short and passed without incident.

"I'm sorry to cause so much trouble," Lorraine said when Fred braked outside her house.

"Not a bit of trouble in the world. You should get that bumper fixed while you're about it." Once again Michael Carmody placed himself smoothly in the centre of her thoughts. "I've been meaning to do so. It's so slight I keep forgetting."

Fred nodded. "Still and all, it takes from the appearance, not to mention the value. Ring me tomorrow afternoon and I'll let you know how I'm getting on."

The repairs took longer than anticipated. Two days later Noeleen drove her to the garage.

"Tricky thing, the electrics." Fred tapped the dashboard, which was, he assured Lorraine, now in perfect working order. "Whoever did the last repairs made a right botch of the job. I'm surprised you haven't had problems before now."

"But this is the first time I've had the car repaired," Lorraine protested. "Apart from a knock on the bumper, it's never had a scratch."

"Maybe the previous owner didn't mention it." Fred rubbed a chamois over the wing mirror. "The bonnet took a right dent and the stereo was ripped out at some stage. That's what damaged the electrics."

"But this is a one-owner car. It was new when I bought it."

He seemed about to argue further then changed his mind. "Far be it from me to contradict a lady such as yourself. If you'd like to settle the bill we'll agree to disagree."

His friendliness had been replaced by a brusque, business-like manner. When she wrote a cheque and handed him a bottle of whiskey as a thank-you gesture for rescuing her, he remained aloof.

"He's got the hump," said Noeleen when Lorraine left the office. "Around here you don't contradict Fred."

"Even when he's wrong?"

"Well, that's the thing," said Noeleen quietly. "He never is."

Chapter Thirty-Two

Brahms Ward
7 p.m.

They've removed the screens from around your bed. Out of danger at last. We can breathe freely again. Did I tell you Meg is home? Your golden girl, back safe and sound from the Big Apple with a wardrobe of new hats and a weight gain of a stone which she finds most annoying. It suits her. I told her she looks wonderful. She said I was fourteen years too late relaying this information. She'll be in to see you tomorrow. Don't be frightened if she cries. You look a little different from the last time she saw you. So do we all, for that matter.

Now that you're stronger, I'm going back there. Over the mountains down by the sea. Unfinished business. My mind buckles when I imagine her driving away. The image doesn't fit. Every time I spoke your name, I watched her face, waited for that flicker of recognition, fear, evasion. All I saw was interest and a desire to know more about you.

The anger is gone, Killian. I gave it up in exchange for your life and now I'm adrift, unable to cling to anything. Shady always struck a hard bargain. I remember so little about her. Faint echoes of her voice, her tears, her perfume, a crumpled piece of tissue. I can't even recall her loss. Just my overpowering love which she was never able to return. Perhaps that's why I demanded so much from you and realised, too late, that love only has substance when it's freely given.

She paints in a stable, Killian. Donkeys used to live there. Philosophical donkeys. Her house is ramshackle, tins of paint and planks of wood, slates crunching underfoot. She still has much to unpack and there are too many empty wine bottles for a woman who spends her time alone.

I pried, Killian. I wanted to see what lay beneath her professional smile and I found it in her drawings. Her sadness leapt from the pages. She was embarrassed to see herself so exposed before a stranger. Jean rang and told me you were slipping away. There was no time for confrontation. I left her standing in the rain.

Raining pouring ... old man snoring ... raining on the pier ... cold ... hide ... run... rain ... pouring ...

CHAPTER THIRTY-THREE

The silence in Virginia's office on a Sunday afternoon was a relief from the usual clamour of phones and endless interruptions. With Adrian in Galway for the weekend, she had decided to spend the time catching up on a backlog of work. At noon she broke for coffee, sliced a fresh Danish she had purchased on the way into the office and ate it slowly, standing by the window. A young girl with black hair ran between cars. The same flyaway hair as Emily Strong and the same belief that fate, like traffic, should give way to her impetuous demands. As always, she was calling the shots.

No matter how much Virginia tried to deny it, the green-eyed monster was rearing its hooves whenever Adrian mentioned his daughter's name – and mention it he did at every opportunity. Emily had taken up horse riding. Emily had an African Irish boyfriend. Emily needed coaxing, gentle handling, understanding. Emily had given birth to a calf, for Christ's sake! He had laughed long and loudly when that particular text arrived.

Since they moved into the apartment, Emily had called only once, arriving one evening unannounced and accompanied by friends – two teenage trolls who were obviously delighted to be in the centre of a family drama. Virginia had offered to send out for pizzas or Chinese takeaways. The trolls declined her invitation. They intended eating in Thunder Road Café and made pizzas sound as appetising as the left-over contents of a dog's feeding bowl. Emily, in the meantime, had observed the table set with candles and wineglasses, a dressed rocket salad and lamb brochettes. A look came over her face. Disgust, resentment, anger, shock – Virginia was unsure what emotion she could ascribe to the stare Emily fixed upon her father. Obviously, the intimacy of a table set for two infuriated her – but what did she think Adrian had been surviving on since she and her mother had moved to Trabawn? Heartache and repentance only? Since then all visits took place in Adrian's father's house or in McDonald's on Grafton Street. He had phoned earlier to say he would be home around six in the evening.

Virginia returned to her computer and clicked into a press release written by Joanna, a key member of her staff. Dross. No impact. She had trained her staff in the language of communication and this inane missive was the result. Tomorrow morning, she would deal with Joanna, call her into the office for a broadside. Shape up or ship out. *Tap, tap, tap.* Her fingers flew across the keyboard. She read the new press release and frowned, returned it to its original dross. She switched off her computer, left her office and walked along College Green. An artist hunkered on the pavement, spraying paint on glass. With his mask and spray gun he reminded her of a nuclear survivor. The fumes dried in her throat. For an instant she was unable to swallow or catch her breath. She allowed her throat muscles to relax and continued on towards Grafton Street. As she entered Brown Thomas, she wondered if she would meet the barrister with the shoe fetish but the shoe department remained resolutely feminine.

Two hours later she emerged with her purchases and continued along the street, passing guitarists and traveller children playing mouth organs. A depressed-looking poet tried without success to sell her a paper-thin volume of his poems. As she cut through Johnson's Court on her way to the Powerscourt Townhouse Centre, she stopped to admire the jewellery in Appleby's windows. A Romanian man selling the *Big Issue* held the magazine towards her. Unable to ignore his heart-wrenching smile, she bought the magazine, determined to shove it into the next litter bin she saw. She looked beyond him to where the lane bent like an elbow and saw her husband striding towards her.

For an instant, she was convinced he was a figment of her imagination. She blinked hard to banish his image but there was no mistaking his swaying, confident stride, his "corner-boy walk", as her father used to say. His trench coat belonged to a detective film – he always dressed too sharply for good taste – and the brim of his hat shaded his face. The wind gusted, flapping the carrier bags against her legs and causing him to hold on to his hat.

"Good afternoon, Virginia." He stopped before her. "Alone on a Sunday afternoon? What a surprise."

"It is indeed, Ralph." Not even the twitch of an eyebrow would reveal her dismay. "What do I offer you? My hand or my cheek? My hand, perhaps? It might be difficult to resist my cheek."

Ralph had no intention of rising to the bait. "Come now, Virginia, that's not a nice way to greet a long-suffering husband." He leaned forward and kissed her cheek. "There now, does that make it better?"

"What are you doing here?" she demanded. "I was under the impression you were in London weeping in my mother's arms."

"I was until Josephine told me a good soldier never looks behind." He smiled, swayed towards her on the balls of his feet then settled firmly back on his heels. "You're looking remarkably beautiful, my darling. Adultery obviously suits you."

A woman entering the gates of Clarendon Street Church cast a started glance in their direction and lingered, hoping to over-hear more.

"Love suits me, Ralph. There's a subtle difference but I doubt if you'd appreciate it." She gazed coldly at the woman who scurried out of sight into the portal of the church.

"No, I never did appreciate your ability to deceive. Isn't that rather strange considering how well I know you?"

She was conscious of a stiffness in her neck and wondered what people saw when they glanced towards them. Protagonists linked in a deadly war – or a couple enjoying each other's company on a late autumn evening? He carried newspapers. Four, if his reading habits had remained the same.

They used to spread the papers across the bed on a Sunday

morning, the two of them drinking coffee, eating croissants, she reading the business and social pages to check if her clients were included then turning to the style magazines. Ralph read the business sections first, underlining information which he could later check out on the Internet. He never felt the cold, propped up against the pillows, turning pages, sometimes drawing her attention to a news item that might interest her.

Unbidden, the span of his bare shoulders, the fuzz of hair on his chest and tapering downwards came to mind. Outside the dignified entrance to Clarendon Street Church seemed a most inappropriate place to ponder such intimate details and Virginia instantly cast them from her.

"Excuse me, Ralph. I'd like to stay and catch up on old times but I've a busy evening ahead of me."

"I believe congratulations are in order. Sheraton & *Strong*." He detained her with a slight sideways movement. "Who'd have believed you'd convince Bill Sheraton to throw his money into a black hole. I'd always assumed him to be an astute businessman."

"Have you finished?" She swept him coldly with her dark eyelashes.

"I love the way you do that, Virginia. It's so daunting. And no, I haven't finished. In fact, I haven't even started. Don't you want to know why I'm in Dublin?"

"Not particularly."

"A very short-sighted approach, if I may say so." He took out his wallet and handed her a business card. His name was heavily embossed in gold lettering against a black background. She noted the address and the name of the company before handing it back to him. "We had an agreement, Ralph. You made a decision to stay in London."

"But I couldn't bear the thought of being so far away from my wife and my very best friend."

"This is direct competition.

"As direct as you can get, Virginia."

"Indeed." She shrugged, shaped her lips in a smile which, she knew, would not deceive him for an instant but appearances had never seemed so important. "Competition should keep us all on our toes. I wish you every success."

"Well said, Virginia." He slid the card back into his wallet and snapped it closed. "We both know how you really feel. You've every right to be frightened. I'm going to wipe him out."

"You're sick."

"You're my sickness, Virginia. A deep, septic and incurable infection."

"Have you finished?"

"For the moment, yes. Who knows what the future holds." He moved aside and allowed her to pass. "I'd better not detain you any longer. It's getting late and Adrian never liked an empty bed." He raised his hand in farewell and walked away.

Outside the Powerscourt Townhouse Centre a young busker danced a wooden puppet off the pavement. The puppet had an idiotic painted grin and blank eyes that stared at Virginia as she passed by. She watched the puppet high-kick then collapse by her feet in a deflated heap. It rose again, pulled on strings. The clicking sound of wooden limbs followed her along the street.

CHAPTER THIRTY-FOUR

Leaves began to fall, crinkled edges fringed with gold. Autumn was almost over, the montbretia wilting on brown stalks, washed-up shoes and plastic bottles – the flotsam and jetsam of a discarded summer – floating in on the tide. Lorraine changed her denim jacket for an old sheepskin coat she had bought in a London flea market during her student days. In a press under the stairs she discovered a pair of furry moon boots that had once belonged to Celia. They were warm and comfortable, ideal for walking the beach.

"Just because we're living through a nightmare doesn't mean you have to dress like an orang-utan with bad taste in boots." Emily shuddered dramatically and covered her eyes when she saw the bilious shade of orange. "Don't you dare wear them to the art classes," she warned. "I'd hate anyone to think I'm descended from a monkey."

She left for Dublin at the end of the week. A weekend hill-walking trip was planned with her grandparents, the last one before winter set in. They had taken her on her first expedition when she was eight years old and she had regularly accompanied them since then.

After returning from the railway station Lorraine decided to walk the beach before commencing work in her studio. Despite not having made any efforts to publicise her whereabouts, she was beginning to receive commissions: one from a local county councillor and Celia's nephew, Eugene Murphy, had sent photographs of his wife, whose birthday was coming up soon.

Hobbs refrained from barking as she passed the farmyard gate. Was she becoming an insider at last, she wondered, climbing the stile onto the beach. Away from the shelter of the fuchsia hedgerows, the wind slapped against her face. She shoved her hands deeper into her pockets. Apart from Con riding his horse in the shallows, the beach was deserted. She reached the half-moon curve and sat in the shelter of the rocks. Already, the old boathouse above her was lost in shadows. The path around the embankment upon which it had been built was a short cut back to the lane but the way was a tangle of heather and briar.

A figure approached, head bent against the wind. At first she thought it was Brendan or Frank, checking for cattle that occasionally strayed onto the beach. She recognised Michael Carmody when he drew nearer and she stood up, surprised that he had not rung in advance to arrange a meeting.

"I called to the house and the studio." He raised his hand in greeting. "The woman in the farm told me I'd find you here. I wasn't sure I'd make it past her dog."

She smiled as they fell into step together and headed back up the beach. "Behind the bluster Hobbs is a shameless jelly."

"I'll take your word for it." Sand whipped along the shore, gritty on their skin. The tide was coming in fast, white horses rearing towards shore.

"When you weren't in touch I thought you'd changed your mind about the portrait."

He shook his head, raised his voice against the roar of collapsing waves. "I've been tied up for the past few weeks. An emergency."

"Had it to do with the phone call you received when you here?"

"Yes." He bent into the wind, looking younger than she remembered. Perhaps it was his hair. The unruly tresses had been neatly cut and he jerked the collar of his leather jacket over his ears as if he had not yet grown accustomed to the chill on his neck.

"You seemed very upset. Is everything all right again?"

"As well as can be expected." He made no further effort to explain the reason for his hasty departure and, as they walked in silence, she became increasingly conscious of her dishevelled appearance, the old sheepskin coat, the hairy orange boots that Emily so derided and which, suddenly, looked ridiculous as she padded along beside him.

"Excuse the boots." She skipped one foot before her then lowered it back to the sand. "They remind my daughter of an orang-utan whose legs have been severed above the shins." If he had laughed at her attempt at humour she would have relaxed but his disconcerting gaze never changed. He studied every move she made — as if each gesture must be observed then absorbed into his memory — yet he seemed detached from this scrutiny, as if his dark eyes viewed her from behind a wall of glass. Indigo clouds gathered above the sea. Kittiwakes screeched above them and the dull thud of hooves pounded against the hard-packed sand when Con galloped past.

"Would you consider having dinner with me later?" he asked. "I'm staying overnight in O'Callaghan's Hotel."

The directness of the invitation surprised her.

"No strings," he said when she hesitated. "Just your company for a few hours. There's something I'd like to discuss with you."

"If it's about cancelling Killian's portrait it's not necessary to offer dinner as an apology. Nor is it necessary if you're commiss-ioning me."

"It's nothing to do with his portrait. There's something else I want to talk about. Would it suit you if I collected you at eight?"

"Eight o'clock sounds fine," she replied. "I'll be ready."

Unable to decide what the occasion demanded, she finally settled on a dove-grey blouse and black evening trousers. Not quite sedate, not too dressy, business-like but softened by the sapphire pendant at her neck. Still no sign of her bracelet. She shrugged, closed the jewellery box, abruptly silencing the tinkling tune, and sat for a moment staring at her reflection. She tried to remember the last time a man had invited her out for a meal and was unable to see beyond Adrian's shoulders, his slim, graceful shoulders that had carefully sheltered her from the truth, from what she had chosen not to see. The pendant, cold against her throat, glittered back at her like a hard unflinching eye. She traced her middle finger over the oval stone, felt the delicate lines of the engraved silver casing into which it had been set. The impulse to snap the chain from her neck was resisted. She watched the jewel rise and fall. Her breath was shallow, too rapid, carrying the voices on the exhalation, the mocking refrain that laid siege upon her whenever she relaxed her guard … all those years of deceit, laughing behind her back, exchanging knowing looks, making excuses, telling lies, seeking hidden places to be together, filling the time in between with longing and lust, all done under her nose, literally under her nose, every day, the four of them working beneath the one roof, sharing cups of coffee, sometimes a drink in the evening before going home, skiing for a week in winter, holidays in France, Italy, Spain, New York, the map of the world at their disposal, and God knows what happened during those weeks, what moments were stolen while she, unaware, accepted, without thought, everything they told her …

Hobbs began to bark. Soon, Michael's car would enter the lane. The hawthorn, stripped bare of leaf and blossom, would lash his wing mirror and he would drive cautiously over the rutted ground, knowing how easily the tyres would puncture over the sharp, jutting stones. Today on the hard-packed sand he had stamped his footsteps next to her own, the double imprint creating an intimate pattern as it wove from the half-moon curve towards the stile. Soon they would sit opposite each other in O'Callaghan's restaurant and exchange tit-bits of information, reveal tantalising aspects of their lives. They both had a history, she was sure of it. These days it was difficult to mark the end of one's thirties without carrying some degree of baggage into the next decade. But maybe she was simply projecting her own misfortune onto him – Emily hurled the "projection" accusation at her often enough. Yet Michael Carmody carried grief like a scar in his eyes and she was curious to know why.

He braked his car outside. She sprayed perfume on her wrists and listened to the creak of the gate as it swung open. Once again she lifted the lid on the jewellery box. A mother-of-pearl bracelet that Donna had brought back as a holiday present from Italy lay among the chains and necklaces. She plucked it free and slipped it over her hand. The bell rang once. She turned from the mirror and walked to the front door. Night and the promise it contained settled stealthily around her.

"I've a vague recollection of coming here once with my aunt." He pulled out her chair and eased it under her. "Church benches for chairs? Back breakers, if I remember rightly."

"There used to be a fire burning over by that wine rack." Lorraine pointed towards the well-stocked wine cellar. "The musicians sat in the area that's now the kitchen."

"You appear to have total recall."

"Total. I loved Trabawn. I first began to paint here … and when I needed to begin my life again it offered me refuge."

"Refuge." He raised his eyebrows, regarded her, unsmiling. "What a strange word to use."

"Solace, refuge, escape, take your choice."

"Sounds like you were running away?"

"My mother called it the height of folly. My daughter still has to forgive me."

He leaned his elbows on the table, rested his chin on his hands. "And your husband?"

"He has no say in any decision I make. We're separated."

"When did you split up?"

"A while ago. I'd rather not discuss him, if you don't mind."

Angie, arriving with the menu and wine list, cast a speculative glance at Michael, no doubt remembering how she had photographed the family gathering on Emily's birthday night. Before taking their order she asked Lorraine's advice about a difficulty she was experiencing with one of her illustrations. After discussing it for a few minutes, she headed towards the kitchen.

"You run art classes?" he asked.

She smiled back at him. "I'm not sure how that came about. Careful manipulation, I suspect, but yes, I do."

His gaze rested on the pendant. "What an intricate design. Very beautiful."

"Thank you. A friend made it. He's a wonderful designer."

"It's an original piece then?"

"Yes. We were friends in college. There's no way I could afford his jewellery now."

She flinched when his fingers touched her throat, remembering how he had faced her in the lane, the wheel brace in his hand, her instinctive fear that he would harm her.

He rested the pendant in the palm of his hand and studied it. "Is it a companion piece for a bracelet?"

"It is, actually. Do you know Karl Hyland's work?"

"I've heard about it." He laid the pendant against her throat and sat back in his chair, his fingers braced against the edge of the table. A group of diners walked towards the table next to them, Sophie and her husband Joe among them. The Sudanese woman winked across at Lorraine, her shimmering yellow thoub attracting attention, as her vivid costumes always did, and Lorraine thought about the night in the slatted shed, the bellowing cow and how Sophie's t-shirt rode high up her back as she wrested the calf from its mother's heaving belly. She told him the story, laughing as she recalled Emily's delight when the new-born calf was named after her, a decision that triggered another round of texts to her friends in Dublin, and how her role as Cow Tail Handler changed in the telling to that of Calving Jack Manager. He joined in her laughter, an unexpected sound, and his face relaxed for the first time since his appearance on the beach. Glancing over at Sophie he shook his head as he tried to juxtapose the glamorous woman reading the menu with Lorraine's description of a farmer labouring to bring forth life in a cow shed.

Angie served their starters, smoked salmon for him, a fan of melon and avocado for Lorraine. He filled her glass again and ordered a second bottle. The rich red Chianti Classico reminded her of Tuscan holidays, vineyards on hillsides, avenues lined with statuesque cypress trees. She was aware that her cheeks were becoming hot from too much wine drunk too quickly yet she drained her glass, allowed him to fill it again.

When the plates had been removed, she rummaged under the chair for her shoulder bag, a shabby leather satchel, useful for carrying a myriad items. She removed a cardboard cylinder and handed it to him. "This is for you."

He weighed it in his hand, his expression puzzled as he removed the lid and drew out a canvas. Unable to hide his surprise he spread it across the table and studied the painting.

"You left one of Killian's photos behind," she explained. "I know it's not the portrait you want me to paint – he's much too young in it. But it was such a dramatic scene, the ferry stealing away between the lighthouses and the little boy on the pier, I couldn't resist painting him. Look upon it as a thank you for dinner."

His face flushed so violently she thought he was going to refuse to accept the painting. As the canvas slowly coiled back in on itself, he made no attempt to open it again. She had stepped over something, an invisible line he had placed between them, and his expression was once again charged with tension. When he finally spoke she could barely hear him.

"He seems so utterly alone."

She nodded in agreement. "I'm afraid it didn't turn out the way I intended. Killian is happy in the photograph yet the mood of the painting developed a life of its own once I started working on it. It's the first thing I've painted in a long time that gave me any satisfaction. I didn't mean to offend you but that appears to be what I've done."

He attempted to smile. The effort it took only increased her embarrassment.

"You surprised me, that's all. I wasn't expecting –" He rolled the painting up and pushed it back into the cylinder. "Thank you. It was a thoughtful gesture. Killian will appreciate it." His words were mechanical. They gave her no pleasure. The cylinder lying between them on the table irritated her. She wanted to sweep it out of sight and he too seemed disturbed by its presence, his gaze constantly flicking towards it and away again.

"It's a very assured painting," he said. "You're obviously familiar with the location."

The main courses had arrived but Lorraine had no appetite for the pasta and chicken dish she had chosen. She twirled tagliatelle on her fork but made no attempt to eat it. "My daughter flew a kite there once. A dog savaged it when it landed. Such hysterics. Poor little Emily."

"And afterwards?" He squeezed lemon over baked sole, twisted the sea-salt container until the particles fell like splinters of ice on his plate. "Did you ever go back?"

"No. We went there just the once. I had a feeling about the place … I didn't like it. Perhaps that's what influenced me when I was painting it. My daughter regularly accuses me of projecting my moods onto her. Perhaps I did the same with your photograph." She realised she was talking too fast, a vulnerable voice starved of attention, giddy from wine and nervous energy, but she seemed unable to stop, just as he seemed unable to hear her.

"You never went back?" The hint of steel in his voice when he repeated the question surprised her.

Puzzled, she laid down her fork, shook her head. "I prefer Howth or Dun Laoghaire if I want to walk the piers. Why do you ask?"

"I used to go there all the time when my son was younger."

"Why do you always sound as if you're hurting when you mention his name?"

He frowned, taken aback by her frankness. "Is it that obvious?"

"To me, yes. Does he live with you?"

"He never lived with me, at least, not in the sense you mean. I had visiting rights."

"Was it difficult being a single father?"

"We made it difficult, Jean and I. We treated him like a possession, not a child. He used to say he felt like a football being kicked from one end of the pitch to the other."

"What a terrible thing to hear. I'm still trying to adjust to being a single mother. Every time Emily mentions her father's name I hear myself snapping back. Sometimes, I don't recognise my own voice. Sometimes I don't even recognise myself. How do you get along with Killian now?"

"It's difficult."

"And his mother?"

He tipped the wine bottle towards her. Throughout the meal he had slowly sipped his wine yet insisted on topping up her glass as soon as the level dropped. "My track record is fairly dismal when it comes to relationships."

"Haven't you ever been in love?"

"Never."

"What kind of man *never* falls in love?"

"What kind of woman risks everything for love?" he replied.

"What do you mean?"

"Your paintings suggest great passion."

"*Painting Dreams* was a farce."

"Surely not. You were painting a dream of love."

"Yes, an illusion. That's why I came here. To kill the illusion." She excused herself and walked quickly towards the Ladies. She held her wrists under the cold-water tap. Her reflection stared back at her, bright-eyed, her flushed face, her hair tumbling over her forehead.

A woman glanced curiously at her before entering one of the cubicles. Lorraine was still standing in the same position when she emerged. "Are you all right, dear?" she asked.

"I'm fine, thanks." Her colour was beginning to recede. She combed her hair, searched in her bag for an elastic band and tied it back. Her hand shook slightly when she applied lipstick.

"You're the new art teacher." The woman washed her hands, held them under the dryer. "Noeleen Donaldson was telling me about the class. Are there any vacancies?"

"I'll take your number and ring you tomorrow." She scribbled the woman's number on the back of a cheque book and returned to the table.

He watched her anxiously as she approached. "You were gone so long. I was beginning to worry."

"Sorry. I met someone." She slung her bag across her shoulder. "Do you mind if I skip dessert, Michael? I've a busy day tomorrow and I'd like to go home now. You finish the bottle and relax. I'll call a taxi."

"Please don't go yet," he said. "I've upset you. I'm sorry."

"It's nothing to do with you. I'm just exhausted."

Angie, approaching their table with the dessert menus, looked surprised when Lorraine asked for her coat.

"Lovers' tiff?" she whispered, returning with it over her arm.

"Nothing that can't be sorted out with a good night's sleep." Lorraine slung the coat over her shoulders and walked quickly towards the exit. Taxis were occasionally parked outside the pub but tonight the road was empty. An elderly man in a luminous yellow jacket patrolled the car-park. He bade her goodnight, called her "Lorraine". She was becoming a recognisable figure in the village.

"I'm driving you home." Michael had followed her from the restaurant. When she tried to call a taxi he placed his hand over her mobile phone. Without another word she walked with him to his car.

A love song played on the radio. They listened in silence. Small talk seemed irrelevant. He concentrated on the road, headlights beaming into the turn at the top of the lane. Their silence became more abrasive as he drove slowly over the uneven surface. Drifting mist winged past the windows and the air was clammy when she stepped out of the car. She moved from the headlights into an inky space and would have stumbled on a tuft of grass if he had not steadied her.

At the front door she searched for her keys, unable to locate them in the jumble at the bottom of her bag. Impatiently, she pulled the zip down too far and the front panel fell open, spilling the contents across the path. The tinkle of a small cosmetic mirror breaking, the jangle of keys, loose coins falling. The sounds cut through the night like discordant music and she was reminded of Adrian's briefcase, the same hapless spewing of everything changing, changing forever. She cried out with annoyance and bent down to fumble in the dark.

"I've a torch in the car," he said.

The porch light automatically switched on before he could move.

"Leave it." Lorraine's hand closed over the keys. "I'll pick up the rest in the morning." Any poise, dignity, privacy seemed stripped from her, spread as randomly before him as the items littering the path.

He reached down and helped her to her feet. "You're trembling," he said. He made it sound like an accusation. "Tell me what I've done to displease you."

"Nothing. As I said already, I'm tired. If you want to discuss the portrait, phone me and we'll come to some arrangement. Thank you for a lovely evening."

Before he could reply she opened the door and closed it firmly behind her. She leaned against it, listened to his footsteps on the path. His car door slammed. She waited for him to drive away. The minutes passed. She could call him back. Her heart shook with reckless yearnings. I want his hands on my body, his lips against my mouth, she thought, and bit down hard on the words, shocked by the response he had aroused in her. She could call him back and he would come. She knew it as surely as the night tide was flowing over sand, eroding footprints and leaving in their place the undulating possibilities of new beginnings. The dog howled, a demented werewolf howl, as if he sensed the turbulence of her thoughts. Finally, the headlights switched on. The engine gave a low growl. The dog continued to howl.

CHAPTER THIRTY-FIVE

Brahms Ward
6 a.m.

Janice thinks I'm crazy coming here so early. Well, ordinarily she would, but she's had a row with her fiancé, something to do with the main event and the afters. She's comfort eating a chocolate bar in the nurse's station. Fruit and Nut. I refused a chunk. Claimed I wasn't hungry. Something in my voice must have registered and she finally snapped herself back from tulle and ivory lace.

"You look like something the cat dragged backwards through a hedge," she said. "Long night, was it?"

She's right. It was a long night. But the roads were empty of traffic. I need to get my head together and Brahms Ward is where reality bites deep and hard. She stole a march on me, Killian. Something opened inside my head when she gave me your portrait. She stared at me across the table, her eyes blue and troubled, sensing but not understanding my confusion. She's used to people responding with pleasure when she presents them with her paintings. What's the matter with me? Why couldn't I be straight with her? She gesticulated when she spoke, made language with her hands, and she spun a funny story about cows and a black woman, who sat opposite us dressed in brilliant colours and a robe that rippled like sails every time she moved. How long since you heard me laugh? Her hair falls red to her shoulders and would, I believe, spark if I touched it. Why couldn't I say it? Come with me to the Brahms Ward ... see what you have done ... see my son. I lied to her from the beginning. Each word we speak swamps me deeper.

I count facts, indisputable bullet points. She owns a silver car. She hides in a lane. She left a husband. She calls Trabawn a refuge. She has a daughter whom she loves yet removed from all that was familiar. She wore a pendant at her throat. It all added up until I looked into her eyes. Sapphire blue, guileless, not cruel or indifferent, which is how they should look ... beguiling eyes ... and her mouth, wide, but not too wide with strong white teeth that match its generous shape. Her wrists were bare. Do you get the picture, Killian? See what I see? Maybe I'm right. Maybe I'm wrong. Maybe I'm crazy. A car in shadow, snatched sounds, Bozo's story; his accusations seemed ludicrous until I drove away and removed myself from her spell.

I wanted to kiss her mouth. Her strong wide mouth. She hesitates before she smiles, afraid that if she laughs she will also cry. How do I know this? Don't ask me to explain. I should have spoken then. I should go back there now and wrench the truth from her. What's the matter with me, Killian? I betray you every time I think of her.

Kisses on eyes ... drowning eyes ... yellow eyes ... yellow eyes ... headlights ... daisy screens ... hands on sheet ... hands on sheet ... hospital!

CHAPTER THIRTY-SIX

Mount Subasio, illuminated with strategic spotlights, rose above them in magnificent splendour.

"Disneyland, eat your heart out." Adrian stared in disbelief at the turrets and the flag which slapped a persistent tattoo against the flag-pole.

"Keep your opinions to yourself," Virginia warned as they mounted the steps. In the past she had attended a number of Andrea's soirées with Ralph and knew they provided an excellent networking environment. She was aware that Andrea's desire for publicity was an important factor in their friendship and Virginia had no objections to being used. Use and be used in turn. It was a fair exchange – and also a significant one. The latest invitation addressed to Virginia and Adrian meant they were now being accepted as a couple in their own right.

Drinks and canapés were served in the long drawing room. The view from the windows dropped towards the distant lights of the city but it was Lorraine's portrait hanging above the mantelpiece upon which the guests fixed their attention. Adrian refused to acknowledge its existence. Not an easy thing to do as

Andrea, flattered by the comments from her guests, coyly preened herself in front of it at every opportunity.

"An impressive piece of work, wouldn't you agree?" Bill Sheraton moved to Virginia's side and nodded upwards. Was he enjoying her discomfort, relishing the incongruity of Lorraine's invisible but dominant presence in their midst?

"It's one of Lorraine's most sensitively executed pieces," she replied. He had the defensive antennae of a self-made millionaire and would be quick to catch the slightest hint of mockery in her voice. Lorraine's portraits had always carried a raw energy and originality. Her focus had been on discovering something unique, a hitherto unnoticed feature or expression, the angle of a head that added a new dimension to the sitter's personality. But this was a painting of plastic people. She wondered if its very perfection was Lorraine's way of mocking her own work, of proving how inconsequential it had become.

"Are you satisfied with it?" she asked.

"Andrea certainly is."

"And you?"

"Technically, it's perfect. What more can I say?"

She knew he hated it.

"What a wonderful study of Lorcan." She felt compelled to comment on the handsome young man staring down at her from the wall, his usually dour young face decisive yet relaxed, his gaze forceful.

"Do you really think so?" Bill studied it carefully. "I'm hoping she saw something in him that I've never managed to catch."

"It's an astute observation." Virginia lied graciously. "I've always found him to be a most charming young man."

"In that case Adrian should have no difficulty taking him on. I've employed my son every summer since he was fifteen and he's never shown a blind bit of interest in what I do. Now, suddenly he wants to go into advertising. I'm anxious to see him settled with people I can rely on."

"Of course, if that's your wish, Bill." She steadied her smile, allowed it to reach her eyes. "But are you sure —"

"Absolutely positive. I suggest he starts next Monday."

"The sooner the better, Bill. I'm sure Adrian will be delighted to take him under his wing."

"There's no such thing as a free lunch." Virginia made the announcement as she undressed for bed. "Bill expects you to take Lorcan into the agency."

"Shit!"

"My sentiments exactly. But I had the good sense to hide my feelings."

"Hiding your feelings is a piece of performance art with you, Virginia." Adrian sounded drunk, morosely so, his face gaunt as he turned around to face her.

"If having good manners and being courteous is performance art then maybe you should consider studying it," she snapped back. "Was it necessary to be so rude to everyone?"

"I wasn't being rude."

"What would you call staring out the window for most of the night and refusing to engage in conversation?"

"I wasn't aware that I was there in the role of a performing dog."

She pulled the sheet to her chin and tried to hide her annoyance. "No, you were there to network, make contacts, do business. Advertising is not just about ideas, Adrian. It's about selling that vision to people who make decisions. I saw Bill watching you. He doesn't miss a trick and now that Lorcan's joining the company he'll have first hand knowledge of all that's going on."

"Can you really see his obnoxious brat lasting more than a week in the business?"

"He could surprise us. I spoke to him at the end of the night. He seems keen and he's got some interesting ideas."

"I thought you said advertising was not just about *ideas*."

"Why won't you be honest and admit the real reason you're so upset?" She switched off the bedside lamp. Somehow, it seemed easier to talk about Lorraine in the dark. "You fell apart when you saw that portrait."

"You never told me he'd commissioned her."

"It was a while ago. I'd forgotten."

"You forget easily."

"Meaning what, exactly?"

He lay silently beside her.

"Don't block me out, Adrian. I want to know what's going on in your head. Are you worried about Ralph?"

"Fuck Ralph! I'm thinking about the lad ..."

Once again, he was forcing her to walk over the same old ground. No matter how hard they tried to forget, the accident cast a long shadow over them, creating panic where none should exist. "I thought we agreed not to discuss him any more?"

"The car could still be traced. With forensics they can tell by paintwork, even glass. We don't know what clues we left behind."

"For a start, it was Lorraine's car. Even if they manage to trace her to Trabawn, all she has to do is tell them she was in New York."

The car had been repaired in a garage where a mechanic, gruff and overworked, took Adrian at his word when he blamed vandals for the damage to the bonnet and the broken glass. Their dread that the boy would die had not been realised. Otherwise they would have read it in the papers – and Virginia read them every day, skimmed them from cover to cover, checking headlines, news in brief, any items that might have repercussions for them. She reassured him, reminded him they were safe, so much time had passed, and, gradually, heard the tension ease from his voice.

"You're so much in control, I envy you," he said.

"Why not kiss me and see how much control I have then?" She was determined to bring an end to the discussion.

It was over quickly. Perhaps it was the darkness that separated them even as their bodies joined and moved together. They always made love with the lights on, open to each other, taking delight in giving and receiving, in watching the passion reflected in their eyes, but now he pressed her face into the pillows and came into her from behind, thrusting deep, and she felt his tension kick into a swift, frantic orgasm that brought relief but no satisfaction to her. He fell asleep immediately.

She listened to the voices. At first they had whispered so softly they were almost inaudible but they were growing louder, more distinct, imitating a grotesque parody of her father's philandering. *"My mummy told me if I was goody that she would buy me a rubber dolly. But when I told her I kissed a soldier she wouldn't buy me a rubber dolly."* Outside Sonya's window the little girls clapped hands and chanted, and in the room where Virginia could not go she heard the puppy sounds. The clock with the cat's face ticked on the mantelpiece and the coloured glass hearts jingled from the ceiling – but nothing sounded as sweet as the canary singing all alone in her cage, like her little throat would burst wide open and all the notes would pour out, spilling downwards, tumbling one after the other onto Virginia's lap. Sonya was a secret, a safe and sound secret that must never be told. Except for Lorraine. In Trabawn she told her cousin. Lying in the darkness of the caravan, she felt the secret lift, as if a hand had released a tight grip on her forehead, and they giggled so hard they had to drink water from the wrong side of the glass to stop the hiccups.

CHAPTER THIRTY-SEVEN

The phone rang constantly. Meg Ruane, home from New York. The county councillor enquiring about the progress of his portrait. Emily's friends from Dublin, demanding progress reports on Emily the calf. Sally Jones rang. She was back from New York and living in Wicklow. She wanted Lorraine to visit her group and facilitate a weekend workshop. Ralph phoned one afternoon when she was walking the beach and left a message on the machine. "Hey there, fellow traveller, how's life in the under-world? Sorry I missed you. Just wanted to know how you're getting on. Maybe I'll drop in on Trabawn one of these days. No red carpet when I call, just a welcome on the mat. Hugs to Emily."

He seemed in high spirits when she returned his call, teasing her about the farmers she was seducing and asking questions about her art group. His arrival back to Ireland had been a surprise but not his decision to set up his own agency, which, he assured her, was off to a flying start. He tossed company names into the conversation, new accounts he had acquired. She recognised some of the names. He was poaching clients from Adrian.

When she made this accusation, he said, "I don't have to poach. It's as easy as shooting fish in a barrel." He promised to call to Trabawn as soon as time allowed. She handed the phone to Emily who launched into a description about the birthing process of calves.

Michael Carmody never rang. No message on her answering machine, no sudden sighting on the beach. The emotions she had experienced that night disturbed her. She was unable to banish him from her mind. For moments at a time she would stop what she was doing and stand motionless, picturing his intense expression, the hint of underlying sexuality about his mouth, his enigmatic eyes that never stopped probing her face. His footsteps ringing on the garden path had trampled against the grief and anger she had carried to Trabawn, trampled over every rational thought until all that remained was her need to see him again.

Eugene Murphy called to collect his wife's birthday present. He shook his head when Lorraine showed him around the house, obviously impressed by what he saw. "I have to admit I thought you were cracked when you told me you wanted to buy the aunty's old house. But you're doing a splendid job."

"I only give the orders. Con and Brendan do the work."

"They're a good pair of workers, all right. But I can see the weight of your hand everywhere. I'm in the business of renovating old houses in Dublin. I'm looking for someone with a bit of flair to advise me on colour schemes. You could be right up my alley. Would you be interested?"

"Why not." The idea appealed to her.

"Ring me when you're next in Dublin. We'll meet up and I'll show you what I'm about."

She accepted his business card, waved him off. What he proposed was different, a challenge. His observations pleased her. The rooms were beginning to take on an identity. Echoes no longer rebounded from the walls. The ghost of a wrinkled woman in a sparkling hairnet sat easily among her new surroundings, keeping watch with her red-eyed dog, cats and donkeys.

She drove to Wicklow and met the members of Sally's art group. They watched slides of the *Painting Dreams* collection and Lorraine entered whole-heartedly into the heated debate that followed. How could they believe a word she uttered, she wondered. The woman who had so confidently painted the languorous, sensuous images no longer existed. When the workshop ended on Sunday afternoon, she drove to Drumcondra and had lunch with her parents. They discussed Christmas, an insurmountable wall that somehow or other had to be breached.

She would drive to Dublin on Christmas Eve. They would celebrate the season as they always did, follow the same engrained traditions. Only Adrian and his father, who had started visiting the Cheevers for Christmas dinner after the death of his wife, would be missing from around the table.

She left as soon as lunch ended, anxious to get as much of the road as possible behind her before darkness set in. Traffic was heavy along the quays. Sunday shopping and the hint of an approaching Christmas had swelled the ranks of consumers anxious to shop early and shop often. Eyes averted, she passed Blaide House and continued onwards until she came to a block of apartments with an arched entry and a sign, "Bellscourt Plaza", etched above it. She wondered which apartment Michael Carmody occupied. A motorcyclist swerved in front of her, causing her to clamp too heavily on the brake. The engine stalled and an irritated driver honked as she tried and failed to restart the car. She lifted her hand in apology and turned the ignition, relieved when the engine started immediately. Rain added to the grey dreariness of the streets and the pedestrians – flitting amongst the traffic, heads down under umbrellas – seemed possessed of a manic death wish.

She braked at traffic lights. The apartments were no longer in view. She clenched her hands on the steering wheel until the lights changed and she could move forward again. Quickly, before she could change her mind, she drove into an empty parking slot and located his business card in her bag. She was almost breathless as she tapped out his number. After four rings she lost courage and was about to abandon the call when he answered. Unable to think of any reason why she should ring him on a Sunday afternoon, she clicked off her mobile and flung it towards the passenger seat. Ready to be plucked and dumped by the first man who pays attention to me, she thought. To be so vulnerable shamed her. She jerked violently when the phone rang.

"Why did you hang up?" His voice rushed into her ear. He must have pressed the return call command.

"The connection broke." She attempted to lie with conviction. "I was driving past your apartment on my way back to Trabawn when I —"

Curtly, he interrupted her. "Where are you now?"

"Not far from here. I shouldn't have bothered you."

"I'm glad you did. Why don't you come to the apartment? Have something to eat before you continue your journey … Lorraine, can you hear me? Are you still on the line?"

"Yes —"

"Then please come. I'd like to see you again."

He was dressed in jeans and an open-necked shirt, the sleeves rolled up above his elbows. From the state of his disorganised work station, it was obvious he had been working when she rang. The computer was still on and a reference book was open beside it. A casual jacket hung from the back of the chair. It was the only untidy area in the living-room, which was small but self-contained, a masculine space, one wall dedicated to music and video tapes, another to books. The paintings on the walls were mainly abstracts, original works. She recognised some of the names; others were unknown. The kitchen was also tidy, as if he spent little time there, the gleaming chrome unmarked by smears or cooking stains. A beef casserole had been simmering in the oven. Steam gushed from the dish when he lifted the lid and tossed chopped parsley over the sauce. Baked potatoes topped with sour cream completed the meal, which, served with the minimum of fuss, tasted delicious.

She discussed the workshop and was surprised, once again, by his knowledge of her career. Remembering her reaction to his questions the last time they were together, she was more cautious in her answers yet, as they continued talking, she began to relax, stimulated by his interest and curious also about his own work. He brought cheese, crackers and sliced apples to the table. She drank water, having refused his earlier offer of wine. It was getting late. An evening drive awaited her yet she was reluctant to leave. When he was in the kitchen making coffee she noticed the painting of his son, which he had had framed in pale wood and hung on the wall. He returned to the table with the cafetière and plunged the lid, filling the room with the aroma of fresh coffee. She made no effort to move from the painting and he, glancing across to see what had occupied her attention, came over to stand beside her.

"I waved goodbye to my mother from that vantage point." He nodded towards the pier.

"You waved goodbye?" She lifted her eyebrows, turned to stare at him. "How final that sounds. Didn't she come back to you?"

"She was killed in a car crash a few days later."

Shocked, she grasped his arm in an instinctive gesture of comfort. "My God, Michael! I'm so sorry."

"It was a long time ago."

"What age were you?"

"Seven years old."

"So young to be without a mother. You must have been devastated."

"I suppose so. It's difficult to remember how I reacted."

"Had you brothers or sisters?"

Dismissively, he shook his head. "No. Just myself and my aunt. I lived with her until I went to university." He was relaying facts, not demanding sympathy, and his arm, feathered with fine dark hairs, had stiffened under her touch, muscle and sinew clenched inwardly against her.

Her hand dropped awkwardly to her side. From the window she could see over the Liffey. The bridges, spanned by spotlights, arched across the river, bearing traffic and people, all of them moving towards an ultimate destination but she, standing too closely to Michael Carmody, had no idea what she was doing in his apartment or why the atmosphere between them could change so rapidly. She remained silent, unwilling to break through his reserve, and he, as if picking up on her thoughts, answered the unspoken question.

"I never knew my father. He left my mother before I was born."

"Did you ever try to trace him?"

He rasped his hand across his chin, two days' growth of

stubble, she guessed, an abrasive shadow as dark as the hairs on his arms. "My aunt said he was a ship that passed in the night. To find him I'd need a compass and a shipping chart."

She felt no inclination to laugh, even when he did, and his face in profile, sharp as a cameo, did not reflect his amusement. From the wall, the boy in the painting seemed to breathe with the same loneliness. She remembered how connected she had been to the photograph when she had pinned it to her easel and begun to paint. Intuitively, she had responded to a force she had once taken for granted and then abandoned, no longer trusting in its subliminal nature. But that night, as Michael Carmody sped eastwards towards whatever trauma awaited him at home, she had tapped into an inexplicable energy and allowed it to take possession of her. She had projected onto canvas the yearnings of a young boy who had lost something too precious to be expressed in words and, in the essence of her painting, he had recognised himself.

"How long have you been waiting on the pier, Michael?" She asked the question gently.

His voice was steady when he replied, "As long as I can remember."

She moved into his arms, or perhaps it was the other way around, and when their lips opened in the heat of that first kiss, it was everything she had anticipated, hunger, longing, relief. She welcomed the harsh scratch of stubble against her skin, his taut strength pressed rigidly against her, and she thought … how differently men kiss … remembering lazy weekend mornings and passion-filled nights and how those interludes became less and less, gradually turning into brief, mechanical performances, snatched when neither she nor Adrian could sleep or as a means of breaking the ever-lengthening silences between them. No more … no more. She wanted him to force such memories from her body, to assault her heart until it beat to a new rhythm.

He wove his fingers through her hair, the palms of his hands caressing her head then curving under her chin, along her neck and shoulders, pressing into the small of her back and she bent into him, willing him onwards. She heard him moan as he lifted her sweater and covered the swell of her breasts, her nipples puckering like ripe berries under his fingertips. Their kisses became more demanding, bruising, pleasure flaring in a hot, almost painful spasm when she unbuttoned his shirt and reached downwards in an intimate searching movement, the sensation of touch so electrifying that she uttered a low surrendering cry against his mouth. Swamped in desire that demanded only one outlet, he forced her against the wall and she was lifted upwards and towards him, her body pliant as clay that he would mould into his own flesh.

Her shoulder knocked against the painting. The wooden frame cracked when it struck the floor. He wrenched himself from her, held her trembling at arm's length. When he turned away from her, there was nothing to suggest that only seconds before they had held each other with such wanton fervour. It could have been a dream, an out-of-time experience, imagination. There was blood on his lip. She must have bitten deep into the soft flesh. Her own lips were swollen, tender.

He bent down and picked up the broken frame. He stared at the painting. "You've absolutely no idea what you've done to me." His voice was a monotone. Anger, shame, fear, grief – she tried to read his mind but he offered her no explanation. "I want you to leave now. Please go."

She grabbed her coat from the back of the armchair and walked quickly past him. Shock had given way to an excruciating embarrassment. Without looking at him she stepped into the narrow hallway and walked swiftly towards the elevator.

"This is a ludicrous situation." She heard his footsteps behind her. "I need to explain something –"

"Leave me alone." The doors of the elevator opened. Furiously, she pushed his hand aside when he attempted to prevent her entering. He mentioned his son's name but now was not the time to discuss anything, least of all his reasons for coming to Trabawn. Nothing could ease the situation except escape yet still he persisted, attempting some futile excuse, his voice grating against her ears.

"There are no explanations necessary. I simply want you to leave me alone." She stepped into the lift and pressed the descend button. Her anger clashed like steel against the confined space and he, seeing her distress and realising the impossibility of explaining anything under such circumstances, made no further effort to detain her.

Emily was asleep in the farmhouse when she arrived home. "Leave her where she is," Noeleen advised. "I'll see she catches the school bus in the morning." She offered to make tea and, when Lorraine refused, insisted on walking back to the house with her. "I know this lane like the back of my hand," she said. "It's all too easy to stumble in the dark."

At the gate, Lorraine impulsively hugged her. "You're a good neighbour, Noeleen. I'd be lost without you."

"Indeed you wouldn't. You'd manage well enough on your own if you had to. You're a survivor, Lorraine."

"Is that how I come across to you?" She was surprised by her neighbour's observation and wondered what Noeleen would think if she had seen her earlier. The memory made her blush and experience once again the humiliation of his inexplicable rejection.

"It's not how you come across. It's what you are." The older woman lifted her hand in farewell and was soon swallowed in the darkness.

Alone in the house, Lorraine undressed and slid between the covers. She was still awake when he rang, as she had known he would before the night was over.

"I told you not to contact me again." She forced herself to speak calmly.

"I wanted to check that you'd arrived safely home."

"Obviously, I have."

"What happened this evening –"

"Yes?"

"I was afraid of what I would do … what I wanted to do … if you'd stayed."

His voice vibrated down the line, lifted goose-pimples on her arms. Kisses that awakened sleeping princesses belonged to fairy stories with happy endings. All his kisses had done was awaken in her the realisation that there was nothing to prevent her pitching headlong into uncertainty and future pain.

"Why do you hate me, Michael? You hardly know me. How *dare* you hate me."

The silence that followed expanded like elastic. She allowed it to stretch, her shoulders raised as if she expected it to snap and snarl back against her face.

"I don't hate you, Lorraine," Finally he spoke. "Believe me, what I feel for you is anything but hatred." His denial sounded genuine yet she heard the skipped beat in his voice, as if his words had to be carefully weighed and considered before being uttered.

"Then what? What do you want from me?"

"Peace of mind. I need to understand –"

"Understand? What's there to understand? Right now, all I know is that you don't make me feel good about myself. I can't cope with ambiguity – or lies. They destroyed me once. I *won't* allow it to happen a second time."

She hung up before he could reply. Her shoulders slumped as if strings had broken. Distracted, all traces of sleep gone, she tried to silence her fevered thoughts. But the heat of his desire was in her veins and there was nothing she could do to still its course. So long – so long. Her hand glided over the curves of her body, hesitantly, as if she was exploring an unfamiliar terrain. His face was above her and she, drowning in his eyes, sank deeply into the pleasure that forced its way through her numbed fingers.

CHAPTER THIRTY-EIGHT

Brahms Ward
Midnight

I lost you once on Dollymount Strand. You must remember the time? We were building a sandcastle. I dug deeper into the trench and you wandered off in search of shells to decorate the ramparts. I didn't realise you'd gone. One minute you were by my side and then you were swallowed in the crowd. I ran among the families, filled with terror, horrifying visions. I looked towards the sea. Far out, a cormorant crested the tide and changed before my eyes into your small lost body. I saw you sliding under the waves, swiftly, silently drawn out to sea.

Minutes later, I found you. Your bucket was full of shells, tears still on your cheeks. I carried you back to our castle but children had been there before us. They had jumped on our creation, trampled it into indistinguishable grains of sand. There was nothing to prove that, only a short while before, a magnificent fortress had stood solidly on the spot.

I haven't the words to accuse her. They are grains slipping through my fingers. Have you the slightest idea what I'm talking about, Killian? You lie there oblivious, your chest rising falling, your eyelids blinking. I can't stand it ... do you hear me? I can't *stand* it.

She thinks I hate her. What could I say? I hate what I believe, or once believed, still believe, don't know, going crazy out of my head, don't know. How could I hold her close and believe she has a heart of stone? It has to stop … *stop*. Love and hate, Killian. How can two sides of a damaged coin have so much power?

One two three coins in a fountain … clinking coins, pennies from heaven … clinkity-clink … jingle-jangle … one two three … clink-clink … stole from wallet … purse … bracelet … Lorcan wait …

CHAPTER THIRTY-NINE

Lorcan had made his entry into Sheraton & Strong Advertising dressed in jeans and a skin-tight top with *I'm It* printed across the front. After a heated discussion with Adrian on the dress code of the company, he started wearing a suit but his attitude remained as insolent as ever. Adrian's name was condensed to "Ado" and he continually referred to Virginia as "Virgin", a form of address usually accompanied by a leer.

"He's an insufferable little cockroach." Adrian complained constantly about him. "With a bit of luck he'll get bored and crawl back under a stone again."

But Lorcan had no intention of crawling anywhere. He shoved his ideas under Adrian's nose, demanding his attention, and sulked when told to perform the most basic office functions. One afternoon, Virginia discovered him sitting on Adrian's chair, swivelling aimlessly from side to side as he chatted on the phone to Marianne Caulfield. At least she assumed "Cauliflower" was the young film-maker who had attended the charity auction. Lorcan was making a date with her. Clubs and pubs, thought Virginia, until the words "prayer meeting" were mentioned. Lorcan, a born-again Christian! The reformed addict's final refuge. With an effort she kept a straight face. Becoming aware of her presence, he abruptly ended his conversation but made no apology or excuse for invading his employer's office.

When asked if Adrian was at a meeting, he replied, "If you say so, Virgin, then I guess that's where he is."

The temptation to wrench him bodily from the chair and shake the cheeky grin from his face was resisted with an effort. No employee would have dared behave with such insolence towards Ralph, whose new company was making an impact. Lots of media attention; he had even featured on a television debate about ethics in advertising, sincerely flashing his white teeth and phoning Virginia afterwards to ask if she had noticed the wink he gave her. The familiar wink from his Sulphuric Acid days when she was dancing before the stage, knowing that he meant, "You think this is music, bitch. Wait till I get you into my bed – then we'll really dance."

He had acquired the Ormond Pharmaceuticals account, as Virginia had feared, blatantly poaching Sheraton & Strong's most lucrative client. Adrian had stormed into her office waving a newspaper that carried a report on the deal in the business section and flung it on her desk. "Let's see what happens when Brian Ormond discovers there isn't a creative bone in his body."

"Ralph nurtured your talent for long enough," she retorted, furious that her suspicions were being realised. This was not the first account that had transferred from Adrian to Ralph.

"Nurtured my talent?" His head shot back, his shoulders squared up to her. "Jesus Christ, Virginia, you make me sound like his fucking protégé. We were partners, remember? I gave one hundred per cent to that company."

"Then why aren't you doing the same now?" She was dismayed at how quickly their conversation had degenerated into an argument. Such thin ice. How easily it cracked under the slightest provocation. "You're all over the place since Ralph pulled out. I don't blame Bill Sheraton for being anxious. He thinks –"

"Have you been discussing my business with him again?"

"Of course not." Virginia placed the newspaper in a shredder and watched the insufferably smug head and shoulders shot of her husband reduced to slivers.

"So what are you saying?"

"The last time we spoke he mentioned Lorcan. He thinks you

should pay more attention to him and you'd be wise to keep Bill on-side. As long as he believes his son is settling into the agency and taking on responsibilities, he won't ask too many questions about poached accounts."

A frown settled between his eyes. "I've enough on my mind without listening to lectures on how to run my *own* company."

"Why are we arguing, Adrian? I'm only trying to help."

"You're smothering me, Virginia. Every time I turn around you're behind me, complaining about something or other. I never asked you to approach Bill Sheraton. I had my own plans but you overrode them. And now you're meeting him behind my back, discussing *my* personal business affairs. How do you think that makes me feel?"

"Smothering you? How exactly am I doing that?"

"Every time I try and talk about it ... the accident ... you shut me up."

"What's that got to do with anything? I was under the impression we were discussing a company that's in danger of going to the wall if you don't pull yourself together."

"I can't ... don't you understand? You won't allow me to *feel* anything. He was so young. Someone's son. He could have been Emily."

"But he *isn't* Emily. And if his parents cared that much about him, why was he down on the pier breaking into cars and robbing whatever he could lay his hands on? How many other cars had he damaged that night before he came to us?"

"What's that got to do with anything? We're the ones who drove away and left him to die." He put up his hand to silence her protests and repeated, "We left him to die."

"We thought he was dead. You felt his pulse. You believed it too."

"How the hell was I to know? Jesus Christ!" He placed his hands over his face. "If we hadn't been together –"

"If you're blaming me for this, you'd better state it loud and clear so that we can deal with it. Do you hear me?" Her voice gained strength. "I refuse to hide like some guilty accusation at the back of your mind."

"Don't you feel any sense of guilt?"

"I'm not like you, Adrian. I don't carry guilt like a knife in my side. It was an accident, a tragedy that should never have happened. But it did and we can't keep beating each other up over it."

"He's on my shoulders, Virginia. I can't shake him loose." He left her office, trailing his fears across her floor. Where had it gone, the delicious anticipation that had sustained them for so many years? She had given up everything for him. In return he had laid his conscience like a rock around her neck.

She dreamed of wolves. They prowled above her in the dark attic and flung their bodies against the trapdoor. She listened to her father. He shouted, demanded that the wolves be released. Her mother's voice pleaded but he refused to listen. None of God's creatures should be imprisoned. He mounted the ladder to the attic and the wolves sprang free above Virginia's head. Such beautiful, sleek creatures, not like the hungry wolves she saw in pictures. Their thick fur shimmered. Their tongues hung loose. Saliva trailed from their mouths as they leapt down the stairs, leapt joyously out through the open window towards freedom.

The dream forced her awake and into the hot airless atmosphere of the apartment. She was used to space, a house with a driveway and tall chimneys, a garden that smelled of lilac and lavender, not chemicals from some polluted and noxious factory that wafted unpleasantly across the bay. No matter what she used, aromatic oil burners, perfume, scented candles, fresh flowers, nothing seemed to eradicate the fumes. She had complained to the interior designer, to the painters and to the agent who sold them the apartment – but no one seemed capable of solving the problem, or even admitting there was a problem.

She switched on the bedside lamp, angled the glow so that it did not disturb Adrian. The dream clung to her like a cold sweat. She entered a small room that they had designated as a home office. The computer was still on. Tropical fish swam across the screen, trailing bubbles, weaving between fronds of seaweed.

Josephine had rung in the afternoon and said, "Truth is stranger than friction." Sometimes, Virginia imagined her mother lying awake at night constructing proverbial distortions to inflict upon her family. On this occasion, she had sounded quite elated. "Guess who came to dinner last night?"

"Edward and his adorable mob?"

"Much and all as I adore Edward's family, I do not suffer little children when I have a table set for two. Guess again."

"Mother, I'm preparing for an important meeting. I've no time for guessing games."

"Your father."

"You can't be serious?" Virginia almost dropped the phone. "Dinner? After all this time?"

"Time is a great sealer, young lady. I'm lonely. So is he, as it happens. We have a lot of catching up to do."

Last year she had rung and announced, "All good things come to those who hate. Guess who's dead?"

Sonya's body had been cremated and her ashes scattered. Ashes to ashes – dust to dust. Virginia had sent apologies for her non-attendance at the funeral. Pressures of work. Her father sent her a memorial card. Sonya and her rabbit teeth smiling from a stamp-sized photograph. Resting safely in the arms of the Lord. And now, it seemed, the old enemies were reunited. Time – the great sealer.

Virginia opened the balcony doors and stepped outside. Faintly in the distance, she heard a siren, an ambulance on an emergency run or a police car chasing joy riders. The night sounds of a city had become familiar to her. What had brought her to this stage, sleepless, haunted by dreams and imaginary fumes that attacked her throat at the most unexpected moments? Her beautiful house was razed to the ground. She could see it so clearly in her mind, the view from her bedroom window, the perfectly restored cornicing in the hallway, the leisurely dinner parties in the long dining room, all gone, destroyed by a property developer who was building luxury apartments on the site. She had driven to Howth for a last look. The garden was overrun with machinery. Ugly purple hoardings surrounded the site.

"Can I do something for you, Missus?" One of the builders had stepped down from a digger and advanced towards her on mud-caked boots. Suddenly, seeing a gaping hole where a silver birch once grew, she was filled with fury. Not with Ralph. They had divided their assets between them and he had been free to sell or not. The anger that spilled from her as she watched a digger claw into the foundations had been directed towards Adrian. He should never have allowed Lorraine room for suspicion. Her evidence was slight, her fears begging to be eased, denied, soothed. But he had fallen apart, the secret on the pier bearing down on him, making him incapable of denying his wife's furious accusations.

Ralph would have withstood the pressure, protected her as she would have protected him.

"You're the only one who will ever see into my soul," he said, soon after Jake died, and handed her the power to penetrate, as delicately as a geologist, each brittle, aggressive strata, chipping away at his tough exterior until he belonged entirely to her. She had seen the estate where he grew up. High-rise council flats, walls covered in graffiti, boarded-up shop windows. The middle child in a brawling working-class family, so different from Edward with his studious glasses and polished accent, and different also from her father, an armchair terrorist, who took the English shilling and muttered vengeance on the Crown. Ralph would have been a real terrorist. Under different circumstances he would have handled a rifle instead of a microphone. He had been the rock upon which she had dashed herself, knowing that his love was strong enough to withstand the demands she would place upon their marriage.

She shivered. Winter was upon them. Over a year now since it happened. Time did not stand still for anyone.

CHAPTER FORTY

Large wooden frames were stacked against the walls of the studio and a number of canvases were in varying stages of completion. The road-works painting was a configuration of bent and crouching figures. The plane trees on the pavement outside her parents' house stood still and black against the sky and the woman in her luminous jacket, her feet in hulking boots and thickly ribbed ankle socks, moved backwards in the spotlight flare, separated from the men yet linked to them by the cable she was unwinding. Lorraine had painted other women. Sophie, her face split in an exhausted grin, a new-born calf between her hands, all slime and glistening life. A canvas titled *Dancing at the Crossroads* revealed the village hall, where middle-aged women in cardigans and sensible shoes danced the salsa. But the painting which attracted Ralph's attention was the one she had painted of bats in flight and a woman watching from the window, a spilled glass of wine on the ledge.

He had arrived in Trabawn with an encyclopaedia on horses for Emily and a bouquet of roses for Lorraine. She had prepared a seafood pasta dish which, after he had toured the studio, they ate in front of the fire. Music thumped from Emily's room, where she had gone to study after regaling Ralph with horsy stories and the daily antics of Emily the calf.

He glanced towards the ceiling. "Who would have believed it? Emily a culchie."

"She's more contented, especially since she made peace with Adrian."

"And you?"

"I'm managing fine."

"By running backwards instead of forwards. Trabawn is a picture postcard, Lorraine, and you're hiding in it. You let them run you out of town."

To return to a place where so much happy memory was invested must seem like the act of a crazed woman, she thought. Ralph would never appreciate her reasons for coming here and she was only now beginning to realise why she had made such a decision. Trabawn with its high sand dunes and teenage yearnings was where a cruel triangle began. She was setting her own imprint on the shifting sands of deceit.

"When the past stinks there's only one thing to do," she replied. "Shake it like a rat. Toss it in the air. Conquer it."

"Such venom!" Surprised by her outburst, he wagged his fork at her and grinned. "Where's the sweet Lorraine I used to know?"

"I'm serious, Ralph. Trabawn belongs to me now, not to the past. It's where I've chosen to begin again."

His voice hardened. "Until it's over, I've no intention of beginning again."

"But it *is* over, Ralph."

"Not until I say so."

He reminded her of a damaged animal, a predator taken off guard, bleeding but still dangerous.

"I'm going to exhibit in the Spiral Staircase gallery," she said.

He turned, surprised, then threw back his head and laughed. "In your old studio?"

"Yes. When I'm ready."

"Will I get an invitation to the opening night?"

"Of course. They will also."

"That should be an interesting occasion. I'll look forward to it immensely." Still smiling, he leaned towards her and wrapped a strand of her hair around his finger, watched it unfurl. Apart from the glow from a table lamp, the room was dim, mainly lit by the flames. "I find myself thinking about you at the most unexpected times. Do you know what I feel then?"

"I'd be afraid to guess."

"Regret that you and I never really got to know each other."

"I've known you for twenty years, Ralph." She smiled back at him, aware that he was flirting with her for the first time ever. But what he said was true. They had never become close, despite all the years of togetherness. They needed space to understand each other but Virginia's dominant personality had never allowed them find it. She had remained the centrepiece in both their lives, the one upon whom they focused their attention. Only occasionally, as had happened on the night Jake died, did Lorraine know him in any emotional sense.

"You were always wary of me," he replied. "Ever since London."

"You were such a bad boy in those days."

"I was a fake. You saw right through me."

She shook her head. "I never knew what to think. Virginia made you sound so dangerous."

"She was right." He pressed his lips against her forehead, butterfly kisses on her cheeks. "I am dangerous when I want something special."

He would not be judged a handsome man by any accepted standards, his features too sharp, a tough city upbringing etched into his face, but the rough edges had been smoothed and what she saw before her was a suave confident man with calculating eyes. She wondered what it would be like to snatch, not just the pleasure he would give her, but also the freedom to walk away from the consequences, as he would do, when the night was over.

"Not a good idea, Ralph." She eased him away with her elbow, keeping her tone light. "Three in a bed is too crowded for my liking."

"Who would be in the middle, Virginia or Adrian?"

"Virginia?"

"Not Adrian?"

"He'll never enter my bed again. Not in real time. Not in dream time."

"But you think Virginia occupies mine?"

"I don't think it. I know it."

"She has nothing to do with us. This is just about you and me, Lorraine."

She shook her head, unable to speak. Michael Carmody was in the room with her, conjured from the heat of the moment, reflected in the desire she saw in another man's face, heard in his voice.

"My poor girl, you're not going to cry on me, are you?" Ralph no longer sounded flirtatious, just concerned.

"No."

"Yes." He rested his finger beneath her eyes. Tears overflowed, trickled over his hand.

"I'm sorry, Ralph."

"Is this about Adrian?"

She shook her head. "I never had his love, not in the way I believed. Why grieve over something that was never mine in the first place."

"Have you met someone since you came here?"

"Of course not."

"That's exactly what Virginia used to say. Unlike you, she was a magnificent liar."

She made the sofa into a bed for him. He would sleep alone tonight. He was nursing a brandy and staring into the fire when they said goodnight.

The following week, in Dublin with Eugene Murphy, she discussed the restoration of a Georgian house. The main repair work was almost completed and, walking through the large, high-ceilinged rooms, she had an immediate sense of how it would look when finished. An hour later she was driving to Drumcondra, having promised Eugene an outline of her plans and some sketches before the Christmas break. She lunched with her parents and was leaving their house when she met Mary Ruane from next door.

"Lorraine, it's good to see you again." The older woman was returning from the supermarket and hurried forward, arms outstretched. She had known Lorraine since she was a baby and the semi-detached houses had been shared with equal freedom by Lorraine and the two Ruane children.

"Donna has been keeping me up to date on everything," said Mary, holding her close as she used to do whenever there were scraped knees and elbows to soothe. "I'm glad you've settled into your new home." They talked for a few minutes about Eoin and his family, who had returned to Ireland from New York.

"What a pity you're not staying longer. They're coming over this evening for dinner," Mary said.

"Give them my love. And tell Meg I'll ring her when I'm next in Dublin."

"I hope you'll see her on Christmas night." Mary hesitated, held Lorraine's hand a little tighter. "Do you think you and Emily will make the party this year? I know it will be difficult without Adrian –"

"We'll be there," Lorraine promised. "Emily would never forgive me if I deprived her of Christmas night in your house."

"What about the little pet? Has she settled?"

"Not so little any more, Mary. It was tough going for a while but I think we're getting there."

"I'm so sorry about everything, love. I wish you were still a tot and I could make it better with a hug. But you're all grown up now. No more magic cures."

"They worked a charm in the past." Lorraine smiled and opened her car door. "I'll see you all on Christmas night."

The afternoon was spent stocking up on painting materials and by late evening Lorraine was driving along the quays, heading west. The peak-hour flow was underway, the traffic slow, hardly moving, the air sluggish with fumes and weariness. She drove past Blaide House and onwards towards a block of apartments with overhanging balconies. Not once did she slow down or turn her eyes from the road.

The sight of fairy lights slung across Market Street added a festive air to the village. Emily attended the lighting of the Christmas tree with her friends and made a wish list that included jodhpurs and riding boots. Horses were an endless subject for discussion and her conversation – which included numerous references to dandy brushes, curry combs and nutrient feeds – was beginning to sound increasingly like the dialogue in a teenage pony novel.

Lorraine forced herself to buy a Christmas tree and decorate it with her daughter. They unwrapped the familiar baubles from tissue paper and hung them from the branches. Along the lane they collected holly and ivy. On the last school day before the Christmas holidays, Lorraine attended the pupils' carol service. She envied the ease with which Sophie wept, her black cheeks glistening as she smiled towards the stage where the pupils were assembled. Sophie had talked about her family, a rebel brother who had joined the Sudan People's Liberation Army and was fighting government forces. Her elderly parents had not heard from him for over a year. She hoped to visit them in the summer but there was much injustice among her people and she lived with a quiet dread that her journey would be too late. Everyone around Lorraine had a story, hidden deep within the reality of ordinary days, but, as the carol service continued, a hushed peace settled over the congregation and the ache in Lorraine's chest eased until she heard only the sweetness of the singing, the solemnity of a message of hope that never changed, no matter how wilfully it was challenged throughout the year.

Adrian had bought a pony for Emily's Christmas present. He had rung the previous day, speaking quickly, his voice low. "I knew how much she wanted one so I rang Con and asked him to organise it. I was afraid to contact you in case you knocked the idea on the head."

"You're free to buy her whatever you want."

"It's what *she* wants, Lorraine. All I want to do is to make some kind of peace with you so that I don't feel I'm trespassing in your life every time I come to Trabawn. We should make this a special occasion for Emily. I was hoping we could have another meal together. The last time meant a lot to her and we could —"

She heard a door open, a voice in the background. Virginia had obviously arrived unexpectedly into the room. She heard his muffled response, imagined his hand over the receiver, his placatory smile, and hung up the phone.

A pony, brown satin coat, cream markings, arrived on the Saturday before Christmas. Lorraine walked towards the farm where the new arrival would be stabled. In the farmyard, the horse box was open and Emily's friends had gathered to inspect the pony. Con ran his hands over her in an experienced way as he explained something to Adrian, and Emily, her face alight with excitement, had her arm around the animal's neck.

Adrian's smile became more confident as the group opened up and admitted Lorraine. A name had already been decided. The new pony would be called Janine. But nothing, Emily declared sternly, would alter the affection she felt for her first love: absolutely adorable, amiable, agreeable, affectionate and accepting Antoinette.

Noeleen came from the kitchen to look at the pony but it was upon Adrian that she settled her shrewd eyes. He retreated from the pungent smell of the stables. Mud caked the ends of his trousers and covered his shoes. It was impossible to imagine him in wellingtons. He belonged to the city and to another life. The atmosphere began to relax. It was almost possible to believe this was a normal gathering of friends and family. Eventually they dispersed, leaving Con to settle the pony in an empty stall.

As she walked back to the house, Adrian fell into step beside her. "Are you annoyed with me?" he demanded, hurrying to keep abreast with her. "Say so if you are. It's better than the ice-cold treatment. I was never able to tolerate it and time hasn't made it any easier to endure."

Without replying she walked faster. If he touched her she would splinter and fall apart. Emily was waiting at the gate, her foot resting on the lower rung.

"Is Daddy coming in?" she asked. "Can we make him something nice to eat? He's had such a long drive to get here."

Lorraine nodded, moved ahead to open the hall door. He breathed into the space she was so carefully creating. His laughter rose to the wooden rafters as he toured the house with Emily. He was lavish with his compliments. It was late by the time he left. Tomorrow Emily would have Christmas lunch with him in O'Callaghan's before he returned to Dublin. He walked to the front door and embraced his daughter. She stood, her hand shielding her eyes, watching until his car disappeared from view.

"He could have stayed here tonight, you know." She turned angrily on her mother. "But I was afraid to ask 'cause I knew you'd have a fit. Why should he be punished so much when it was all *her* fault?"

"Did he say that to you?"

"More or less."

"And you believe him?"

"He wouldn't have left us otherwise. She's a vicious slag."

"Stop it, Emily. Virginia didn't hold a gun to his head."

"Why are you standing up for her? You hate her as much as I do."

"Hating her has nothing to do with it. It's too easy to package the whole messy thing up and stick a label on it saying 'Virginia's Fault'. Your father made choices and one of those was to move in with Virginia."

"Only because you threw him out. He never wanted to leave us. We could have divided the house in two and then I wouldn't feel like I'm splitting *myself* in two every time I want to see him." Her bottom lip swelled mutinously as she brushed past Lorraine and ran up the stairs.

The spray was blowing strong off the sea. The hedgerows crouched into the wind, stilted limbs braced against the coming storms.

CHAPTER FORTY-ONE

Brahms Ward
7 p.m.

"You don't understand it, Michael," you cried one night when it seemed another beginning was possible and, for that instant, I was tempted to lose myself in the cold power of a needle. To share with you the ultimate deadening hit. To reach Nirvana. Was that what it was like, Killian? Wanting, not wanting?

I was singing her name when I awoke this morning. Sweet Lorraine ... when I marry Sweet Lorraine. I loved that song once. Nat King Cole, the smooth crooner, evoking mystery and glamour and the hint of happy-ever-after endings.

Christmas will soon be here. A Santa Claus on every corner and reindeers on the roof. You were reluctant to stop believing in Santa Claus. No matter how often Lorcan placed irrefutable proof in front of you, you refused to accept reality. I hope that fat old man with his Coca-Cola beard is still alive in your mind tonight. Magic is important in a child's heart.

She's in my veins, Killian. I want to lie beside her and never rise. Her voice runs over my skin. This delirium can't last. All I want is oblivion but her name sings in my head and I'm bereft.

She's not the one. Don't ask ... I just know! Hold my hand,

do you hear me? *Damn* you ... hold my hand. Oh Jesus, this is unendurable. I love you, Killian. OK ... where were we? Let's talk some sense tonight. The next series of *Nowhere Lodge* starts production in the spring. I've started writing a new one. Roz O'Hara is pleased. How I love the world of fiction.

Look at the moon. Full as a rich man's belly. Maybe we're all a bit touched by its madness. You always wanted to catch the moon. Remember how we chased it, running behind it as it swept across rooftops, skidded giddy as a hoop around corners, somersaulted behind monkey-puzzle trees and lampposts. When we stopped defeated, and we were always defeated, there it was, still resting securely on your horizon. An old devil moon that cows jumped at random while the dish and the spoon ran fast and far away from home.

Want the moon ... the moon ... chase the moon ... wired to the moon ... too many Killians ... hospital ... screens around the bed ... Killian is my name ...

CHAPTER FORTY-TWO

It was too much. Virginia forced her way up Grafton Street, ignoring carol singers whose cheerfulness and jingling tambourines increased her irritation to boiling point. The Sunday before Christmas, their first real Christmas together, and he was in Galway with his daughter. Surely Virginia would not deny him the opportunity of seeing Emily and wishing her a happy Christmas, he demanded when she protested. She knew better than to continue the argument. Christmas and family were sacrosanct. Her own parents always signed a peace pact for the season of goodwill and allowed harmony to reign over the turkey.

She was waiting at the tail end of a queue to exit the car-park when a text came through on her mobile: *Virginia – why are you alone on a Sunday afternoon? For answer meet me in our favourite restaurant. Unlike us, it remains unchanged. Some things were meant to last.*

Quickly, she texted back. *Piss off Ralph and get a life!*

He responded immediately. *I'll be waiting for you at the usual table by the window at 7 p.m. Don't be late. I've something important to tell you.*

How did he know she was alone? Guesswork, she decided, cheeky bastard. Her hopes that Adrian had arrived home before her were dashed when she opened the door of the apartment. She rang his mobile. He was apologetic, hassled. The visit had taken longer than expected and he was just about to leave his

247

father's house. With the holiday traffic on the road, God knows what time she could expect him home. At six-thirty she showered, dressed and took a taxi into the city.

Temple Bar was noisy, a seamless flow of people enjoying the festive atmosphere. The glass-fronted restaurant – decorated with silver bows and bells and twinkling lights ordering her to be of good cheer – still managed to look unnervingly familiar, as did the sight of Ralph in a sharply tailored navy jacket rising from the window seat to greet her. He was dressed formally in a shirt and tie, the effect more suited to the office than a restaurant where the majority of diners were wearing reindeer horns and Santa hats.

"Virginia, you never fail to astonish me. Your text read like a she-devil's jingle but here you are, as angelic as ever."

"You said this was important." She slid into the seat opposite him and linked her fingers on the table. "My time is limited. Make it snappy."

"First things first." He accepted the menu from the waitress, choosing, as Virginia had known he would, a fillet steak, rare. She ordered prawns and he smiled, as if he had also anticipated her choice. After the waitress departed with their orders he glanced around. "As you can see, it's hardly changed at all."

"What did you expect?" she snapped. "A changed décor to match our changed circumstances?"

"Yes, I keep expecting everything to be different. Don't you?"

"What do you want to discuss with me?"

"All in good time," he said. "Happy Christmas."

"Perhaps you've time to waste but I can't stay long."

He bent towards her and traced his finger along either side of her lips in a provocative semi-circle. "Do you know something, Virginia? I believe you're getting a disgruntled mouth. Is the sanctity of a monogamous relationship already beginning to pall?"

She felt her skin contract, as if his touch had already furrowed her smooth skin. No matter how much she tried to deny the facts, there were deepening lines around her eyes and in the mornings her complexion was puffy until she applied make-up. Lack of sleep was the problem, not age, she assured herself. But what was she to do about it? Sleeping tablets helped but they only provided fitful relief.

"Why did you ask me here?" She sat perfectly still until he took his hand away.

"I want a sensible answer to a sensible question. Why him, Virginia? The others I tolerated. Like fleas, they could be eradicated. But him? Why take that step too far?"

"I was in love with him."

He shook his head slowly. "You never intended leaving me. I know you too well, my darling. You scorch your wings but you never fly too close to the flame. You went with him for a reason. Don't call me a fool by pretending it was love."

The waitress returned and laid their meals before them.

"*Bon appetit*, Virginia." He cut deeply into his steak. A thin drizzle of blood ran across the plate. "How is business?" He raised his eyebrows quizzically.

"Excellent." She bit down on a prawn, tasted ginger and garlic. "And Adrian?"

"The same."

"The days of lying to me are gone, Virginia. I'd advise you to keep a close eye on him or he'll drag you down when he hits the deck."

"Such concern," she mocked. "It would be touching if you were not such a vindictive bastard. I know what you're trying to do to him."

"Trying?" He shook his head. "I think succeeding would be the operative word. Where is he today?"

"Minding his own business."

"Minding his own business in Trabawn, you mean. Be warned, Virginia. No matter how many times he goes to Trabawn, Lorraine won't forgive him. But, this is a teaser, will Adrian be able to forgive you? And, more importantly, will he ever be able to forgive himself? As for me ..." He paused, his fork in mid-air. "Now that is the *real* million dollar question."

For an instant her composure deserted her. "Not that it's got anything to do with you but Adrian does not go to Trabawn."

"Even when he visits his daughter?"

"They meet in Galway."

"Geography was never my strong point so correct me if I'm wrong. I was under the impression that Trabawn was in the majestic kingdom of Kerry. At least it was the last time I saw Emily." He continued to carve his steak into small tender pieces and she felt cold suddenly, even though they were seated near the open kitchen where flames leaped from ovens and grease spat viciously against the bars of the grill.

"What are you suggesting?"

"Nothing at all. If Adrian says he's in Galway who am I to suggest otherwise? We both know he *never* lies."

"You're the one who's lying."

"Always the optimist, Virginia. But I never believed you to be a credulous fool." He stretched back in his chair and watched her rise to her feet. "Going so soon? What a pity. I was hoping we'd have the rest of the evening to enjoy each other's company."

"You're pathetic, Ralph. You can't bear the thought that I could be happy with someone else."

"Your happiness was all I ever wanted, Virginia. All I'm advising you to do is be alert. As your mother would say, 'Love in rose-tinted glasses is such a blind bitch.'"

She searched his pockets, the drawers where he kept his underwear and socks, found his briefcase keys and discovered the photographs. She spread them across the kitchen table. Emily with her arms around her boyfriend. Emily blowing out birthday candles. Proud parents sharing the moment. The man's arm around the woman's shoulders. Red hair spilling. Lorraine's smile straining the corners of her eyes.

"Sorry I'm late." It was after eleven when he finally arrived home. "When will the government get off its arse and sort out the traffic problem? I must have been forty minutes coming through Enfield, not to mention –"

"How is your father?" She rose from an armchair, cut across his apology.

"In good form. He sends his love."

"Don't patronise me, Adrian. If your father was to send me anything it would be a hand grenade with a defective pin."

"Give him time. He's coming round."

"Like Emily?"

"Definitely softening up."

"Did you invite her to visit us over Christmas?"

"Of course I did. But she's still very negative about staying here. I just have to keep pushing the door open a little further each time." He crossed to the drinks cabinet. "Jesus, I need a drink after that drive. Want to join me?"

When she nodded he poured two generous measures of whiskey, added ice and water, handed a glass to her. "Cheers."

"Cheers," she replied. "Tell me about Trabawn. Has it changed much over the years?"

He paused, startled. "I was in Galway. I told you. Emily took the train over to meet me."

"We lived inside a lie for too long, Adrian." Her voice remained calm. "Truth was the one thing we always promised each other. Remember? If we couldn't trust each other we had nothing. Don't lie to me now."

He lowered his glass and placed it on the table. His stricken expression when he noticed the photographs added to her fury.

"Would you like to explain what all this is about?" She swiped the photographs and sent them flying to the floor.

"I'm sorry Virginia. I wanted to tell you but I knew you wouldn't understand. Emily won't come here, so Lorraine decided the best solution was for me to visit Trabawn."

She stood rigidly before him when he tried to draw her into his arms. "How often have you met Lorraine?"

"Just the once. It was Emily's birthday. For her sake, we had to spend the evening together."

She lit a cigarette, dragged smoke deeply into her lungs. "Where did you do that? In the barn or the haystack?"

"For Christ's sake, Virginia! You saw the photographs. We were in O'Callaghan's." His defensive tone softened, became placatory. "You wouldn't believe how much it's changed. It's quite up-market now and the restaurant is –"

"I'm delighted O'Callaghan's slum-clearance programme has been successful," she snapped. "Tell me, did my name come up during this intimate little celebration?"

"Not that I can recall."

"You can't recall? What are we dealing with here? Amnesia or

Alzheimer's? Have I become so unimportant that you can't even remember if I was a subject for discussion?"

"Why are you being such a bitch?" Unable any longer to control his temper, he banged his fist off the table. "I've lost my wife, my daughter, my home. All I'm trying to do is put a small piece of my life back together again and you're not even willing to try and understand. I won't be able to see Emily on Christmas Day because she refuses to come here and it's not – "

"How *dare* you assume the lion's share of pain!" Furiously, she interrupted him. "What about me? I'm trying to hold on to Blaide House by my fingernails. I'm the one making contacts, trying to lift you from this mess while you spend your time moaning because your family doesn't love you any more. What did you expect? You made your choice when you left –"

"And what have I got in return?" he shouted. "Neurotic jealousy and a cheapskate apartment that reminds me of a fucking shop window."

"How *dare* you!"

He ducked when she lifted her arm and flung the whiskey glass towards him. The crystal shattered against the wall. She watched the whiskey trickle towards the floor.

Shocked, he stared at the broken shards. "I lied because I knew this was how you'd react. I'd no intention of seeing Lorraine but I had to mend bridges. Emily is all I care about. You have to trust me, Virginia."

"No more weekends apart," she said when their anger finally subsided. "You've signed O'Callaghan's upmarket register for the last time. If Emily wants to see you she comes here. Otherwise, you don't come home to me."

In bed, she waited for him to join her. We should be making love now, she thought, banishing angry words, finding the energy to keep going.

At last, unable any longer to endure the empty space, she entered the living-room. He was slumped in front of the television, aimlessly changing channels. The stations flicked in rapid succession, weather forecasts, shoot-outs, political debate, war zones. She removed the remote control from his hand and switched off the television. Without a word he rose and followed her.

CHAPTER FORTY-THREE

On Christmas Eve they left Trabawn in the early afternoon and headed for Dublin. Emily, who had cried leaving the horses, fretted whenever Lorraine drove over a pothole in case the jolt caused the collapse of the Christmas cake she had made in her domestic-science class. They stopped at Sophie's house where she exchanged presents with Ibrahim. This changeover took such an inordinate length of time that Sophie was forced to bang on his bedroom door and order them out. It was dark when an exhausted Lorraine finally reached Dublin.

Her parents' house was filled with determined good cheer and the smells of herbs and spices. Christmas Day passed in a haze of activity. Adrian rang, maudlin, reminiscing. She handed the phone to Emily and returned to the kitchen to baste the turkey. The annual party in Ruanes' was well underway when they went next door to join the festivities. A crowd had gathered around the piano where Eoin was playing Christmas songs for the children. Meg and Lorraine slipped into one of the bedrooms to talk. Meg had put on weight since New York. It added a stateliness to her neck and shoulders. She had tied a headband with coloured stones around her forehead and this ornate bandanna shimmered every time she shook her head. The friendship that followed after Meg commissioned her husband's portrait needed little more than an occasional meeting between the two women to sustain it and Meg listened without interruption while Lorraine talked about the previous year. When she admitted her suspicion that she was probably the last to find out about her husband's affair, Meg shook her head.

"I never suspected anything was going on or spoke to anyone else who did."

"But I *did* know." Lorraine gave her head thee hard knocks. "In here I had a sense that everything wasn't right. It was intuition rather than suspicion, the inner voice ordering me to wake up but I simply wasn't prepared to listen. What does that make me? Deaf, blind, stupid, pathetic – or all four?"

"The inner voice is always loudest when it sings in hindsight." Meg laughed as the sounds of familiar carols floated upwards. Mary banged on the bedroom door and ordered them down to join in the singing.

"We're throwing a party at the end of January," said Meg before they went downstairs. "It's a chance to see our friends in one fell swoop. We'd love you and Emily to come."

"If we can make it we will. But you and Eoin have to come down some weekend. I'm getting the house in order at last. The girls can bring sleeping-bags. Emily would love to show them around Trabawn."

"It'll be summer before Eoin has another weekend free."

"He's obviously in demand as much as ever."

"More than ever." Meg sighed. "I thought New York was busy but this is manic. Mary, God bless her, has offered to move in and mind the kids when Eoin is touring the UK so I'll be able to accompany him for a change. It's so long since we've had a chance to be alone together."

The friends rejoined the party. They stood in a circle and sang carols, as they did every year, and if anyone missed the fine tenor voice of Adrian Strong, the deeper baritone of Ralph Blaide and the perfectly pitched soprano notes that poured so effortlessly from Virginia's throat, no one commented. Lorraine, as always, sang rapturously inside her head, but softly mouthed the words. The frog in the school choir, she knew her limitations.

CHAPTER FORTY-FOUR

Brahms Ward
10 p.m.

Harriet phoned before I left, Killian. She scolded me for being alone. A social indiscretion on Christmas Day. She'd been partying on a house boat for two days and sounded tipsy from some home-made Maori brew; rot-gut, I would imagine, but she has a stomach like an ox. She sends her love by the armload.

She was trekking through thermal springs, bathing in New Zealand mud, when she heard about your accident. She flew home immediately. A leathery existence with her home in a rucksack leaves little space for tears yet she shed them freely as she willed you to respond. You were still sleeping when she flew away again. Like me, she has a deadline to keep. Dear Harriet, journaling ... journeying, eccentric as a road runner.

I didn't have to spend the day alone. Many invitations came. Roz and Meg and your mother. Didn't she look lovely when she was in earlier? And Laura? From gawky to gorgeous in one fell swoop. Jean worries about the belly stud and the pierced tongue. I reminded her that she once wore jeans with a slashed backside. For the first time we were able to look back on the weekend that made you and smile, remembering.

The city is empty tonight. Except for the illuminations. Trees dressed in silver, shooting stars above the bridges, even the cranes are festooned with flashing lights but there is silence everywhere. I rang her before I left the apartment. I couldn't stop myself. Like a mad fool I rang her house and listened to her voice on the answering machine. Twice. I won't do it again.

We'll sit out the late shift together and sing carols. O the holly bears a berry as blood it is red. And Mary she bore Jesus who died in our stead ...

I didn't die ... didn't die ... didn't die ... hear me!

CHAPTER FORTY-FIVE

When the phone rang, startling them from their sleep and jerking Virginia upright, she answered it with a sense of dread. Edward was calling from London. Their father had suffered a massive aneurysm and been pronounced dead on arrival at the hospital. Josephine had accompanied him in the ambulance. Edward spoke sombrely, still in deep shock, then handed the phone to his mother.

"Time and tide wait for no man," announced Josephine. Her voice quivered, sobbed. "I need my family around me. How soon will you be able to get a flight?"

Still unable to believe that her father should die so effortlessly, Virginia was already calculating which business meetings could be postponed or delegated. "I'll have to cancel a business trip. I'm supposed to fly out to Madeira in two days' time. I'll ring back when I've more definite information."

Bill Sheraton was understanding when she rang. A family bereavement was first priority. He would cancel their flights and rearrange the trip. Sheraton Worldwide Travel wanted to launch a media promotion of their winter holidays and Madeira was one of the chosen destinations. Virginia had intended visiting the island and drawing up an itinerary that would appeal to a select group of journalists whom she would bring over at a later date.

She was skilled at summing up locations, her intuition honed to the story that would trigger interest, create a colour feature, inspire enthusiasm. He phoned her back a few minutes later and told her he had organised a flight for her to Heathrow Airport that afternoon. A strange man, she thought, putting down the phone. An irascible bully yet capable of kindness when the occasion demanded it.

Edward was waiting in the airport to drive her to their childhood home in Forest Hill. They had no sooner left the airport than he assumed the lofty tones of the righteous and said, "You've been making a lot of mischief since we last met, sister mine. How long was it going on before Lorraine had the good sense to kick him out?"

She ordered him to mind his own business and he retorted, "As I happen to be closely acquainted with all the parties involved, this is my business. Dare I ask if you and Adrian are happy?"

"Of course we are."

"Liar, liar, dirty –"

"Shut up, Edward." They always fell back into childhood roles, bickering and teasing each other within five minutes of meeting. If he had nudged her with his elbow and told her to shove over in the seat she would not have been surprised.

"Will Lorraine be at the funeral?" he asked.

"I haven't the faintest idea. We're not exactly in close communication these days."

"Don't be so defensive. It'll be an extremely difficult occasion for everyone involved. Mother is distraught enough without this added tension."

"Distraught! She wanted to turn his head into a bowling ball when he left her."

"Which should give you some indication about how Lorraine feels about you."

"We never wanted to hurt anyone, especially Lorraine."

"Well, as mother would say, you can't make a omelette without breaking hearts."

"Give me a *break*." How pompous he sounded, in his gold-rimmed glasses and Caribbean tan, sitting like a proud chubby child behind the wheel of his Mercedes. He dyed his hair, not a hint of grey anywhere, but she could see tell-tale red tinges when it caught the light. Adrian was going grey, just a smattering and difficult, as yet, to distinguish among the blonde – but it remained a disquieting reminder of all they had been through.

Instead of the discreet and private cremation she had anticipated, Des Cheevers had left specific instructions about the type of funeral he wanted. Death notices had to appear in the Irish newspapers. His body was to be flown to Dublin and buried in Glasnevin Cemetery. Certain hymns for the burial service and, afterwards – when the clay was finally flung over his bones – he had left money to pay for a slap-up feed for his relations and childhood friends.

"I can't believe Mother is going through with this ridiculous charade." She ranted at her brother who agreed it was appallingly tacky – but they should be thankful their father had not also requested a gun salute from men in balaclavas.

"Everybody wants to go to heaven but nobody wants to die." Josephine wept in Virginia's arms and continued to repeat this truism whenever anyone called to offer their condolences. Virginia had no sooner stepped over the threshold when she was led upstairs to inspect the bedroom where her errant father had breathed his last.

"He was sitting up in bed eating a boiled egg when it happened. He just keeled over in front of my eyes." Josephine managed to look both grief-stricken and coy in the same instant. "He always liked a boiled egg after –"

Virginia's expression prevented any further discussion on the subject and Josephine contented herself by pointing to a stain on the yellow duvet. "That's where he knocked over his mug of tea."

Horrified to think her parents had been sleeping together, Virginia refused to ask the obvious question. She hurried from her mother's bedroom, resolving to wash the duvet cover as soon as Josephine's back was turned. Perhaps that was the reason for his aneurysm. Over-exertion. Her mind skidded away from the image. His sexual capers had finally killed him in the arms of his ex-wife. Funny old thing, life. As Josephine would say, "Truth is stranger than friction."

Adrian rang every day. It was impossible for him to get away from the office. A slight hiccup had occurred, nothing to worry about, everything was under control. The dismay in his voice when he heard the funeral would take place in Ireland was palpable.

"Josephine is determined to carry out his last wishes." Virginia sighed.

"But the funeral will be horrendous. When is he being buried?"

"No date yet. It depends on when the undertaker is ready to release his body and how quickly it can be flown over. I'll ring and let you know as soon as I've more information."

"Do you think Lorraine will attend?"

"She will," Virginia replied. "She'll do it simply to prove she can. And so will Ralph."

Rigor mortis had set her father's lips into their thin final position, banished his smile, so embracing and mercurial, and placed, instead, a slack-jawed incredulity on his face, as if he had been caught unaware when death crept up behind him. But Virginia saw also in his raddled mouth the weakness of a man who had lied with conviction, charm and utter sincerity.

She had betrayed him when she was seventeen. Betrayed. The word sounded strange on her tongue. She repeated it again, a breathless-sounding, sly, Judas word. Disconcerting to speak it now when he was stretched cold before her, reposing grandly on purple satin.

It had been raining the night she betrayed him, falling like needles under the street lamps, trickling coldly down the back of her neck. She opened the front door and silently entered the house. The hope that her parents were sleeping, oblivious to the fact that she had spent the small hours on a tumbled blanket with a man called Razor Blade, was quickly dashed when her father summoned her into the living-room. They were waiting up for her, sitting on opposite armchairs, as inflexible as judges and united for once in common purpose.

"Slut!" he roared and grabbed her hair, pulled it so hard her eyes stung with shock. "Where were you until this hour?"

Virginia laughed, holding her cheek, remembering the heat of Razor's hands on her hips, his lanky frame stretched beneath her, and she above him, controlling him, her hot-blooded, angry punk.

"It's none of your business," she retorted and tried to push past him.

"Answer me, slut." He shoved her back against the wall.

"Don't bully me," she shouted. "I'm not a kid any more."

He lifted his hand again and struck her cheek. She turned on him, her anger as strong as his own, and answered him. "We were fucking in Razor's flat. It took longer than expected because we did it twice."

Horror-struck, Josephine lifted her hand to her mouth.

"You foul-mouthed tramp," he roared. "How dare you use such language in front of your mother. I'll make you give up that punk bastard if it's the last thing I do." He struck her again and again, his face flushed so deeply she thought he would have a stroke. "There's plenty more where that came from if you don't stop behaving like a little whore."

There was always more where that came from. When she was young she believed there was a magic spell in Sonya's house that took all the angry lines from her father's face. But the spell only lasted until they reached the end of her road. She had grown up with the sting of his hands on her legs, her arms and her face, his bullying voice loud in her ears. She had loved and hated him in equal measure. It was her love that kept Sonya a secret and her hatred that released it that night, when she screamed, "What about your slut, Sonya? When are you going to give her up? How many years now … how many years have you forced me to lie?"

The sound her mother made reminded Virginia of pups. The same helpless, whimpering cry she used to hear from the room where she could not go. Only now it held anguish and the acknowledgement of a truth long denied. A truth that longed to be denied. It was the loneliest cry in the world.

Her father moved out the following day. Shortly afterwards she also left home and moved in with Razor. Her mother joined a bowling team.

At last his body was flown to Dublin. The atmosphere in the funeral parlour was restrained, polite greetings, whispered condolences. No tears were shed as the mourners filed before the open coffin and Virginia, shaking hands, smiling, accepting sympathy from her father's Irish relatives, wondered how soon the charade would end. Josephine, arrayed in widow's weeds that looked as if they had rested in mothballs since the reign of Queen Victoria, was the only person who wept, and this she did with relentless force. Edward's plump arm comforted her. His children, two boys and a girl, all endowed with his earnest, round face and their mother's pale complexion, gazed longingly towards the door when Josephine ordered them to kiss their grandfather's forehead in farewell.

Brian Cheevers bowed his head in prayer then stepped back from the coffin. Donna took his hand and they stood together, offering condolences to Josephine, refusing to make eye contact with Virginia. The ingrained veneer of civility working against the odds, she thought. Still no sign of Lorraine or Ralph.

They followed the coffin into the church and sat in the front row. Behind them, the whispering, fidgeting and coughing gave way to an anticipatory silence. Virginia did not need to turn around to see whose footsteps clicked sharply up the aisle. The friction of separate particles rubbing together and igniting. Adrian shifted in his seat, as if he too could feel the electricity in the air, and moved slightly away from her.

The funeral mass was swift. The priest had never heard of Des Cheevers and had no inclination to eulogise a stranger. Wafted with incense, doused with holy water, the coffin was wheeled briskly back down the aisle. Statues and stations of the cross wavered before Virginia's eyes. Burning hearts offering everlasting forgiveness – but there was no forgiveness in the cold gaze of Lorraine Cheevers, who stared unflinchingly as the small family procession approached. The brash red jacket she wore should have clashed with her hair but it added luminance to her appearance, a vibrant statement. Virginia knew it had been chosen with care.

More handshaking outside the church. Virginia smiled at the elderly men who came forward and told her what a card her father had been. A great man when it came to the wine and the women. As if the latter fact needed verification, a woman in a Zimmer frame twinkled up at her and confessed that she and Des had quite a thing going in the olden days, not a twinge of arthritis between them, the pair of them as frisky as young goats. She guffawed loudly and shuffled back into the crowd. Ralph had also arrived during the funeral mass. He shook hands with Edward and kissed Lorraine for longer than was appropriate at a funeral ceremony. Virginia signalled the undertaker to depart for the cemetery. The day was gathering its own momentum, sweeping them haplessly on its back.

At the graveside they stood opposite each other, Lorraine flanked grimly by her parents. The hole into which Des Cheevers was being lowered was only a fissure in the distance separating them. After the burial people hung around the graveside. Virginia wanted to clap her hands and scatter them. The Irish had no sense of decorum. They turned every gathering, even a funeral, into a party. Her jaw locked painfully when her mother again related the boiled-egg story, this time to Ralph, who listened, his head tilted to one side, and asked if it had been hard or soft boiled.

Firmly, Virginia escorted her mother back to the mourning car. She slammed the door on her protests and walked back to Ralph. "Thank you for coming." Her tone was as formal as her handshake. "Don't let me detain you any longer."

"Des was a fine man. He'll be sadly missed."

Her smile glittered. "He was a bad-tempered bully who never cared where he landed his fists. I remember he planted them in your teeth once. It's a memory I'll always cherish."

"Indeed ... memories. Where would we be without them. Fancy your father dying in Josephine's bed. Who knows? There's hope for us yet, my darling."

The mourners filed from the graveside and were joined by a man who had been standing slightly apart from the main gathering. Virginia had no recollection of seeing him in the funeral home or the church. When Lorraine approached with her parents he stepped forward and spoke to her. She drew back, surprised by his appearance, then shook his hand.

Virginia was sure she had met him before. His face was

familiar, the angular boniness and narrow chin, an expressive face, but arrogant too, and it was this arrogance that clicked the memory into place. He had come to Blaide House demanding Lorraine's address and been unnecessarily rude when she refused to give it to him.

Lorraine stood talking to him. She allowed her parents to walk on ahead and laughed at something he said. So long since Virginia had heard her laughter. The sound shocked her. When she allowed herself to think about Lorraine, she thought only of tears and ranting grief.

CHAPTER FORTY-SIX

They had lunch in a restaurant close to his apartment. Lorraine pointed to the first item on the menu.

"Same for me." He placed his order without once taking his eyes from her face.

"What did we order?" he asked after the waiter departed.

"I've absolutely no idea."

Her answer made him smile and reach across the table to take her hand. She had been shocked at his appearance in the cemetery and now, sitting opposite him, she was able to observe the difference in him. He looked carefree, happy to be with her, his body relaxed as he described how he had read her uncle's death notice in *The Irish Times* and had arrived at the cemetery on the off-chance that he would find her among the mourners.

"You've no idea how much I wanted to contact you but I was afraid you'd hang up on me. Not that I would have blamed you. I should never have let you leave my apartment."

"Why did you tell me to go?"

"I was caught up in something, Lorraine. It's very personal and has nothing to do with you. But, at the time, I wasn't able to make that separation."

"If you're involved with someone else —"

"*No.*" His denial was instant, emphatic. "It has to do with my son. I'd like to talk about it soon … but not now. I want the day to belong to us." His gaze warmed her face, nothing hidden, none of the confused signals she had picked up every other time they were together.

"I accused you of hating me when you phoned that night," she said.

"I remember our conversation."

"I still can't understand why you made me feel that way."

"It was unforgivable of me. I love you, Lorraine. I've wanted to say that to you for a long time."

His energy came towards her in waves, giddy, intoxicating, and his expression, free from ambiguity, seemed lit from within. Their time together had been so fraught with contradictions and confusion. Now, suddenly, everything seemed different but she was unwilling to trust the fusion taking place so effortlessly between them.

"I'm not ready to fall in love, Michael. It's too soon."

"As long as there's a possibility that some day you'll love me, I'll wait forever."

Their food was placed before them. Beef burgers, heaped with onions, luminous carrots on the side, a trickle of congealed gravy over mashed potatoes.

They stared at their plates and then at each other. Their laughter was spontaneous, so hearty that people dining nearby looked curiously across. He pushed his plate to one side and said, "I'll make something to eat in the apartment, if you'd like to come back with me?"

She could leave him now and return to her refuge. The walls were strong, reinforced. There was wine in the fridge and a glass ready to be filled. But an afternoon stretched before them and the promise it contained shimmered like an oasis on parched sand. It was so easy, effortless really, to decide. He paid the bill. They walked together from the restaurant.

He drew the curtains to close out the day. The sun filtered through a chink and filled the room with shadowy light. Somewhere behind her a clock ticked, measuring time that no longer had relevance. Only a few hours ago she had stood in a cemetery between her parents, fragile as an invalid exposed to sunshine after a long illness. Her body shaking with the knowledge that there would be other family occasions when she would have to endure the sight of them together. Now she lay in another man's arms, her lips racked with his kisses, feeling him hard against her, shockingly erect, no awkwardness between them as they undressed each other and stretched across his bed, soaking up each other's nakedness. He could have spent a lifetime knowing my body, she thought, knowing the pitch of my pleasure, the depths of my passion. His hands traced across her thighs and she opened to him, her limbs receiving him, holding him captive. She was above him, beyond him, and he, within her, filling her, his eyes devouring her, drove deeper until there was nothing left except the sundering of body and mind. She wanted to hold the sensation yet she compelled him onwards until she felt the shuddering spill of his passion inside her and he, hearing her cry out, hearing her abandonment, buried his face in her hair, engulfed.

Afterwards, there was time to lie in each other's arms. They talked until the room grew dark and the sounds in the apartment block began to change. Balcony doors slammed, a radio played next door and there were voices outside, a brief staccato of sound that quickly faded. They drew life histories from each other, exploring their contrasting childhoods; the leafy suburbs of Drumcondra and the commune where he had spent the first four years of his life.

His mother's parents had died when she was young and, after the death of her father, which occurred just before her sixteenth birthday, Shady Carmody emigrated to America with her older sister. At first they lived in New York, then moved to California and on to Arizona, where they settled in Sedona, attracted by the boulders and rugged canyons they had seen so often in cowboy films. They were told stories about Native American tribes practising ancient religious ceremonies in secret caverns and, having been reared under the shadow of Croagh Patrick, where pilgrims stumbled bare-foot over stones, they were at ease with mystery and rite. They moved into a hippy commune and learned to meditate and weave lengths of fabric which they sold to tourists. But the older sister grew tired of sunshine and chanting in the shade of red-faced crags. She felt it was time to explore Alaska.

"Harriet Carmody," he said, and paused as if he expected Lorraine to recognise her name. "The travel writer," he added, seeing her puzzlement, and she nodded, remembering a book she had once read about India.

Shady refused to leave the commune. Unknown to her sister she had fallen in love with a young man who was showing her other ways of travelling. When he spoke about his mother, he could have been describing an ephemeral being, floating by on fairy dust, and Lorraine pictured a young woman in a long skirt, hair to her waist, beads around her neck, smoke from a joint spiralling through her fingers. The sisters agreed to separate, one moving outwards, the other travelling to distant places in her mind. Michael was born twelve months later.

His memories were fragmented, wonderful descriptions of sunsets and towering rocks and of his mother weaving lengths of golden fabric. The women in the commune mothered him. They carried him in a sling, played for him on sitars and bongo drums, brought him food to a table under vines. There were men in the commune, beards and sandals; they all looked alike to him and he called none of them his father. Nor did he have any concept of fatherhood. He belonged to a community, not a family. When he was older, he discovered that his father had exchanged his sandals for deck shoes before he was born. On the last sighting, he was crewing on a yacht in the Bahamas.

It would be a few more years before Scott McKenzie turned San Francisco into a garden for flower children and "make love not war" became a cliché with a bitter aftertaste – but for Shady Carmody, the dream was already turning sour. Once, he found her unconscious. Many times he heard her crying in her sleep. She swung him high on elation, beat him down with her despair. Her hair fell below her waist but it was matted and her feet were caked with clay. He could not understand why she sang and cried on the same breath. He was four years old when his aunt returned to the commune and held him in her arms for the first time. She placed her sister and her nephew in the back of a pick-up truck and drove away.

Shady stayed in hospital – he had no idea how long, to him it seemed an endless time – and after she was discharged the sisters returned to Ireland. They lived in Dublin where Harriet quelled her wanderlust and set about writing her first book. His mother, restless and adrift, waited tables. In the summer of '67 she travelled to Woburn Abbey, where The Festival of the Flower Children, England's answer to Woodstock, was taking place.

"A little holiday," said Harriet, who had been unable to prevent her going. He still remembered the rows and his mother crying on the stairs the night before she left. He was filled with foreboding and the belief that she was returning to the commune, terrified he would never see her again. He waved goodbye to her from the pier. Harriet said they would have a good view from there. Afterwards, she took him to the Broadway café on O'Connell Street and treated him to an ice-cream flavoured with raspberry syrup.

For three days Shady Carmody danced to the anthem of an era – turn on, tune in, drop out. The car crash occurred on the night before she was due to return home. The young man driving escaped with minor injuries. She died on the spot. A flower child with daisies in her hair. Shortly after her funeral, his aunt brought him to Mayo, to the house where she had been born and where, she said, he would be safe.

Lorraine drew him to her. His heart pounded against her breast. She thought about her own childhood, playing safe in a suburban garden with Eoin and Sally Ruane, their mothers in the kitchen exchanging recipes for chocolate cake, keeping a wary eye on their children playing safely on see-saws.

"I love you," he said. He repeated her name, as if the sound was a foreign language on his tongue. "My sweet Lorraine … I love you."

CHAPTER FORTY-SEVEN

Brahms Ward
Midnight

How could I have got it so wrong? She was in New York. I want
to say it again. Listen carefully, Killian. She was in New York. A
continent away. In an Irish bar in the East Village, she sang "Ladies
of the Canyon". She sings off-key, said Eoin, always did. But she
knows how to paint a quirky portrait. A railway station, of all
places. Meg said it usually hangs in his study but they decided to
show it off for their party and there it was in the living-room, a
splendid thing to see.

We live in a small world but a magical one. How strange our
paths never crossed before. Perhaps they did. Meg's parties are
crowded jamborees, as this one was, with crowds spilling into
different rooms and forming huddles wherever there is space.
Lorraine Cheevers should have been there. She rang and
accepted the invitation than rang again to cancel. She had a
funeral to attend.

Killian, my boy, my silent patient boy, I've no right to feel
delirious but I'm wild with it. We talked about everything but the
right thing. I told her about the commune, all of it, the dirt and
neglect and how your grandmother lay like a crushed bird with

no hope of ever flying free until Harriet lifted her up and tried to heal her. I've never spoken so freely about it. Not even in Slane. I wanted to lie beside her forever and feel her warm breath on my face but in the end she left and I'm here with you again. Back on the night shift.

I should have been honest with her. Yes, of course I should. Don't give me that sideways look. I'll tell her everything when I see her. It won't be easy but she'll understand. I'll bring her here to meet you and you'll see why I'm daft with happiness.

What will I say? Not to worry; I'll find a way. There'll be time to explain and she will listen. Just as she listened today when I laid those years before her. She's afraid of love, mistrustful. What have I done? How could I have been such a fool? You brought us together but it was along a very crooked road. How can I even begin to describe it to her?

Snow is forecast, Killian. It's drifting towards us on a north-easterly. But not yet. I've a trip to make before it falls.

Snow fall. Snorting snow. Coke-head Marianne. Wired to the moon. Marianne Lorcan me. Mammy Daddy Terence. Three blind mice. Three coins in the fountain. Maggie has three biscuits. Arrowroot Custard Cream Gingernut.

CHAPTER FORTY-EIGHT

Ice on the runway delayed take-off for over two hours. At last the plane glided into the air. Stress fell from Virginia as effortlessly as the slanting patchwork of snow-covered fields dropping below her. She sipped a gin and tonic and flicked through the latest edition of *Prestige*. Andrea Sheraton smiled from the glossy pages. Her husband grunted when Virginia showed him the colour spread and returned to his lap-top. Although she knew little about the island, except that her mother always enjoyed a glass of Madeira sherry before her Christmas dinner, it would be easy to explore, especially with a guide and car at her disposal. Darkness had descended when they reached their destination. The volcanic slopes rose around them in invisible rocky layers and the lights of Madeira were woven like golden needlework into the fabric of the night.

From the hotel balcony Virginia heard the faint strains of dance music floating upwards through the open doors of the bar. She sat at the dressing table and applied her make-up, lining her lips then softening the inner curves with lipstick, stroking the tube back and forth.

"Beauty is only skin deep, young lady," Josephine had warned the young Virginia whenever her daughter stared overlong at her reflection in the mirror. "It's the mote in the eye of the begrudger."

Whether people begrudged or beheld her loveliness remained a matter of indifference to Virginia. What was the sense in possessing a beautiful inner self when no one could see it – and the mirror reassured her that her beauty remained skin deep and unblemished. The restaurant Bill had chosen for their evening meal gave them a bird's eye view of the island. He was only staying for one night and planned to fly from there to Portugal. They discussed the new campaign, their manner remaining business-like despite their relaxed surroundings. Virginia never mixed business and pleasure, despite the regular propositions she received from clients.

"Avoid complications," an experienced public-relations executive had advised her when she first became involved in the business. "If you want to play away from home make sure you don't do it on office time."

The band was still playing when they returned to the hotel bar for a nightcap. Bill cupped a goblet of brandy in his hands while she sipped a cocktail. They watched couples dancing around the small circular floor in vigorous quicksteps or gliding into a waltz. Some of the younger guests, defeated by the old-fashioned dance rhythms, settled around the bar. A young man sitting on a high stool gazed speculatively across at her. She ignored him yet his scrutiny ignited her conversation, sparked her laughter.

"You're good, Virginia." The businessman watched her carefully from behind a wreath of smoke. "Sharp as a tack when it comes to publicity and promotion. But I'm beginning to have my doubts about Adrian. He needs to understand I don't carry dead soldiers. Is it possible he's too stressed out with his family situation to cope with the demands of the job?"

"That is an outrageous assumption, Bill! It's most unprof-essional –"

He held up his hand, unperturbed by her outburst. "Your personal life is your own business as long as it doesn't interfere with my profit margins."

She inclined her head in acknowledgement. "You've made your position perfectly clear. I'm sorry you feel it necessary to have this conversation with me"

He nodded curtly. "I also regret it. You and I have always had a sound working relationship. But perception is important in the advertising industry. If word gets about that an agency is losing its punch the inevitable starts to happen."

"What has Lorcan been saying?"

"Lorcan has nothing to do with this conversation. But while we're on the subject of my son, his efforts are still not being appreciated."

"On the contrary, Bill –"

"He's come up with some excellent ideas which Adrian hasn't even looked at."

"I assure you –"

"Don't assure me. Assure him. I'm anxious that Lorcan makes a success of this job. As you know, he was running with a wild bunch for a while." He puffed vigorously on his cigarillo. The foul smell seeped into her clothes, stung her eyes. "At one time we honestly didn't believe he'd make it back."

Virginia stirred her cocktail and glanced casually across the bar. The young man stared boldly back. He was sallow-skinned, obviously local, dressed in white slacks and a casual polo shirt. He lifted his glass in a discreet salute. A smile flickered meaningfully at the corners of his lips.

"That explains Lorcan's prayer meeting." She turned her attention back to Bill. "I overheard him discussing it on the phone. I did wonder at the time. He never struck me as particularly religious young man."

"Lorcan religious? I think not." He drained his brandy glass and set it back on the table with a decisive clink. "That's me finished for the night. No, Lorcan's definitely not religious. At this stage, I'm happy to settle for sensible. The prayer meeting was arranged by friends of ours. I'm not a great man for the church myself but if prayers can move mountains then Jean Devine-O'Malley has said enough to shift the Alps."

Virginia lifted an olive from the dish beside her and bit hard into the acrid flesh. The taste was bitter, sickeningly so. She swallowed, forced herself to smile. She wanted to be a child again, her fingers stuffed in her ears, but Bill Sheraton kept talking about basket cases and how the police who were so good on speed checks had done fuck all to find who was responsible for the hit and run. On the circular dance floor two elderly women tangoed together. The smaller of the two wore a short kilt with pleats that kicked out as she danced. She held her shoulders stiffly, her expression never changing, even when her companion bent her backwards or spun her around. Her sturdy barrel figure reminded Virginia of her mother. "Eyes to the front, Virginia. Best foot forward."

"How very sad," she murmured. "I hope Lorcan's friend recovers."

"I don't think there's much chance of that." He stubbed out his cigarillo. The barman came and removed the ashtray, left a clean one in its place. "It's hard to get your head around it. Our kids have everything yet they dice with death and come up again for a second round. Are you heading up to bed or can I get you another drink?"

"I'll nurse this one for a few minutes longer, Bill. See you in the morning before you leave."

She watched him walk from the bar. He had a confident stride, almost a strut. As soon as he disappeared the young man glided towards her. His name was Rafael. In heavily accented English he told Virginia he lived in Funchal. He owned a vineyard and a winery. He knew her official guide, his mother's second cousin, easily deposed. Tomorrow morning Rafael would take personal charge of her. He held her closely as they danced. His fingers pressed lightly but insistently against the thin material of her dress. Later, in her bedroom, she watched it slide from his fingers to the floor.

The relief of not having to justify, defend, comfort, console, pacify, pretend. Virginia had forgotten what it was like simply to be herself. Madeira's height and corkscrew roads, the terraced farms and vineyards hacked from volcanic rock, were easy to explore. She walked in shaded parks blazing with Bird of Paradise flowers and trekked through the levadas. In bed, Rafael was a demanding lover, leaving her exhausted but satisfied when he slipped quietly from her side in the early hours. She suspected a wife or, considering his age, possibly a fiancée, but she had no interest in his personal life. Nor did he ask questions about the life awaiting her at home.

On the day before she was due to leave, he parked the car in a small mountain village. The shops were closed, siesta time. They sat on a stone bench beneath an overhanging tree and picnicked on cheese and wine. Lizards darted under the shade of stones; leaves rustled above them. She stretched out and rested her head on his knees. The spill of purple bougainvillea was a wafting scent, reminding her of the sweet-smelling pot-pourri in Sonya's cushions, and she drifted deeper into childhood – hearing the canary singing and the glass hearts tinkling as they danced from the ceiling. She forced herself awake, the sun hot on her face, her mouth dry. As they gathered the remains of the picnic and returned to the car the beginnings of a headache throbbed against her temples.

Rafael continued his drive along the mountain, climbing higher and higher until they were travelling through a labyrinth of tunnels. Streams of water cascaded from the cliff face and played a dull rumbling tune against the side of the car. He assured her that a restaurant with a magnificent view over the coast awaited them at the end of their journey. It was owned by his friend who would be delighted to entertain a group of Irish journalists. She must definitely add it to her planned itinerary. He entered another tunnel. The car's headlights cast a frail light into the pitch black interior. Each time they emerged into sunshine, Virginia thought they had reached the summit. Yet the road continued to narrow and rise. The view became even more spectacular. Scaling volcanic rock loomed on one side and, on their side, a narrow ledge separated them from the long drop to the ocean below. Tour buses increased in numbers. The bravado of the coach drivers had ceased to fascinate Virginia. They thundered towards the car, arrogant daredevils who signalled impatiently at Rafael to make more space and he, shouting insults back at them, casually manoeuvred the car closer to the edge. She huddled against the seat, eyes closed, her stomach churning. When she screamed the sound was detached, as if another entity had entered the car and was careering downwards with her towards the glittering ocean.

Rafael steered the car into a lay-by and tried to calm her down. Perspiration soaked her skin. He ordered her to breathe deeply, everything would be OK … OK … they were nearly there. He sounded bewildered, helpless in the face of her terror.

"Calm down. We're safe … we're safe. I know these roads like my own hand."

This realisation made no difference. She wrenched open the door and was violently sick, her stomach shuddering, the bilious taste of wine making her eyes water. A bus thundered past, swerving treacherously around a bend, breaks squealing, exhaust fumes belching. She breathed deeply. Ten deep breaths would do the trick. Concentrate on the future. The future was all that mattered.

CHAPTER FORTY-NINE

"It will snow before nightfall." Noeleen called to the house on her way to the village and cast an experienced gaze towards the sky. "It's waiting to happen. Stock up on anything you need. We won't be going anywhere in a hurry over the next few days."

Brendan arrived shortly afterwards to make sure the central heating was in order. He was followed by his father with a trailer of logs, which his sons helped stack against the outside kitchen wall. In the afternoon Lorraine drove to the supermarket. Snow dashed lightly against the windscreen as she entred the car-park. Sophie was at the check-out, swaddled in a brown padded coat, her vibrant colours hidden. In the art class she painted sunshine. Golden orbs high in the sky, black upturned faces.

"This weather is destroying my life blood," she moaned. "Each winter I say, no more, no more, but what can I do?"

The initial flurry of snow stopped as suddenly as it had started. Clouds were whisked aside and on the journey home the sun shone with sparkling clarity on the snow-covered hills. The branches, caught in the flash of sunlight, reminded Lorraine of supplicating arms reaching upwards into the wintry sky. She was relieved to see the school bus pulling away from the top of the lane. Emily was walking fast, her hands plunged deep into the pockets of her school coat, her scarf flapping wildly behind her.

"I'm freezing to death," she whined, climbing into the car. "Everyone says we're going to be marooned. I'd better make sure Antoinette and Janine are comfy." She leaned forward to peer through the windscreen. "There's a car outside our house. Were you expecting someone?"

"Not as far as I know."

His car was parked against the hedgerow, already blanketed with a light dusting of snow, empty. She recognised it instantly and felt the wheels of her own car glide dangerously towards it. She had not expected him to arrive so soon. He had left the car doors unlocked. *The Irish Times* was folded on the passenger seat beside his mobile phone. A manuscript lay on top with pencil notes scribbled in the margins.

Emily was stacking groceries into presses when she entered the kitchen.

"Who owns the car?" she asked

"Michael Carmody."

"My God! What's he doing here? You said he wasn't coming back again."

Lorraine reached upwards to place the last of the groceries out of sight. "I can't always be right, Emily."

"Where's he gone?"

"I don't know. Perhaps he went to the farm to see when I'd be back."

"I'll check it out for you." Emily grabbed her parka jacket and left.

Silence settled over the countryside. Even Hobbs was affected by the hush. Only the rooster, determined to outwit nature, crowed triumphantly into the muffled evening. Emily rang to report that Noeleen had earlier seen him crossing the stile and heading towards the beach. The snow was falling again, heavier now, and beginning to swirl on the wind. Lorraine hesitated no longer. Lights were already shining from the windows of the Donaldsons' house. The beach was deserted. If he had left footprints they were already obscured. A cormorant was tossed like parchment against the pewter sky and the kittiwakes huddled on ledges, were silent for once. She called his name, forcing the sound forward into the rising storm. Again and again she shouted, cupping her hands to her mouth, her fear growing as the moments passed.

She heard something. It could have been an echo or the screeching of the cormorant. The old boathouse, barely visible, hulked above the rocky ledge on the half-moon turn. Boats had once slid effortlessly down the jetty when she was a child but over the years much of its wooden structure had collapsed into the sea. Only the shell of the building and its corrugated iron roof were still intact. She climbed from the sand into a tangle of dead fern and heather, searching for the trail that would lead her upwards. Again, she shouted his name. This time his reply was stronger, nearer. The mildewed smell of rotting seaweed reached her as soon as she approached the entrance. She gave a startled shriek when a rat scurried into a rocky crevice.

"Thank God." He ground the words through clenched teeth, his back slumped against the wall. In the gathering gloom his face was a pain-stricken blur, his brown eyes shadowed with exhaustion. "I thought you might have been on the beach. It started to snow and I tried to find a short cut back to the lane. I hauled myself in here and hoped to Christ you'd find me before the waves did." He rocked forward in agony. "I think I've gone and broken my bloody leg. Stupid ... stupid thing to do."

She removed her coat and put it over him, pulled her cap over his head, held his face between her hands. "Michael, listen to me. You're safe here. The sea seldom rises to this height. I'm going for help."

When he tried to move the pain jerked his head back with such force that she heard the thud of flesh on rock. He gripped her hand tightly. "Lorraine, I wanted to see you so desperately."

"We'll talk later. Everything's going to be all right."

She emerged from the shelter and heard, all around her, the fury of the sea as it struck the rocks, and the high screech of the wind, carrying its burden of snow. Unhindered by hills or walls, it almost tossed her off her feet. The Donaldsons responded immediately. Noeleen rang for an ambulance while Frank grabbed blankets and ran with his sons to the boathouse.

"Put this coat on you, for the love of the Lord Jesus." Noeleen rushed after her and flung a coat over Lorraine's shoulders.

Michael fainted when they lifted him and laid him carefully on a plank covered with blankets. It formed a make-shift stretcher with Lorraine carrying the fourth corner. The journey back to the lane was hazardous and completed in darkness. Emily led the way, holding aloft a storm lantern. Lorraine felt the cold sinking into her bones. She imagined him dragging his body towards the boathouse. He must have screamed many times before he reached it. Perhaps he lost consciousness on the journey.

"The hospital can't guarantee an ambulance for at least an hour." Noeleen, dwarfed under a bright yellow oilskin jacket, met them at the stile. "I'm just hoping it'll be able to make it down the lane."

"I'll bring him in the jeep." Frank spoke with authority. "Even if the ambulance comes within the next hour it won't get through to us. The man's in deep shock. There's no time to waste."

"Better be on your way then." Noeleen stared nervously into the night. "I'll phone ahead and tell them to expect you."

"I'll go with you," said Lorraine and held Michael's hand as he was moved into the back seat of the jeep.

Accident and emergency was crowded. After an initial examination Michael was moved on a trolley into a cubicle. A young nurse apologised. Hopefully, tomorrow morning, a bed would be available. The woman in the next cubicle coughed persistently. An elderly man, injured when his car skidded into a ditch, loudly demanded attention.

"We'd better be starting back." The drive to the hospital had been slow and Frank was becoming increasingly worried. "I'll let you say your goodbyes. See you in the car-park, Lorraine."

She lifted her coat from the chair. It felt damp and heavy, a wet-wool smell seeping from the fibres. Michael gripped her hand, pulled her closer to the trolley.

"I owe you my life, Lorraine." He spoke quietly, his eyes half-closed, already drifting on the medication he had received.

"Why didn't you tell me you were coming?"

"I needed to talk to you."

The snow was turning into a blizzard. She could see it swirling past the window and imagined it settling on the lane, banking high between the hedgerows. She bent over him and kissed his cheek.

"I'd better not keep Frank waiting. We'll talk another time. For now, you need to rest. If I'm able to drive I'll be in to see you tomorrow. Do you want me to phone anyone … Killian?"

Her hair brushed his face. His eyes darkened, as if he remembered the spread of it on his bed. He tried to rise. The effort made him gasp and collapse back against the pillow. "Don't worry about Killian," he said. "I'll take care of him."

At the door she turned and waved.

"I love you." He mouthed the words towards her.

Her fingers curled tightly into a fist. All the love she would ever need flowed across the distance and was accepted by her.

The countryside held its breath for three days as snow floated lightly from branches, crunched icily beneath their footsteps. The occupants of the lane moved within their marooned ambit, separated from the main road by sculpted drifts that sparkled like crushed shards of crystal but showed no signs of thawing. School was cancelled and Emily struggled regularly through the snow to check on the well-being of horse and pony. Frank and his sons arrived with spades to help Lorraine clear the way to her studio. An unfamiliar shape hung over everything. The clinking sound of shovels, the hidden caw of crows, the bold chirp of a robin on the window ledge and the gnawing wind, forcing its way through the trees, played an eerie melody as they worked.

The urge to paint was strong. If the bats flew above the windbreak trees she did not notice. Darkness was everywhere when she left her studio on the third night. Even the glow from the windows of Donaldsons' farmhouse had been extinguished. Snow crunched underfoot. A new moon disappeared behind clouds and emerged again to float in its silver aureole. A distant reach. A promise waiting to be fulfilled. She walked forward into its pale, filtering light.

"The specialist says I'll be climbing mountains as soon as I'm back on my feet." Michael's leg had been operated on and he had rung earlier in the day with a progress report. "Are you still cut off?"

"It's possible Frank will be able to drive the tractor to the top of the lane tomorrow," Lorraine replied. "If he can, I'll follow in his tracks. The main roads are gritted. They should be fine for driving."

"I don't want you to take any risks," he warned. "Promise you'll only come if the way is safe?"

"Promise."

"I want to talk about Killian." His voice was still slurred from the anaesthetic. "It's important that we meet as soon as possible."

The following morning the thaw was underway. Water dripped from the eaves of the old house and the crunch beneath Lorraine's feet became a squelch. Snow slid easily from Michael's car. She opened the door and removed his manuscript and mobile phone. As she expected, the phone was dead. It was the same model as her own and she plugged it into her battery charger. Emily, muffled in scarves and a woolly cap, opened the kitchen door and stamped water over the floor.

"This weather is driving me *nuts*. Con won't let me ride Janine until it clears." She buttered bread, sliced cheese and tomatoes, switched on the sandwich maker. The smell of toasting cheese filled the kitchen.

"I can't believe I rescued the creator of *Nowhere Lodge* from certain death," she said, noticing his manuscript on the table." She carried it and the sandwich to the sofa where she read avidly for the rest of the morning. "My friends will never believe this." Occasionally, she chortled. "I bet I'm the only person in the world who knows what's going to happen in the next series. Can I visit him this afternoon? I've a number of suggestions to make. Some of his plot lines are way off target."

"You certainly cannot visit him. He's recovering from serious surgery."

"Then I'll make some notes. Be sure and give them to him. Tell him I'm prepared to accept ten Jason Judge autographs as payment. Otherwise –" she paused for dramatic effect, "I'll reveal everything to the tabloids."

"I'll warn him."

"I like it when you laugh and mean it."

"Glad to know something meets with your approval."

"Are you all right about me staying in Dad's apartment next weekend?"

"I already told you. It's fine."

"It's not fine at all. But he's under house arrest. She's such a calculating, conniving *cow*. No! That's too insulting to the mother of my calf. She's a blistering, bollocking bitch!"

"Emily!"

"Stop pretending to be Saint Lorraine. If I were in your shoes I'd take out a contract on her. She was supposed to be your best friend and all the time she was cheating behind your back."

"Stop it immediately. Do you hear me? *Stop* it."

"It's never going to be all right again with Dad, is it?"

"Not the way it was. I can't turn the clock back, no matter how much you want me to."

"If you went for counselling, it could help. I read an article on mediation. This woman said it gave her and her husband a whole new perspective on their marriage. I cut the article out of the paper for you."

Lorraine had a sudden desire to slap her daughter. A sharp smack on her backside which would silence her instantly, stop the aimless drivel she felt obligated to fling at her mother whenever the opportunity rose. With the pony, Adrian had broken through the last of Emily's defences. Lorraine had been aware of a shifting in the balance of blame. Somehow, Adrian, working gently, persuasively, had managed to obtain his daughter's support and the two women who had been in the centre of his life for more years than Lorraine cared to count were now assuming responsibility for his marriage break-up. She stared at the set of her daughter's mouth, the wilful expression disguising her confusion, and knew that Emily was as adrift as she was, battling too many conflicting emotions, dreaming too many impossible dreams.

The sudden flash of anger drained away and Lorraine was overwhelmed by all they had lost. It was a pure feeling of loss. Nothing else, no fury, disbelief or jealousy. She sank to the sofa and began to weep. Emily held her close. The reversal of roles was instantaneous and her daughter's arms were strong. Later, they could reclaim their rightful order in the echelons of family life but for the moment there was just the comforter and the comforted.

A phone call from the hospital came as Lorraine was preparing to leave the house. The nurse was apologetic. Complications had arisen and Michael was under observation until his temperature settled. Could Lorraine postpone her visit until tomorrow? The nurse was reassuring but her brisk voice did nothing to lessen Lorraine's apprehension. She remembered the urgency in his voice when he mentioned his son, his anxiety to see her as soon as possible. She moved indecisively around the kitchen, unable to settle. The opportunity of painting for the afternoon held no appeal. The studio was cold and the earlier bout of weeping had drained her energy. Emily was also suffering from severe cabin fever and intended cycling through the slush to visit the friend whose house was closest to Stile's Lane. She emerged from her bedroom in black cycling trousers, a yellow puffa jacket and bicycle helmet. "Don't say it," she warned her mother. "I know I look like an obese wasp but you will insist on the helmet. Can I sleep in Fran's tonight?"

"That depends on whether we're discussing a male or female," Lorraine replied, still puzzled on the gender issues surrounding this particular friend.

"You think Fran's a *girl*?" Outraged, Emily stared at her mother.

"It's the eye shadow that makes me uncertain."

"So? Has anyone ever stopped you wearing aftershave?"

"I don't wear aftershave."

"But Fran wouldn't stop you if you wanted to. Why can't he wear eye shadow? Your generation are always labelling people. It's so … *so* old age stuff."

"All I asked was – oh, never mind. I'll ring his mother and check if it's OK."

"We're planning a surprise birthday party for the goths." She bared her teeth, stuck two index fingers to the sides of her mouth. "We're going to dress up as vampires and invite them over to his house. Then we're going to jump out on them from behind the kitchen door."

"Have you considered the possibility that Janis and Joplin could drop dead from shock?"

"Then we suck their blood." She guffawed heartily.

Mother and daughter had reverted to their natural roles.

CHAPTER FIFTY

Killian

Snowflakes in a glass orb. Still and peaceful, shining like a diamond on his grandmother's mantelpiece. He shakes the world. Shakes it in his fist. Watches the snowflakes swirl. Watches them settle. He waits for the night shift.

A broken tibia, Killian. What on earth was your father doing in Trabawn? Never heard of the place. Don't fret, he'll be back soon. Duncan got a star in school today. Best boy in class. He's with me now. Say hello to Killian.

Hello … hello … can we go home now?

Another boy band in the charts, Killian. White suits, ugh! I've got a rose tattooed on my shoulder. See? Mum is threatening to lock me up and throw away the key. Lorcan's a suit. Can you believe it? He showed me his business card. Advertising Executive. He's even carrying a briefcase. Says it impresses the hell out of his old man.

Knock Knock. Who's there? B-4. B-4 who? Let me in B-4 I freeze to death. Ha Ha Ha.

The job's crap, my mate. Guy's a snowflake. He doesn't see me. Just the old man's money. She's a bit of all right but a real ball breaker. Wake up, Killian. Wake up! I want to talk to you proper.

My daughter text tonight. She has a boyfriend now. A biker boy. Angel from hell. I worry he will go too fast. Soon I see my family. Soon, little soldier, soon.

Killian, it's Meg. See what I've got. The Cat in the Hat! *Bet you remember every word. But I'm going to read it again, anyway. Eoin's here too. He brought you a xylophone. Listen to the notes ... doh ray me fah soh lah tee doh. Listen again ... and again ... sing with your heart, Killian, and we will hear you.*

I've put on weight. Comfort eating. My wedding dress is too tight. Fuck! Why did I ever say yes?

There you are, Loveadove. I'll park my trolley and we'll begin. Am I holding biscuits in my hand? One blink for yes, two for no.
    Blink.
    How many biscuits am I holding up?
    Blink! Blink! Blink!
    Three it is. A genius ... a bleedin' genius, that's what you are! What's with those goats in their white coats? Don't know their arses from their elbows. Goats in white coats – listen to me. I'm a bleedin' poet. Isn't that what I am?
    Blink!

Killian my wandering boy. Where have you gone? Further than any of us, I should imagine. Wait till I tell you about the Milford Sound! Such magnificence. Such adventures. I'll bring you with me next time. Maggie says you're counting. How many fingers have I got? Three, you say. Three fingers and a thumb. Lost one in Alaska. Bet it's preserved better than I am. Where on earth is your father? Lucky I had the key to his apartment or I'd have spent the night on the corridor. His phone is off. It's not like him to be out of contact. Must ring Jean, see what's going on.

PART FOUR

Chapter Fifty-One

"Is this Michael's phone?" The voice at the other end had the huskiness of a heavy smoker.

"Yes, it is," Lorraine replied.

"Can I speak to him, please? I've been trying to contact him since last night."

She had been clearing the breakfast dishes from the table when she remembered his mobile phone. The call came shortly after she removed it from the charger and switched it on.

"I'm afraid he's still in hospital."

"Jean told me about his accident. How is he?"

"He's over his operation. Yesterday, his temperature was still high but I've been speaking to him this morning and he sounds fine."

"Who are you, my dear?"

"My name is Lorraine Cheevers. Michael's accident happened close to where I live. I'll be visiting him shortly."

"I'm his aunt, Harriet Carmody. Could you give me the telephone number for the hospital? I flew in from New Zealand late last night but he wasn't expecting me back for some weeks yet."

Lorraine flicked among the papers on the telephone table and called out the hospital number.

"I'll ring him right away." The woman thanked her. "He must be extremely worried about Killian."

"Is Killian all right?"

"There's no change, at least not that I can notice. But I'm afraid the prognosis remains as bleak as ever."

"Prognosis?"

"I'm in the clinic with him at the moment. How long does Michael expect to be in hospital?"

"I'm not sure ... are you saying there's something *seriously* wrong with Killian?"

"There's no deterioration in his condition, if that's what you mean. He's still in a deep coma but I was talking to the tea lady before I rang you and she insists there are signs of an increased response. She may have something there. It's so hard to be certain. If the doctors knew what she's doing they'd have apoplexy."

"But Michael said ... are you telling me that Killian is in a *coma?*" Lorraine's voice faltered, fell silent.

"Hasn't Michael told you about his son?" The woman sounded surprised.

"No." His mobile phone was heavy in her hand. "What happened to him?"

After the phone call ended, she sat at the table and stared towards the window. Her skin felt hot, attacked by a heat rash or a fever. Water dripped like tears from the eaves, shimmered in the glare of winter sunshine. Her eyes were dry as she left the house and drove towards the hospital.

She knew the Hammond Clinic, a small private hospital where one of Donna's friends had died after being in a coma for a month. Afterwards, a short memorial service had been held in the oratory. Her abiding memory of that occasion was the deep peaceful silence that filled the corridors. A deceptive silence, born out of desperation as relations waited for a signal, a sigh, a whisper from their loved ones who lay sleeping behind closed doors.

Snow lingered on the hospital roof but the flower beds were splashed with green. Early crocuses poked spiky stalks above the earth and the snowdrops were once again visible. He sat outside the bedcover. One leg was heavily encased in plaster of Paris from thigh to shin. The devastation on his face confirmed that his aunt had already been in touch.

He winced when she flung his mobile phone on the bed. "You have to give me a chance to explain," he said. "Please sit down, Lorraine."

"Why?" she demanded. "What possible explanation can you give me? You wanted me to meet your son. To paint his portrait. I don't understand –" She was unmindful of the other patients, the visitors who paused in their conversations to glance curiously in their direction.

"I was going to tell you today. I don't know what I was going to say – but I hoped to make you understand. I'd no idea Harriet was returning so soon from New Zealand."

"She said Killian was knocked down in a hit-and-run accident."

"Yes."

"Why did you lie to me? What possible reason could there be to tell such a terrible lie?"

"I believed you were responsible for his accident." The words fell dully, shockingly, between them.

Seeing her expression grow more incredulous, he pleaded. "Please give me time to explain properly, Lorraine."

She tried to concentrate on what he was saying. His voice seemed far away, unconnected. She pushed the chair back from his bed. She needed distance if she was to hold herself together. He stretched out his hand to comfort her, a jerking movement that disturbed the cast. The pull of his cheeks revealed his pain.

"Where did the accident happen?" she asked.

"On the Great South Wall."

A boy on the pier, the ferry sailing towards the horizon. Every word they had spoken was meaningless, every gesture misunderstood. Their loving … she closed her eyes, unable any longer to look at him. How he must have hated her, even as he kissed her mouth and stirred her with emotions she believed had been buried forever. He had raped her with his thoughts, desired what he despised, swallowed her in his dark, deep eyes. "Don't say anything else. I can't bear to hear another word. Every time we were together I sensed it. But I couldn't understand –"

"I never meant to fall in love with you. It didn't make sense. You've no idea how hard I fought against those feelings but they cut through everything, the evidence and suspicions, all the anger. I went to Trabawn to accuse you." He forced her to listen. "But that time in your studio … Killian almost died. We didn't believe he'd make it back."

Tears rushed into her eyes. She willed them away. She had shed too many tears over love.

He mentioned Meg's name and other names that meant nothing to her. She was unable to absorb what he was saying. His voice was too fast, incoherent almost, his breathing shallow, his complexion as translucent as wax.

Before Meg and Eoin went to the States, they had thrown a farewell party. The house was so crowded that people spilled out into the back garden. Had Michael Carmody been among the crush of people who raised their glasses and wished Eoin success in his sabbatical? Had they noticed each other among the crowd then passed on by, never registering the moment? Surely she would have remembered his searching gaze. But she would not have been the object of his attention, not then, not when their worlds were intact and secure.

"I'm leaving, Michael." She willed her legs to hold her upright.

If she walked from the ward she could reach her car in five minutes. Spine erect, eyes looking straight ahead. He pleaded with her to stay but then, realising the enormity of his accusation, his head fell back against the pillows and he was silent.

She ignored the urge to run but once outside the hospital she hurried towards the car-park. She gripped the steering wheel and drove carefully away. How was she to make sense of anything? A portrait of his son. She was mired in lies. Surrounded by illusions.

He rang her house and left messages. She ignored his entreaties, his declarations of love. He was discharged from hospital. Fred Byrne arrived and removed his car. The grass where it had rested was flat and withered.

His manuscript arrived in a Jiffy envelope a week later, sheets of printed paper stapled together. He had handwritten the brief note accompanying it.

I wrote this when I was in a dark place. Please read it and try to understand how I could have been so wrong.

She read about his son. The bitter struggles to claim his love, his loyalty. What a picture he painted. Tug love eventually replaced by tough love. She read about a wino with a clown's name, a vandalised car, painting materials in the boot, a bracelet in the dashboard, uniquely designed, stolen by a homeless youth called Ferryman.

Silver was a colour of many hues: the moon above the sea, a shimmer of mist on hedgerows, the gleam in the edge of a sharpened blade. It reflected in the plunge of a needle, glittered on a woman's wrist. In the dead of night, silver was a bullet waiting to strike.

CHAPTER FIFTY-TWO

Brahms ward
5 p.m.

Killian, I'm here now. Don't mind me lumbering around the ward. I'm an awkward ass on these crutches. What a time I've had of it ... what a time. Never mind. Onwards march, as Meg says. She gave me a right tongue-lashing, I can tell you. You look stronger today. Good colour on your cheeks. I like the new pyjamas.

Maggie says you're pressing her hand, blinking with your eyes, sending signals.

"Goats in white coats." She thinks she's the new poet laureate. "Your lad has a grip as tight as a crab's claw and he means business. Go on, see for yourself."

Here's my hand. Tell me – did you miss me when I was in Trabawn? Ouch, Maggie's right. A real bone crusher that was ... oh Killian ... Killian ... don't mind me. I'm a fucked up mess. I'm sorry for staying away so long. As they say, the matter was out of my legs. Sorry, bad joke. Almost as bad as Terence's knock knockers.

Count my fingers. Five blinks, excellent. How many fingers has Harriet? All present and correct, my man. I was fifteen years old when I told her I wanted to follow in her footsteps, figuratively speaking, not literally. Unlike your great-aunt, I'd no interest in paddling the waters of the Ganges or trekking to the roots of the Grand Canyon. I filled pages with unremarkable poems which she slashed with her eyes and said, "Dead words, Michael. I want to live inside your head, not stare at your thoughts through a window that shines too brightly from other people's elbow grease. Bring me on a journey where I touch, smell, see, breathe, love."

I sent your story winging through the post, addressed to Trabawn. Did she read it, I wonder, or did she scatter the pages to the wind? She never replied. She found me in a boathouse, a gaping mouth facing the sea. She held me in her arms. I didn't care about the pain. That's the way it is with love.

You remind me of my mother when you look at me like that. Eyes like pennies. Lorraine's eyes closed me out. Her face seemed to break apart when I tried to explain. From the beginning we were on different wavelengths yet they joined together and everything seemed possible. Strange things, telephone calls. The one that brought an ambulance to the pier saved your life. The one Harriet made destroyed mine.

Do you think your father is a crazy, sad old man? Blink once for yes. Twice for no.

∽

Blink!

CHAPTER FIFTY-THREE

Emily was still undressed, slouched across the armchair in her pony slippers and horse-printed pyjamas. "Gary's parents are moving to Australia. He'll be forced to go with them so that's him out of the series – which is brilliant. Ibrahim thinks he's an *absolute* abysmal asshole and I agree. Jessica's career as a singer with Love Bytes will collapse in ruins. She's *such* a bossy, belligerent, bellicose bitch. The way she treats Jason Judge makes me sick. Naomi becomes pregnant." She shook her head in amazement. "Naomi! Can you believe she'd be so stupid, especially doing it with Gary – *ughh!*"

Virginia sighed wearily and resisted the urge to glance at her watch. "Emily, I haven't a clue what you're talking about. Are these friends of yours because if they are –?"

"Don't be ridiculous!" Emily's laughter had a distinctly whinnying quality. Too much time mucking out stables, from the sound of it. "They're the characters in *Nowhere Lodge*. I already explained that to you. My mother's boyfriend writes the series. I rescued him from certain death."

"Yes indeed. You *did* already tell us the story." Adrian's indulgence had been severely tested over the weekend. "Can you please change the subject and talk about something intelligent?"

Virginia had armed herself with a full schedule for Emily's visit. Cooking chips and burgers, or whatever glutinous

298

concoction teenagers were fed, was not on the agenda. After collecting her from the train on Friday evening they had dined out. A visit to an equestrian centre took care of Saturday afternoon. Pony paradise. The three of them went riding together. What a picture they cut, trotting through Pine Forest in jodhpurs and riding boots. Adrian was still sitting down with extreme caution and complaining about a shifting disc in his lower back. The evening had ended with pub grub on the way home and Emily had gone straight to her room.

Apart from constantly demanding her father's attention, and playing on his guilt by mentioning Lorraine's name at every conceivable opportunity, she had behaved like any normal pubescent horsy teenager over the weekend. One last visit to a restaurant – Virginia had decided on Thunder Road Café as a special treat – and then it was time for the train journey home. Sweet blissful relief.

"You'd better get dressed, Emily." She forced enthusiasm into her voice. "We'll soon be leaving for Thunder Road."

"We're not eating out a*gain*?" Emily lifted her shoulders to her ears in amazement. "Don't you ever do home cooking? Mum is the most brilliant cook, isn't she, Dad? Remember the pavlova she used to make for dessert on Sundays? Deliciously delightful, delicately –"

"You heard Virginia." Adrian sounded close to breaking point. "We're eating out and then we're driving you to the station."

"Bloody brilliant."

"Don't swear."

"Fucking fantastic."

"Emily! We've tried very hard to make this weekend work." In a battle of wills Virginia was not going to be bested by a spoilt sixteen-year-old. "The least we can expect from you is a degree of courtesy."

Emily crossed her knees. The heads of her pony slippers bobbed threateningly. "Craven, cringing common courtesy."

She sulked her way through brunch, nibbled around the edges of a burger and asked for the remains to be wrapped in a "horsy bag".

Adrian had bought her a pony for her birthday. His business

was floundering and he was squandering money on a pedigree pony. Shortly after Christmas, Virginia had discovered the receipt in a drawer in his office, an innocuous-looking document with "Received with Thanks" stamped across it.

"If she wanted a pet so much why not a hamster?" Outraged, she had waved the receipt in his face. "Why did it have to be a pony?"

He had accused her of spying, forced her to go on the defensive, afraid that he would discover how thoroughly she had searched his office. The amount of unpaid bills in his files had alarmed her. She had read letters from his bank manager, his accountant and the leasing company which provided much of his office equipment. Among the unpaid bills was a demand from Ginia Communications for rent arrears.

Heuston Station was crowded with young people returning to the city after the weekend. Emily hugged her father, suddenly a vulnerable, repentant daughter. Virginia knew the wisdom of avoiding any contact other than a farewell nod.

"We really enjoyed having you to stay, Emily. You must come and visit us again soon."

"Thank you so very much for having me, Virginia." Emily's contrived politeness was more difficult to tolerate than her rudeness.

Virginia willed the train to move. For an instant she saw it jolt forward. Her heart jerked with the same sensation but it remained stationary. Only her heart continued to race in sharp, painful palpitations.

"Well, Virginia, I think a stiff drink is in order, don't you?" Adrian lifted his chin in relief as the train finally eased out of the station. "Don't worry. It's sure to be much easier the next time."

CHAPTER FIFTY-FOUR

The central heating purred. No cracks or dampness marred the walls. The last crate was emptied, contents stored out of sight. What was not needed was dumped in jumbo plastic sacks and flung into the skip. Faintly, Lorraine heard the sounds from the farm, the clink of buckets and churns, the lowing of cows, the rumble of Frank's tractor. The remains of Emily's breakfast were on the table. She lifted a cornflake, nibbled it, grimaced at the stale taste. She made beds, brushed a duster over the furniture. In her daughter's bedroom a framed photograph of Adrian sat on the dressing table. The large montage of family photographs was mounted on the wall. Smiling days. She pressed her face into them and closed her eyes.

The bracelet had fallen from her arm one night when she was at the theatre. She was unaware of her loss until she was leaving and her foot kicked accidentally against it. Adrian had promised to have the clasp repaired but she had no memory of this having been done.

An intertwining rope of silver, two separate strands, coiled but not soldered, softly curved. "A romantic piece," Karl Hyland had declared when he delicately embedded pure blue sapphires within the coils to represent the stepping stones they would cross through their marriage. "I will never make another bracelet like this one. Let it become a love heirloom passed on from one generation to the next."

Karl had been her best friend in college. He was much given to dramatic gestures and flamboyant phrases.

"Amazing." Emily arrived home from school and stared around the tidied house. "Just when I'd adjusted to life in a tip-head you turn my world upside down again."

"I've been searching for my sapphire bracelet." Lorraine pushed her hair from her eyes and sank onto a kitchen chair. "Did you see it anywhere?"

"Have you checked your jewellery box?"

"Obviously! Can you remember packing it when we were leaving Churchview Terrace? *Think*, Emily. I'm exhausted searching for it."

"How should I know? My life was falling apart, if you remember that far back. I wasn't exactly cataloguing everything I packed. Maybe he took it and gave it to *her*."

"Don't be ridiculous."

"Why not?" Emily flung her school satchel into the corner of the kitchen. "He gave her everything else."

Fred Byrne took his reputation seriously. Since Lorraine had refuted his opinion on the state of her car, his manner towards her when she drove into the forecourt for petrol had been polite but distant. In his office, she sat opposite him and spread her hands apologetically towards him.

"I'm here to apologise," she said. "Since the last time we spoke I've discovered it's possible my car was in an accident."

"Possible?" Fred's nostrils narrowed. She had offended him again. "I don't deal in possibilities. If I did my customers could end up in a ditch on the side of the road – *dead*."

She swallowed, forced the words from her. "My car *was* involved in an accident. I'd really appreciate it if you could show me what made you suspicious?"

Fred marched from his office to the forecourt. All that was missing from his demeanour was the wag of a triumphant tail. He lifted the bonnet of her car and peered into the interior.

"It's the little tell-tale signs that give it away. Look closely, now, and see what I'm about. The grommets should be black but they're silver. So are these bolts. It's a dead giveaway that the bonnet's been resprayed. A car would never leave the production line in that condition."

As Lorraine followed his directions she also noticed tiny slivers of silver paint adhered to the front window frame.

"It's a botched job, if ever I saw one." Fred snorted derisively and pointed to a bend in a bar stretching across the front of the engine. "The cross member's dented. The bonnet must have taken a right dint to bend it. And, like I said before, the stereo was ripped out at some stage. I knew it as soon as I started working on the wiring. I'd have a word with the dealer who sold you this car. If you like I'll write down everything and you can show him my signature on the bottom. Cowboys, some of them bastards." He slammed the bonnet closed.

"Thanks, Mr Byrne. You've been very helpful. I'll follow it up."

"No trouble at all. Call me Fred. I hear the art classes are great gas altogether. The wife was talking about maybe giving them a go."

She tried to concentrate on what he was saying. His face swam in and out of her line of vision. She accepted the signed sheet of paper and drove home.

The following day she travelled to Dublin.

The title *Dublin Echo* had always reminded Lorraine of paper-boys with sandwich boards. The interior of the newspaper office with its warren of dark corridors did little to banish this perception. She eventually found the library where the back issues of the newspapers were filed. A frail elderly man led her towards a viewfinder and stooped over her, demonstrating how it should be used. His pasty face blended into a fuzzy white beard. She imagined him living his life within the archival reaches of the building, seldom venturing into the brash modern world outside. She found the reports she needed without any difficulty and paid at reception for the back issues. Then she walked the short distance to Temple Bar where Karl Hyland's jewellery design studio was located.

Karl greeted her with open arms. "Darling girl, too long – *too* long. What's this I hear about you becoming a rustic maiden?" He removed imaginary straw from her hair and hugged her again. "How long are you staying? We have to do dinner. But not tonight. Tomorrow? No? Oh dear, cows calling you back so soon? My heart broke when I heard about you and Adrian. As for Virginia, darling – with friends like that who needs a very best enemy? How's the little one? Cute as ever or has she become one of those revolting teenagers with tongue studs?"

He led her through his shop into the back room where his studio was located. The clutter was in marked contrast to the shop floor where the hushed reverence of a tomb prevailed and an austere young woman in black laid his designs before the public. Karl's patter remained as fast-paced as ever. He filled Lorraine in on who was doing what and living where and with whom, and how they should all get together for a reunion – a suggestion that filled them both with instant enthusiasm and the guilty knowledge that it would probably never happen.

"I wanted to ask about my bracelet." She finally managed to interrupt him.

He stared at her wrist and shook his head in mock disappointment. "An inspired design. Why aren't you wearing it?"

"I've mislaid it for the moment. But I'll find it, don't worry." She stilled his horrified reaction with a smile. "I just wanted to enquire if you'd made any other bracelets using that particular design?"

"*What?* I'm mortally wounded. When Karl Hyland says *unique* that's exactly what he means. How could you even *ask* such a question?"

"I thought there might be others with a similar pattern."

"Not with my name on it, how could there be?"

"Did Adrian leave it in to be repaired?"

"It's some time ago, but I remember. Seeing it again reminded me that I was born to design beautiful things."

"When did he leave it in?"

"Can't remember exactly. Let me check the records." He clicked into a computer, scrolled through names. "Last year,

November 20th. Paid for and collected. I'll cut my throat if you tell me he never gave it back to you."

"No need for such drastic action. I'll find it. Moving house has been such an upheaval. Everything's misplaced."

"Tell me something I don't know." He sighed dramatically. "Twice in the last year I've pulled up roots. The first place was a hole, an absolute coal hole, and the cost! Darling, you wouldn't believe what I was shelling out in rent." She allowed his voice to wash over her. Karl was easy to be around. No hidden fissures.

Adrian was waiting outside Bewley's Café. They entered and made their way towards the self-service counter. The din of voices rising towards the stained-glass windows, the aroma of coffee, croissants and bacon, the glow from the open fire, the rustle of newspapers, everything was comfortingly familiar. Breakfast in Bewley's on a Sunday morning was a treat when Emily was a child yet the very core of their lives had changed and the bustling café was filled with uneasy ghosts. She was not hungry but Adrian insisted on ordering coffee and croissants. He emptied sugar into his cup and stirred it rapidly before speaking again. "You look exhausted. What's wrong?"

"I've lost my bracelet."

"Surely that's not the reason for those shadows under your eyes?"

"I was wondering where you left it after collecting it from Karl. I spoke to him yesterday. He has a record of the repair."

"I left it back in your jewellery box. Why?"

"It's not there now."

"Then you must have left it somewhere else." He smiled across the table. "It's a beautiful piece of jewellery but the memory I have of giving it to you is even more precious. Do you remember the night −"

"Perfectly." Her voice was expressionless. "I remember you presented it to me as a symbol of devotion and fidelity."

"I wish to Christ I could make amends and start again."

"Is the dream not living up to your expectations?"

"I never stopped loving you ... despite everything."

"We've already had this conversation, Adrian. Don't bore me by repeating it. Just give my bracelet back to me."

She watched him run his finger nervously around the rim of his coffee mug. "I told you I don't have it. Why are we fighting, Lorraine? We've hurt each other enough as it is. Surely there are more important things we can discuss?"

"I only asked you to return what belongs to me."

"I gave it to you as a gift. Why should I take it back?"

"You took my trust and flung it away. There's no reason why you should respect a piece of jewellery."

"Jesus Christ, Lorraine." His anger was as instant as she remembered. The flash of temper, the persuasive smile, the dismissive shrug. His gestures were as familiar as his ability to render her questions meaningless. A sleight of hand with the truth. "You can't wait to serve divorce papers on me yet, when you finally decide to contact me, all you do is whinge about that bloody bracelet. What the hell is going on here?"

"I want it back, Adrian. I'll be in touch next week. Have it for me."

I loved this man, she thought, rising to her feet. I loved him to distraction and now, when I look at him, when I talk to him, I feel nothing. Emptiness. She rose from the table, fought against the nausea that threatened to overwhelm her. The fire burned brightly as she walked away, embers falling from the grate and settling into grey ash.

A woman reading beside a bed. Photographs and cards pinned to a wall. The scent of flowers and aromatic oils. Impressions whirled before Lorraine's eyes when she stepped into the ward. The young man lay stiff as an effigy, his body hardly raising the bedcover. Tubes from his body sustained him, drained him. His chin was shadowed with a faint stubble. How calmly he slept. As if aware of her presence his eyelids fluttered and his leg gave a sudden jerk, dislodging a panda bear propped at the foot of the bed. A mangy fur coat, one eye, obviously much loved, much used.

Tears rushed to her eyes. Was he warm or cold, she wondered. Did his heart beat fast or in a slow, uncertain rhythm? A prayer came to her lips. She had never thought of herself as religious, especially since her teenage years, yet, in the presence of such unconsciousness, prayer seemed a natural response. An earthenware bowl filled with oil sat on the locker beside a xylophone. She stepped backwards as the woman raised her face from a book. The lucent quality of her skin added a frailness to her appearance, as if she was recovering from an illness or suffering from deep exhaustion. She wore loose trousers and a silk blouse tucked into the waist. A half-smile softened her mouth when she stood up. The material moved, billowed slightly then settled like a sigh around her.

"Have you come to visit Killian?" she asked.

"I'm sorry. Wrong corridor." Lorraine backed from the ward. "Please forgive my intrusion."

How stilted she sounded, unconvincing. Outside in the corridor she leaned against the wall. The back of her neck was damp with perspiration.

"Are you all right?" The woman quietly closed the door behind her and handed Lorraine a glass of water. "I thought you were going to faint. Would you like to sit down for a moment?"

Lorraine straightened, pushed her hair from her forehead. "I'm fine … really."

"Drink the water. You're still very pale. It's probably the heating. So terribly stifling at times."

Lorraine sipped the water and laid the glass on the window ledge. Down below, beyond the hospital grounds, a swathe of green spread before her. The grey mountains fused into grey cloud. Unable to stop herself, she stared at the closed door of the small private ward. "The young man – he seems so still."

"He's my son."

"I'm so sorry. What you're going through must be unendurable."

"Every day I keep thinking it will happen. When I rise in the morning, I believe today will be the day. He'll call my name, look into my eyes and see me. If it's not today I won't be able to go on. But I do. Day after day after day, wondering if he's dreaming, remembering, feeling pain, hearing noises. If his thoughts are peaceful or tormented." She walked to the window and stared through the glass. "Do you think it will rain this evening? It seems to be coming down from the mountain."

"According to the forecast, yes."

"My younger son can't handle it any more. If it wasn't for my daughter – do you have children?"

"I have a daughter."

"An only child?"

"Yes. I wanted more children but my husband –" Lorraine stopped, took a step backwards. The outpouring of emotion from the woman had released a similar need in her. "I'm keeping you from your son. I'll pray he recovers soon."

"It's our punishment. We demanded from our son what we had no right to demand. Children are God's possessions, not ours. When Jesus is ready to forgive us he will awaken Killian."

"How can that be true?" Lorraine shrank from the agony in the woman's voice. "It's a merciless God who would punish you like this."

"Could I ask you –?" Jean Devine-O'Malley fingered a cross hanging around her neck. The scent of rosemary was on her hands. "Would you pray with me for a short while. The power of prayer is all I've left."

Lorraine resisted the urge to run. The conviction flowing from the woman made excuses meaningless. She thought of Emily riding her pony, running down the lane with Ibrahim and the goths, her endless chatter and moans about life being a bore, so much energy and noise from one young person. This woman's son was a portrait, still and silent, framed by a bed from which there was no escape.

The prayer was short, intense. When it was over Jean Devine-O'Malley made the sign of the cross on her son's forehead and closed her eyes. A tremendous weariness settled on her face.

"Why don't you take a break for a little while?" On her way in Lorraine had noticed a small café off the reception area of the clinic. "I'll sit with your son until you return."

Sometimes he seemed peaceful, his body lying motionless beneath the cover, neither fidgeting nor flailing his limbs. His eyelids fluttered and a grimace, almost too subtle to notice, flashed over his face. She had noticed this fleeting expression a number of times when his mother was praying. It reminded her of the almost-imagined smiles that flit across a baby's face and are often dismissed as wind. He flicked his fingers on one hand, as if they were lightly running over the keys of a piano. She was almost afraid to breathe in case she disturbed his concentration. Suddenly, his eyes opened. His intense stare, so instantly reminding her of his father, caused her to cry out in shock and he, in turn, moved his head slightly, as if the sound had brushed against him. She lifted his hand and pressed it against her cheek.

"My name is Lorraine," she spoke softly. "Your father has told me about you." The pads of his fingers jerked as if stung by faint currents of electricity. "Do you understand me, Killian? Squeeze my hand if you do." The pressure he exerted was weak yet she could not mistake its meaning. She remained in that position for a moment, isolated from the sounds, smells and movements of the clinic.

"Killian, I rage at the thought of them together, driving away, leaving you. How terrified they must be. I don't want them to escape. But Emily, my daughter, what about her? I've watched her struggle to find a way back to her father. This will break her heart. That's the problem with truth. It hurts. Do you hear what I'm saying?"

He batted his eyelids once, a prolonged deliberate blink, before his hand became flaccid. A faint clanking sound outside on the corridor grew louder and stopped outside the door. She watched his long eyelashes flutter with excitement.

A woman entered the ward with a tea trolley and came towards Lorraine. "Jean thought you might fancy a cuppa." She poured tea and laid two biscuits on the saucer. "Friend of the family, are you?"

"I'm keeping her son company for a little while," Lorraine replied.

"He's a real charmer is our Killian, with an eye for the women. Isn't that right, Loveadove?" She tapped the xylophone, startling Lorraine as she struck a scale, then laid her hands on the boy's face, smoothing his forehead with firm even strokes. From the curve of her hand to the turn of her cheek and her solid little body with its determined stance, she was linked to the boy. "See you later, Loveadove."

Jean Devine-O'Malley returned shortly afterwards. She looked more resolute, calm.

"Thank you," she said. "You've been incredibly understanding. What ward do you want? I know every corner of this clinic."

"I was on the wrong floor. Don't worry. I'll find my own way there."

She hurried along the corridor, following the exit sign, and entered the lift. On the ground floor visitors swarmed through the glass doors. Flowers spilled from the entrance of a gift shop. She noticed Michael standing inside the door. For an instant, the crowded vestibule seemed to shrink into a breathless space holding only the two of them. His leg was still in plaster. He moved awkwardly on a crutch towards the counter and spoke to the shop assistant, smiled at some comment she made. Their manner towards each other was familiar. He probably knew everyone, the security staff and nurses, the medical team who kept his son alive. He lifted his head and stared into the mirror behind the assistant's back.

He had come to Trabawn seeking answers, information, building a profile of the woman he believed responsible for the destruction of his son. What if Emily had been tossed on the side of the road and left to die? She would have scoured the earth until she found who was responsible. Her breath shortened as if she could feel the thud of metal, hear the screech of brakes, the surging roar of acceleration. How could they … how could they … to drive away and leave him lying broken in the dark, intent only on keeping their secret world intact.

From the beginning deceit had marred her relationship with Michael Carmody, but now it had become a different kind of deceit. She remembered Adrian's briefcase falling, the crumpled papers with the rust-coloured smears. Blood on their hands. The police would come to her house. They would confiscate her car. There would be forensic examinations, questions, statements, a court case, and Emily, struggling to make sense of her devastated world.

A group of people surged past Lorraine on their way to the

exit. She moved behind them and walked in their footsteps, knowing it was not only physical distance she was putting between herself and Michael but also any hope they had of building a future together.

Ralph asked no questions when he entered her car. Lorraine drove towards the quays. Lights blazed from anchored ships. Small pleasure boats listed on the Liffey breeze. Massive cranes straddled the landscape like the bones of ancient dinosaurs. They walked the length of the pier and stopped at the red lighthouse. Lights spiralled along the headlands. Howth with its thrusting cliffs and hill-top houses and, far into the distance, the fading outlines of Dun Laoghaire winding upwards towards Killiney Head.

She adjusted her camera and began to take photographs. The wings of gulls wove ghostly flight patterns above the waves.

CHAPTER FIFTY-FIVE

Brahms Ward
7.30 p.m.

I see her everywhere. Her smile, her eyes, the shape of her head, her long straight back. It's as if fragments of her being have been soldered to the bodies of strangers. I can't escape her. Even on the way up here, a shake of red hair disappearing into the crowd.

You're calm tonight, Killian. Can you see the fingers I'm holding in the air? Three blinks. Exactly right. Look, I bought you a CD. I rang Laura and asked her advice. She recommended The Streets. Says it's your kind of music. I'm putting on your disc player. Do you like it? Thought you would.

I was on the Internet again last night. The message board was busy as I contacted others who have slept the deep sleep and awoke. Rip Van Winkles who answered my questions, gave me hope, encouraged me to be brave. Some of their stories fill me with terror. But there are also stories of courage and endurance that lift my spirits and keep me believing that miracles can happen.

Your specialist agrees that you are responding to stimuli but he remains cautious. How can he refuse to give us hope when there is hope all around us? I see it in your gaze. Our language is silent but we speak it well. He was outraged when I pointed out that Maggie was the first to communicate with you. Tea for two, two for tea, cha cha cha lady.

The cast is coming off soon. You wouldn't believe the itch. All in all, I'm in good nick. Red hair … I thought for a moment … what the hell. The mind plays crazy tricks. It's enough to make one believe in moving statues.

Hear me, daddy, hear me. She came into the ward. I smelled her perfume. I heard her voice.

CHAPTER FIFTY-SIX

The staff of Ginia Communications officially recognised each other's birthdays with a celebratory cake. A single sparkler was a diplomatic way of marking but not acknowledging the advances of time, and when Virginia's office door opened on the afternoon of her birthday, a heavily decorated Black Forest Gâteau fizzed towards her desk. She switched on a grateful smile as her staff gathered around her and sang "Happy Birthday" and, less enthusiastically, "For She's a Jolly Good Fellow".

The sparkler spluttered into silence and the cake was ready for cutting. Paper plates were produced by Joanne. A bottle of champagne was held aloft by Adrian and uncorked. Lorcan clowned on the floor, pretending to drink the frothing liquid.

The toast was proposed by Adrian who spoke eloquently. "Raise your glasses to a woman who combines beauty, charm and success. To Virginia – who has carried us forward with her energy and dedication. May she remain an inspiration to us all."

She searched his face for signs of mockery. How could he utter such nonsense and sound as if he meant every word? The staff sipped champagne and seemed infused with the same bubbling twaddle. No one appeared remotely inclined to leave her office or quell the party spirit. Helium balloons with her name and birthday wishes bobbed from the corners, and Lorcan reduced the staff to hysterical laughter by imitating a chipmunk. His linen suit was crumpled, but fashionably so, and accessorised with a crisp white shirt. Take away the prisoner-of-war hairstyle, change his belief that the world was a kip and Lorcan Sheraton could be quite a prepossessing young man.

Mara Robertson, the owner of the art gallery, arrived, armed with more champagne. Only for Kathleen, the receptionist, who had remained steadfast at her desk fielding phone calls, they might as well have closed the shutters for the next hour. As the noise level increased, Virginia slipped outside to the corridor and hurried towards the elevator. On the reception desk Kathleen was glumly painting her nails.

"How's the party going?" she asked.

"It needs you to make it swing, Kathleen. I'll take over while you have a glass of champagne."

"Oh no, that's not necessary, it's your party. It wouldn't be right —" Kathleen tried to hide her surprise at this unexpected gesture.

"One glass of champagne and a slice of Black Forest, then you report back here. And tell my staff that I want everyone's heads bent over their desks by the time I return. Now scoot! You're wasting precious time."

Kathleen needed no further encouragement. For twenty minutes Virginia answered the phone. She clicked into her e-mail and noted that another one had arrived from Ralph. She read it twice before deleting it.

Sent: 7 March 2.00 p.m.
Subject: Birthday wishes

Happy Birthday, Virginia. Did he bring you breakfast in bed? Was there a red rose on your tray? Did he lay you back against the pillows and kiss every inch of your delectable flesh? How well I remember my sexy birthday girl.
Razor

A motorbike courier obeyed the notice to remove his helmet before entering Blaide House and walked towards reception.

From his satchel he removed a large foil-coloured envelope and handed it across the desk. She signed her name to the delivery form and laid it to one side.

Usually Ralph's e-mails came at night or in the early hours, as if he too were sleepless, waiting for the dawn. They had started arriving two weeks ago. Sometimes she deleted his messages without reading them but he persisted, growing bolder, more demanding, signing himself by that ridiculous nickname, drawing her back into the rough embrace of another era. He would tire of the game eventually and leave her alone.

Kathleen returned to reception in a decidedly giddy frame of mind but the office staff had recovered some sense of decorum and were busily engaged in various functions when Virginia returned. Their busyness did not fool her for a moment. She resigned herself to a wasted working afternoon. It was time to call a halt to this ridiculous tradition of downing tools just because someone had added another year to life's quota. She retreated into her own office to open the envelope that had been delivered by the courier. She lifted out a birthday card, a tasteless picture of balloons and champagne, similar in style to the scenario her staff had forced upon her. She scanned the card for a signature but there were only words written in block capitals. *HAPPY BIRTHDAY VIRGINIA. IS THE PAST FINALLY CATCHING UP WITH YOU? XXX.* A black and white photograph had been placed in the centre of the card.

Once, when she and Edward were small, they found a small bird caught in chicken wire at the bottom of their garden. She remembered the frantic beat of the bird's wings as Edward tried to save it, beating away its rescuer even as it struggled desperately to be free. Her heart beat at the same frantic pace. She laid the photograph on her desk and stared down at the picture of a late-night ferry casting reflections on the water as it sailed towards the North Wall terminal.

She did not show the photograph to Adrian until they returned to the apartment that evening.

"Jesus Christ, Virginia. Someone knows." His Adam's apple jerked violently.

"Someone thinks they know," she replied.

"How can you be so calm? Don't you understand anything? Someone *knows*. What are we going to do?"

On the wall behind him a Picasso print hung slightly to one side. Her hands itched to straighten it. "We do nothing. Whoever sent this is trying to spook us. What can they prove?"

"What can they prove?" Savagely, he mocked her accent. "They can blackmail us, report us to the police, destroy our lives." His expression reminded her of a cartoon rabbit, petrified at the end of a gun barrel.

"But first they need proof. Without proof they have nothing. This is bluff, Adrian. Nothing more, nothing less."

"What if you're wrong? We should have gone to the police as soon as it happened but you were so adamant, so sure of yourself. Oh Christ, why did I listen to you?"

"Stop it!" Her anger forced him into silence. "We had no option but to drive away. If we'd gone to the police it would have ruined everything."

"It was ruined anyway." His laughter verged on hysteria.

"Is that how you see us? A ruin?"

"Stop putting words into my mouth."

"Then what do you mean?"

"We could have worked something out between us. Made up an explanation as to why we were on the pier –"

He was burrowing into her strength, diminishing it. "Don't be ridiculous. There was only one reason why we were there. It wouldn't take a rocket scientist to figure that one out."

"I don't care. The accident wasn't our fault, as you're so fond of reminding me. No judge would have blamed us."

"Since when did you become an expert on the judicial system?"

"I'm telling you –"

"No! Let *me* tell you the consequences of what you're suggesting. If he dies we're on a murder charge, as well as being responsible for leaving the scene of an accident and hiding the evidence. We have to continue as normal. Otherwise –"

He seemed unable to hear her. "It's damage limitation, Virginia. You of all people should understand the concept. We need a good lawyer –"

"Go to the police if that's what you want to do. Go on – *go*!

See what good that will do. It won't make any difference to the boy. And what about Emily? What will she think of you? Forget any future with her. It's over."

"But it's the past that's the problem, Virginia. Not the future."

Sent: 9 March 2.00 a.m.
Subject: Loneliness

Virginia ... remember? A Chinese takeaway, beanbags on the floor. We played the Buzzcocks over and over again. "Ever Fallen in Love" was our song. I tasted your hot mouth. Oh, how I tasted you. You laughed when we came together, laughed into my shoulder, bit hard into my flesh and rested – but only for a short while – in the crook of my arm. Remember Virginia – remember the magic? Rain on the windows, you and I locked indoors against the world. Answer me. My witch, my bitch. Tell me you've forgotten. I'm lonely tonight, Virginia.
Razor

Virginia's personal assistant entered with the post and daily papers, which she laid across her employer's desk. Most correspondence only needed a cursory glance before being passed on to various members of staff but it gave Virginia an overview of everything that was going on throughout her company. It also afforded her an opportunity to view the newspaper clippings supplied by the cutting agency employed to track publicity material about her clients.

She picked up a large manila envelope and slit it open. The newspaper clipping was heavily underlined. POLICE SEEK INFORMATION ON HIT-AND-RUN ACCIDENT. The same anonymous message that accompanied the birthday card was stapled to the clipping. Not a muscle moved in her face as she read the report. She glanced towards her assistant, wondering if she too was aware that the air had suddenly been sucked from the office, but the young woman was breathing calmly as she moved to the window and opened the blinds to the exact angle ordained by Virginia.

The afternoon passed. Adrian's mobile phone had been switched off. Lorcan said he was at a meeting. She discussed a forthcoming product launch with Joanne. A rapid-bonding adhesive, no matter how sticky and revolutionary, was such an uninteresting product to promote that even Virginia's professionalism had faltered when assembling the press kit. It was late in the afternoon when Lorcan rang through. Adrian had returned to his office. He would see her now.

He stood with his back to the door, absorbed in watching the progress of a blue-bottle across the windowpane. When she called his name he turned and walked towards his desk. She noted its tidiness, empty of clutter, no ideas roughly sketched, no catchy slogans, storyboards, transparencies. He slumped into his chair and waved her into an armchair with wide-angled arms. She sank deeply into soft cushions. The fly swept over her head and dive-bombed around the office before fluttering back to the window.

"Poor bastard." Adrian sighed. "How long will it take before the light dawns?"

"Fly watching may be an interesting pastime but it's not going to solve our problems." She did not like sitting in such a low chair. "I assume your untimely departure from your office had to do with this." She struggled to her feet and laid the clipping before him.

He gestured towards the litter bin where he had dumped the shredded clippings from his own copy. "What can I say, Virginia? We're fucked and it's all your fault."

Sent: 13 March 5.30 p.m.
Subject: Sighting

Another day over, Virginia. Did you miss me ... even for a moment? At lunch-time today I caught a glimpse of you crossing Nassau Street. Your hair was blowing in the wind. I followed you past Trinity College, watched your long legs striding ahead of me. You broke the lights. Impetuous, as always.
I miss my vampire bitch.
Razor

The lure of good wine and tasty canapés brought a sizable gathering of journalists to the Congress Hotel to launch the revolutionary adhesive. Virginia's experienced eyes gauged the numbers. They were mainly from trade publications but two social diarists from the nationals had made an appearance and a consumer-affairs journalist from RTÉ. They were handed vellum folders, bound with the new adhesive, and a gift box of the company's products. One journalist, arriving late, addressed her as Veronica and brushed aside the press release with a dismissive flick of her hand.

"Don't add to my clutter, Veronica. I can only give the product a few lines, if at all." She tapped her pen impatiently. "Surely it's not beyond your reach to condense it for me."

"Which publication do you represent?" Years of experience in the business of public relations helped maintain Virginia's composure.

"*Dublin Echo*."

"I thought they were sending their science correspondent, not their social diarist?"

"You thought correctly." The journalist's smile flashed warningly.

"Then you'll find everything you need, including photographs, in the press release. If you have any problem with the information, please contact my office."

"You PR types would denude the world of trees if you had your way." The journalist shrugged and shoved the press release into her briefcase. "So much paper and not a sentence worth reading." She glided into the press reception where she was loudly greeted by friends.

The speeches were over and the journalists had scoffed the canapés when Ralph arrived.

"I wasn't aware your name was on my invitation list." She glanced pointedly at the list in front of her.

"I haven't been on your invitation list for a long while, Virginia."

"Then why are you here?"

"To see you, of course. I miss my sparring partner."

"In case you haven't noticed, I'm busy running a press launch."

"A sticky situation, what?"

"I'm not in the mood for jokes, Ralph."

"I keep hoping you'll reply to my e-mails."

"I delete them instantly."

"Not even a sneaky little look?" He smiled. His teeth looked whiter than she remembered.

"What do you want from me?"

"I thought we could engage in a little light banter over dinner."

"I hate to dash a man's hopes but needs must."

"You can tell me all about tonight's success." He glanced towards the open doors of the Ivy Suite where the hum of a large gathering was audible. "It has been successful, hasn't it? Only my Virginia could persuade a bunch of free-loading journalists that glue was a worthwhile present to carry home in their goody-bags."

She found herself smiling. How the smile reached her lips, let alone her eyes, astonished her. The evening had been successful, despite the attitude of the *Dublin Echo* reporter whose svelte body and Bambi eyes had reminded Virginia of a faun and filled her with a hunter's instinct to aim and fire.

In the past, she had always met Ralph after a press launch and relaxed down with a drink or a meal. He would listen to her rehash the evening, laughing at her anecdotes and the gossipy tit-bits she had picked up from journalists. The temptation to accept his invitation was fleeting. Beneath his affable smile, he was ruthless when crossed in business. She had no reason to believe he would behave differently when crossed in love, and he did still love her. She could see it glinting in his smile, his eyes, his speculative stare. But was he ready to forgive her? The answer, she suspected, was in the negative.

Adrian was sleeping when she returned to the apartment. He had started snoring, not an undignified, rampaging snore but a gentle, whistling whine through his nose that drove her from his side and into the chilly living-room where her computer flickered, beckoned.

Why, Ralph had asked, the last time they were together. Why him? Why take that one step too far? She had wanted to scream the answer back at him and was shocked by her desire to do so. The boy. It always came back to the boy. He had bound her in a sinister secret, forced her into hasty, unplanned decisions, sent her scurrying into a foxhole of an apartment which she hated and where her lover's body – so fervently desired when it was unobtainable – now lay shivering in his own fear.

Sent: 14 March 1:45 a.m.
Subject: Lonelines

After I left you, I went to the Horseshoe Bar. Packed as always. The women were beautiful. But I drove home alone. There was only one woman I wanted in my bed. How many ways can a man love a woman – a woman love a man? Once upon a time we tried each one then started all over again. I keep thinking about what might have been – should have been. You and I were never meant to be sparring partners. Virginia, where did you go when I foolishly averted my gaze? I miss my vampire bitch.
Razor

The third envelope arrived a week later. The sender had cut Virginia's photograph from *Prestige* and placed it beside a silver car. The sea lapped against the wall of the pier.

An hour later Lorcan called into her office and asked if she knew where Adrian had gone. He was due to give a presentation in thirty minutes.

"Cancel it, Lorcan," she said. "He won't be back on time."

When he left, she shredded the anonymous photograph. She tidied her desk, pens, staplers, paper clips and the letter opener shaped like a dagger. She carefully placed each item into its allotted space. A place for everything and everything in its place. When her office was in order she called in her staff for a brainstorming session on how to engineer publicity for a forthcoming award ceremony.

After the meeting ended, she entered Adrian's office, unable to believe he was still missing. Lorcan was on the phone, his face in profile as he made excuses to an irate client. The insolence that had been so irritating in the early days had disappeared and he was beginning to acquire a confident business-like manner which reminded Virginia of his father – but without the abrasive edge.

"He's still not back, Ms Blaide. I expect he was held up with a client." His attempts to pacify her only increased her anger. It was becoming more difficult to smile. "I'm sure that's true, Lorcan. When he does contact you, tell him I need to speak urgently to him."

He removed a folder from a drawer in his desk and held it towards her. "I keep working on these ideas. Would you mind looking over them? I'd appreciate your opinion."

"Of course I will, Lorcan. But this is Mr Strong's area. Have you shown them to him?"

"He's not remotely interested." His reply was matter-of-fact. "But I'd respect your opinion."

She opened the folder, glanced quickly through the contents, surprised to see how meticulously everything had been prepared. She examined the visuals he intended using to promote Sheraton Travel. Satellite pictures taken at night from outer space, pinpricks of global light linking continent after continent, the vast and the sparsely dotted regions – a filigree as delicate as early morning cobwebs on hedgerows, and in that instant, as she absorbed the image, she was running fleetly, barefooted, down a country lane and Lorraine was running with her, Old Red Eye panting between them, and the world was hazed with wonder. She shook her head, scattering dewdrops, and concentrated on how Lorcan Sheraton would link these visuals into the world-wide concept of his father's travel agency. His ideas had a raw energy that excited her. With the right training he could be good. Ralph would have picked up on his talent immediately.

"I'm impressed, Lorcan." She snapped the folder closed and handed it back to him.

"You don't have to pretend." He made no attempt to smile back at her. " I asked for an honest opinion. I want my father left out of this."

"I'm being honest, Lorcan. Your ideas are good. They need refining but there's no reason why they can't translate into a viable advertising campaign. As a matter of fact, your father and I had quite an interesting conversation about you when we were in Madeira."

"I can imagine."

"Actually, he's very proud of you. He mentioned a friend of

yours who had an accident. The two of you were very close, I believe."

His face flushed. For an instant she thought he was going to burst into tears. "Killian was my best mate."

"I hope he recovers soon."

"Thanks, Ms Blaide. I'll tell Mr Strong you were looking for him."

She wondered where anger lay. Throughout the day, as one phone call after another relayed the same message from Adrian's answering service, it moved arbitrarily from one body zone to the next. It cramped her stomach, tightened her chest, clenched her teeth. It was after ten before he returned home.

"Where the hell were you?" she demanded. The walls of the apartment were thin. Often, they heard music at night, and raised voices, thudding footsteps, toilets flushing, the creak of beds. Tonight she no longer cared who overheard. She followed him into the bedroom where he dropped his shoes on the floor with an unnecessary clatter. He slowly wound one sock into the other and flung them towards the laundry basket. He missed the target and the bunched socks crouched like a baleful rodent on the wooden floorboards.

"I left about a dozen messages on your mobile. You must have realised I was frantic with worry but you never even *bothered* returning my calls."

"I was at a meeting."

"Don't bullshit me, Adrian. What meeting?"

"A meeting with myself."

"That must have been utterly fascinating."

"Pathetic would be a better description. I went to Church-view Terrace, met some of the old neighbours. Mr Thomson, sad to say, is dead. Emily will be choked when she hears. She adored him. But I'm glad to say the rest are as fit as ever. A hardy bunch, those pensioners. The house looks the same but different, like it's acquired another skin. They have a jeep parked outside, for Christ's sake. Then I went to the warehouse where Lorraine had her first studio. There's an office block in its place. Surprise, surprise. After that, where did I go? Oh yes, I had a drink in our *special* hotel. Under new management, would you believe? The staff actually noticed me. Wouldn't be safe to go there any more – that's if we needed to, but of course we don't because we have this cosy little love nest all to ourselves."

She picked up his socks, flung them out of sight into the laundry basket. "You're hysterical. Hopefully, you'll talk sense in the morning."

"He stole Lorraine's bracelet."

"What?"

"It was in the glove box. Lorraine keeps demanding it back."

"What bracelet?"

"The one I gave her ... never mind what bracelet. She keeps phoning, insisting I have it. We should have stopped! I wanted to but you wouldn't listen. You never listen. It always has to be your way."

He began to sob, an ugly grating sound that repelled her. She knelt before him, forced him to look at her. "Are you telling me Lorraine has been sending us that shit?"

"I'm not telling you, I know it. You should have seen her face when she demanded her bracelet back."

"When did you meet her?"

"A while ago. She kept harping on and on ... She knew my car was going to be serviced when she was away. She's figured it out, Virginia. All that publicity ... it's not surprising. And it's only a matter of time before she goes to the police. That's if she hasn't gone already."

"Listen to me, Adrian." She knelt before him, forced him to hear her. "Lorraine is fucking with our minds. But you can lay bets she hasn't gone anywhere. Emily will be her first priority. She won't expose her to a scandal. But you must talk to her, find out exactly what her game is."

"Jesus Christ! What am I supposed to say? We hit and we ran but please stop sending us those nasty letters in the post. I can't face her. I *won't*."

"You must."

"How come you've never once expressed guilt or remorse, Virginia?"

"I'm tired, Adrian. All I want to do is sleep."

"Will anything have changed by morning?"
"Sleep in the other room tonight."
"It will be my pleasure."

Sent: 22 March 11.30 p.m.
Subject: Jake

Virginia — do you remember the night you told me about Jake?
Your fingers on my spine. Remember how I danced you around
our bedroom and told you I would treasure our child forever. You
said I didn't know the meaning of love. Only the grit and hatred
I spewed from a stage. But we removed the masks that night —
what a night. And you lay beside me content. I know you did,
even though you say differently now. If you had told me about him
I would have let you go. I had no desire to love a captive bird. But
you never mentioned his name, not by the flick of an eyelid or the
tremor in your voice. Why was that, Virginia?
  I remember being washed in your tears when our child died.
How you cried and clung to me. I kissed your tears and shed my
own in private. I rested my head on your soft empty belly and
said, "I will fill you with life again." You never allowed me to keep
my promise. Why was that, Virginia? Running away from the
past was never the answer.
  Razor

CHAPTER FIFTY-SEVEN

March had been a boisterous month, clouds as skittish as new-born lambs. The wind buffeted the trees and flattened the early daffodils. Swallows dived like bombers, foraging for twigs and straw, busily nest-building in the eaves above her studio. So much energy and activity. The need to paint, a nervous, creative excitement filled Lorraine, exhilarated her. Yet she was also frightened by the energy coursing through her. It reminded her of the last time, the dream paintings, the trip to Venice when the rapturous singing of a mad woman had awoken her from a long sleep. The woman was probably dead by now or locked up in some safe asylum, her songs of praise silenced – but her voice was a loud exhortation every time Lorraine's energy flagged.

She moved from one surface to the next, her mind clear, her strokes decisive. Three paintings linked by a single thread. Each time she approached the triptych, she was filled with the challenge of filling such a large space. She allowed her instincts to guide her. Sometimes she brushed out what she had done the previous day and began again. This lack of progress did not disturb her. She was prepared to allow the paintings to grow at their own pace. When she finished each session, she locked the triptych in the darkroom, out of sight of her daughter's curious gaze.

"Is this another dream painting?" Emily came into the studio one afternoon when she was working on the painting of the boy.

"No. It's about a life."

"It's more like a fairy story. All those briars. Who's going to awaken him?"

"Faith, I expect."

"Are the shadows meant to be birds or people?"

"They're whatever you want them to be."

"I hate it when you go on with all that abstract stuff. What's *The Cat in the Hat* doing there?"

"It's a voice in the boy's head."

"Who's the subject?"

"Just a boy."

"Are you going to work through the night again?"

"Yes."

"You're painting some very weird stuff. You're not doing drugs, are you?"

"I promise you'll be the first to know if I start."

With each stroke she willed him back to his family. At night she lay in bed and thought how he too was lying with his face turned to the ceiling, breathing in a floating space between thought and dreams. The volcanic force of his desire to communicate – his eyelids fluttering, the clench of his fingers, his grunts and jerking movements – she imagined his mind as a chaotic galaxy, hurtling furiously through a solid veil of stillness. Sometimes, she seemed to breathe in harmony with him and she would sink into a heavy dreamless sleep which only lasted a few hours. Then she arose refreshed, her energy driving her from her bed to the studio where she would paint until the dawn spread silver shale across the sky.

CHAPTER FIFTY-EIGHT

Brahms Ward
10 p.m.

Look at me, Killian. I could dance a jig, a highland fling, the samba and the tango. I might even take up trekking – who knows what the future holds? Harriet says it holds her garden. She wants to plant flowers and doze in the sun. Claims her trekking days are done. Too old for such adventures. I don't believe a word of it. Her book will be a success, she'll do some interviews, chat shows, she might even pull a few weeds, and then she'll spin the globe and be off again. You once called her a stick insect in mountain boots. Remember? Tears ran down her cheeks she laughed so much.

She's the reason I wasn't in yesterday. I drove her back to the cottage. She has a month to finish her next book, no title as yet, and needs peace. On the drive down we talked about Shady and childhood and her parents and Mayo and men who wanted to marry her but she'd lost her wedding-ring finger, on purpose I'd swear. Her first book was called *Giving My Finger to the World*. She always had a weird sense of humour. I told her everything, Killian. It didn't help. She called me a fool, and not for the first time, but she was my lifeline after Shady died and one doesn't let lifelines slide too easily away. I told her about the crooked road that led me to Trabawn and how it quickly became a road going nowhere. "I've walked many crooked roads in my day," she said. "Bush, forests, mountains, deserts. Sooner or later, they always arrived at a destination."

When you're better I'll bring you to the cottage. I should have done it before, given you a feel of your own roots, but Jean would have … Oh, what does that matter now? It's where I lived after Shady died. Harriet believed I'd be safe under the shadow of Croagh Patrick and she was right. When we go there we'll fish the lakes and climb the mountain. No problem to me when I was a boy, agile as a mountain goat, I was, and barefoot too.

After I left her I stopped off at the cemetery. I can't remember the last time I was there. Cowslips and buttercups are blooming on her grave, stars in the long grass. There were horses in a nearby field, their coats as sleek as melting chocolate, and they ran together when they heard my car, tossing their heads, their manes, their hooves dancing; and the rooks gathered on the branches above them, chattering like old women in black shawls. It's a good place for Shady to rest. I left flowers on the headstone. I asked her for nothing except your life. Everything else, passion, desire, love, yearning, is immaterial. I will survive anything except losing you.

See you tomorrow, Killian. It's been a long night and we have done much talking.

I hear you … see you … smell you … touch you … taste you … need you …

CHAPTER FIFTY-NINE

Adrian flicked the invitation with his nail. The thwacking sound reminded Virginia of fine bones snapping, like the wishbone she always broke on Christmas Day, herself and Edward gripping the delicate turkey bone with determined fingers, fighting for the wish. She always won.

The invitation had arrived in the morning post. Unlike the other envelopes, which had been delivered by courier to Blaide House, this one was postmarked Trabawn and had been posted two days previously. It contained an invitation to the opening of an art exhibition. The logo on the invitation ended any last lingering doubt; a ripe melon moon shining plump above a deserted pier. Even the title of the collection, *Falling into Night*, resonated with suspicion.

Virginia inserted the compact disc accompanying the invitation into her computer and opened the attachment. There was nothing surreal or abstract about the painting that flashed on her screen. It had inspired the logo on the invitation but the pier she now gazed upon was not deserted. A silver car had been added, shards of shattered glass, and beyond the car, two entwined figures against a high wall. The man remained in shadow but each feature in the woman's face had been painted in exquisite detail. The jaded satisfaction of her smile. Her lips slightly open, swollen like a flower-head about to burst into bloom.

Virginia's friendship with Lorraine had survived because there were compartments in her mind that closed and opened at her will. Only occasionally was she swamped with the enormity of her betrayal. Then, guilt was a wolf clawing her throat. Lorraine had waited until now to avenge herself on the people she once loved, the people who had betrayed her. The wolves had been sprung from the attic, freed.

The car with its rusty chassis was long gone and the sand dunes were eroding, coiling inwards like a forlorn row of question marks. Music came from an open window where Celia Murphy had once watched for the arrival of the holiday makers. A vase of daffodils sat on the ledge. After trying to attract attention and failing, Virginia walked to the side of the house. She ducked beneath a dash of yellow forsythia and entered the studio. Discarded paint brushes rested in a jar of spirits. The sink was splashed with red, as if a blood bath had taken place within its enamel confines. Canvases in the process of being primed and slabs of painted wood rested against the walls. Three paintings had been grouped together, almost hinged in their closeness, the vivid imagery creating such uniformity that the scenes – although distinct and different – merged effortlessly together. She had already seen the first painting on her computer but the reality of it – the layered texture and thick impasto, the precision of each brush stroke and shimmering glaze of oils – shocked her anew. The second painting contrasted the luminosity of the terminal building and its reflection on the water with the muffled pier on the far side of the bay. A silver car was held in a blur of speed and a young man's body danced upwards, spinning, falling. She had turned to the third painting when Lorraine's voice cut like a whip through the studio.

"Why are you trespassing on my property?" She closed the door quietly behind her. "I asked you a question, Virginia. Why are you here?" As she advanced towards Virginia she tracked sand from the soles of her sandals across the floor.

"I want an explanation for the anonymous post you've been sending us."

"Anonymous?" Lorraine raised her eyebrows. Her voice

sounded different, no quiver of uncertainty, not even the weeping anger she had displayed so openly when her marriage broke up. "Surely the term 'anonymous' signifies a mysterious sender?"

"There's no mystery. It's obvious you're responsible. It has to stop, Lorraine. I know how deeply we've hurt you. I'm not going to pretend you haven't good reason to hate us but choosing this way of getting your own back is madness."

"Beware the vision of the insane, Virginia."

"I'm worried about you. There were times in the past … I wondered. I could see it in your paintings … And now this – this obscenity." Virginia's gaze skittered towards the triptych and away again.

"It's not an obscenity, it's a triptych. An eternal triangle. An unholy trinity. I've decided to call it *Exposé on the Great South Wall*. I've always liked unambiguous titles."

"Jesus, Lorraine, have you any idea what you're doing to yourself? You ran away without giving me a chance to explain anything and locked yourself away from everyone who cares about you. No wonder you're losing touch with reality. I can understand your anger. What happened with Adrian was a stupid crazy mistake. I'll regret it to my dying day but I was going through such a wretched time with Ralph and Adrian listened. We never intended hurting anyone, you least of all. I was on the verge of ending it, I swear to you, we were going to finish it and I was returning to London, cutting all ties with him. Ralph hated living here. We'd have gone back sooner only I knew that if he left Adrian in the lurch the company would fold. I was so torn, Lorraine, unsure of the best course of action to take. When you rang that night you not only ended your own marriage, you destroyed mine in the process. But the most devastating thing was the loss of your friendship. I don't expect you to understand … How could you understand? … But it's true, I swear. I deserved everything you said, and I agreed with you too … only you wouldn't listen. How many times did I ring you? I pleaded with you, begged you to meet me. I desperately wanted us all to find a way forward. There were others to consider, Emily, for instance, and your career, Adrian's business. It wasn't just about you and me but no matter how hard I tried to make amends –"

"I'd stopped listening for the knock on the caravan window."

"What?"

"It doesn't matter. Please, don't let me interrupt. I now appreciate why Ralph called you the Princess of Spin."

"I'm not spinning, Lorraine. I'm telling it as it is. You've had too much time to brood over everything. This is your way of getting back at us. It's cruel and upsetting –"

"But effective, don't you think?"

Virginia slowly released her breath. "I never meant to break up your marriage. I know you find that impossible to believe –"

"On the contrary, I find it utterly believable. You had it all, devoted husband, compliant friend, vigorous lover, successful career. Why would you change anything when life was so bountiful?"

"If you can't forgive me then I must accept it as the price I have to pay. But I won't allow you to invade my life with these malicious accusations. I didn't steal your husband. Adrian came to me of his own free will."

Lorraine combed her fingers through her hair, brushed it back from her forehead. Her face, revealed in its entirety, seemed alien, formidable, the skin drawn finely under her eyes. Sleepless nights. Virginia recognised the signs.

"Free will? What an interesting concept. Did my husband leave the Great South Wall of his own free will? Did he decide to keep silent of his own free will? And you. Where do you stand on the subject of Killian Devine-O'Malley? Don't look so puzzled, Virginia. Surely you haven't forgotten his name? Look again if you can't remember." She nodded towards the last painting. "You left him for dead. Free will. Remember?"

Her eyes dulled as they rested on the imagery Lorraine had crafted with such deliberation and which seemed to expand outwards while drawing Virginia into its centre. A car speeding away and the moon shining an accusing beam on the face of the boy they had left behind. She had refused to give him an identity, imposing on him an identi-kit image: brutish features, a crude protruding forehead, hard staring eyes. But she saw him now, his young stricken face, his mouth slackly open, as if he had lost consciousness on a cry of terror.

"This is *outrageous.*" Her knees shook in a sudden violent spasm. "Does Emily know you entertain such vile notions about her father?"

"Emily is not your concern."

"She adores Adrian. What will she do when she realises her mother is suffering from crazed delusions?"

"Don't waste my time, Virginia. I'm preparing for an exhibition."

"You'll never exhibit in that gallery."

"You have no say in where I choose to exhibit. That decision has been made by Mara Robertson." Lorraine gestured towards the paintings. "This triptych will form the centrepiece of my collection. You and Adrian have already received invitations. Opening nights can be such interesting events. Quite revelatory, on occasions. On my last opening night I discovered that you and I both loved an insubstantial man."

The glass jug was heavy in her hands when Virginia lifted it from the table, the smell of spirits almost overwhelming as she flung the cloudy liquid against the canvas. Oil and spirits collided, ran like blood from the painted faces. The features blurred, massed into abstract humps and hollows, no longer recognisable.

"See a shrink, Lorraine." She placed the empty jug back on the table. "It might help get this shit out of your system. Next time you paint my portrait ask my permission first."

Apart from the twitch of muscle below Lorraine's left eye, her face was impassive. She walked to the door and held it open. "I know what you and Adrian did, Virginia. Always remember that I *know.* I want you to leave now. You're not welcome in my house."

The apartment complex was in darkness except for the globe-headed security lights in the courtyard. Virginia listened to the drip-drip-drip of raindrops falling from the balcony. The wind blew moist on her face. Adrian was sleeping in the spare room. They had hardly seen each other for over a week. When they did meet in the corridors of Blaide House they greeted each other with a sullen calm that signified the inevitable ending of their relationship. She did not want to think about him, not now.

Tomorrow, perhaps, she would tell him it was over. He was too locked into his own self-absorption to protest. Unlike the night her marriage ended, this relationship would cease with a whimper not a roar. Emily would welcome him back. For all her tantrums and attention-seeking wiles, she missed him desperately. But Lorraine – forgiveness was beyond her.

A movement in the courtyard below attracted her attention. For an instant, something flitted through it, a dog, perhaps, or someone hurrying, running slantways through a splash of light before disappearing out of sight behind the red-brick blocks. The young man spun before her eyes. Her skin tingled as if tiny electrical currents had being switched on over her entire body. Her heart began to palpitate, the fast thumping beat causing a swelling sensation until it seemed as if it could no longer be contained within her chest. She returned to the living-room and sank into an armchair. When she could move again she poured a brandy and sipped it neat. The need to awaken Adrian was overwhelming but nothing would be served by opening the subject up again. She was determined that the ghost made flesh was not going to destroy her. She switched on her computer and watched the screen come to life.

Sent: 6 April 11.30 p.m.
Subject: Sleeping Beauty

Virginia – why are you chasing sleep? Counting sheep? I used to call you my sleeping beauty. Sometimes, I switched on the light and watched you, the rise and fall of your breath, your mouth curled in surrender. I would turn you gently and slide deeply into your moist dark cunt and you would stir, call my name, a sleepy signal, and oh … Virginia … I can't go on.

Meet me. Make love to me again. Tell no one but your heart. Is it possible? Answer me, Virginia.
Forever yours,
Razor

CHAPTER SIXTY

From the outside Blaide House had looked the same yet once inside Lorraine could see the changes. A finance company had taken possession of the entire ground floor where Strong–Blaide Advertising once sprawled. But it was in the atmosphere rather than the physical transformation that the change was most apparent. The young people who had formed the creative heart of the partnership no longer spilled out into the corridors and the finance house had a more sedate work-force hidden behind slatted blinds. Adrian's company, she noticed from the signpost, was now on the same floor as Ginia Communications. She allowed the elevator to continue upwards to the next storey and walked the length of the corridor towards the familiar spiral staircase.

In ten minutes' time her exhibition would officially open. No one would come. She had been forgotten. If people did arrive they would laugh silently before drifting away. The art critics would slice her in two, their harsh judgements forcing her to crawl back to Trabawn for cover. Having rapidly run the entire gauntlet of first-night nerves she stepped forward to greet Mara Robertson.

The transformation of her one-time functional studio amazed

her. Mara had used the space ingeniously, creating brightly lit display recesses in areas Lorraine had previously used for storage. The ceiling seemed higher, the walls wider, more spacious. The Donaldson brothers and Ibrahim had done a splendid job hanging her paintings. Only the triptych was missing.

Painting the triptych should have been a dramatic gesture, worthy of some form of liberation. An escape from the hurt and anger that had held her in thrall for so long. She had breeched their secret, exacted a nasty revenge which brought her no comfort. She had waited for Virginia's arrival, knowing she would be unable to stay away, but, after she departed, driving too fast and furiously from the lane, Lorraine had collapsed into a chair and hugged her arms to her chest until she was calm enough to carry the ruined paintings to the end of the back garden. The flames licked the wood and canvas then roared into an incandescent flare and devoured their secret. It was over in an instant.

Adrian arrived in Trabawn the following day. Unable to disguise his fear, he had approached her with bluster and denials. He demanded to know if the stress of their broken marriage had reduced her to making insidious and dangerous accusations. He called her neurotic, vindictive, crazy. He demanded an end to her conniving dangerous games. He covered his face with his hands and begged her to forgive him. Emily found him in this position on her arrival home from school. He left shortly afterwards.

"He hates his apartment," she announced when she returned to the kitchen after waving him off. "If you snapped your fingers he'd crawl back, I know he would." She came over to inspect the roasting tray Lorraine was removing from the oven. "You could at least have asked him to stay for dinner. He *adores* roast chicken."

"He was in a hurry to leave." Lorraine placed the tray carefully on a heat mat and pierced the tender flesh with a fork.

"No way! He wants to be here with us."

The argument that followed was predictable and resulted in Emily bursting into tears as she ran up the stairs to her bedroom. The door slammed, the music thumped and texts flowed back and forth between her and Ibrahim as she demanded sympathy and understanding.

Lorraine's forehead felt bruised and tender. A headache that had been throbbing gently all afternoon developed into a painful spasm. Painkillers would take care of her headache but there was nothing in her medicine cabinet to protect her from Emily's hopeless optimism.

The invited guests filled the gallery. Meg and Eoin Ruane arrived, followed by Lorraine's parents. The road-works crew were there in force and gathered around the portrait, teasing the woman who had dressed for the occasion in an off-the-shoulder red dress and dangling earrings. The Trabawn art group came *en masse*. Emily abandoned her combats for the occasion and wore a black, skin-hugging mini. Aware of the impact she made as she sashayed around the gallery, she delighted, once again, in being the daughter of an infamous artist. Lorraine heard her saying, "Extraordinarily effulgent and expressively executed," to Ibrahim, who replied, "Spit out the dictionary, girl, and kiss me." Adrian and Virginia did not make an appearance.

Lorraine greeted old friends and familiar journalists. She smiled into cameras and uttered convincing sound-bites. Bill Sheraton held her hand in a forceful grip. She was air-kissed by Andrea. Lorcan made an impressive entrance, dressed in a black velvet suit and red frilled shirt. He seemed taller than she remembered, more confident, capable of smiling without pain. He introduced his girlfriend, a thistledown young woman called Marianne, who appeared to have an opinion on every painting in the collection.

"Very noir-*ish* and filmic. Edward Hopper influences. I like your honesty, Lorraine. You're not afraid of realism."

Bill Sheraton purchased the road-works painting. "Marianne claims it signifies the underground dominance of the matriarchal structures in post-modern society or some such crap," he said in an aside to Lorraine. "For my part, I fancy that tough little woman with the cable. Reminds me of my mother."

Andrea's mouth tightened. The colour scheme was obviously not to her liking.

Other paintings had acquired "Sold" stickers, including the

salsa women and the birthing of the calf, the latter proudly purchased by Sophie's husband.

Mara stood beside her, smiling. "Lorraine, I'd like to introduce you to the buyer of *Sand Blizzard*."

She turned and found herself face to face with Michael Carmody.

Her paintings had been admired, criticised, analysed, misinterpreted, praised for their iconoclastic images of desolation, isolation, alienation, inclusion, exclusion – dismissed as being too representative, photographic, trivial – and now the gallery was in darkness.

"A most successful opening," beamed Mara Robertson before she led the Trabawn contingent towards Dawson Street and drinks in Café en Seine. Ibrahim had left with Emily whose grandparents were treating them to a meal in a Chinese restaurant.

To be alone with him was the height of folly but he had asked her to go somewhere quiet and she had nodded, unable to refuse. Their footsteps beat time against the Liffey boardwalk. The city was restless, traffic still heavy on the bridges. Soon the pubs would empty, spilling young people onto the streets, and the air would be redolent with kebabs and violence. A young woman in a slip dress shouted as she walked past, a rag doll stumbling drunk. Her face beneath tendrils of blonde hair was hazed in the overhanging lamps, her plump body lurched forward on heels that were too high. Her companions surrounded her. They laughed and bore her away, accepting with good nature the casualties the night had to offer.

Lorraine was conscious of his stillness when he stopped and rested his arms on the river wall.

"Nothing has changed," he said. "I love you. But you can't forgive me. I see it on your face. You're fighting against me as hard as I once fought against you."

"This is not about forgiveness, Michael."

"Then what? I know we can make it work. I've never been more positive about anything in my life."

"My marriage was built on deception. How can I begin another relationship when it was founded on lies?"

"We have no secrets now."

"But you're still tormented by what happened to Killian. You won't rest easy until you find the people who are responsible."

"Would you be able to rest easy?" he demanded. "Knowing that if they'd stopped and called an ambulance immediately the trauma to his brain would not have been so severe. What would you do in my place?"

"Exactly the same." Her words dropped like stones into the sullen water flowing below them.

"What happened to Killian no longer has anything to do with us." When she made no reply he moved closer. "I've never been in love until now. I'll never fall in love again. This will stay with me until I die."

The love he demanded would be soldered with passion and tenderness. Her love would be fiercely insistent on honesty, trust. One vision, one truth. If she stood with him a minute longer she would never be able to leave. Her voice shook then steadied. "I can't give you the love you need, Michael. And anything less between us would be a sham. We've said goodbye so often. This has to be the last time. Forgive me."

The river tossed seagulls on its crest, eddies spinning, twisting and turning as it wended under the luminous arch of the Ha'penny Bridge and continued its restless passage towards the sea.

CHAPTER SIXTY-ONE

Brahms Ward
Midnight

Perhaps the experts are right. Cannot be awoken ... have not yet ... Who am I to be the judge of anything? Reflex actions, fluttering eyelashes, your tight convulsive grip, I come here night after night seeking signs, hoping, praying, willing you – all of us willing you back to us. I'm no good tonight. Your grip gives me comfort but it changes nothing. My heart is a stone. She has left me bereft. The trail to the Great South Wall is dead.

I went back there today, back to where the sea laps the pier and seagulls swoop through fumes of gas and oil. Dublin is in the grip of a renaissance, Killian. Office blocks are mushrooming along the quays, apartments, hotels. The motorways are marching onwards for Ireland; cement labyrinths carrying traffic outwards to the four provinces. Under ground, over ground, tunnels, tracks and grid-lock. On the docklands there is a new heart beating and only the old Customs House sprawling white along the quays prevents this city becoming a stranger to me.

I walked the wall between the rocks and the sea and tried to imagine what you were trying to recapture each time you strayed there. Childish memories, stories of mysterious sea voyages – or was I weighing you down with my own dead memories? It rained while I was there. I let it wash over my face and when it stopped a rainbow spanned the lighthouses that guard the mouth of Dublin Bay. A white ferry passed beneath its arch. I saw you sliding deep into the indigo, hiding away from all of us, Jean, Terence, Laura and sulky brat Duncan who loves you so much he's mixed it up with hate because that's the only way he can cope. Love and hate, Killian. Two sides of a damaged coin. I spun a silver coin and found it to be baseless.

Afterwards, I collected my painting. The exhibition is over. A new artist will soon take her place on the walls. *Sand Blizzard*, she called it. Snow on sand and a woman slight as a twig looking upwards towards the old boathouse. The gallery owner said it's a good choice. *Painting Dreams* was illusion, fantasy, unfulfilled desire. There was no strength in her paintings, only yearnings. This collection is different. Energy jumps from the canvases. The night is magic.

I stood among the cool white walls of the gallery and imagined a studio where donkeys used to live. I saw palettes of burnt sienna and yellow ochre, the luminous splashes on the walls, the canvases still drying. I saw her painting you … or was it me? That's the way it will always be. I can deal with it. Rainbows are illusions. They disappear.

On the way down I shared the elevator with Virginia Blaide. If she remembered our last meeting she gave no sign. She smiled and wished me good day.

The tide has receded. Black horses at rest. One by one, two, three and four, the stars appear, pinpricks shimmering, sparking. Dawn will come soon. The world will be green. What a colour that will be. A green new world. He stirs and reaches for the moon.

CHAPTER SIXTY-TWO

MIRACLE RECOVERY OF COMA VICTIM

A courageous young man has defied medical opinion and is recovering in hospital from horrific head injuries incurred when he was critically injured in a hit-and-run accident. For seventeen months Killian Devine-O'Malley lay in a post-coma vegetative state with little hope of recovery. Supported by his family and friends he fought back and is now in a stable condition. His reawakening has been greeted with amazement by the medical team at the Hammond Clinic.

"We never lost hope that he would recover," said his father, Michael Carmody, whose TV series Nowhere Lodge *has won him legions of young fans.*

"For Killian to reawaken after such a traumatic injury is nothing short of a miracle," said an overjoyed Ms Devine-O'Malley, whose vigil by her son's bedside was constant.

The family plan a quiet celebration when Killian is released from hospital.

Gardaí hope to interview him when he is strong enough to answer questions. It is hoped he can provide them with relevant information on the circumstances surrounding his accident.

"In the meantime we are renewing our appeal to anyone who was in the vicinity of the Great South Wall on 20 November 2001 between 11 p.m. and midnight and noticed anything suspicious," said Garda Sergeant Murray. *"The case is still open and we are particularly interested in interviewing the owner of a silver car (make unknown) which was seen in the vicinity shortly before the accident occurred."*

The fax machine in Virginia's office clicked into receive mode. A document came through, slightly darkened in transmission. Not a muscle moved in her face as her eyes scanned the headline from the *Dublin Echo*. Adrian's office was empty, his computer still on, a half-empty mug of coffee cooling. The faxed clipping had been shredded and flung into the wastepaper basket.

The touch of lace on her skin. The cool whisper of silk. Virginia fastened hooks and suspenders. She stepped into a dark purple dress that flattened across her stomach, outlined her breasts. She applied lipstick, a damson streak, and sprayed perfume on her pulses.

Temple Bar was crowded with cinema-goers and diners. The night was mild enough for young people to gather on the pavements outside the pubs, where they converged in groups. She entered an apartment block and took the elevator to the top storey.

"I didn't think you'd come." Ralph opened the door wide and drew her inside.

"Just hold me," she said . "We don't have to talk."

She knew his body intimately yet, now, it was as if she touched him for the first time. His lovemaking, once so demanding, moved at a slow, leisurely pace. She remained passive in his arms, willing to allow him control, knowing he was enjoying the languid lie of her body, her slow sensuous response. She remembered the violence of their early years, her delight when he twisted her arms above her head, locked her in a grim embrace, and how she had fought him, feigning resistance, teasing him into exhaustion, their excitement heightened to a point where it could no longer be contained. Youthful games that seemed so trivial after Jake died. Life taking its toll on fun and games, even war games.

It was after midnight when she phoned Adrian. "I won't be home tonight," she said. "I'm staying overnight with friends." She hung up before he could reply.

"I never believed I could forgive you." Ralph leaned on his elbow and stared down at her, smiling his sharp wolf smile.

"But you haven't forgiven me."

"If that's what you believe why are you here?"

"We always played games, Ralph."

"Games are for children."

"Games are for those who want to play them."

He pulled her roughly towards him. "Let's play some more then."

The bells for Sunday mass were ringing as she drove through the city and out towards Clontarf. Joggers ran along the promenade, elbows tight to their sides. A flotilla of yachts swooped past Howth Head, white sails billowing towards harbour. What had they talked about? So many subjects to be skirted. No-go areas where she must tread with caution. But it was possible to recreate those early days, move back to London, make a fresh start together. The Celtic Tiger economy was slowing down, companies cutting back, hi-tech US giants repatriating their profits or seeking cheaper labour markets further afield. It was only a matter of time before Bill Sheraton took action. She was tired of Ireland with its constant inward navel-gazing and scandals. Time to bale out.

Adrian was sitting by the window, a bottle of whiskey almost empty. All night long he had been waiting, she realised, looking at the overflowing ashtray, the congealed remains of an evening meal.

"Ah, Virginia, just in time to share the last glass." He carefully poured the remaining whiskey into two glasses and handed one to her. "To us. To happiness. Are you going to tell me where you were?"

"I was with friends. I told you I was staying overnight with one of them."

"Don't make me laugh, Virginia. You have no friends."

The weight of desolation dragged his face downwards, his eyes, his cheeks, his lips, everything sagging like a sad clown. Whiskey fumes, paint fumes, fumes of guilt; she was tired struggling. As he bent forward unsteadily to place his glass on the low marble-topped table it slipped from his fingers and shattered.

"Broken glass – look, broken glass. Better not touch." He laughed wildly and held his hand before her, pointing to a white scar across his palm.

She forced him back from the table, suddenly terrified he would lift a shard and press it into his flesh or turn, in his befuddled and furious state, on her. "Leave it, Adrian. I'll clear it up."

He sank heavily back into the armchair, his head bent forward, watching her with a bleary but focused stare. "You were with a man last night. I can smell him on you." He gripped her wrist, pulled her downwards with such force that she lost her balance and collapsed on top of him. "Leave me and I'm going straight to the police."

"I've no intention of leaving you. You're drunk, Adrian. We'll discuss this again when you're sober."

"I'm drunk and I'm serious. For better or worse. That's us, Virginia."

"For better or worse," she replied and opened the window to let the fresh morning air blow through.

CHAPTER SIXTY-THREE

Lorraine sat quietly beside his bed. His eyelids flickered. A familiar sign, seen on her previous visit. He moved his head slowly against the pillows and coughed. How fine his skin looked, almost translucent. She noticed, for the first time, his damaged arms, scarred pinpricks, still fading. He lifted one arm, reached across to touch his other hand and squeezed it a number of times. Pins and needles, she wondered, watching his clutching movements becoming stronger. Holding on, she thought. Terrified he would slip away from them again. She placed his painting against the wall. He would see it as soon as he awoke.

His father's voice had been choked with emotion when he rang. Unrecognisable until he gasped her name and said, "Lorraine, he's awake. He opened his eyes and recognised me. Then he smiled and went back to sleep again. I thought it was my imagination and I waited ... I waited until he woke up again. He spoke my name."

Struggling to compose herself she sank into a chair. "Thank God, Michael – oh thank God!"

"He spoke my name. I wanted you to know. Do you understand what I'm saying, Lorraine? Killian is awake."

"It's wonderful – wonderful. I'm so happy for you."

"Please come and see him. Share this with me. I'm only half alive without you. Please come now."

She longed to drop the phone and run to her car, drive without stopping, breaking lights and speed limits, barriers, road-blocks, throwing caution helter-skelter out the window, not stopping until she was crushed against him, rejoicing together in this joyous moment. This longing, which he shared – she could hear it in his voice, in the anticipatory silence as he waited for her to speak – drained the last vestige of energy from her. The kitchen door opened. Emily entered and flung her bag into the corner. Afterwards, Lorraine was unable to remember what she said to him. Platitudes, probably, but they signalled the end of their conversation.

A week had passed since his phone call. At reception she had checked that his son was alone before entering his ward. She was about to leave when Killian stirred. His eyes opened and fixed on her, the glazed fear slowly clearing. Awake, he seemed frailer, his cheeks sunken, his mouth almost bloodless, but there was a strong rhythm to his breathing and his stare held knowledge. No longer a boy held captive in a realm beyond dreams.

The word he spoke was muffled, almost inaudible, and when he repeated it she realised it was his father's name. His gaze slowly travelled over her face and onto a painting where shadows played across a fairy-tale forest of briars. Dense with dangerous thorns, the forest held him captive, but hanging from the briars Lorraine had painted many things: a xylophone and a cartoon-type cat with a hat, a manuscript, a prayer book, a teapot, get-well cards, medical equipment, a Walkman and, glinting with sapphire lights, a silver bracelet.

CHAPTER SIXTY-FOUR

Ralph raised his wineglass, tipped it towards her in a laconic salute. "To the most beautiful woman in the restaurant."

To bask in her husband's admiration. The irony was not lost on Virginia. Who would have believed it? She wondered what her mother would say if she knew. "Time is a great sealer" seemed like a predictable response.

He had chosen a restaurant with horse prints on the walls and heavy oak beams stretched above them. Their table was secluded behind a partition with stained-glass portholes through which she glimpsed the other diners. Not that prying eyes should matter. She smiled inwardly but decided it would be unwise to share her thoughts with Ralph. He was only too aware that he was seducing his wife under her lover's nose.

He signalled for the bill. She studied his hands, his broad knuckles, the flourish with which he signed his signature on the payment slip, adding a lavish tip for the waitress.

"Thank you for a wonderful meal, Ralph," she said.

"My pleasure." He quirked an eyebrow, smiled. "I hope you're not going to play Cinderella tonight. I've booked somewhere private … intimate."

He took her elbow and they walked from the restaurant. In the foyer the waiter brought her coat, held it out for her as she placed her arms into the sleeves and nestled the fur collar against her neck. Mock-antique lanterns shone from the walls and cast an amber glow over the mirror behind the reception desk. She glanced automatically into the dulled recess. They looked so perfect together it was possible to imagine they had never been sundered by her own foolish recklessness. She moved her head for a final look and saw her father staring back at her. She recognised his lips, the bloat of pleasure on them when he emerged from Sonya's room, the room where Virginia must not go, the lazy satiated smile that Lorraine had painted with such devastating precision. Virginia locked into his dead gaze then slowly, deliberately, she forced him away until she saw only her own taut cheekbones and vivid mouth. The most beautiful face in the restaurant, Ralph had said, toasting her.

"We should never have come to Ireland," she said as he drove from the car-park. "You've no idea how much I regret —"

"No regrets," he said. "It's not your style, Virginia."

He switched on a CD of love ballads. The music was gentle, relaxing, but her face felt different, overlaid with her father's stamp, and she cursed Lorraine who, with such cruel precision, had etched an indelible impression on her mind. He braked at the Merrion Gates. They watched the DART speeding southwards. A few dog owners were walking their pets on the Sandymount esplanade. A Yorkshire terrier and a large bulldog sniffed each other in mutual fascination until their owners jerked them apart. She wondered which hotel he had booked for the night. When she asked he winked and said, "Curiosity killed the cat," which, as an answer, lacked a certain maturity but she purred against his shoulder, teasing him and gently clawing her nails down the side of his face.

"Have you told him yet?" Ralph asked.

"Not yet."

"Why won't you just go, walk away?"

"He's sick, Ralph. It's all been too much for him. I need some more time but it's over, finished."

The love songs ended. Ralph replaced the CD with a tape. The clashing screams of punk filled the car, music once so familiar, now so alienating. Sulphuric Acid. Blast from the past. She drew back from the savagery of the lyrics, uneasy when he sang along, his voice older now, a deeper resonance. As he turned right and drove swiftly in the direction of the East Link Bridge, he slapped his hand off the steering-wheel in a rhythmic drum beat. She liked speed but not on a road with bends and roundabouts.

"Where are we going, Ralph?" She spoke loudly above the music.

"As I said, Virginia, somewhere special."

"Then take it easy." She laid her hand warningly on his arm. "We'll get there soon enough."

She watched the speedometer climb higher. "Why can't we go to your apartment?"

"It needs redecorating."

"It's only new. Why should it need to be redecorated?"

He swerved sharply at the South Port roundabout. "You stayed there, Virginia." His smile flashed in the darkened interior. "You left your perfume on my sheets. You contaminated my air."

She pressed down on the belt clasp but her hands trembled so much she was unable to release it. "Stop the car immediately. I don't know what you're playing at but it's not remotely funny."

She opened the belt but he was driving too fast for her to do anything except stare in horror as he drove past the oil depots and container yards, the traveller families safe in their caravans, past the derelict buildings with their murky, empty doorways and the sprawling outlines of the generating station. The Pigeon House chimneys spilled smoke into the air and, in the distance, standing squat and alert at the foot of the Great South Wall, a red lighthouse flung a warning beam across Dublin Bay.

"You're mad," she sobbed when he braked, tyres screeching, at the entrance to the pier. "Insane. We could have been killed."

"Imagine that," he said. "Dead on the pier and no one to tell."

She gulped, forcing moisture into her mouth, but still she felt her throat contracting. Everything depended on her staying in control. The alternative was to run screaming into the night.

"You've had your fun, Ralph." Finally, she managed to speak. "I want to go home now."

"Our home is in rubble, Virginia."

"Please, Ralph, this is crazy –"

"Revenge is a dish best served cold." She flinched from the mockery in his voice. "Get out of my car, Virginia." His voice rose impatiently when she refused to move. "Get out before I drag you out."

She stepped onto the surface of the pier. To run was useless. Once she was outside the cone of light she would be unable to see in front of her. He moved quickly from his side of the car and grabbed her arm, walked her into the shelter of the shed.

"Was this where you fucked him?" He cupped her face in his hand, tilted her chin towards him. "Or did you do it in the car? Fill me in on the details, please."

It was too dark to see his expression but she imagined it, wolfish, a casual brutality, raw and sexual. Her angry punk with his contrived fury, spewing his lyrics above the heads of his fans and she, holding him on the reins of her pleasure, controlling him.

"Answer me, Virginia."

"Make me," she whispered. She grasped his hair, dragged her mouth across his throat. "Is this what you want?" Her moist lips opened to him and he, in turn, lowered his face, his hands on her buttocks as he pressed her forcefully against the wall.

"You betrayed me with indifference," he whispered into her ear, his breath hot against her skin. "You betrayed me with ease. Time and time again you came to my bed and lay down beside me, held me, looked into my eyes, lied to me. So many *many* times." Still holding her with his body, he encircled her neck with his hand, his thumb and fingers tightening.

"Why are you doing this, Ralph? I don't understand."

"Stop lying, Virginia." His tone suggested he was chastising a mischievous child and was more terrifying in its gentleness. "No more games." One by one he lifted his fingers from her throat until only his thumb remained impaled on her skin. "I could kill you with that same indifference, that same ease. I could leave you lying here, helpless, then drive away, just as you did, and never think about you again." His thumb eased away. "But I know I can't. You'd haunt me forever. Cold and hard and beautiful as a diamond, that's what you are, Virginia. So I'm walking away. You're not worth a single day of pain. You never were."

His footsteps rang against the concrete. Already he was

disappearing into the darkness. Unable to believe he was abandoning her, she called after him. Her legs trembled as she ran forward to the centre of the pier. She watched him climb into his car and start the engine. Her foot caught against a wedge of concrete and she fell, her ankle twisting, one shoe off, her stockings torn. Desperately, she crawled away from the engulfing headlights, screamed into her hands as he drove past, the wheels spraying grit and dust over her. He stopped, reversed and turned, came towards her again. Then he was gone and she was alone in the darkness.

Her ankle throbbed painfully. Already, it was beginning to swell above her shoe. She searched through her bag for her mobile phone, her movements becoming more frantic as she realised it was missing from its customary pocket. It must have fallen on the pier when she tripped. She scrabbled in the dark, concrete grazing her fingers. Unable to find it, she realised he must have removed it from her bag at some stage during the night. She wept with the indignity he had imposed upon her but mainly she raged against herself. How could she have allowed herself to be so deceived? Honeyed e-mails eating up her sleepless hours. Anonymous mail eating up her days. Worn out with worry and lack of sleep she had allowed him to gradually chip away at her defences and, oh, how he had chipped, teasing, flirting, enticing her back into his arms.

Rain began to fall. She huddled against the wall. She imagined him in jail, kidnapping and assault, locked safely behind bars, his wolf smile banished forever. In the distance she saw headlights dipping and swaying towards the pier. She huddled deeper against the wall, terrified he had returned.

The car drew closer. She heard tyres thudding over the ridged entrance to the pier. A door banged, a voice called her name. She shielded her eyes, limped forward.

"He phoned me, told me I'd find you here." Adrian led her, weeping, towards his car.

She collapsed against the passenger seat, her hands over her eyes as he turned and left the pier behind. The wheels buckled over the uneven surface, creating a thudding sound that jolted her body against the seat.

"He forced me to come here –"

"Ralph has never forced you to do anything in your life, Virginia. He spared no details when he phoned. But then why should he? I stole his whore."

Warm air from the heater blasted her face. She felt her colour rise, her scalp prickling. "You believe I'm here by *choice*? Answer me," she shrieked. "Do you believe I deliberately asked him to bring me here?"

"I believe you were with him tonight by your own choice. I believe he made a fool of us." His fury seared through her. "I believe it would be a relief if I never set eyes on you again. I believe you've plundered my soul."

"Plundered!" She mocked him with her laughter. "I thought he was going to kill me and all you can do is talk about your *plundered* soul."

"Be quiet." His tone was dismissive. "This madness has to stop somewhere. We're going straight to the police."

"The only reason we'll go to the police is to charge him with assault and kidnapping."

"Stop lying, Virginia. I've made up my mind. Ralph knows. Lorraine knows. It's only a matter of time before it's general knowledge. I'll confess to driving the car. I don't give a tinker's curse any more." The weariness with which he spoke was more frightening than his earlier anger. "If we don't stop it now it will go on forever. I can't take it any more."

"Yes, you can. And you will. Everything passes, Adrian. Everything! The kid is recovering. He'll be out of hospital soon. It will pass and be forgotten. Listen to me –"

"It's over. I don't hear you any more."

"But you must – you must. You can't do this, Adrian. I won't let you."

"There's nothing you can do to stop me."

Across the black sea she smelled the fumes. Such a pungent, suffocating smell of paint rising above the pier wall and rolling towards her. Its oily residue was in her nostrils, her throat. Adrian turned a corner and there, leaping from the shadows, turning to stand motionless before them, was the young man, his mouth open on a scream, his woollen cap low over his eyes, but not low enough to prevent him staring, such a fierce penetrating stare, into her eyes, and she screamed a warning, screamed before it was too late, forced Adrian to swerve, dragged at the wheel with all her strength until the tyres skidded, spun haplessly across the empty road towards the looming steel barrier on the far side. She watched as the steering wheel wrenched free from his hands and he bent forward, graceful as a dancer accepting applause, to meet it with his chest.

The crunch, she would always remember the crunch, and the sense of utter incredulity that life could be so whimsical; so easily given and arbitrarily taken away. Adrian died instantly. She knew he was gone before she touched his slumped body. She heard someone screaming. The sound was far away and there was an empty road before her … empty … empty …

Later, minutes, maybe hours, a car braked. Footsteps ran towards her then slowed cautiously. She heard voices and was able to call back, to tell them she was injured but safe. A man forced open the passenger door, turned her face into his shoulder when she began to shake. The ambulance came quickly.

"A miracle," said the driver as she was lifted onto a stretcher. They laid a blanket over Adrian's face. It seemed insulting to cry. So utterly futile. He would still be dead, no matter how violently she rent her grief into the night.

CHAPTER SIXTY-FIVE

His funeral was well attended. A sombre occasion as befitting a man who went before his time. Lorraine stood by his grave, her arm around Emily's shoulders, their backs ramrod straight. The grieving widow. People gave her the respect this deserved, uttered the obligatory words of sympathy, carefully disguising their curiosity. Ralph stood beside her. Once, when the priest mentioned Adrian's name, he clasped her hand. His touch was cold, his eyes red-rimmed. No one mentioned Virginia's name. Her absence added to the power of her invisible presence.

She heard traffic passing outside the cemetery wall. The air was heavy with the scent of pine. They stood on a carpet of dead needles. It is over, she thought as she walked from his grave, shocked anew by the finality of death. All his energy and vitality, the space he once occupied in the world, all gone, quenched, folded over.

Michael Carmody came to the funeral. He made no effort to utter trite words of solace. They stood together for a moment, not moving, not speaking. When she stirred, aware of Emily's bleak gaze, he said, "I met Ralph Blaide yesterday. I'm aware of everything that happened on the pier."

"I can't talk about it yet, Michael."

"I told you once I'd wait for you forever. Nothing will change my mind."

"How is Killian?"

"Strong. He's responding to physiotherapy. But he's a long way to go yet. Thank you for the painting."

She nodded, rejoined Emily. Time was at a standstill. It would move forward again but for now she could only live in the moment.

Epilogue

Six months later

The Donaldson brothers dropped in on their spare time to finish small jobs. She started work on the garden. After the overgrowth had been removed she had a clear perception of the space she had to manage. Sometimes, Emily worked beside her. Her friends called regularly, cycling down the lane, their noise and exuberant good humour drawing her out of her silence, returning colour to her cheeks, light to her eyes.

Old Celia used to have lilies in her front garden, tall and stately as church candles, and so it was lilies that preoccupied Lorraine one evening when she heard Hobbs barking. She would plant the lilies in the turned earth near the front of the house and fill the air with their scent. A car braked outside the gate and she knew, without turning, that he had arrived. Emily came to the front door and stood waiting. Hobbs' barking abruptly stopped when Noeleen's commanding voice rang out and, for an instant, when the engine switched off, the only sound to break the silence was the faint pulse of the sea.

Michael Carmody helped his son from the passenger seat. The young man's legs looked too slender to support his weight. His face twisted from the effort of standing upright but he was able to place one foot before the other, and, leaning heavily on his father's arm, step forward to greet Lorraine. The sun hovered above the headland, as if drifting on smoke, before disappearing into a dark rim beyond the brow.

Rain would fall before dawn. She could taste it, smell it, feel it on her skin, hear it falling softly from clouds scudding dark across the sky. So much to do, a desk diary filled with appointments, breakfast meetings, receptions to organise, phone calls to return. Virginia pulled open the balcony doors and stepped outside. Across the bay, a mosaic of flickering lights crowned the skyline, spiralled upwards towards the summit of Howth Head. The balcony rail was cold against her hand. A door slammed in a neighbouring apartment and, in the courtyard below, she saw him dance. He moved forward into fluorescent pools, spun and fell and rose again to bow before her. She pressed her hands against the rail and allowed the fear to consume her, acknowledging its source, knowing it would take time to pass. And it would pass. It always did. Everything passed. The courtyard lamps continued to burn between the high anonymous spires. A string of jewels surrounding the secrets of the night.

Acknowledgements

I'd like to extend my thanks to the many people who helped me throughout the writing of *Deceptions*.

For their willingness to provide advice and information: Michael Burke, Tony Considine, Michelle Considine, Paul Flanagan, Ursula Fraser, Des O'Toole and Una Ratcliffe.

To my extended family and my friends, those who write and are always available with support at the end of a telephone line – and those who order me to press Log Off and go for coffee. Writing is a solitary occupation but the value of such friendships prevents it becoming a lonely one.

To the team at New Island, who have made the publication of *Deceptions* such a enjoyable and painless experience: my publisher, Edwin Higel, my editor, Emma Dunne, PR and marketing manager Joseph Hoban and production manager Fidelma Slattery. Thanks also to my agent, Faith O'Grady, for her commitment.

My gratitude to Roddy Flynn, Fran Power and Simon Joyce can only be expressed in kilobytes. They have done their utmost to convince me that a computer is not closely related to a black hole and show an unfailing tolerance, no matter how often I seek their assistance.

A special thank you to my husband Sean, my son Tony, and daughters Ciara and Michelle. Their love, loyalty and support has been constant throughout my career and is much appreciated.

Finally, I'd like to honour the memory of my beautiful niece, Linda Mullally. She was much-loved and precious.